Bone China

ROMA TEARNE

Bone China

HARPERCOLLINS PUBLISHERS LTD

Published by HarperCollins Publishers Ltd

Originally published in Great Britain by Harper*Press* in 2008
First published in Canada by HarperCollins Publishers Ltd in this
original trade paperback edition: 2009

'Love is the Sweetest Thing' Words and Music by Ray Noble © 1932.
Reproduced by permission of Francis Day & Hunter Ltd, London w8 5sw.

Quotations by E.M. Forster used by kind permission of The Provost and
Scholars of King's College, Cambridge, and the Society of Authors as the
Literary Representatives of the Estate of E.M. Forster.

HarperCollins books may be purchased for educational, business, or sales
promotional use through our Special Markets Department.

HarperCollins Publishers Ltd
2 Bloor Street East, 20th Floor
Toronto, Ontario, Canada
M4W 1A8

www.harpercollins.ca

Library and Archives Canada Cataloguing in Publication
Tearne, Roma
Bone china : a novel / Roma Tearne.

ISBN 978-1-55468-416-8

I. Title.
PR6120.E27B65 2009   823'.92   C2008-907961-2

Printed and bound in the United States
RRD 9 8 7 6 5 4 3 2 1

For Barrie,
Oliver, Alistair and Mollie.

And in memory of my parents.

'He who never leaves his country is full of prejudices.'

CARLO GOLDONI

Secrets

1

FROM THE ROAD ALL THAT COULD be seen of the house was its long red roof. Everything else was screened by the trees. Occasionally, depending on the direction of the breeze, children's voices or a piano being played could be heard, but usually, the only sound was the faint rush of water falling away further down the valley. Until this point where the road ended, the house and all its grandeur remained hidden. Then suddenly it burst into view. The car, approaching from the south side, wound slowly up the tea-covered hills. Passing one breathtaking view after another it climbed higher and higher until at last it rolled to a halt. For a moment Aloysius de Silva sat staring out. The house had been in his wife's family for more than two hundred years. Local people, those who knew of it and knew the family, called it the House of Many Balconies. All around its façade were ornate carvings punctuated by small stone balconies and deep verandas. The gardens were planted with rhododendrons and foxgloves, arum lilies and soft, rainwashed flowers. 'Serendipity,' the Governor had called it, 'somewhere deep in the Garden of Eden.' It was here, in this

3

undisturbed paradise, viridian green and temperate, that the dark-eyed Grace had grown up. And it was here that she waited for him now.

Sighing heavily, for he was returning home after an absence of several days, Aloysius opened the door of the car, nodding to the driver. He would walk the rest of the way. It was early morning, on the first day of September 1939. Thin patches of mist drifted in the rarefied air. In his haste to return home he had caught only a glimpse of the newspaper headlines. They could no longer be ignored. The war in Europe was official, and because the island of Ceylon was still under British Crown Rule he knew it would affect them all. But this morning Aloysius de Silva had other things on his mind. He was the bearer of some rather pressing news of his own. His wife, he remembered with some reluctance, was waiting. The next few hours would not be easy. Aloysius had been playing poker. He had promised her he would not, but he had broken his promise. He had been drinking, so that, as sometimes happened on such occasions, one thing had led seamlessly to another. One minute he had had the chance to win back, at a single blow, the unravelled fortunes of his family, the horses, the estates. But the next it had vanished with an inevitability that had proved hard to anticipate. A queen, a king, an ace; he could see them clearly still. He had staked his life on a hand of cards. And he had lost. Why had he done this? He had no idea how to tell her the last of her tea estates had gone. It had been the thing he dreaded most of all.

'They're crooks,' he declared loudly, a bit later on.

No good beating about the bush, he thought. They were sitting in the turquoise drawing room, surrounded by the Dutch colonial furniture, the Italian glass and the exquisite collection of rare bone china that had belonged to Grace's mother. Family portraits lined the walls, bookcases and vitrines filled the room, and a huge chandelier hung its droplets above them.

'Rasanayagaim set me up,' said Aloysius. 'I could tell there was some funny business going on. You know, all the time there was some sort of message being passed between him and that puppy, Chesterton.'

His wife said nothing and Aloysius searched around for a match to light his cigar. When he found none he rang the bell and the servant boy appeared.

'Bring some tea,' he said irritably after he relit his cigar. 'I was set up,' he continued, when the servant had left the room. 'As soon as I saw that bastard Rasanayagaim, I knew there'd be trouble. You remember what happened to Harold Fonsaka? And then later on, to that fellow, Sam? I'm telling you, on every single occasion Rasanayagaim was in the room!'

Aloysius blew a ring of cigar smoke and coughed. Still Grace de Silva said nothing. Aloysius could see she had her inscrutable look. This could go on for days, he thought, eyeing her warily. It was a pity really, given how good-looking she still was. Quite my best asset most of the time. He suppressed the desire to laugh. The conversation was liable to get tricky.

'It was just bad luck, darl,' he said, trying another tack. 'Just wait, men, I'll win it all back at the next game!'

He could see it clearly. The moment he fanned out the cards there had been a constellation of possibilities. A queen, a king, an ace! But then, it hadn't been enough. Too little, too late, he thought, regretfully. All over Europe the lights were going out. As from this moment, Britain was at war with Germany. Bad luck, thought Aloysius, again. She'll be silent for days now, weeks even, he predicted gloomily. She knows how to punish me. Always has.

The servant brought in the tea on a silver tray. The china

was exquisite. Blue and white and faded. It had been in the family for years, commissioned by the Queen for the Hyde Park Exhibition. Does it still belong to us? Grace thought furiously, looking at them. Or has he signed them away too? And what about me? she wanted to shout. I'm surprised he hasn't gambled me away. Aloysius watched her. He was well aware that his wife was corseted in good manners, bound up by good breeding, wrapped in the glow of a more elegant world than the one he had been brought up in. But he also knew, underneath, she had a temper. The servant poured the tea. The porcelain teacups were paper-thin. They let in a faint glow of light when she held them up.

'It isn't as bad as you think,' he said conversationally. No use encouraging her silence, he decided, briskly. What's done is done. Move forward, he thought. 'We'd have had to give up the house anyway. The Governor wants it for the war. It's been on the cards for ages, you know, darl,' he told her, not realising what he was saying.

Grace de Silva pursed her lips. The flower in her hair trembled. Her eyes were blue-black like a kingfisher's beak and she wanted to kill Aloysius.

'So you see, sooner or later we'd have to move.'

He waved aside his smoke, coughing. The servant, having handed a cup of tea to Mrs de Silva, left. Dammit, thought Aloysius, again. Why does she have to be so hard on me? It was a mistake, wasn't it? Her silence unnerved him.

'The fact is, I'm no longer necessary to the British. We were useful as sandbags, once,' he continued, sounding more confident than he felt. 'Those were the days, hah! It was people like me, you know, who kept civil unrest at bay. But now, now they have their damn war looming, they don't need *me*.'

Is she ever going to say anything? he wondered. Women were

such strange creatures. He moved restlessly. Not having slept he was exhausted. The effort of wanting to give Grace a surprise windfall had tired him out.

'So, it's only the estate we've lost,' he repeated uneasily, trying to gauge her mood. 'I don't want to be a manager on a plantation that's no longer ours. What's the point in that? I've no intention of being one of their bloody slaves!'

Grace stirred her tea. Aloysius was a Tamil man who had, by some mysterious means, acquired a Sinhalese surname. He had done this long before Grace knew him, having taken a liking to the name de Silva. When he first began working as the estate manager at her father's factory he had been young and very clever in the sharp ways of an educated Tamil. And he had been eager to learn. But most of all he had been musical and full of high spirits, full of effervescent charm. Grace, the only daughter of the planter boss, had fallen in love. In all her life she had never met anyone as intelligent as Aloysius. He was *still* clever, she thought now, but his weaknesses appalled her. Soon after their marriage he had started gambling with the British officers, staying out late, drinking and losing money. Only then did Grace understand her father's warning.

'He will drink your fortune away, Grace,' her father had said. 'The British will give him special privileges because of his charm, and it will go to his head. He will not be the husband you think.'

Her father had not wanted her to marry Aloysius. He had tried to stop her, but Grace had a stubborn streak. In the end, her father, who could deny her nothing, had given in. Now, finally, she saw what she had done.

'The children have been asked to leave Greenwood,' she told him, coldly. 'Their school fees haven't been paid for a year. A *year*!'

Hearing her own voice rise she stopped talking. She blamed herself. Five children, she thought. I've borne him *five* children. And now this. Her anger was more than she could bear.

'Stanley Simpson wanted me to play,' Aloysius was saying. Stanley Simpson was his boss. 'It would have been incorrect of me to refuse.' He avoided Grace's eye. 'I have always been his equal, darl. How could I suddenly refuse to join in? These English fellows have always relied on me to make up the numbers.'

'But they know when to stop,' Grace said bitterly. 'They don't ruin themselves.'

Aloysius looked at his feet. 'When it's your hands on the wheel it's so much easier to apply the brake,' he mumbled.

They were both silent, listening to the ticking of the grand-father clock. Outside, a bird screeched and was answered by another bird.

'Don't worry about the children, darl,' Aloysius said sooth-ingly. 'We can get Myrtle to tutor them.'

Grace started. *Myrtle?* Had Aloysius completely taken leave of his senses? Myrtle was her cousin. She hated Grace.

'We'll start again, move to Colombo. I'll get the estates back somehow, you'll see. And after the war, we'll get the house back too. I promise you. It's just a small inconvenience.'

Grace looked at him. I've been a fool, she thought, bitterly. I've no one to blame but myself. And now he wants to bring Myrtle back into our lives. She suppressed a shiver.

Outside, another day on the tea plantation continued, regard-less. The early-morning mist had cleared and the coolies had brought in their baskets of leaves to be weighed. Christopher de Silva, youngest son of Grace and Aloysius, was sneaking in through the back of the house. Christopher had brought his mother a present. Well, it wasn't exactly for her, it was his really.

But if he gave it to Grace he knew he'd be allowed to keep it. The older children were still at school and no one had seen his father for some time. It was as good a moment as any. He hurried across the kitchen garden and entered the house through the servants' quarters carrying a large cardboard box punctured with holes. The kitchen was full of activity. Lunch was being prepared. A pale cream tureen was being filled with a mound of hot rice. Napkins were pushed into silver rings.

'Aiyo!' said the cook, seeing him. 'You can't put your things there. Mr de Silva's back and we're late with the lunch.'

'Christopher, master,' said the servant boy who had just served tea for the lady of the house, 'your brothers are coming home this afternoon.'

'What?' asked Christopher, startled.

The box he was holding wobbled and he put it down hastily. He stared at the servant boy in dismay. Why were his brothers coming home? Just when he had thought he was rid of them too. Disappointment leapt on his back; he felt bowed down by it. He was only ten years old, too young as yet to attend Greenwood College with Jacob and Thornton. And although he longed for the day when, at the age of eleven, he could join them there, life at home without Thornton was very good. Thornton monopolised his mother and Christopher preferred his absence.

'Is Thornton coming too?' he asked in dismay.

'Yes,' said the servant boy. 'They're *all* coming home. Alicia and Frieda too.'

His eyes were shining with excitement. He was the same age as Christopher. They were good friends.

'You're all going to live in Colombo now,' he announced. 'I'm going to come too!' He waggled his head from side to side.

'Namil, will you never learn to keep your mouth shut?' cried

9

his mother the cook, pulling the boy by the ear. 'Here, you nuisance, take these coconuts outside to be scraped. And Christopher, master, please go and wash your hands, lunch is almost ready.'

'What's going on?' muttered Christopher. 'I'm going to find out.'

Then he remembered the cardboard box in the middle of the floor. A muffled miaowing came from within.

'Namil,' he said, 'can you put this in my room, carefully? Don't let anyone see. It's a present for my mother.'

'What is it?' asked the servant boy, but Christopher had gone, unaware of the horrified expression on the cook's face as she watched the cardboard box rocking on her kitchen floor.

Further down the valley Christopher's older brothers waited on the steps of Greenwood College for the buggy to collect them. Jacob de Silva was worried. They had been told to leave their books before returning home. Although the real significance of the message had not fully dawned on him, the vague sense of unease and suspicion that was his constant companion grew stronger with each passing minute.

'Why d'you think we have to go home?' he asked Thornton.

'I thought you said they hadn't paid our school fees,' Thornton replied. He was not really interested.

'But why d'you think that is?' insisted Jacob. 'Why didn't they pay them?' Thornton did not care. He was only thirteen, the apple of his mother's eyes, a dreamer, a chaser of the cream butterflies that invaded the valley at this time of year. Today merely signalled freedom for him.

'Oh, who knows with grown-ups,' he said. 'Just think, tomorrow we'll wake up in our own bedroom. We can go out onto the balcony and look at the garden and no one will mind.

And we can have egg hoppers and mangoes for breakfast instead of toast and marmalade. So who cares!' He laughed. 'I'm glad we're leaving. It's so boring here. We can do what we want at home.' A thought struck him. 'I wonder if the girls have been sent back too?'

On their last holiday they had climbed down from the bedroom balcony very early one morning and crept through the mist, to the square where the nuns and the monkeys gathered beside the white Portuguese church. They had had breakfast with Father Jeremy who wheezed and coughed and offered them whisky, which they had drunk in one swift gulp. And afterwards they had staggered back home to bed. Thornton giggled at the memory.

Jacob watched him solemnly. He watched him run down the steps of Greenwood College, this privileged seat of learning for the sons of British government officials and the island's elite, his laughter floating on the sunlight.

'I want to stay here,' he said softly, stubbornly, under his breath. 'We can go home any time. But we can only learn things here.'

He frowned. He could see all the plans for his future beginning to fade. The headmaster had told him he could have gone to university had he stayed on at school and finished his studies. His Latin teacher had told him he might have done classics. Then his science teacher had told him that in *his* opinion Jacob could have gone to medical school. Jacob had kept these conversations to himself.

'Oh, I can learn things anywhere,' Thornton was saying airily. 'I'm a poet, remember.' He laughed again. 'I'm so lucky,' he said. And then, in the fleeting manner of sudden childhood insights, he thought, I'm glad I'm not the eldest.

'Come on,' he added kindly, sensing some invisible struggle, some unspoken battle going on between them. 'Race you to the gate.'

But Jacob did not move. He stared morosely ahead of him, not speaking. Both boys wore the same ridiculous English public-school uniform, but whereas Thornton wore his with ease, already in possession of the looks that would mark him out for the rest of his life, Jacob simply looked hot and awkward. Again, he was aware of some difficulty, some comparison in his own mind, between himself and his brother. But what this was he could not say. Thornton's voice drifted faintly towards him, but still Jacob did not move.

'I can't.' His voice sounded strained. 'You don't understand. Someone must stay here to wait for the buggy.'

He was fifteen years old. He had been brought up to believe he was the inheritor of the tea plantations that rose steeply in tiers around him. The responsibilities of being the eldest child rested heavily on his small shoulders. As he stood watching his brother chasing the butterflies that slipped through the trees, he was suddenly aware of wanting to cry. Something inexplicable and infinitely precious seemed to be breaking inside him. Something he loved. And he could do nothing to stop it.

The buggy never arrived. After a while an older boy came out with a message.

'Your parents have rung,' the boy said. 'Looks like you're going to have to walk. They don't have a buggy any more. Perhaps it's been sold off to pay your father's debtors,' he grinned.

'We have no debtors,' muttered Jacob, but the boy had gone.

Eventually the brothers began to walk. Jacob walked slowly. The long fingers of sun shone pink and low in the sky as they left the driveway of Greenwood for the very last time. Rain had fallen earlier, dampening the ground on this ordinary afternoon, one so like the others, in their gentle upcountry childhood. The air across the valley was filled with the pungent scent of tea, rising steeply as far as the eye could see. In the distance the sound of the factory chute rattled on, endlessly processing, mixing and moving in time to the roar of the waterfall. The two boys wandered on, past the lake brimming with an abundance of water lilies, past clouds of cream butter-flies, and through the height of the afternoon, their voices echoed far into the distance. Returning to their home nestling in the hills of Little England.

To his dismay, Christopher discovered the servant boy had been right. Jacob and Thornton were coming home. Alicia and Frieda, still stranded at the Carmelite Convent School, were waiting fruitlessly for another buggy to pick them up. In the end the priest, taking pity on them, drove them home and it was teatime before Grace was able to break the news to them all. The servant brought a butter cake and some Bora into the drawing room. She brought in small triangles of bread spread with butter and jaggery. And she brought in king coconut juice for the children and tea for Grace. The servant, knowing how upset Grace was, served it all on Grace's favourite green Hartley china tea service. Alicia opened the beautiful old Bechstein piano and began to play Schubert. The others ate quietly. For a moment Grace was distracted. The mellow tone of this sonata was one she loved and Alicia's light touch never failed to surprise her. She waited until the andante was over.

'That was lovely,' she said, putting her hand gently on her daughter's shoulder. 'It's come along a lot since I last heard it.'

'That's because we've got a new piano teacher. She's wonderful, Mummy!' Alicia said. 'She said I must be careful about the phrasing of this last section. Listen,' and she played a few bars over again.

'Yes, I see,' Grace said. 'Good! Now, I want to talk to all of you about something else. So could you leave the piano for a moment, darling?'

Five pairs of eyes watched her solemnly as she spoke.

'We're moving to Colombo,' she told them slowly. 'We're going to live in our other house by the sea.' She took a deep breath. 'Because there's going to be a war the British military needs this house, you see.' There was a surprised pause.

Alicia was the first to speak. 'What about the piano?' she asked anxiously.

'Oh, the piano will come with us, of course. Don't worry, Alicia, nothing like that will change. I promise you.'

She smiled shakily. Jacob was watching her in stony silence. He had guessed correctly. The Greenwood days were over.

'Myrtle will live with us,' said Grace, carefully. 'She'll give you piano lessons, Alicia. And she'll help in the house generally.'

No one spoke. Thornton helped himself to another piece of cake.

'There's a war on,' Grace reminded them gently. 'Everyone has to economise. Even us.' She looked pale.

'Good,' nodded Thornton, having decided. 'I think Colombo will be great. And we'll have the sea, think of that!'

Grace smiled at him with relief. Christopher, noticing this, scowled. But all he said was: 'Can I give you your present now?'

The servant boy, who had been hovering in the background, grinned and brought in the cardboard box. The family crowded around and the miaowing inside the box increased.

'What on earth's in there, Christopher?' asked Alicia, astonished.

'It's a cat,' guessed Thornton.

'But we've already got one,' said Frieda, puzzled. 'We can't have another. They'll fight.'

'Have you been stealing kittens again?' asked Jacob, frowning.

'Well, well, what's going on now?' asked Aloysius, coming in.

Having left his wife to break the news to his children he was now in the best of humours. A nap had been all he had needed. Glancing at Grace he assessed her mood correctly. There was still some way for them to go. The miaowing inside the box had turned to a growl. Everyone looked mystified and Christopher grinned.

'What is it?' asked Grace faintly, wondering how many more shocks there were in store for her.

Aloysius's news had not come as a surprise. Grace had always known that one day they would have to leave the valley where she had been born. There had been too many rumours, too many hints dropped by the British planters during the past few months. It had all pointed to this. So much of their own land had gradually been sold off. British taxes, unrest among the workers and general mismanagement of the estates had all played a part. Her drunken husband had merely speeded things up. And with the onset of war they would lose the house anyway. She felt unutterably tired. The effort of waiting for something to happen had worn her out. Now, knowing just how bad things were, she could at least try to deal with them. In Colombo, she would take charge of her life; manage things herself. It should have happened years ago. In Colombo, things would be different, she told herself firmly. And when the war was over they would come back. To the house at any rate. Of that she was certain. Christopher was holding a box out to her. But what on earth had he brought home this time? she wondered, frowning.

'It's for you,' Christopher said. 'To take to Colombo.'

Slowly she opened the box.

'Yes,' said a hollow voice from within. 'Hello, men.'

Then with a sharp rustle a small, bright-eyed mynah bird flew out and around the room, coming to rest on the grandfather clock, from where it surveyed them with interest. There was a shocked silence.

'It's a mynah bird,' said Christopher unnecessarily. 'And it can talk. We can teach it all kinds of things. It can say lazy boy, and –'

'Lazy bugger,' said the mynah bird, gazing at them solemnly.

'Good God, Christopher!' cried Aloysius, recovering first. He burst out laughing. 'What a present to give your mother!'

They were all laughing now. The servant boy was grinning, and even Jacob was smiling.

'But he's wonderful,' said Grace, laughing the most. 'He's a wonderful present!'

Later on she said, to Christopher's intense joy: 'I shall call him Jasper! And we'll take him to our new life in Colombo.'

It was in this way that Grace de Silva dealt with their reduced family circumstance. Easily, without fuss, without a single word in public of reproach to her husband and with all the serene good manners that were the hallmark of her character. Aloysius breathed a sigh of relief. Whatever she felt, she would now keep to herself he knew. Outwardly, she would appear no different. And so, as the rumours of impending war on the island grew stronger, the house beside the lake with all its balconies and splendid rooms was emptied. Its furniture and chandeliers, its delicate bone china were packed away, and even as they watched, their beloved home was closed forever and given up to the British for their military efforts. In this way the de Silva family, cast out from the cradle where they had lived for so long, moved south to Colombo. To a white house with a sweeping veranda, close by the railway line where the humidity was very often oppressive, but where the sweet, soft sound of the Indian Ocean was never far away.

2

AUGUST WAS A DANGEROUS MONTH, when the heat, reaching unbearable proportions, created an oasis of stillness. Every flutter, every breeze, vanished, leaving an eerie calm. Nothing moved. Dogs stretched out on the dusty roads panting, too exhausted to move out of the shade, too parched to bark even. Dust lay tiredly on everything, on buildings, on the soles of the feet of the rickshaw men, on the sides of the old London double-decker buses. Disease scurried through the sun-crisped grass; some said there was typhoid in the south, others that the malaria season had begun. No one knew the truth. A pack of rabid dogs moved up the coast at a trot, and elsewhere in the crowds at Galle Face, baby-pink, raw-faced monkeys chattered and sometimes bit a passer-by. But this was August, when sanity was stretched to its limits.

Four years had vanished in the blink of an eye. Swallowed up beneath a peacock sky while the de Silvas grew and expanded into their new life by the sea. Five de Silva childhoods gone in a flash while the war still limped on unnoticed. It existed in places that were merely names on a map. Vichy, Paris, Dresden,

Berlin, Vienna, London. But the hardships in these distant lands barely touched the fringes of the coral-ringed island. The war was a muffled drum, beating elsewhere and leaving the island largely untouched and unconcerned. Grace de Silva hurrying home after one of her trips to Colombo heard the familiar strains of piano music drifting through the long French windows that opened out into the garden. The music cascaded out onto the bougainvillea and was absorbed by it. As she slipped in through the front door, escaping the wall of blistering sunlight, the music rose and swelled and fell delicately. Jasper, the mynah bird who sat by the meshed window in the wide cool hallway, watched her beadily. He had grown enormously.

'Hello,' he greeted her. 'Hello, men,' and he shifted on his perch.

Grace, who had been trying to be quiet, giggled.

'Good morning,' continued Jasper severely. 'Good morning, men.'

Having been silent and alone all day he found it difficult to stop talking. Grace looked away, suppressing a smile. She kicked off her shoes, ignoring him. Any attention, she knew, was likely to make him garrulous. She poured a glass of icy water from the fridge, gasping as she drank.

The sound of the piano drifted through the interior of the house. It travelled softly across the shuttered rooms and along the yellow stick of light that escaped through them. Alicia was playing the second movement of a Mozart sonata with start-ling tenderness in one so young. Grace stood listening, holding her breath, waiting as though hearing it for the first time. On and on and on played her eldest daughter in an unbroken dialogue with the music. The notes ran like quicksilver through her fingers. Grace closed her eyes. Her body ached sweetly. Without a doubt, she thought, distracted by the music, Alicia ought to be studying at the Conservatoire. But she knew discussing the financial implications of this with Aloysius was an impossibility. Better to give a monkey a ladder, thought Grace wryly. All she would do if she voiced her anxieties was provide him with an excuse to start his poker up again. No, she decided closing her eyes, *I* will have to find the money. There was still some of her legacy left that Aloysius knew nothing about. Grace had hoped to keep it for a rainy day. She frowned.

'Perhaps I shall have to sell the land after all,' she said out loud.

'Yes,' said Jasper as though he understood.

'Do you think so?' asked Grace absent-mindedly, forgetting for a moment who he was.

'Hello, yes, yes, men,' said Jasper imperiously, preening himself and ignoring Grace's peal of laughter. Then he squawked flatly and turned his back on her.

Outside, the air was heavy with the smells of late afternoon. The servants were cleaning out the clay pots from lunch, laying them out in the sun to dry. The heat flattened the noises all around into slow hollow slaps as the convent clock struck the hour in a strange flat monotone. Grace paused in the darkened room listening to these unfamiliar southern noises, of crows cawing and bicycle bells. She listened to the lilting sound of the Beethoven study Alicia was now playing. It was interspersed with her husband's drunken snores in the next room. While the steady ticking of the metronome drew and fused all of it, weaving this fleeting moment in time forever. Grace sighed with pleasure. In spite of the difficulty, her family had made the transition into their new life with ease. Their circumstances had been reduced, but they were happy. The freedom of the big city and the unbroken views of the sea had made up for a lot. She poured herself another glass of water.

Myrtle Cruz, hearing the front door, sat up in bed. She had been resting. The heat in Colombo was intolerable. She missed the cool greenness of the hill station where she had been a governess to the British family. She missed the order and calm of the English children she had taught.

'This place is a madhouse,' muttered Myrtle, switching off the fan and getting out of bed.

The English family had long gone. And this, thought Myrtle, *this* is my karma. She disliked her cousin Grace. It had happened long ago when they had been young, when Myrtle had first met the new estate manager at her uncle's factory. He had been penniless but handsome and ambitious, often invited to dine at the House of Many Balconies. In those distant, halcyon days Myrtle had understood nothing of the world. She had fallen hopelessly in love with the young Aloysius, with his intelligence, and his good looks. It had been an act of transformation, blinding and total. Unthinkingly, assuming his friendliness meant he felt as she did, she had revealed her feelings. She had not known his interests lay elsewhere. All she had seen was her own compulsive need, her own desperation, so that throwing caution to the winds she had declared her passion. The shame was unbearable. Afterwards she felt it was the single worst thing she had ever done in her life. He had looked at her, first with horror, and then with embarrassment. Aloysius had had no idea she felt that way. He had been bewildered but kind. His kindness had been her greatest humiliation and later on, when she saw all those things he had left unsaid, she realised there had never really been a chance. The presence of the wantonly beautiful Grace in the house would have stopped anything. Her hopes had fallen like ashes of roses, at his feet. No amount of visits to the astrologer, no amount of prayers or offerings made at sacred shrines, had altered anything. Karma was karma,

Myrtle had realised with bitterness. She fled her uncle's house imagining they were all laughing at her. She had not come back for the wedding; she had not seen Grace for years after that. By the time she finally met them both again, Grace had other things on her mind. All their money had gone, frittered away. Oh the sweet irony of it! Her cousin was still as beautiful, but Myrtle could see she was no longer happy. Five children and a useless marriage, she had thought, with a small glint in her eye, that too was karma. How different life might have been for Aloysius had he married her instead. *She* would never have let him go to the dogs. *She* would have loved him.

Myrtle could hear Grace moving around the house. She glanced at the clock. Then she pulled out her diary.

Two fifteen, she wrote. *This is the second time in a week! So where the devil has she been? She's missed lunch; she's had no breakfast and it's three o'clock. The shops would have shut long ago. So where's she been?*

Myrtle paused, staring out at the plantain tree outside her window. Two bright sunbirds hovered briefly on a bush before disappearing from view.

There are several things that interest me, she continued, writing furiously. *One, why does she have to work with the Irish nuns in Colombo? Why not work in the convent here, why take the train to Colombo all the time? The chauffeur drops her off at the station, he picks her up, she comes in and goes straight to bed. There is something very, very fishy going on. Two, what is this work she's so involved in?*

Myrtle knew it was useless asking the children. Frieda and Alicia had only the vaguest idea of what their mother did and the boys were never home, anyway. *Is she some sort of spy for the British? She certainly knows plenty of them.*

Myrtle stared at what she had written. Like mother like sons, she thought sourly. Then she closed her diary and went off to have a wash.

The truth about Grace was simpler. She had taken a lover. Well, why not? She was still young. Had she not been a good mother, a good wife too? Did she not deserve a little happiness, having remained with the husband who had squandered her inheritance? Well then, thought Grace, who could argue with that? Grace's lover was called Vijay. He worked in Maya's Silk Merchants in Pettah. One day, soon after the de Silvas had arrived in Colombo, she had gone over to buy her daughters some saris and he had served her. She had noticed him even then, a lean, handsome man probably in his mid thirties, but with the air of someone much older. A few weeks later she had returned for more silk. He had looked at her in the way that she was used to, in the way men had looked at her all her life, but without, she felt, the suggestiveness that usually accompanied such a look. His look had struck her forcefully. Vijay's eyes had been soft and full of exhaustion and something, some long-forgotten emotion, had stirred within Grace. Years of neglect on Aloysius's part had taken its toll. Suddenly, and without warning, she saw that she had grown indifferent without realising it. Her patience had been stretched for too long. Perhaps her marriage had simply reached its outer limits. Perhaps the end had come long ago. Once Aloysius had been her whole world. But no more. So that eventually, after what felt like a moment's blinding desire, before she could consult her better judgement, say a prayer or argue with her conscience, she found she had given herself to Vijay.

On the first occasion it had happened with a swiftness that took them both by surprise. Grace had been ordering silk. Yards and yards of the stuff. For Frieda and for Alicia.

'I have two daughters,' she had told Vijay.

23

'Then you will have to come back often,' Vijay told her softly.

He had not smiled. She heard him as though from a great distance. On the second occasion he had brought out a roll of pale, flamingo-pink material, letting it flow through his hands, letting it stream to the floor.

'See,' he said. He could not take his eyes off her. 'Feel it,' he said. 'This is pure cashmere.'

'Yes,' she agreed, feeling a constriction in her chest.

No one noticed. She saw, from this, they already talked a secret language. Her hand brushed the cloth and accidentally touched his. Something happened to her throat, something ancient and familiar, closing it up as though it were a flower. The shop had become stuffy in spite of the ceiling fan. She had felt she might faint. So that, stepping back, she pretended to look at other things while waiting for the room to clear. And afterwards, after she had bought her saris and given her address for them to be delivered, she had gone out into the blazing sun, only to hear a radio playing somewhere in the distance.

> *Love is the sweetest thing,*
> *What else on earth could ever bring,*
> *Such happiness to everything . . .*

Even though she continued to walk on, she was struck by the silly coincidence of the words.

> *Love is the strangest thing . . .*
> *I only hope that fate may bring*
> *Love's story to you.*

Grace stood rooted to the spot listening. She was not a superstitious woman. Nor did she believe in fate, but she had left her umbrella in the shop. Turning round, as though there was no time to lose, as though he was calling her, as if she had *promised* him, she ran back. Like a young girl with foolish dreams in her eyes.

By now the shop was half shuttered. It was midday and the heat had spun a glistening, magical net around everything. The street was empty. Grace stopped abruptly. Why had she expected him still to be there? Perhaps, she thought in panic, it was a terrible mistake. He did not want her after all. Uncertain, feeling ridiculous, she looked around her and saw him standing silently in the doorway. Watching her. Relief exploded in her face. Desire rose like a multicoloured fountain. Happiness somersaulted across the sky. In that moment neither gave a thought to the dangers. Vijay simply waited in the shadows. It was beyond him to summon up a smile and Grace saw the time for smiling had not arrived. In spite of the heat she began to shiver, swaying slightly, mesmerised by his eyes.

'Grace?' he said.

He had walked towards her, something seemed to propel him, something he clearly had no control over. How did he know her name? Hearing his voice, Grace felt electric shocks travel through her. Vijay's voice sounded threadbare, as if he had worn it out with too much longing. Like a bird that was parched; like an animal without hope. Seeing this Grace was overcome by sleepy paralysis. So, holding the heavy weight of her heart, with slow inevitability and leaden feet, she went towards him and placed her head against the length of his body. The door closed behind them. Softly, and with great care. Vijay was too frightened to speak. He rocked against her. Then he unravelled her, shedding her sari as though he were peeling ripe fruit, sinking into the moment, tasting her. A first sip of nectar that left him weakened and snared by his own desire.

Slowly he removed the pins from her hair. It was as if he was detonating a bomb. His hands caught against her skin, caressing it, tricked into following a path of its own across her body. Digressing. Grace swallowed. She felt the untold disappointments of years loosen and become smooth and clear and very simple. Vijay kissed her. He kissed her neck and her ears. He pulled her gently towards him and somewhere in that moment, in the three or four seconds it took for this to happen, they crossed an invisible point of no return. The clock ticked on like a metronome. Grace waited. Soon he would kiss her in every conceivable place, in every possible way. Her eyes closed of their own accord. Her eyes seemed to have gone down deep into her body, to some watchful place of their own. She felt his ear against her navel as he listened to the hot shuddering sighs within her. He found a cleft of sweetness and felt the room spin. Then he wrapped himself around her in an ever tightening embrace as they rushed headlong into each other. Later on, exhausted, they slept, half lying, half sitting against each other and time stood still once again. She awoke to feel his mouth against her and then, hearing the beat of his heart marking time like a drum, she knew that he had begun to count the cost of what they had done. Prejudice, she saw, would march between them, like death. Uncompromising and grim. Everything and nothing had changed. She saw without surprise that there was little more she wanted in the world. As he began again, turning her over, feeling his way back into her, defiantly and with certainty she knew, no one would ever keep them apart. Afterwards, he was filled with remorse, so that sitting between the bales of turmeric-coloured silks, surrounded by the faint perfume of new cloth, she reached out and touched him. He was from another caste. To love beyond its boundaries was outside any remit he might have had. He understood too well the laws that must not be disobeyed. As did she. They stood in the darkness of the shop, cocooned by the silk and she read his thoughts for the first of many times. She felt the fear within him grow and solidify into a hard, dark, impenetrable thing. The death of a million silkworms surrounded them, stretched out into a myriad of colours. Grace was unrepentant; she felt as though a terrible fever had just passed her by and she was safe at last. Stroking the dips and slopes of his body, seeing only the smooth brownness of muscles, the long dark limbs, unashamed by his caste, or her class, she smiled. What could Vijay do after that? In the face of such a smile? He could hardly recognise his own hands let alone turn away. His hands belonged to her now. It was an unplanned passion, swift and carefree, carrying with it the last glow of youth.

Alicia was playing something new, something she had never played before. The notes floated hesitantly and with great clarity across the shuttered house. Vijay was a Tamil man and these days madness shadowed the Tamils. Luck was no longer on their side. Who knew what the future held. In the early days none of this had meant anything. She had gone on unthinkingly, acting on her instincts, a huge euphoria propelling her to his door. The sky had shouted her happiness. But no one heard. She had launched her delight into the air like a white paper kite. But no one saw. It was only lately that she had begun to think of the future.

This morning Maya's Silk Merchants had been closed so Grace had visited Vijay in his lodgings instead. They were towards the east side of Colombo, which was why she had been late getting back. She smiled, remembering the moment, as it rose and fell to the sound of Alicia's music.

'I've just been listening to the radio,' Aloysius said, coming in noiselessly, fresh from his afternoon nap. 'You know, darl, it really is going to be quite bad for the Tamils when the British leave.'

Grace was startled. 'Will they really leave, d'you think?' she asked.

Aloysius might be a fool over money but when it came to the British, he was shrewd.

'Of course they'll go, and sooner than you think. I imagine there'll be some sort of a backlash after that.'

Aloysius poured himself some water. He didn't want to frighten Grace but rumours of a different kind of war were circulating. Sinhalese resentment grew daily, a resentment which would demand acknowledgement. Soon, *they* would be the majority, with unstoppable power over the Tamils. Grace shivered. Independence had begun to frighten her. Aloysius opened the shutters and stared out at the sea. He was sober. He did not like the feeling. It forced him to think of their uncertain future.

'Is that Thornton, coming up the hill?' he asked. 'Good God, how can he ride his bicycle in this heat?'

Grace did not answer. She had just left Vijay's small airless room, walking away from his rattan mattress back to her marble floors. Leaving some essential part of herself behind, carrying the sound of his voice home with her. Alicia was playing Schubert. Recently Grace had met a British officer she had known long ago as a young girl. There had been a time when she had thought she might have married him instead of Aloysius. Now she wanted to go to this man, to ask him if the British would really leave. Would there be an independent government at last? And did he think there would be civil war? But the price for such information was too high. The British, she decided, were best at arm's length. For suddenly Grace was beginning to understand, painfully and with fear, just what might happen to her beloved country. Propelled by this late last love, she had wandered towards frontiers not normally reached by women of her class. She was walking a dangerous road. A secret door in her life had swung open. It could not now be easily closed.

'Sweep the devils out, men,' Aloysius said, handing his empty glass to the servant who had walked in, 'and who knows what others will come in. The Sinhalese won't stay marginalised forever.'

Alicia had stopped her practice; the metronome was no longer ticking.

'I'm going to have a shower,' Aloysius said, shaking his head. 'Too much foreign rule is bound to tamper with the balance of this place.' And he went out, bumping into Thornton who had just come in.

'Ah! The wanderer returns!' Grace heard him say.

Thornton de Silva was seventeen. In the years since they had left their old upcountry home, he had grown tall and very handsome while his smile remained incontestably beautiful. Colombo suited him. He loved its bustle and energy around him. He loved the noise. The British talked of a Japanese invasion, the navy was on constant alert, and the newspapers were full of depressing predictions. But what did Thornton care? Youth held unimaginable promise. Possibilities festooned his days like strings of coloured lights. Earlier this afternoon he had gone to meet his brother Jacob. The harbour had been a tangle of sounds; muffled horns, and shrill whistles, and waves that washed against the jetty. The air was an invisible ocean, salt-fresh and wet, with a breeze that seemed to throb in time to the sound of motor launches. Further along, in the entry-strictly-prohibited parts of the harbour, brass-buttoned British officers revved their jeeps, while stick-thin boys stepped out of rickshaws carrying native food for important personnel, balancing tiffin tins precariously on their heads. Thornton had brought Jacob his lunch. He had been wheeling his bicycle along the seafront watching the frenzy of activity when he had bumped into two English girls, one of whom he vaguely knew. She had called out to him and Thornton had smiled, a beacon of a smile, a searchlight of happiness, making the girl giggle. She was drinking a bright green limeade through a candy-striped straw. Thornton watched her lips wrap themselves around the straw. Then, regretfully, remembering that his brother was waiting for him, he had waved and moved on. But Jacob, when he met him, had been full of his usual gloom. Thornton sighed, only half listening.

'Crown Rule,' Jacob declared loftily, following some thread of his own, 'my boss says it's a privilege the Indian Empire doesn't have. Which is why they are in such a mess!'

Thornton had not the faintest idea what his brother was talking about. The girl with the candy-striped straw filled his head.

'Crown Rule is what keeps the elephants in the jungle and stops them trampling all over the parks.'

Jacob paused, considering his own words. It was true the parks *were* beautiful. And he could see, Crown Rule did keep the grass green with water sprinklers. It gave the island its economy of rubber and tea. So really, he decided, on balance, it was probably a good thing. Thornton remained silent. Personally he didn't care if the elephants walked on the railway lines, or the grass all died, or the rubber trees dried up. He had no idea what went on in Jacob's head.

'Let's go to the Skyline Hotel tonight,' he had suggested instead. 'There's a jazz band I know playing there.'

'I can't,' Jacob said shortly, 'I've got overtime.'

Since leaving their old home, since he had turned sixteen, Jacob had been working for the Ceylon Tea Board. He was almost nineteen now and he detested Colombo. The trees here were dull green and dirty and the air, when it was not filled with water, was choked with the dust from the spice mills. His childhood was finished and the life that he had so loved gone with it. There was nothing more to say on the subject. These days his only ambition was to leave this wretched place and sail away to the United Kingdom. Life there, so he'd been led to believe, was much better. Just as soon as the war was over he planned to escape.

'Why don't you get a job instead of loafing around,' he asked, his irritation barely concealed.

Thornton had stared dreamily at the sea. It lay like a ploughed field beyond the harbour wall and the day was thick and dazzling and humid. It was far too hot to argue. The air had compressed and solidified into a block of heat. It pressed against Thornton, reminding him once again of the girl with the limeade drink. Her dress had been made of a semi-transparent material that clung to her as she walked, hinting of other, interesting things. He imagined brushing his hands against her hips. Or maybe even, he thought, maybe, her neck. Thornton had a strong feeling that a poem was just beginning to develop. Something about breasts, he thought, smiling warmly to himself. And soft, rosy lips.

'Thornton.' Jacob's irritation had cut across this delicious daydream. 'It's no joke, you know. You have to *plan* your future. It won't simply happen. Don't you *want* your own money?'

What? thought Thornton, confused. All around him the heat shimmered with hormonal promise. His brother's voice buzzed like a fly against his ear. I wonder if I'll be allowed to go to the concert on my own, he thought, whistling the snatch of jazz he had heard earlier. No, he decided, that's not quite right. I haven't got the timing right. When I get back, if Alicia has finished on the piano I'll try to play it by ear.

'Or are you planning on taking up gambling? Carrying on the family tradition perhaps?' Jacob had continued, unable to let the subject go.

'Oh God, Jacob!' Thornton had laughed, refusing to be drawn. 'Life is not simply about making money. I *keep* telling you, I'm a poet.'

'What does that mean, apart from loafing around?'

Thornton had done an impromptu tap dance. Sunlight sparkled on the water.

'I'm not loafing around! *This* is how I get my experience,' he said, waving his hands at the activity in front of them. 'There is a purpose to everything I do. Can't you see?'

'You're getting worse,' Jacob had said gloomily, throwing some crumbs at the seagulls.

Thornton, trying not to laugh again, had decided: his brother simply had no soul.

'I've sent another poem to the *Daily News*,' he offered. 'It's about fishermen. Maybe it will get published. Who knows? Then I'll be rich *and* famous!'

'That proves it,' Jacob told him, satisfied. 'You're a complete idiot!'

Having finished his lunch, having had enough, he stood up.

'Right,' he said briskly, 'I must get back to work. You should think about what I said. I could get you a job here, you know.'

And he was gone, leaving Thornton to his daydreams.

Having washed her face and feeling a little cooler, Myrtle went to the kitchen in search of a piece of cake. From the sound of the jazz being played she guessed Thornton was back. Myrtle pursed her lips. The boy was always playing jazz, or swimming, or wandering aimlessly around Colombo. In the past, whenever she had tried tackling Grace on the subject of Thornton's laziness, it had had no effect. Grace merely smiled indulgently; Thornton could do no wrong.

'He's still young,' was all she said in a voice that brooked no argument.

Myrtle had given up. Thornton would learn a lesson one day. She had seen it in the cards. Her cards never lied.

Myrtle cut herself an enormous slice of cake, ate it and went looking for Grace. But Grace was nowhere in sight. Thornton was still at the piano, and Jasper, moving restlessly on his perch, eyed her with interest.

'Good evening,' he said slowly. 'Where've you been?'

Instantly Myrtle averted her eyes, not wishing to provoke him, but Jasper let out a low whistle. Myrtle retreated hastily into her room, closing the door. Then she got out her pack of cards and began to lay them out. It was her daily practice to see what misfortune might befall the family. The jazz had stopped and a door slammed. A shadow fell across her window. She caught a glimpse of Christopher disappearing into the kitchen. Ah! thought Myrtle, alert again. So *he's* back. For some time she had suspected that Christopher was stealing food. It wouldn't have surprised her if he were selling it on the black market. One way or another they were all up to no good. What else could one expect from a family of gamblers and drunks? The cards were dealt. She began to turn them over, one by one. Perhaps they would offer her an explanation.

Christopher left the house through the back with a parcel under his arm. The servants were resting and so, he hoped, was his mother. No one else mattered. No one else took much notice of him. Now fifteen, Christopher found that Colombo had made little difference to the way he lived his life. He still came and went as he pleased and he still loathed Thornton. He would never forgive his father for sending his brothers to Greenwood while he had never even been to school. Rage, never far off, threatened to overtake him whenever he thought of Thornton. To distract himself he remembered his secret. For Christopher had a secret that of late had brought him immense happiness. None of his family knew that he had fallen in love and was conducting the most wonderful romance. The object of his adoration was a little girl called Kamala whose father ran a sherbet and betel *kadé* on Galle Face Green. It was to Kamala, with her emaciated body and her poverty, that he went with the outpouring of all those things he kept hidden from the rest of the de Silvas. With furious energy and great passion Christopher showered her with his stolen presents. He took food, money, books; anything he could think of that might bring her happiness. This afternoon he had found a cardboard box with some silk in it. His mother was always buying saris. Christopher felt sure she would not miss one. Picking up the box and a packet of English biscuits lying on the kitchen table, he hurried out. Jasper, who had moved to his lower perch, watched him leave with narrow-eyed interest.

'Careful, my boy!' he said, copying Aloysius.

But Christopher only grinned and tweaked the bird's tail feathers affectionately before sauntering out into the sun. He crossed the road and headed towards the seafront. To his surprise he saw Thornton hurrying ahead of him. Christopher slowed down. Thornton was the last person he wanted to meet just at this moment. A bus passed and Thornton ducked suddenly, and then vanished. Christopher looked around, puzzled. There was nowhere Thornton could have gone. He glanced down the road but there was no sign of him. His brother had disappeared. Perhaps he had been mistaken, Christopher thought, continuing on his way. Stepping off the bus on his afternoon off, Jacob looked across the road. He too was certain he had glimpsed Thornton. Heading off furtively in the direction of the Jewish Quarter of the town.

Having decided to do something about Alicia's musical education, Grace went to see the Director of the Conservatoire. She had known his family from many years before, in the days when her mother was alive and used to hold concerts in their house in the hills. All she wanted, she told the Director, was an opinion on Alicia's ability. Then she would sell her land to pay for her daughter's studies.

'Bring her to me, Grace,' the Director said, smiling at her. 'Let's hear her play, let's see what she can do first.'

The Director had a soft spot for Grace. He had never really understood why she had thrown her life away with Aloysius de Silva. Seeing her lovely, anxious face, he was determined to help if he could.

Grace needn't have worried. Three weeks later Alicia was accepted on her own merits, securing a scholarship for the entire three-year diploma. Her daughter's talent would not be wasted and the last of Grace's legacy would remain untouched. Waiting for that rainy day.

When he heard the news Aloysius looked with admiration at his talented daughter. Alicia was sixteen. Her future was bright.

'You see, darl,' he said beaming at Grace. 'She's got our talent! Thank goodness one of them has, eh?'

'Well, I think we should all thank Myrtle, first,' Grace said, handing the letter of acceptance to her cousin. 'Without her lessons, Alicia, you would have been nowhere!'

'You'll be able to play on a Steinway, Alicia,' Thornton said, pleased for his sister. 'And *everything* sounds wonderful on a Steinway!'

'This calls for a celebration, darl,' Aloysius decided, much to Grace's alarm. 'Our family will be famous yet, you'll see!'

And he went out to play a game of poker, to win some money and buy his clever daughter a present. Or if not a present for Alicia, thought Aloysius unsteadily, moments before he fell into the sea at Galle Face, then at least some whisky.

Myrtle watched him go. Afterwards, she wrote in her diary.

Thursday, September 4. So, my cousin thanks me as though I am her servant. How she loves to play the good mother while neglecting her husband. As for Aloysius he will die of drink.

Towards evening, an Englishman from the Tea Board brought Aloysius home. Grace would not go to the door. She was too ashamed. She sent the servant instead.

'He's had a slight accident,' the Englishman said tactfully to the servant, helping Aloysius into the hall.

There was a brief pause.

'Is Grace de Silva at home by any chance?'

Myrtle, hearing the commotion, opened her door stealthily and listened for a moment. Then she went back to her diary.

Four o'clock, she wrote, grimly. *And Aloysius is drunk again. I shall continue to record what goes on in this house. Who knows when it might come in useful? If Grace is doing something illegal, if she is caught, my diary will be useful evidence.*

Grace was furious. She recognised the man's voice. How could Aloysius make such a fool of them both? *He* might not mind being humiliated, but what about her?

'Charming bastards,' said Aloysius staggering in, stopping short at the sight of his wife skulking in the doorway. 'Why on earth are you hiding, darl?' he asked cheerily. 'I know he's *white* but he's not such a bad fellow, you know, underneath. My clothes made rather a mess of his jeep, I'm afraid!'

He laughed. Grace glared at him. She would never raise her voice in front of the servants.

'They don't like me much any more,' continued Aloysius mildly, unaware of her fury. 'They think I'm no use with the local idiots.' He wagged a finger at her. 'They think I don't know what's going on, that I'm a bloody fool! But I know what the British are up to. I know what's going on.' He leaned unsteadily against the door. 'Divide and rule. That's been their game for years, darl. These fellows don't give a damn about *any* of us.' He made a gesture as though he was cutting his throat. 'I think I'll have a little lie-down now, if you don't mind, darl.'

And off he went, first to wash off the seawater and then to pour out a small hair of the dog, after which, he informed the servant sternly, he would have a late afternoon nap.

All her life, Myrtle wrote, *G has had everything she wanted. The looks, the wealth and the man I wanted. But she'll never be happy. And he has wasted his life because of her.*

In a month from now Alicia would leave for the Conservatoire. She would be a full-time boarder. Myrtle paused, staring out at the bright afternoon garden. That would leave Frieda, she thought.

The shadow, she wrote, *whom no one notices!*

3

THE WAR ENDED. IN SPITE OF ALL the predictions, Japan had not invaded. The enemy, it seemed, was within. The writing on the wall was no longer possible to ignore. A hundred and fifty years of British Rule, guided by Lord Soulbury, drew to a close and the island became a self-governing dominion. One day it would no longer be called Ceylon. A few days before independence was announced Aloysius was offered early retirement.

'They want me out of the way,' he told Grace, avoiding her eye.

Ostensibly his retirement was due to his ill health. Privately, all of them knew it was a different matter. His drink problem had never gone away, his liver was failing, his eyesight poor. On his last day he came home early.

'Well, that's that,' he announced. 'The end of my working life!'

There were several vans with loudspeakers parked outside on the streets delivering party political broadcasts.

'Of course I drink too much,' Aloysius shouted above the racket, glaring at the servant who handed him a drink. 'But they kicked me out for a different reason.' He was more subdued than Grace had seen him for a long time. The servants closed the shutters to muffle the noise.

'I'm a Tamil,' Aloysius said, to no one in particular. His voice was expressionless. 'That's not going to change, is it? They can give their damn job to one of their own, I don't much care any more.' He was beginning to sound cornered. 'The old ways are finished. These fellows have no need for courtesy. Or good manners. Life as we have known it will shrink. We've been sucked dry like a mango stone!'

Discarded, thought Grace. That's how we'll be.

'I shall breed Persian cats,' declared Aloysius.

He looked with distaste at the cloudy liquid in his glass.

'I've forgotten what decent whisky tastes like,' he muttered.

Christopher, standing in the doorway, looked at both his parents in amazement. Why did his mother remain silent, why couldn't she stop his drinking?

'Hah!' Aloysius continued, grimacing as he drank. 'The Sinhalese have been waiting years for this. Well, let's see what happens, now they've got the upper hand.'

He's like a worn-out gramophone, thought Grace wearily. In all the years of their marriage she had never told him what he should do. But she was tired. Aloysius switched on the radio and raised his voice.

'It was bound to happen. I told you! Independence will change *everything*.' He was getting into his stride. 'The Tamils won't be able to keep a single job.'

Pausing, he took a quick swig of his drink.

'The English language will become a thing of the past.'

'Don't!' Grace said, sharply.

'What d'you expect, men? The minute the *suddhas*, these white fellows, are gone and Sinhalese becomes the official language, what d'you think will happen? They'll forget every bit of English they've learned. In schools, in the offices, all over the bloody place! It's obvious, isn't it? And then,' he gave a short laugh, drained his glass and poured himself another drink, 'not only will the Tamils suffer but we'll be cut off from the rest of the world. Who the bloody hell except the Sinhalese will speak their language?'

He held his glass up to the light and peered at it for a moment.

'Here's to the new and *independent* Ceylon!'

Christopher waited uneasily. He knew the signs. His father would gradually become louder and his arguments more circular. The six o'clock news finished. Evening shadows lengthened in the garden and a small refreshing breeze stirred the trees. Somewhere the liquid, flute-like notes of a black-hooded oriole could be heard calling sweetly to its mate: *ku-kyi-ho*.

'Our Sinhalese peasants will be the new ruling class,' Aloysius declared, waving a hand in the direction of the servants' quarters.

Christopher was horrified. Well, *don't* for God's sake antagonise them, he wanted to say. Don't just get drunk, *do* something. His father was all talk.

'On the other hand,' Aloysius continued, the arrack taking effect, 'can one blame these fellows? The British have been snubbing the Sinhalese for a century. Is it surprising they are angry?' He paced the floor with furious energy. 'They lost their language and their religion was totally discarded. How d'you think you can suppress a large majority like this without asking for trouble? Huh? Tell me that, men?'

He glared at his wife as though it was her fault. No one spoke. Grace closed her eyes and waited while Aloysius drained the last drop in his glass, triumphantly.

'Having finished playing merry hell the British fellows are off now, leaving us to pay the price. Is this fair play? Is this cricket?' He was working himself into a frenzy. 'Soon we'll all be talking in Sinhalese. Except I can't speak a bloody word of course.'

He belched loudly. Christopher made as if to leave the room but Aloysius held out his glass absent-mindedly.

'Get me some ice, will you, putha?' he said.

The radio droned on. It was beginning to give Grace a headache. She went over and switched it off. Then she looked at her watch. Although she knew he was right, Aloysius in this mood was best ignored.

'That's enough,' she said finally. 'Dinner will be ready in an hour. Myrtle,' she smiled at her cousin, 'can you tell the others, please?' She would not have talks of politics at the dinner table. 'And stop frowning, Christopher,' she added. 'Tonight we are celebrating your father's retirement.'

She spoke firmly, hiding her anxieties. The signs of civil unrest had been growing steadily for months. Two weeks before independence had been declared a series of riots had broken out in the north of the island. The poorest outcasts, the coolies, had had their vote withdrawn. Predictions of trouble swarmed everywhere with a high-pitched whine. Rumours, like mosquitoes, punctured the very flesh of the island. Discrimination against the Tamils, it was said, had already begun in the north. When she heard the stories it was always Vijay that Grace thought of.

Their affair had run on for several years. It had exceeded all their expectations. It had proved that rights and wrongs were complicated things with mysterious inner rhythms. It had given them hope when they had expected none. Vijay was the most disturbed by this. Grace, having discovered her conscience was smaller, steadier than his, had never been as frightened as he was. It was Vijay who struggled to accept what had been given to him. He submerged himself in her, making no demands, never probing her on her other life which was so patently different, never questioning her on her sudden long absences. He loved her with a burning intensity, impossible to quench, existing only for her visits, trustingly, utterly faithful. His understanding still astonished Grace. Whenever she appeared at his door, tense and worn, he would unravel her sari and massage her with sandalwood oil, waiting until the strained anxious look left her face before he accepted what she offered. Silently. He did all this silently. Instinct kept him so. Instinct made him give her the passion she seemed so desperately to crave.

Occasionally, when news from his home town could not be ignored, he would talk about his childhood. Grace, unable to help him, listened as his anger burrowed a hole through his life. Vijay had grown up in a smallholding where the red-brick, earth and the parched years of droughts had made it impossible to grow much.

'Our land was always tired,' he had said, stroking her hair, lulling her to sleep, his voice husky. Usually it was after they made love that Vijay did most of his talking. 'But my parents never stopped working.'

After his father died of dysentery Vijay's older brothers took over the farm. His mother struggled on and although food was scarce there was always a pot of dhal and some country rice on the fire.

'I couldn't bear to watch my mother and my brothers becoming old before their time.'

He was the youngest child. He was bright. The schoolteacher, before he had lost his job, had wanted Vijay to continue with his studies, and maybe one day try for the university.

'I thought, if I moved to Colombo, I could find work and send money home. Maybe I could even begin to study again.'

But it was not to be. The only work he could find in Colombo was tiring, and difficult to come by, and Vijay soon became dispirited.

'There are too many prejudices towards the Tamils,' he said. 'And in this country, if you are born into poverty there is no escape.'

At first, alone and homesick, all he had been able to do was survive. He had never expected to stumble upon Grace. She had not been part of any plan, he told her, smiling a little.

'I remember exactly how you looked, and where you stood!'

The light slanted down on them through his small window, casting long purple shadows on the ground.

'I saw you first, long before you even noticed me!' he told her, delighting in teasing her.

He had dropped a bale of silk in his astonishment, he remembered. The silk had slipped and poured onto the ground, so that he had to gather up armfuls of it before the manager saw him. He had stood holding the cloth, cool against his face, watching as Grace went out of the shop.

'Do you remember? You had a young girl with you,' Vijay told her, smiling. 'I could see, one day she would be like you.'

Alicia. Grace had been glad that he had seen Alicia. She longed to show him the others, reckless though it was. She wanted him to meet Frieda and Jacob, her solemn son, and fierce, angry Christopher, and beautiful Thornton. But every time she voiced this thought Vijay shook his head.

'It is enough for me to imagine them.' Grace felt her heart contract.

Everything about him, his voice, his words, soothed her. Like the coriander tea he made whenever she came to him, exhausted from dealing with Aloysius. She found it unbearable that he asked for so little. It was the hopelessness of their love that hurt her most of all. But when she told him this he dismissed it lightly, with a small shake of his head.

'It's just a dream of ours,' he said. 'How can a high-caste woman like you make a life with someone like me? Let's just dream!'

It pained her to hear him speak this way, so accepting of his place in society, with no attempt to change his lot. There were no words to express her own feelings. Not since her father had died had she felt so cherished.

'But he loves you, doesn't he?' Vijay asked her once, refer- ring to Aloysius. 'How can he *not* love you? He cannot be a bad man, Grace, not if he loves you.'

She loved him for his generosity.

'Yes,' she had said, Aloysius loved her. It was not Aloysius's love that was the problem any longer.

'We belonged together in another life,' Vijay liked to say. 'In some other time. In another place. Perhaps you were my child, or my wife. Only the gods will know.' Vijay was a Hindu. It was easy for him to think this way. 'After you died,' he said, his eyes shining as he kissed the hollow in her neck, 'my grief was such that the gods told me, wait and she will come back to you.'

She wanted to believe him. Often, kneeling in the church, she heard his words. But when she looked all she saw was a cross.

'You are such a courageous woman,' he would tell her. 'D'you know that? You have insights far in advance of these times we live in.' He had learned much from watching her. Slowly he had begun to understand the rich Tamils in this country. 'This gambling and drinking is just one more sign of what is happening.' They had lost their way, he told her, earnestly. In the wake of British Rule, they shared a thread of hopelessness with the poor. 'Aloysius is no different from the others,' Vijay said, in his defence.

When he ran his hands over her fair, unblemished skin he felt as though he touched all the despair of the island, all their collective troubles, their desires, their confusions, here on this lovely, warm and unlined body.

'For all of us,' he told Grace, 'are doomed in our different ways. Both rich and poor, it makes no difference. We are caught, in the wheel of history.'

Dinner that night was quieter than usual. For a start there were only five of them present. Alicia was at the Conservatoire, Jacob was working late and Thornton was out. Christopher and Frieda were silent. Myrtle watched them without comment. She could see Grace was very agitated while Aloysius was not so much drunk as in a state of rage. The loudspeakers continued to pour out their endless stream of messages in Sinhalese.

'Why can't they move away from this road?' Aloysius said, irritably.

'Take no notice,' Grace told him, quietly. And she asked the servant to close the dining-room shutters.

'No!' Aloysius bellowed, flinging his napkin down. 'Why should we be stifled inside our own home? Wait, I'm going to have a word with them.'

He stood up. But they would not let him go outside.

'What's the point?' said Christopher, unable to keep silent any longer, glaring at his father. 'This isn't the way to do it.'

'Christopher,' Grace said, softly, 'that's enough.'

'Where's Thornton?' asked Myrtle, challengingly, looking at Grace.

45

Grace continued to eat, her face expressionless. She refused to be needled by her cousin. The servant brought in another jug of iced water and refilled the glasses. The election vans were moving off to another street but the tension remained.

'Thornton's visiting a friend,' Frieda said, quickly.

'Who?' Aloysius asked, sharply. 'Who is it this time? Some girl, I suppose. Why doesn't he just get a job and make himself useful, for a change?'

'He'll find it harder and harder to get a job, now we have independence,' Christopher reminded them, slyly, helping himself to more swordfish curry.

'Well, that should suit Thornton, then,' Myrtle said. She laughed hollowly.

Grace stopped eating. She was no longer hungry.

'He's a poet! He can't do any old job,' protested Frieda.

No one seemed to hear her. Frieda felt like crying. She wished Thornton were here; she loved his cheerfulness. She wished her sister wasn't at the Conservatoire; she missed her terribly. I hate Myrtle, she thought, glancing at her mother. Grace looked around the table. She too wished Thornton were present, with his uncomplicated cheerfulness and his easy affection.

'We must stay calm,' she said at last. 'There's no point in letting all this talk of civil trouble upset us. Nothing has happened. It *will* be all right,' she added, with a certainty she did not feel.

Later that evening, after the servants had cleared the plates, she went out into the garden. The loudspeakers had stopped spewing out their propaganda and the sound of the sea could be heard again for the first time that day. Across the city, as the Independence Day celebrations began, fountains of fireworks rose and sparkled in the darkening sky. The scent of jasmine drifted towards her on the cool breeze and mingled with the faint smell of the sea. Grace walked to the end of the garden where the coconut trees rustled and whispered in the grove. Vijay was out again tonight. He had gone to a meeting organised by a group of Tamils from Trincomalee. Grace had not wanted him to go, but he had told her, in the future, the Tamils would need to stick together. She heard the sound of *baila* music somewhere in the distance. Small lights twinkled in the trees beyond the coconut grove. The Burgher family were having a party. What was there to celebrate? Grace wondered. She would have liked to slip out, to go and find Vijay, but in the last week she had suddenly become conscious of Myrtle watching her. Every time Grace had come back from the city Myrtle had stared at her, meaningfully.

'I wish she would leave,' Grace had told Vijay. 'I can't ask her to go but I don't want her living with us any more. She hates me!'

Vijay had not taken her seriously. He could not imagine anyone hating Grace. Grace, however, remained uneasily watchful. She had tried talking to Aloysius about Myrtle but he too had dismissed her fears.

'She's harmless, darl. What's the matter with you? Of course she doesn't hate you! That business before we got married was long ago. She's forgotten about it. She wouldn't be here if she hadn't.'

But Grace was no longer so sure.

Having retired to her room after dinner Myrtle took out her diary. Grace had done her disappearing act and Aloysius would undoubtedly be drinking himself into a stupor. There would be no interruptions.

October 8. Aloysius left work today and the de Silvas will now be in a serious financial mess. So, where has all their privilege got them? It's true they still have some influence, should it be needed, but they're no longer wealthy in the way they once were. When all is said and done, this is a Tamil family. It will take more than a Sinhalese surname to change that! They look Tamil. And the head of the family is a perfect drunk! What a liability. One wrong word and he'll cause trouble. Tonight, Grace managed to stop him making a fool of himself over the election vans but how long can she go on stopping him? Poor, useless Aloysius can't see beyond his bottle. Perhaps it is time for me to think of leaving, going back to Jaffna? Perhaps it might be safer there?

She paused and gazed grimly out of her window. The stars were out. Once, her cousin had had everything. Now, however, the planets were moving, they were changing houses. Life did not stay the same forever.

Walking back to the house Grace decided she would begin a novena tonight. She had no control over Aloysius, but this did not bother her. It was Vijay she was thinking of. Last week, he had lost his job at the silk merchants. The manager was new; he was a Sinhalese man. He had told Vijay, since the war finished, cutbacks were necessary in the silk business. Naturally he was sorry to lose Vijay, but, he had shrugged, things weren't so good for small businesses any more. He would not look at Vijay as he spoke. Later on, Vijay told Grace, he found the other staff would be remaining at Maya's. They were all Sinhalese. Grace had been speechless with anger. She had wanted to go to the silk merchant and talk to him. But Vijay would not let her.

'To think of all the business I gave that man,' she cried. 'I'll never shop there again.'

'Forget it,' Vijay had said. 'I'll find another job.'

I will say a novena for him, thought Grace, staring at the sky. I will go to church especially for him, tomorrow.

Somewhere in the distance a train hooted. Grace shivered.

She heard the sound of the gate shut behind her. It was Thornton coming home. In a few weeks Alicia would be graduating at the Conservatoire and they would be all together once more. I must not despair, she thought firmly. Faith was what she needed. Turning towards his footsteps, with a small smile of gladness she waited for her favourite son to walk up the path.

The concert hall, controlled by the last of the Westernised elite, was packed. They arrived late. Heads turned as they took their seats. The de Silva family out in full force for the occasion were very striking. Thornton watched the audience with interest. This is how it will be one day, he thought going into his favourite daydream, when *I* am famous! This is how they will come to hear me read my poetry. He felt a little nervous on his sister's behalf. Frieda too was nervous. She had gone to Mass that morning to pray for Alicia. Frieda had been longing for this evening. Weeks and weeks of longing. A lifetime seemed to have passed since her sister had left home. Frieda had never stopped missing her. Now, at last, Alicia would be returning. We'll be able to be together, thought Frieda happily, her heart beating with joy. We'll be able to talk properly instead of her constant rushing backwards and forwards. Crossing her fingers she watched the stage expectantly, waiting for Alicia to appear.

Christopher moved restlessly in his seat. After the concert, he was going to see Kamala. He had decided to teach her to read in English. It had only just occurred to him to do this and he was looking forward to seeing the expression on her face when he told her. Jacob was deep in a conversation with a man from work. The Tea Board had been taken over by the Sinhalese, it was not run as efficiently as when the English had been there, but Jacob did not mind. His job was secure enough. He spoke

Sinhalese and was generally liked. Besides, what did he care? He was still saving up for his passage to England.

'Jacob has lots of friends among the Sinhalese,' remarked Aloysius in a benign mood, watching his eldest son. 'How does he do it?'

'Oh look, there's Anton Gunesekera,' said Thornton excitedly. 'He's from *The Times*. Shall I tell him about my poetry?'

Idiot, thought Christopher.

'There's a girl staring at you, Thornton,' Frieda said, giggling. Happiness bubbled up in her. At last, sang her heart. The three years were over. Hurray! They would all be together again. Forever and ever. Her lovely family.

'She's been looking at you for ages,' she told Thornton, happily.

'Well, there's a surprise,' said Myrtle. 'Let's hope she's rich!' She laughed at her own joke.

The auditorium was buzzing. Proud parents, talent scouts, even the national newspapers were here. Thornton grinned with delight. It was all so thrilling. The Director of the Conservatoire came over to them.

'Welcome, welcome, Grace, Aloysius,' he beamed. 'How lovely to see all of you here together, supporting Alicia. I promise you there's a wonderful treat in store for you this evening.' He rubbed his hands together. 'Drinks backstage afterwards, don't forget.'

Aloysius hadn't forgotten. He watched the Director's receding back and then, observing Grace's annoyed expression, he burst out laughing.

'That fellow's keen on you, darl!' he told her.

Aloysius too was relaxed tonight. Looking around the concert hall with unusual pride he thought how beautiful his wife looked. They sat for a while longer, fanning themselves with their programmes. Then without warning the lights dimmed and the noise subsided. The first item was a Beethoven trio. Aloysius sat up, instantly alert. He knew the piece well.

'Good!' he said afterwards, above the applause, as the musicians took a bow. 'Well, quite good, a difficult choice, really. For their age, I mean. Don't you think, darl? It's a difficult piece.'

Grace agreed. Myrtle looked at them, at their bent heads, and felt a knife twist in her. It had been music that had first brought them together, long ago.

'Here we sit waiting for our daughter to appear!' Aloysius remarked, but he was looking at Grace. How radiant she is, he thought, genuinely surprised. 'No different than on the day I first set eyes on you!' he told her, loudly.

Myrtle winced. Yes, thought Grace, sadly, aware of the look, you think I'm someone who has everything.

'We should go out more often, darl,' Aloysius said. He was in an expansive mood. 'Now I've retired, now I've more time. D'you remember the concerts your father used to put on?'

She nodded. All she had wanted then was him, and his children.

'Of course, these Sinhalese philistines might stop the concerts,' Aloysius continued, unable to resist the thought. 'They're bound to see Western music as part of the British Empire, just like the language!'

Jacob sighed, pointedly. Grace seemed not to hear. She was lost in thought, engulfed by a sudden wave of sadness, an unspeakable loneliness. Vijay would never share this part of her life. Bending her head, she stared with unseeing eyes at her programme.

'Alicia has become more and more like you,' Aloysius burbled on.

Myrtle, unable to stand any more of such remarks, turned her head away. Must be the thought of the backstage party, she decided, sourly.

In the end, thought Grace, as she waited for Alicia to appear, I am alone. Perhaps after all the Buddhists were right and, ultimately, one was always alone. But, as she waited, musing over these things, her face softened with longing, the lights dimmed again and there she was, on the stage. Slim, beautiful Alicia. Poised and very calm, her long hair was pinned up, making her appear strangely older. A replica of her mother, yet not quite so. The other de Silvas, watching her, gasped. Is this my daughter? thought Grace shaken, astonished, forgetting everything else. For Alicia was playing Schubert. In a way they had never heard her play before, with an effortless passion they had not known she possessed. Revealing something about herself none of them had noticed. Had it always been present? Perhaps she had always played in this way; maybe it simply had slipped their attention in the bustle of everyday life. The sounds fell perfectly, parting the darkness as though it were a path, pausing, running on, lifted by Alicia's fingers, cascading into the silent hall, until finally they rose and floated to rest, gently, somewhere above them in the darkness. Where had such music come from? Will she live her life as she plays the piano? Grace wondered, transfixed.

She brought the house down. The applause, when it came, flooded the concert hall. Nothing matched her after that.

'*Brava!*' the audience shouted when she re-appeared at the end. '*Brava!* A star is born!'

People were staring at the de Silvas. Flashbulbs exploded like flowers.

'Tomorrow,' mouthed the music critic Anton Gunesekera, looking at Grace, pointing to his notebook, 'buy the papers tomorrow!'

So young, everyone said. Such talent! Astonishing! Aloysius looked at his wife, his eyes shining, visibly moved. They were both speechless. United for once, thought Myrtle, bitterly. Thornton was writing furiously on his programme. Christopher, glancing at him, burst out laughing.

'Not another bloody poem,' he said, but the applause drowned his words. His own hands ached with clapping.

'Come on,' Aloysius shouted boisterously over the noise. He waved them onwards. It was so long since they had something to celebrate. 'Backstage, everyone. Come on, come on. I *always* knew she was talented. You see, darl,' he told his wife, 'I always said she should study at the Conservatoire!'

Grace felt laughter explode in her. The tensions of the last few weeks, the new independence, her daughter's music, all of it, gathered in her, making her eyes shine with unshed tears.

Backstage, all was noisy celebration. Alicia stood among a crowd of fellow students holding a spray of orchids. The de Silva children were startled. Was this their sister, this self-assured, beautiful stranger? Shyly they watched. It was in this way that Sunil Pereira first caught sight of her.

'My name is Sunil,' he said above the noise, daringly, having fought his way towards her in the crowd. 'I sent you those.'

He pointed at the flowers she held. Alicia, delighted, took the hand he offered.

'The Schubert was beautiful,' Sunil added.

He hesitated, not knowing how to go on. He felt overwhelmed by the sight of this girl, filled with an unaccountable joy. He was unable to do more than hold her hand.

'Hello, Miss de Silva,' said another voice. 'I am Ranjith Pieris, Sunil's friend.'

Ranjith Pieris was older than Sunil. Putting his arm around his friend, he grinned. Then he too shook Alicia's hand.

'Don't believe a word he says, will you? Sunil's a philistine about music. No, really,' he added as Alicia laughed. 'Truthfully! I'm telling you, he's completely cloth-eared! What he really means is *you* are beautiful. Now, although I would agree with that, *I* thought you played magnificently, as well!'

Ranjith Pieris winked teasingly and Alicia blushed. She opened her mouth to speak but Ranjith continued, making Alicia laugh a little more.

'As you can see, my friend is unable to speak for himself. Fortunately for me he's lost his voice! So, may *I* use this rare opportunity to invite you to the Mount Lavinia dance next week?'

From the corner of her eye Alicia could see Aloysius. But where was her mother? She smiled again, fanning herself, dropping the spray of orchids, which Sunil bent and retrieved for her.

'Why don't you come and meet my family?' she asked him, starry-eyed.

Her mother was deep in conversation with the Director of the Conservatoire. Alicia waved urgently trying to catch her attention. And that was when she saw Frieda. And Thornton and Jacob and Christopher, all together in an awestruck group, all looking uncomfortable. She burst out laughing. Tonight she felt as though she had wings.

Aloysius advanced towards his daughter, beaming. He had noticed Sunil Pereira when he had first walked in. Why, the boy looked as though he was in a trance. Hmm, thought Aloysius. A Sinhalese boy! It could have been worse. His eyes narrowed with interest but he kept his thoughts to himself.

'Splendid! Splendid!' he said out loud.

And having kissed and congratulated his daughter, he asked Sunil what he did for a living. Sunil hardly heard him and it was left to Ranjith Pieris to speak to Aloysius.

'We both work for the External Trade Office,' Ranjith said.

'How interesting!' Aloysius nodded. Civil servants, he thought, pleased. Well, well, how very interesting. I may be an old dog, but I can still spot a winner, when I see one. How fortunate, they were fluent both in Sinhalese and in English.

'So,' he asked, casually, 'you work in our new government, huh? How d'you find it there? Now that the British have gone?'

Christopher frowned. His father was looking shifty. 'What's he up to, now?' he muttered to Jacob.

Aloysius was thinking furiously. Being in the new government meant access to British whisky and British cigarettes. Aloysius was sick of arrack and unfiltered Old Roses. Being in the government meant better rations and a superior quality of rice. With his eyes firmly on the main chance, he watched Sunil talking to Alicia. His daughter, he observed, with a growing sense of well-being, had changed in the last three years. The promise of her childhood good looks appeared to have come to fruition. Until now her life had been filled exclusively with her music. She had spent her days in a dreamworld hardly straying from the confines of her Bechstein. Never mind, thought Aloysius, delightedly, all this was about to change. Tonight had brought the first public recognition of her talent. What else had it brought? Seeing his wife approaching, he waved, excitedly.

'Darl,' he cried, 'come and meet Sunil Pereira.'

And without a moment's hesitation, before his wife could comment, he invited this courteous young man home. The romance, for clearly it was to be just that, was to be encouraged.

'He seems very nice,' Grace admitted later, a little doubtfully. Left to herself she would have waited a while before issuing any invitations. 'Aren't we being a bit hasty though?' she ventured. 'Perhaps we should find out a bit more about him first? Her future is just beginning and this is only the first one.'

'Nonsense, she's the perfect age, darl,' said Aloysius, looking sentimentally at her. 'The same age as you were when your father gave me your hand.'

Yes, thought Grace, sharply, and look what a mess I made. But she kept her thoughts to herself.

'Why do I have to be there when he visits?' complained Jacob, who had planned to work overtime. 'I don't have anything to say to him.'

'Oh for heaven's sake, Jacob,' Aloysius replied, annoyed, 'show some family solidarity, will you?'

The day after Alicia's graduation the newspapers were full of reviews of her performance. Her talent, her youth, her future, all these things were suddenly of interest. Already she had been offered two concerts.

'Beethoven *and* Mozart,' she said, in a panic, 'all in a month. How will I learn them?'

The de Silvas were staggered. Overnight, Alicia had become something of a celebrity. A photographer came to the house and her picture appeared in a music magazine. The family felt as though they were seeing her for the first time. And suddenly there was an admirer as well. Two more weeks went by. Sunil Pereira came to call. He had thought of nothing else but Alicia since the concert. He waited, impatient for the visit, a prey to Ranjith Pieris's teasing. He hardly slept, dreaming constantly about her.

'Go and see them, men,' Ranjith teased. 'Put yourself out of your misery, or I'll have to!'

So, plucking up his courage, unprepared for his meeting with her, much less her eccentric colonial family, he went.

Let loose at this first encounter, the de Silvas reacted each in their different ways.

'Hello, Sunil,' said Thornton, shaking hands with him, smiling in a new and dazzling way. It was clear he needed to do nothing else. 'Why don't you come with us to the party at the Skyline Hotel next week? There's supposed to be an extremely good jazz quartet playing.'

Ah, yes, why not? thought Myrtle. Why not show off in our usual fashion?

Christopher, resigned and silent as always, saw no point in getting annoyed with his family. They were completely crazy. Any friends of theirs were bound to be crazy too. What *am* I doing here? he thought. I don't belong.

'Where do your parents live, Sunil?' asked Grace tactfully, thinking, first things first. A few discreet enquiries never went amiss. Earlier that day she had discussed Sunil with Vijay. Lying in his arms, she had told Vijay about their first encounter.

'He has an open, friendly face,' she had said.

Seeing him again, she felt she had been right. The young man seemed unaffected and honest.

'My father worked for the railways,' Sunil told them. 'He was killed in the riots of '47: Now my mother lives in Dondra.'

He hesitated. Would a family such as this have heard about the riots in '47? Grace nodded, encouragingly. Of course she remembered.

'He was crushed in an accident,' Sunil said. His father, he told them, had been working his shift at the time. He had not been part of the riots but in the skirmish that followed he had been trampled to death. 'My mother couldn't get her widow's pension because it was thought my father had taken part in the demonstration. She should have taken the matter to a tribunal but, well . . .' He spread his hands out expressively.

Alicia was listening. There was not a trace of bitterness in Sunil's voice. In the silence that followed, Grace read between the lines. She had heard how terrible things had been, how many people had been killed. Sunil's childhood would have been very hard as a direct result. Being a Sinhalese woman, Sunil's mother would have been ignored by the British. She would have had no idea how to get any compensation. Aloysius nodded. One brown face, he guessed, would have been the same as any other. Aloysius was unusually silent. The talk turned to other things. To Sunil's political ambitions for the new country they were building. Good God, thought Aloysius astonished, I must be growing old. This boy's optimism is so refreshing.

'Our only way forward is through education,' Sunil told Alicia, earnestly. It was a simple thought, he admitted, apologetically, but the discovery was a turning point for him. Christopher, about to leave the room, stopped in surprise.

'All the foreign rule we've been subjected to is bound to affect us as a country,' Sunil continued. 'We have become a confused nation. What we desperately need now is free state education. For everyone.' He was talking to them all, but it was Alicia he was looking at. 'Sinhalese, Tamils, everyone,' he said.

There was no doubting his sincerity. Ah, thought Jacob, cynically, here we go again, same old story. Well, what does he think he can achieve alone?

'I went from the village school to being a weekly boarder in town,' Sunil told them. 'Then I took the scholarship exam for Colombo Boys School.'

A self-made man, thought Aloysius, impressed. They are the best. It's men like this we need.

'I found it paid off,' Sunil smiled at Alicia. 'After that, I could send my mother some money.'

But he's wonderful, Alicia was thinking. He's *so* wonderful! Christopher too was listening hungrily. Here at last, in the midst of his idiotic family whose sole interests were concerts and parties, was someone he might talk to. Here at last was a real person. Someone who might care about the state of this place. Suddenly Christopher wanted desperately to have a proper conversation with Sunil. But there were too many de Silvas present. He stood sullen and uncommunicative, hovering un-certainly in the background, not knowing what to do next.

Sunil had no idea of the tensions around him. The family behaved impeccably, plying him with petits fours (where, he wondered fleetingly, did they get *them*?) and tea, served in exquisite white bone-china cups, and love cake on beautiful, green Hartley china plates. Alicia played the piano for him and Jasper watched the proceedings silently, gimlet-eyed and newly awake from his afternoon nap.

The conversation became general. Grace and Aloysius were charming hosts. All those house parties, those weekend tennis events had not taken place for nothing. Even Jacob became cautiously friendly, talking to Sunil about his work exporting tea. Sunil was interested in everything. Aloysius told him about the tea estates that had once belonged to Grace while Thornton showed him some of his poems. But this last proved to be too much for Christopher. Taking the cats with him, he disappeared.

'Thank God, sister!' shouted Jasper, who loathed the cats.

Sunil was enchanted all over again. How could he not be? Jasper alone was a force to be reckoned with.

'Have you ever played poker, Sunil?' asked Aloysius.

'Oh no, please, no!' exclaimed Grace. But she was laughing.

'Wait, wait,' Thornton cried. 'Let's all play. Come on, Jacob, you too!'

The evening meandered on. The card table was brought out; ice-cold palmyra toddy in etched Venetian glasses appeared as if from nowhere; and, with the unexpected arrival of the aunts, Coco and Valerie, the family launched into a game of Ajoutha. It was a magical starlit evening, effortlessly filled with the possibilities of youth. Alicia was persuaded to play the piano again, this time for Sunil's friend Ranjith Pieris who arrived just before dinner was served out on the veranda. Sunil could not remember another time as wonderful as this.

'You know, I have Ranjith to thank for meeting you,' he told them, beginning slowly to relax, feeling some inexplicable emotion glowing within him each time his eyes alighted on Alicia. For it had been Ranjith, he told them, shyly, who had bought the tickets for the Conservatoire recital. It had been Ranjith who, persuading Sunil to accompany him, had sent him reluctantly out into this bright looking-glass world of elegance, from which there would be no going back.

The wedding was set for December when it would be cooler. The invisible forces of karma worked with effortless ease. Gladness filled the air. Sunil was a Buddhist, but in the face of Alicia's happiness, no one cared much. For Alicia was radiant. Everyone remarked on the change in her. Her career was taking off. Having given two more concert performances in Colombo she was invited to take part in a radio series in the New Year.

'After that, who knows?' said the Director of the Conservatoire. 'An international tour perhaps? Grace, your daughter is an extraordinary girl.'

'Let's get the wedding over with first, for goodness' sake!'

begged Grace. The world seemed to be spinning madly with so many things happening at once.

'Yes, yes,' agreed Aloysius joyously, helping himself to the whisky the bridegroom-to-be had just brought him.

The marriage was arranged for the last day in the year, a Poya day, a night of the full moon. An auspicious sign, a good omen.

'Come along, everyone,' cried Aloysius with gusto, 'let's drink to the wedding of the year!'

It was the first proper whisky he had drunk in months. It was clear he was going to get on with his future son-in-law like a house on fire.

'What we need is a small windfall,' he added with a small gleam in his eyes. 'A little poker might do the trick, what d'you think, darl? Huh?'

Grace ignored him. She was still ignoring him, when, four weeks later the windfall turned out to be in the form of a broken arm.

'Don't worry,' Aloysius told her, finding it hugely funny. 'It's only August after all. By Christmas I will be out of the sling!'

Grace had other things on her mind.

'Father Giovanni wants the bride and groom to attend matrimonial classes together,' announced Frieda, who was in charge of helping her mother on all such matters. Frieda was to be the bridesmaid. 'Otherwise, there can't be a church wedding, he told me.'

'Hindu bastard!' screeched Jasper, not following the story very well. He was feeling the heat.

'Be quiet, Jasper,' said Grace absent-mindedly.

'Bastard!' said Jasper sourly.

'That bird should be shot. He's a social embarrassment. I'll do it, if you like, darl,' offered Aloysius, whose right hand was still capable of pulling a trigger. 'This is entirely Christopher's doing, you know. God knows what he'll come out with when the guests start arriving.'

But naturally everyone protested and Jasper was spared yet again.

Meanwhile, in all this commotion, no one noticed Thornton's frequent mealtime absences. Jacob, the usual guardian of all the siblings, was preoccupied. In just over a year's time he hoped to secure a passage on one of the Italian ocean liners that crossed and recrossed the seas to England. He told no one of this plan which had been fermenting quietly for years. His sister's wedding, his brother's whereabouts, these things had increasingly become less important to Jacob. If he noticed his family at all these days, it was from a great distance, their chatter muffled by the sound of the ocean, that heartbeat of all his hopes. So Jacob, the sharpest of them all, the one who noticed everything, failed to notice that Thornton was often absent. Which left Thornton free to do just about whatever he wanted. At last that wonderful smile was paying off. These days, his dark curly hair shone glossily and his large eyes were limpid pools of iridescent light. Such was his laughter when he *was* home, planting a kiss on his mother's head, tweaking his sister's hair, deferential towards his father, that nobody really registered those times when he was not. Except Jasper that is. Jasper was always saying crossly, 'You're late!'

'I know,' laughed Thornton, coming in with great energy, sitting down at the piano, playing the snatch of jazz he had heard only moments before as he walked up to the house. 'I've been looking for a new mynah bird, old thing!'

'Oh Thornton!' exclaimed Alicia, rushing in. Being in love made her rush. 'You are so clever. I wish I could play by ear.'

Thornton laughed, delighted. The piano under his fingers

took on the swagger of the dance floor. He would be playing at his sister's wedding.

'Will you play "Maybe" and "An American in Paris" at the reception?' begged Alicia, her arms around his neck, hugging him.

'Yes,' said Thornton. 'Yes, yes, yes!'

And he laughed again with the sheer joy of it all, pushing his hat down over his eyes, sticking a cigarette in the side of his mouth Bogart-style, foot pressed down on the loud pedal, until he deafened them all with the vibrations. Alicia, because she was happy, assumed naturally that his happiness was due to her. Naturally, being in love, what else could she assume? But Thornton was filled with an exuberance, a secret glow that was nothing whatsoever to do with the sunshine outside, or his sister. It was a tingling feeling that made him belt out 'As Time Goes By' one minute, and 'Maple Leaf Rag' the next.

The house was almost continuously filled with activity, music pouring out of its every window. Love was in the air. Even the stifling heat of the dry season could not dispel it. Everyone was completely wrapped up with this, the first marriage in the family. The visitors' list grew daily. Relatives from across the island, from Australia, and from as far away as Canada were coming.

'We mustn't forget Anslem, you know,' said Aloysius. 'Oh, and that fellow, what's his name, darl, you know, the chap from the hill station?'

'Harrison?' asked Grace. 'Yes. He's on my list. What about Dr Davidson and his wife?'

'Don't forget the Fernandos,' Frieda reminded her. 'And is Mabel coming?'

'What about Anton?' asked Thornton. 'I hope he's coming.'

'He is,' said Grace frowning, looking at her list again, harassed.

'Alicia, is Ranjith Pieris *definitely* Sunil's best man? I need to know.'

'Yes,' shouted Alicia from another part of the house.

'Oh good!' said Thornton. 'Hey, Jacob, Anton's coming!'

'Good,' said Jacob, hurrying out. He was late for work.

Having sold off a piece of her land Grace prepared to throw open their doors for a party bigger and grander than anything in living memory. Bigger than Grace's own wedding and grander than the party thrown by her father at the birth of Jacob. Grace was orchestrating the whole event, and Aloysius . . . Aloysius could hardly *wait* for the celebrations. A huge wedding cake was being made. As rationing was still in operation this was no easy task, but in this, at least, the bridegroom was able to help. The list of ingredients was frightening.

'Rulang, sugar, raisins,' said Frieda importantly, 'sultanas, currants, candied peel, cherries, ginger preserve, chow-chow preserve, pumpkin preserve, almonds, Australian butter, brandy, rose water, bee's honey, vanilla essence, almond essence, nutmeg, cloves, cinnamon, one hundred and fifty eggs.'

Even Myrtle was drawn in and for once joined forces with the cook to weigh, chop and mix the ingredients, while Sunil was consulted on the little matter of the eggs. His mother in Dondra was instructed to round up all the hens she could find. Sunil volunteered to fetch the eggs, returning with all one hundred and fifty, travelling on the overnight steam train that hugged the coconut-fringed coastline, lit by the light of the phosphorescent moon.

It was hot and airless in the train and several times during the night Sunil went out into the corridor where the breeze from the open window made it cooler. A huge moon stretched a path across the water. From where he stood it shone like crumpled cloth. Sunil stood watching the catamarans on the motionless sea and the men silhouetted on their stilts, delicate nets fanning like coral around them. It was the landscape of his birth, the place he loved and had grown up with. It was part and parcel of his childhood. Now, with this sudden momentous turn of events he was leaving it all behind to begin his married life in Colombo. Soon, very soon, he would have a wife to support. And then, he thought with wonder, then, there would be children! In the darkness his face softened at the thought. He had been an only child. He could not imagine children. His and Alicia's. He knew his mother worried about this unexpected match to a Tamil girl. She had said nothing, but he knew what was on her mind. Sunil, however, was certain. He had given his heart, and his certainty was such that nothing would go wrong, he promised her. If the United Ethnic Party came into power, as he fervently hoped, then his political ambitions and all his wishes for unity on the island would be fulfilled at last, and the vague and reckless talk of civil war would be averted. It *will* be averted, thought Sunil determinedly. One day, he had promised his mother, brushing aside her anxieties, climbing aboard the train, with his parcel of eggs, they would build a house in Dondra, at the furthest tip of land by the lighthouse, overlooking the sea. So that she might live at last surrounded by her memories, so that he and Alicia, and all their children could be frequent visitors. Peering out of the carriage window, with the sea rushing past, his thoughts ran on in this way, planning, dreaming, hoping, as the Capital Express sped along the coast, hissing and hooting plaintively into the night. The ships on the horizon looked out from the darkened sea at the delicate necklace of lights on this small blessed island, as Sunil, gazing at the moon, carried one hundred and fifty eggs back for his beloved's wedding cake.

4

By LATE OCTOBER THE HEAT IN Colombo had become impossible. There had been no rain for months and the garden that had thrived under Grace's care began to wilt. The air was thick and clammy and humid but still there was no sign of any rain. Every day the sky appeared a cloudless, gemstone blue, joined seamlessly to the sea. One morning, when the preparations for the wedding were fully under way, Grace decided to leave early for Colombo. These days she was always shopping in Colombo. There was Alicia's entire trousseau to buy; there were clothes for the other children. And there were her own saris, too.

'Start lunch without me,' she told Frieda, as she waited for the taxi.

'I won't be in either, darl,' Aloysius warned her.

He had joined a new club where he could play poker undisturbed. Grace nodded. She had seen to it that Aloysius had only a limited amount of money each month and she was happy for him to spend it as he pleased. Once this allowance was gone, she told him, firmly, there would be nothing more until the next month. Sitting in her taxi, driving across the heat-soaked city, she dismissed him from her mind. It was Vijay who filled her thoughts. She was on her way to visit him. It had become increasingly difficult for Grace to escape, harder to find suitable excuses to leave the house. But although she was aware of an increased risk, she saw Vijay as often as she dared, seldom leaving it longer than a week. After two months of unemployment Vijay had finally got a new job as a cook in a restaurant. It meant he worked late and was only free during the mornings and although in some ways this made things easier for Grace, she missed seeing him in the evenings.

'I've been longing to see you,' she cried breathlessly, coming in quietly, noticing how cool his tiny room was. Noticing the white sheet on his makeshift bed and the spray of jasmine in water on the table. She loved this room with its pristine cleanliness and its sparse austerity. Vijay was looking at her with a tender expression that made her heart turn over.

'I have all morning,' she said, sounding like a young girl, feeling the luxury of her words. They had no need to rush.

Afterwards, lying side by side, she saw there were hours left. Vijay lay with one arm around her staring at a patch of light flickering on the ceiling. Grace could see fragments of them both reflected in the mirror that stood beside the door. A leg entwined with a foot, indistinguishable from a smooth hip. Joined as one. Skin to skin. Turning her face towards his, she pulled him gently away from his private reverie, her eyes dark and very beautiful so that, unable to resist her, unable to remain melancholy in the face of her certainty, he buried his face in her. And began to kiss her, slowly and methodically, inch by inch, with an urgency he had not shown before. Outside the morning sun rose higher in the sapphire sky, shortening the shadows, increasing the heat, unnoticed by them. When finally she could speak again Grace told him about a party she had been invited to. She liked to tell him about her days and what the family did. She wanted him to know everything about her life.

'It's being held in the old Governor's House,' she said. 'Next Saturday.'

They washed each other in water Vijay brought up from the well. The water smelt of damp moss. Vijay began preparing a little lunch. He would have to go to work soon.

'You know the place?' Grace said, pinning up her hair. She leaned over and he fed her some rice. Then he kissed her. 'It overlooks Mount Lavinia Bay. You can see this part of town from their garden. I'll stand on the veranda and think of you,' she said tenderly.

'You're going *there*?' Vijay asked her in alarm. 'On the night before the eclipse?'

'What difference does the eclipse make?' Grace asked him, laughing. She was aware that for Vijay, as for most other Sri Lankans, the eclipse brought insurmountable fears with it. Superstition threaded darkly across the lives of the Buddhists and the Hindus. But Grace had grown up untouched by all these complicated rituals and she found it hard to take him seriously on this subject.

There had not been a total eclipse for eighty-eight years. The island was feverish with excitement. It prepared itself for the event in different ways. The British (those who remained) brought out their telescopes and their encyclopedias. They were interested in the life cycle of the universe. The Roman Catholics ignored all talk of it. The Buddhists, ruled as they were by the light of the moon, were understandably nervous. Unable to move away from the cycle of their own karma, they, like the Hindus, were trapped in darkness, hoping the vibrations of their prayers would protect them. Only Grace remained fearless.

'Oh, you mustn't give in to the ignorance of this place!' she told him, knowing he wasn't listening, hoping to tease him out of this nonsense. She stole up behind him as he prepared the food and put her arms around his waist. 'You of all people shouldn't let these old wives' tales rule your life. Vijay, you *know* it's all rubbish!'

Vijay shook his head stubbornly. The old traditions were ingrained in him and he was not prepared to listen. He would have to go to work in an hour; he would not see Grace for another week, perhaps longer. There was no time for arguments.

'Tell me about the wedding,' he said, changing the subject.

'Well, the cake is made,' Grace said, smiling, not wanting to argue either. 'Frieda and Myrtle made it together. With the cook's help.'

She hesitated. There was something else, something she could not put her finger on. It was nothing much, but her suspicions about Myrtle were growing. This morning Grace had had a strong sensation of being followed. Could it be possible that her cousin knew?

'What about Alicia?' asked Vijay. He was boiling some water. Grace had given him one of her mother's old teapots and he was making tea in it.

'She's blissfully happy, of course, but . . .' Again Grace hesitated. Alicia's future made her uneasy. Out of loyalty to her daughter she had not discussed it, but what would happen when Alicia had children? As a family the de Silvas had their own strong Tamil identity. What would happen to that?

'What will it be like for Alicia's children?' she asked tentatively. 'Their father will be a Sinhalese. What problems will this cause?'

Vijay handed her a cup of tea and smiled broadly. It was his turn to tease her.

'Aiyo! So you have fears too,' he said. 'Are *you* worrying about becoming a grandmother? Even before the wedding?'

'No, no, I –'

'It's a *good* thing,' Vijay said earnestly. 'Don't you see? You should be *glad*! The only hope this country has is through inter-marriage.' He paused. 'It's too late for us, but for Alicia there is hope.'

He smiled and the ever-present sadness lifted from his eyes making her wish her life back, to live it all over again, differently. But then, just before she left him, he brought up the subject of the eclipse again.

'It's not a very good time, you know,' he fretted. 'Do you have to go to this party?'

'Vijay?' she said.

She had never seen him so worried. She could feel his heart beating. Vijay took her face in his hands, kissing her luminescent eyes. He should have felt dirty beside her, he told her. A scavenger straying out of his domain. But he felt none of these things, such was the healing strength of her love, pouring over the poor soil that was his life, overwhelming him.

'You and your superstitious country ways!' she teased him, hiding an unaccountable heaviness in her heart. She knew he went to watch the many demonstrations springing up in the heart of the city. She knew there was no stopping him, and she, too, was afraid. 'I can come back next Saturday morning,' was all she said before leaving him. 'I shall say I'm visiting the nuns. Will you be here? Will I see you?'

Vijay nodded. He did not want her to leave. A terrible fore-boding had overtaken him. Next Saturday was more than a week away.

Sitting in the taxi, going home, she felt the heat spread like an infectious disease. It carried with it an ugly undercurrent of destruction that hovered wherever one went in the capital. It was not good. The British, sidelined by choice, watched silently. Waiting. Those who loved this island, and there were many who did, were saddened by what they saw. But most of them, Grace knew, had predicted the elephants would soon be out of the jungles.

Having finished her chores, having eaten her lunch alone, Frieda decided to go shopping. There was no one to go with her into Colombo. No one was at home, no one cared, but the fact was, she told herself with a trace of resentment, she felt very lonely. She needed to buy a present for the bride. Today was as good a day as any. Alicia's wedding, just two months away, was threatening to give her a permanent headache. Myrtle's constant questions didn't help. Her mother was preoccupied. They were *all* busy with their own things. I might as well go out, thought Frieda, her eyes filling with tears. The sunlight was a blinding curtain, a bright ache of unhappiness thumping against her heart as she walked. Unhappiness shadowed her as she crossed the dusty streets. I am only a year younger, she thought dully, frowning with concentration, but look at the difference in our lives.

Before her sister had gone to the Conservatoire they had been inseparable, sharing bedrooms, clothes, secrets. She had known this would change when Alicia left home but Frieda had been looking forward so much to her return. And then, unexpectedly, hardly had she completed her diploma than she found Sunil. Frieda had not anticipated this. She had certainly not expected such a quick marriage. The last few months had been terrible. Her headache worsened as she walked. A pair of cymbals clashed together in her head. Nothing will ever be the same, she thought, mournfully. Everything has changed. Once

I was her only friend but now Alicia belongs to another. The words went round and round, beating into her head, competing with the boiling sun. Alicia has Sunil *and* she has her music. Thornton has his poetry. What do I have? Nothing. Absolutely nothing. So thought Frieda with a drum roll going on in her head as she hurried down the road to Pettah.

On the way, much to her astonishment, she saw various members of her family. First she saw Thornton. He hurried past furtively and jumped onto a number 16 bus heading towards the east side of town. The Jewish Quarter, thought Frieda, puzzled. Who does he know there? Her favourite brother looked harassed. It wasn't like Thornton to scowl. What was the matter with him? Next she saw Myrtle walking towards Mr Basher's house. Frieda paused, wondering whether to call out to her. Mr Basher was a palmist. Myrtle avoided the main door. She rang the bell at the side entrance and went in, hurriedly. Why was Myrtle seeing a palmist? Then she saw Christopher. He rushed past on the other side of the street looking hot and fierce.

'Goodness,' muttered Frieda, startled, 'we're all out and we're all in a bad mood!'

She felt a little cheered, without quite knowing why. There was nothing very unusual about Christopher's presence in town. Since the age of thirteen he was more out than in. What was more worrying was that he had two large cardboard boxes tucked under his arm.

'Oh no,' Frieda exclaimed aloud, suddenly alert, forgetting her woes. 'He's stolen some wedding cake!'

Why would he do a thing like that? Making a mental note to count the cake boxes when she got back she continued on her way. A slight breeze had sprung up. She was nearing the waterfront. Frieda entered Harrison's music shop intent on finding a particular gramophone recording for Alicia. She was uncertain of the name. Lost in thought, she wandered around looking at the recordings, humming to herself, unaware of the fair-haired young man who watched her quizzically.

'Can't you find what you want?' the young man asked, eventually.

Frieda, puzzling over the problem, replied unthinkingly, 'No, but I can sort of sing it. I think it's a Beethoven piece.'

She hummed loudly, marking time with her hands. She did not look up, mistaking him for a sales assistant. The boy laughed, amused.

'At any rate, you can sing,' he said. 'Although I doubt it's Beethoven.'

'Why?' demanded Frieda, without thinking. 'What makes you so sure?'

The boy grinned and Frieda looked at him for the first time. But he's *English*, she thought, confusedly. And he's got *golden* hair!

'Well,' said the boy, 'does it sound like this?'

He sang the opening bars, conducting it with both hands and accidentally knocking a record off the counter. The assistant hurried towards them. The boy was right; it was not Beethoven at all but Smetana with his river. How foolish she felt. And how strange was the quality of the light, she thought faintly, noticing it as it caught the sharp blueness of his eyes. They were dazzling, like the sea at noon. Something constricted in her heart.

'Robert Grant, at your service,' the boy said, bowing over her hand as if he was acting in a play.

Suddenly it felt as though a whole orchestra was playing in Frieda's head.

'I'm Frieda de Silva,' she said, wondering why it was so hot. 'My sister is getting married soon and this is a present for her.'

The boy's eyes were hypnotic. Frieda was unable to look away. Never had she seen such eyes.

'She's a concert pianist too,' she said, her voice faint.

'Oh? What's her name?'

'Alicia. Alicia de Silva.' Then, with a boldness that was to astonish her, afterwards, she added, 'Why don't you come to the concert she's playing in, next week?'

Robert Grant grinned again. He had been bored, but now he was less so.

'I'd love to,' he said with alacrity. 'Where's it on and at what time?'

The assistant, who knew the de Silva family, handed Frieda her gramophone record and smiled.

'Hello, Miss Frieda, I read a very good review about your sister in *The Times* last week.'

Frieda nodded. The orchestra in her head was playing a coda.

'Is she famous?' Robert asked as they walked out, and again Frieda nodded.

'Yes. Yes, well, I mean, she's getting famous,' she stammered. 'Come and meet her, meet my whole family.'

Outside, the heat was solid and impenetrable. Robert wrote down the time of the concert and shook hands with her. There was a small flash of startling blue as he glanced at her, then he was gone. It was as though the sea, ultramarine and wonderful, had seeped into her day. Opening her mouth to call after him, watching his receding back, Frieda stopped abruptly, for what on earth did she think she was doing? Turning, quickly, she began to walk home and entirely missed seeing her mother slipping out of a dark unfamiliar alleyway beside the station, into the afternoon sunshine. As she opened her umbrella and lifted her sari off the ground, Grace had the look of a softly bruised and ripened fruit, with a bloom, not usually found on the face of a woman who had borne five children and lived with a man such as Aloysius. She looked like a woman ten years her junior. But Frieda hurrying home in the scorching heat, with her heart on fire, and a set of wings attached to the soles of her feet, her sari sweeping up the dust of all Asia, saw none of this. Her mother's dazed and secret look was entirely lost on her. For now at last, finally, Frieda had a secret all of her own.

'Yes?' asked Jasper as she entered the house stealthily, adding to himself, when she did not reply, 'Up to no good.'

Frieda, pouring herself a long, cool glass of water, adding many ice cubes to it, ignored him, certain, even as the liquid slipped down her throat, that her world had changed forever since lunchtime.

Myrtle switched on her ceiling fan. Then she unlocked the drawer in her desk and took out her diary. Refilling her fountain pen she began to write.

October 28. A profitable morning. Followed G as far as the Elephant Hotel but then lost her. The taxi driver was exceedingly stupid and did not seem to understand what following a car meant. However, Mr B was very helpful. I gave him the information about the wedding and he agreed with me that the marriage is not a good one. Time will tell, he kept saying, shaking his head, gloomily. When I asked him how much time, he spread the cards. He is a very thoughtful and clever man and I am inclined to believe him. By the looks of things this marriage is going to be in serious trouble. Mr B asked me why I wanted to know so badly. There was no point in going into the details, no point in telling him about G and my suspicions about her activities with the British. I simply told him I wanted to save the rest of the family from further harm. Mr B nodded his head and told me I would not have long to wait. Months, perhaps, he said. But I had the distinct feeling he meant weeks. Then he gave me something else to stop the marriage. He told me what to do. I daren't write the instructions down. All this has cost me a hell of a lot of money.

Myrtle paused. She could hear someone moving about in the hall. Jasper was saying something. She opened her door gently.

'Up to no good,' Jasper was saying morosely. 'Up to no good!'

Robert Grant could not believe his luck. Having finished his degree at Oxford earlier that summer, he had arrived in Colombo to visit his parents. Sir John Grant had only a few more months as High Commissioner, after which he would return to England. Robert's mother had decided it was a good thing for him to travel across the empire, before following his father into the Foreign Office. To begin with Robert had been bored. The embassy was filled with stuffy old people and the only locals he met were shopkeepers or servants. Then, just as he began to wish he were back in England again, quite by chance he had met Frieda de Silva. On her invitation he had gone to Alicia's concert the following Monday and met the rest of her family. Mrs de Silva invited him to have dinner with them afterwards.

'I know your father!' Grace exclaimed when she had discovered who he was. They had finished eating and were now in the drawing room. 'We're very old friends. How lovely to meet you at last. I knew you were coming over here, but not when.' Grace was delighted. 'We used to play together as children, you know. He used to visit us at the House of Many Balconies. Your grandfather and my father were good friends. How funny! We've just had an invitation to your father's farewell party at Mount Lavinia House.'

Robert was pleased.

'How long will you be in Colombo?' asked Grace.

'I'm sailing back just before the New Year.'

'Oh what a pity. You'll miss Alicia's wedding!'

Robert was startled. And then dismayed. So the girl Alicia was engaged to be married? Gosh! he thought, not knowing what to say. Suddenly Sunil's presence made sense. He felt a sharp sense of something having passed him by. Something irretrievable and very important.

'I forgot,' he mumbled. 'What a pity.'

'Never mind,' Grace told him cheerfully, 'we'll see you at the party on Saturday.'

'Do you have a telescope?' Aloysius asked suddenly. 'You know we're having an eclipse soon?'

In spite of herself Grace shivered. Perhaps, she thought, confused, there will be rain soon. Briefly her eyes met Myrtle's.

'I expect my father has,' Robert said, distractedly.

He was unable to take his eyes off Alicia who was laughing with Thornton. Catching sight of him looking at her, Alicia called him over to join them.

'You know, darl,' Aloysius said, turning to Grace, 'hundreds of staff on the railways walked out today. The factory workers from the rubber plantations are joining them tomorrow. The copra workers will strike next. The Sinhalese are blaming the Tamils for taking their jobs. I heard on the news yesterday, the government expect things to explode around the time of the eclipse.'

'I know,' said Grace softly. She looked at Sunil.

'Come on, sis,' Thornton was saying, 'don't be so boring! Let's play a duet. Tell her, will you, Sunil?'

Sunil smiled. They were both such children! He turned to Grace.

'The government told the factory workers to go back to work

or lose their jobs,' he said, his face serious. He shook his head. It was utterly unbelievable. 'Trade in rubber and copra had fallen, you know. There's not much demand for these materials any more. That's the reason the factories are closing. It's nothing to do with the Tamils.'

'Of course, men,' Aloysius agreed, joining in and beginning to get agitated. 'This is nothing new, we all know this. Of course, of course. The Tamils haven't taken the jobs. There *are no* jobs. It's the fault of the war! Why don't the Sinhalese blame it on the war instead?' he asked belligerently.

Thornton and Alicia had begun to play a duet, laughing and stumbling over the notes, pushing each other off the piano stool. Sunil hesitated, his eyes on Alicia. She was so much younger than him. More than anything else in the world he wanted her life to be trouble-free. He wanted her to live a life of peace.

'I was out on the streets all of last week,' he said. 'Canvassing for the United Ethnic Party.' Robert had gone over to the piano and was watching Alicia. Sunil lowered his voice. 'It wasn't too good.' He shook his head, gesturing helplessly. 'There's a lot of ignorance, a lot of aggression.'

He stopped, seeing Grace's face. He could not tell her; what he feared the most was a bloodbath.

Christopher scowled at Robert. White fool, he was thinking. Go back to where you belong. You've done enough damage with your empire-building. Christopher edged nearer to the door. He had hoped to visit Kamala tonight but now it didn't look possible. Thornton's laughter drifted towards him. 'Oh why don't you shut up!' muttered Christopher, distracted. Looking around at her family, aware of certain tensions, Grace sighed. There was a guest present; she could not let Aloysius start an argument. She could see that Christopher was unhappy about something; she could hear Jasper making barking noises, he was probably thirsty. It was not the time for discussions; she would talk to Sunil later, when they were alone and she would find out what he really thought. But for now she needed to change the subject.

'Christopher,' she said, raising her voice, 'could you make sure the servant has given Jasper enough water to drink? It's very hot at the moment and he seems restless.'

She smiled at him, but Christopher continued to scowl, ignoring his mother.

'Idiot!' screeched Jasper suddenly, breaking a longer than usual silence. 'Imbeciles!'

He fluttered somewhere in the darkness above them. Myrtle could hear his unclipped claws scratch, on heaven knows what antique piece of furniture. Myrtle hated the bird most of all.

'Idiot! Bastards!'

'Jasper!' said Grace sharply. 'That's enough. Don't be so *rude*.' She smiled at Robert, a smile as sweet as Alicia's, adding somewhat unnecessarily, 'Jasper is our mynah bird, Robert. Unfortunately he has no manners. We're really not sure what to do about it, but we do think he's a bit of an oracle!'

Everyone laughed except Myrtle and Aloysius who looked meaningfully at his wife. Who knows what Jasper might say at the wedding? his look warned. But Robert, like many before him, was entranced. A talking bird, he thought. How exotic! The household, the whole family, everything about the de Silvas, was delightfully eccentric. Why had he ever thought this country boring? England suddenly seemed a very long way away.

On the day of the Prime Minister's party for the High Commissioner Grace brought Vijay a mango freshly picked from a tree in Jaffna. It had been given to her by a servant. No other mango tasted as sweet as those from the north, Vijay told her. But he did not look happy. Carefully he cut into it with his penknife, the juice running down his arm, and all the fragrance of his childhood, all the yearnings of his youth, gathered and fell to the floor. This morning, during their lovemaking, he had hardly looked at her. Sensing some desperation, she tried questioning him afterwards, but he avoided her eye.

'What is it, Vijay?' she asked, frightened suddenly. 'Has something happened?' She knew he did not want her to go to the party tonight and meet the Prime Minister. He hated this figure-head in a puppet government. She wondered if this was the problem.

'I had a letter this morning,' Vijay said slowly. And then, in a rush of unaccustomed bitterness, he told her about his niece, his brother's daughter. He had often talked about the girl. 'You know she was five last month.'

Grace nodded. Vijay looked terrible.

'She became ill with diphtheria a few weeks ago. My brother was very worried. He took his bullock cart into the town where the doctor lived. He walked in the burning heat, the road was covered in red dust. My brother took two pots of curd, hoping to find a doctor he could afford. One that would treat a Tamil child.' He stopped talking.

'What's happened?' asked Grace.

Vijay was staring at the floor. 'They sent me the news, today,' he said barely audibly. 'They could not find such a doctor. Now they want me to make a *puja* for her.'

The child had died. His brother was inconsolable.

'One more Tamil death is not important,' he said quietly.

'Oh my God! What kind of people have we become? Where will it end?'

'There is something wrong with a country that will not unite.

There is something wrong with a nation that hates its own people.'

Grace could see that things were breaking inside him, and would not be easily mended. The night before there had been a police attack on a crowd of Tamil office workers and tonight there was a large demonstration taking place near Galle Face. Vijay would go to it, Grace was certain. What could she do? He was stubborn and angry, he had been hurt for so long, Grace could not stop him. She stayed as late as she dared. Then she left to get ready for the party.

Towards six o'clock, in the sudden darkness that descended, Vijay went out into the city. The talk was that there would be another march followed by anti-government speeches. He felt a desperate need to be part of it. Just now the darkness lent a little substance to the city. There was no twilight in this part of the tropics. The heat had brought out the local families. Small children played on the beach, lovers strolled, young men loitered, buying sweep tickets, hoping to win the money to purchase a dream. All along the roadside were small shanty *kadés* glowing with green and white lights, selling everything from cheap plastic toys and brooches and bangles, to multi-coloured drinks and string hoppers, hot sambals and sweetmeats. The betel seller rolled his leaves, red and white goo dribbling from his toothless mouth. He waved at Vijay. But Vijay did not stop to talk tonight. His niece's death had been in his thoughts all day. He was certain: two more deaths would follow. He walked on through the meat market, with its stench of rancid fat and congealed blood. The heat of the day had penetrated even here, even into this subterranean part. There were flies on every surface, on the vaulted ceilings, clinging to the carcasses, their blue wings hanging like drops of moisture. Vijay walked on seeing none of this, his feet picking their way swiftly and fastidiously through the filth. Unseeing, towards the clock tower, a lone figure in a white sarong, trembling into the distance, silhouetted against the darkened sky.

At some point during the evening, out of a sense of nostalgia and probably because he was bored, Aloysius looked around for his wife.

'This is entirely your mother's fault,' he told Frieda grumpily. 'Why do we have to be here, wearing all this finery, suffering this silly party?'

Frieda was watching Robert. She too wished they were at home. Percussion instruments jarred in her head. One look at Alicia and I no longer exist. No one cares, he has forgotten about me! On and on went Frieda's thoughts, round and round. She felt dizzy. Aloysius, thinking his younger daughter seemed a little glum this evening, helped himself to his third whisky and wandered off. Grace was standing on a balcony overhanging the private beach. She could see the top of Mount Lavinia Hill, with its whitewashed houses and its funfair. Someone on the beach below was flying a box kite and its tail flickered lazily in the wind. As always, whenever she was alone, Grace's thoughts strayed back to Vijay. She had told him she would look across the bay and think of him. Tonight the view was hazy and the horizon had become blurred by a storm far out at sea. In the distance, forked lightning speared the water. The sky was heavy and full of menace. Soon the storm would reach the shore.

'I see Thornton has found all the good-looking women again,' Aloysius greeted her peevishly, breaking into her thoughts.

Grace laughed lightly and went inside to see for herself.

It was quite true; Thornton was having a wonderful time. He saw no reason to be as morose as his elder brother Jacob, or bad-tempered like his younger brother Christopher. Not, of course, that anyone knew where the devil Christopher was. Gone, no doubt, to some political rally. Thornton could never understand how anyone would deliberately choose a meeting over such a good party. Well, wasn't that Christopher all over. Always making life difficult for himself. Still, Thornton was not one to try to change the world. No, no, he thought, seriously, shaking his head, frowning a little. He did all of that with his poetry. In the new 'voice' he was developing.

'Can I read some of your poems, Thorn?' asked the pretty nurse he was chatting to, anxiously seeing his frown. She hoped she wasn't boring him.

Thornton smiled, and the world tilted. Before righting itself again. The girl's knees locked heavily together, making her sway towards him. Thornton did not notice. He had begun to recite one of his poems.

'Oh!' the girl said breathlessly when he had finished. 'I think that was wonderful!' She felt that she might, at any moment, swoon with desire.

'Oh please,' asked another girl, joining the group belatedly, looking at Thornton's glossy hair. 'Please say it again. I missed the first verse.'

Jacob, deep in conversation with someone very dull, glanced up just as his brother was tilting the world again. There was nothing new here as far as Jacob could see, nothing suspicious, he thought, satisfied. Although, he paused, frowning, it suddenly occurred to him that lately Thornton had been out rather a lot. Feeling his elder brother's eye on him, Thornton coolly tried tilting the world at him too, with no success. Jacob merely shook his head disapprovingly and went back to his dull conversation. Oh dear, thought Thornton regretfully, no *joie de vivre*. None whatsoever.

The Prime Minister had asked their sister to play the piano. He had made a little speech about the lovely Miss de Silva. He told them all how proud he was of this home-grown talent. Then he led Alicia to the piano. Everyone fell silent as Alicia began to play. She played as though she was alone. As though she was at home, and the Prime Minister had not held her hand and smiled at her. She played as though there was no one there at all. Life was like that for her, thought Frieda, standing beside Robert with her breaking heart, watching him watch Alicia. Life was so easy for her sister. On and on went Alicia's fingers, galloping with the notes, crossing boundaries, lifting barriers, drawing everyone in this elegant room together without the slightest effort. Aloysius reached for another drink. No one noticed.

Sunil watched Alicia from the back of the room. Words like 'majority language' did not matter to her. Her language was simpler, older, less complicated. If only life could be like Alicia, he wished, filled with tender pride. It had been a useful evening for Sunil, meeting the Prime Minister, being noticed. His hopes for a united country were strengthened in spite of all the talk of civil unrest.

Alicia was playing when a telephone rang for the Prime Minister. She was still playing when he received the news that rioting had broken out all over the city. The police needed the Prime Minister's authorisation to deal with it. She was still playing as he left the party in his dark-tinted limousine with Sir John and the Chief Constable. No one saw them go. Sunil, suspecting an incident, went in search of more information. He learned that the rioting had got out of hand. What had been a slow protest, a silent march, days of handing out leaflets had turned into crowds of angry people, voices on the end of a megaphone. Someone had been injured. Then the number had risen and there had been some fatalities. A petrol bomb had been thrown.

It was a night of the full moon, this night before the eclipse. There was a rumour that a Buddhist monk had been involved. An unknown passer-by had seen a young priest running away, a thin smear of saffron in the night. If a Buddhist monk had really been involved Sunil knew it would be bad for everyone. It would only take one single gesture, he thought, one furious shaven head, for centuries of lotus flowers to be wiped out forever.

Alicia had just finished playing when the intruder broke in. Walking swiftly past the guard, past the doorman who tried and failed to stop him and past the servants who then appeared, he burst in, blood clinging to his shirt. His face was streaked with sweat and dirt. He was no more than a boy, his hands were cut and bruised, one eye was swollen and bleeding. There was glass in his hair and he smelt of smoke and something else. Someone screamed. The servants, having caught up with him, twisted his arms behind his back. The boy did not struggle. He stood perfectly still, searching the faces in the room until he found the face he had been looking for, crying out in anguish,

'They killed them! They killed them! I saw them burn! Oh Christ! I saw them burn!'

Grace, recognising him before anyone else, stepped forward saying in Sinhalese, in a voice seldom heard in public, coldly, sharply to the servants, 'Let him go! He's my son!' And then in English, 'Christopher, who has done this to you?'

Outside, the rain they had all longed for began to fall with a thunderous noise, in long beating waves. Drumming on the earth, on the buildings, lashing against the land in great sheets. But no one heard.

5

THE RAIN DESCENDED WITH A VENGEANCE. It filled the holes in the road, it beat a tattoo on the fallen coconut shells and moved the dirt, transforming it swiftly into mud. It fell on Grace, standing stock-still and statue-like in the coconut grove, sari-silk clinging to her, flowers fallen from her hair. There was no escape. The land became a curtain of green water. Pawpaw leaves detached themselves, floating like large athletic spiders to the ground. The rain spared nothing. There were so many rivulets to form, so many surfaces to hammer against. Although it was still quite early, huge black clouds gave the garden an air of darkness. Even the birds, sheltering, waiting patiently, could barely be heard above the chorus of falling water. Earlier on, in the dead of night, a servant swore she had heard the devil-bird scream. It had come out of the forest because of the rain, the servant said, in the hope of escape. But escape was no longer possible.

'Aiyo,' wailed the servant, for she knew this was an ill omen.

'You must leave an offering on the roadside,' said her friend the cinnamon seller. 'If you heard the devil-bird you must pray to God for protection.'

So the servant woman took a plantain leaf and some temple flowers. She wrapped a mound of milk rice and rambutans in it, decorated it with fried fish and coconut, and left it outside the gate. She hoped the gods would be pleased. But the gods were not listening. They were too busy with the rains.

Then just as suddenly, without warning, it stopped. The noise and the roar of the water ceased, and the early-morning traffic picked up from where it had been held up. Bicycle bells rang, the rickshaw men ran, and the crows that had been sheltering under the eaves of buildings came out again and continued their scavenging in the rubbish as though they had never left off. The ground steamed. The mud remained on the road of course, and passers-by still held up their umbrellas to catch any stray drop of wetness, but by and large the rain had stopped for the moment. It was as though someone had turned off a tap. What a difference the sun made, bringing out all the everyday symphony of sounds, of callings and cawing and whistling and scrapings, and because she had slept in late after last night's event, Alicia's scales and arpeggios, joining in where the rain left off.

The servant, having made her offering to the gods, on this day of total eclipse, brought in the breakfast. It consisted of milk rice, coarse jaggery, seeni sambal and mangoes.

'For the lady,' she said, beaming at Grace.

It was meant as a pleasant surprise, but Grace, coming in just then (where had she been at this hour? wondered Myrtle), soaked to the bone and ashen-faced, did not look pleased.

'What is this?' she had shouted. 'Who gave you permission to make milk rice? Who *told* you to make this auspicious dish? Do I pay you to make food without instruction?'

Myrtle was astonished. Her cousin seemed beside herself. She was not normally a woman to show her temper in this way. Grace did not look well. She looked on the verge of collapse.

'Where've you been, darl?' Aloysius asked, astonished. 'We've been looking for you everywhere. You're soaking. Here, give her a towel, will you, Myrtle? Thornton, pour your mother a drink.'

'I have a headache,' Grace said abruptly, seeing Myrtle staring at her. 'I'm going to bed.'

She disappeared to her room.

'What on earth is going on?' asked Myrtle slyly.

Aloysius, ignoring her, walked abruptly out of the room.

'What's wrong with your mother?' Myrtle asked Frieda.

But Frieda did not want to talk either.

'I think I'm coming down with a fever,' Frieda mumbled. And she too disappeared into her room.

Some party, no? thought Myrtle. She nodded her head from side to side, as though having a heated conversation. Jasper watched her intensely. He was on his higher perch this morning and felt much better since it had rained. The air had thinned out and it was generally much cooler. He felt his old self again. Almost. He shuffled round and round the perch.

'Hello, bastards,' he said, and when Myrtle ignored him he jauntily whistled a snatch of *The Magic Flute*, the bit he knew the best. Then he did his impersonation of the neighbour's dog and for an encore he whistled the Schubert that Alicia always played. Then, when his saw-drill noise had finally driven her from the room, cursing, he began to repeat a new sound he was learning. Softly at first, for Jasper always perfected his repertoire softly, he practised the sound of the devil-bird. Last night he had been woken up several times. First, there had been the sounds of sirens rushing past. Then Christopher had come crashing in.

'Good morning, men!' Jasper had remarked, though, unusually for him, Christopher had not replied.

The rest of the family followed, making no effort at being quiet. And finally, sometime towards the early morning, he had awoken again to a long and awful scream, so long and so strangled that Jasper, lifting his head, sleepily protested.

'Be quiet, men!'

The sound had gone on and on, not waking anyone else, but it had stayed in Jasper's head and he remembered it now with his usual clarity.

During the shocking, hurried journey home, shocking because no one had ever seen Christopher in quite this way before, hurried because of the embarrassment, they had all been subdued.

'It was a good party you missed,' said Thornton tentatively, not wanting to upset Christopher any more by questioning him too closely.

What was the matter with him? he wondered uneasily. Had he been in a fight?

'Time we left anyway,' Aloysius said by way of comfort. He looked shocked, Thornton noticed, while Grace seemed almost too upset to speak.

'What on earth were you doing at the demonstration?' asked Jacob. The thought of what might have happened frightened him, making him sound furious. 'What did you expect, you fool, if you go to dangerous places like that? I told you to keep away from the riots. I told you. You're lucky to have got away with burnt hands!'

'That's enough now, Jacob,' Grace said quietly from the back of the old Austin Morris. Her voice was that of a stranger. It was hardly audible. In the darkness her face looked deathly pale.

'I hope Sunil will be all right,' Alicia said anxiously, for, in spite of all her pleas, Sunil had gone back to the UEP head-quarters to send a telegram.

'Don't worry, darling,' Grace said, 'he'll be fine.'

She sounded as if she was gasping for air. Thornton's unease grew. Christopher too seemed to be struck dumb. His head-long flight to find his mother, his astonishing uncontrollable grief, was followed by silence. As soon as they got back to the house, he disappeared. No one could make any sense of what had happened, no one could work out why he had been anywhere near the riots. Unobserved by any of them, Christopher slipped away and rode his bicycle all the way back to the beach at Galle Face.

It was now almost four o'clock in the morning. The rain had perfumed the air, only the sound of the sea gnawing at the shore remained, a reminder of the storm. Far away on the horizon a streak of lilac struggled to appear against the sky. The boats were coming in with the day's catch. On the quay, seagulls circled around the fishermen, waiting for a pause in the activities, hoping for a morsel of food. Christopher stared at the beach, miraculously ironed smooth with the morning, every blemish swept as though by an unseen hand. Grief, like nothing he had ever felt before, broke, riding roughshod over him. He was distraught.

Last night was a million light years away. Remembering Jacob's foolish questions he began to heave. Jacob, he thought, busy sucking up to the *whites*. And Thornton, the empty-headed beauty, what did *he* care about, except how he looked and what everyone thought of him? Only his mother, thought Christopher, incoherent now, only his mother had under-stood.

'Come back,' he screamed. 'Come back!' His voice was whipped by the sea breeze and caught in the roar of the waves.

He stood screaming and choking as the seagulls circled the sky. 'I'm finished,' he cried. 'It's over.'

He had not gone to watch the riots as Jacob suspected, or to join in the demonstration. His thoughts became disjointed. Everything that had followed was blurred. Racked by sobs, broken, desperate, he fell to his knees on the soft white sand. Raising his face towards the sky, he whispered, 'I can't go on.'

Only a few hours earlier he had visited Kamala with a heart that brimmed over with hope. Carrying the tenderness that he showed no one else. Kamala had been ill, but seemed to Christopher's anxious eyes to be much better.

'You *are* better,' he recalled saying fiercely, willing her to be. And Kamala, laughing (he always made her laugh), agreed.

Her father was at his Galle Face stall, selling plastic jewellery. White butterflies trapped in Perspex, flecked with gold, dozens of bangles, pink, yellow and green. There was to be a demonstration tonight, and a march organised by the railway and factory workers. A peaceful march. Christopher met Kamala at the stall.

'Let's walk along the beach,' he had said, for he had brought money with him. 'I want to buy you some fried crab and Lanka lime. Then we can be happy.'

Yes, that's what he had said. He remembered it very clearly, being happy was something he could only do with Kamala. As they walked he had talked, as he often did, of his passionate desire for free state education. It was his favourite subject, his dream.

'It *must* be offered to everyone,' he had said. 'Not just the rich but the coolies, the servants. In any case . . .' he paused, while Kamala gazed admiringly at him, 'why do we need servants anyway?'

Kamala listened not fully understanding, but agreeing with

everything. Full of pride. He had told her the Greenwood story again. He was always telling her that story. How many times had she heard it? But on each occasion she listened patiently.

'By the time it was my turn the money had run out. They gave it all to that fool Thornton. And what did he ever do with it?' he had fumed, unable to stop himself. He had known Kamala hated to hear him talk about his brother in this way.

'You mustn't,' she had said, earnestly. 'You mustn't say these things. Your family is a gift, Chris. It's *bad* for you to talk like this.'

It hadn't stopped him though. He had taken no notice of her. Last night he had begun again, moaning on and on about Thornton and the price of a decent education in this country. Never knowing how he was wasting time. Kamala had pulled his hand and teased him into a better mood.

'Next year, after my sister's wedding,' he told her, 'we'll get married. I'll speak to my mother. Just wait,' he said, as if it was Kamala and not he who was in a hurry, 'you'll see, I *will* become a journalist.'

He hated to think of Kamala sleeping in the shack with the *cajan* roof that let in the monsoon.

'Soon,' he promised, 'you'll sleep on a proper bed in a clean, dry bedroom with a roof made of tiles. Our children will have decent educations. *All* of them, not just a chosen few.'

He had said all this. Only last night.

The Galle Face had been crowded with people. But Kamala's father let her take a walk along the beach with Christopher. He knew his daughter's illness was not curable. It was her karma. So he let them walk together along the seafront, letting them enjoy what brief happiness they could. Two young people with no idea of what their future held, but planning it anyway.

After a while they decided to go back up the hill towards

the centre. Someone said there was a street fair and Christopher thought they might try the tombola. He had forgotten about the Tamil strikers' demonstration. It was Kamala's father, catching sight of them retracing their footsteps, who remembered. But by the time he had found someone to mind his stall they had vanished from sight. The crowds had grown. Away from the sea breeze the smell of sweaty bodies mixed with the fetid slabs of meat in the market as he hurried through the maze of stalls. An air of nervous tension hung over the neighbourhood. Outside, close to the Fort and behind the market, a few mounted policemen in white uniforms waited expectantly. Most of the shops in this area were shut or closing, there was no sign of the fair, and no sign of Kamala or Christopher. One or two men on bicycles rode by. A few dogs scavenged in the gutters. Kamala's father quickened his pace.

The whole of this part of the city was in darkness. A muffled sound of voices, the faint throb of a loudspeaker could be heard in the distance, but still he could not see anyone. Out of the corner of his eye he thought he saw a movement, but when he turned there was nothing there. He hurried on knowing he could not leave the stall for long. He needed to find Kamala and Christopher, to warn them to keep away from the demonstration. He was now in St Anthony's Road and in front of him was the great Roman Catholic cathedral. Close by was Temple Tree Square where the Bo trees were tied with offerings. Kamala's father breathed more easily, for this was a sacred site with an open aspect and lights. Through the trees, on the other side of the square, he could see the reason for the silence. The demonstrators, with their banners, had gathered together to listen to the speaker. The march had ended peacefully after all and as he approached Kamala's father saw with relief that Christopher and Kamala were on the edge of the crowd.

'Kamala,' he had called. 'Kamala, Christopher. Come here.' He waved urgently, becoming suddenly, unaccountably afraid.

Only then did he see the shadow of a saffron robe. Only then did he smell the petrol and see the ragged flames, one after another, until too late, a circle of fire surrounded him. Drawing closer and closer. A Kathakali dance of death.

'Watch out,' he had shouted in vain. 'Be careful. Chris, Chris, take her away.'

They heard him shout but the words were indistinct. Kamala turned and ran towards him. For a brief moment, in the flare of the burning rags, Christopher saw them both clearly, her wide bright eyes reflecting the light, her hair aglow. Then he heard only their screams, father and daughter, mixing and blending together with the sound of his own anguish. Flesh against flesh, ashes to ashes.

The night was nearly over now. For Christopher there would never be such a night again. He stared at his hands. They oozed liquid through the bandages his mother had used. The burns covered both palms, crossing his lifeline, changing it forever. He had heard afterwards, there had been many others. One of them, he had cried, hardly registering the look on his mother's face, had been the man she knew as Vijay.

The dawn rose, the sun came out. Beach sweepers began clearing the debris from the night before, but still Christopher stood motionless, Kamala's name tolling a steady refrain in his head. A newspaper seller shouted out the headlines, riots, petrol bombs, fourteen dead, seven injured. The government was to impose a curfew. But Christopher heard none of this. It was the day of the total eclipse.

They found his bicycle first. It was another four days before they found him. He had wandered for miles along the outskirts

of the city, without shoes, his bandages torn off, his hands a mass of sores and infected pus, his face covered in insect bites. He did not see the eclipse as the moon slipped slowly over the sun. Or the many thousand crescent shadows that drained the warmth from the earth. Or hear the birds, whose confused, small roosting sounds filled the sudden night. And, as his family searched frantically for him, Christopher remained oblivious of the darkness that slipped swiftly across the land before sinking at last, gently, into the Bay of Bengal.

6

GRACE, FACE DOWN, FISTS CLENCHED, was lying across the bed. She was trying to control herself. Somewhere far in the distance a train hooted. The sound sliced the air. She shuddered as though she had been hit by it. Aloysius was frightened. Closing the bedroom door, he stood for a moment staring at her in horror.

'What is it, Grace?' he asked in a whisper. 'Nothing happened to Christopher in the end. What's wrong?'

Her face was thrown against the pillow and she was shaking. No sound came from her. Nothing. Just the clenching and unclenching of her fists. 'Grace,' said Aloysius, fearfully. He took a step towards her, the room blurred for a moment. Not even when he had told her they were leaving their home in the hills had he seen her this way.

'Grace,' he said again.

His own voice sounded unrecognisable. He hesitated, suddenly terrified. Then he knelt down beside the bed and tried to take her in his arms. Her sari clung to her, dripping wet with filth from the road. She was shivering.

'What is it, Grace?' Aloysius asked again, pleading, half not wanting to know. 'It isn't Christopher, is it?'

Something in the tone of his voice made her turn blindly towards him and he caught her as she fell soaked and weeping into his arms. He had no idea how long he stayed in this way, with her cold body and her heart beating against him. Eventually there was a knock on the door. It was Thornton.

'Not now,' Aloysius said quickly, before Thornton could see the state his mother was in.

Then Aloysius undressed her, drying her hair, her arms, wiping her face even as she cried, getting her into bed, unquestioning. Concerned only that she would lie down under the mosquito net, with the lights off and the shutters closed.

'I'll call the doctor,' he said, when it was clear that her grief would not abate. 'Please,' he said, huskily. 'Please, Grace. Wait, I'll be back.'

And he went out, shutting the door softly behind him, to make his phone call and send Thornton and Myrtle away, telling them Grace was ill with stomach cramp and the doctor would be here soon.

Outside the rain increased and thunder beat against the sky. The air had cooled rapidly and small insects invaded the house. Aloysius woke the servant woman and asked her to make some coriander tea for Grace. Then he waited for the doctor to arrive.

Frieda iced the wedding cake while Myrtle read the instructions out loud.

'"To Ornament Your Wedding Cake."'

With only two months to go there was still a lot to be done. Frieda's head ached with a fever. It was raining again, heavy rain that vomited out of the sky, thrashing the branches of the coconut trees. Every word Myrtle uttered, every crack of thunder made the veins in Frieda's temples pulsate harder. How her head ached. The rain had brought in several uninvited guests. Large garden spiders thudded against the walls and a rat snake slithered in through the front door, curling up by the open fire in the kitchen. The cook had been blowing into the flames when she saw it.

'Missy, missy,' she shouted to Frieda. 'We have a visit from the Hindu God. It is good luck, missy. It is a good omen for the wedding.'

The cook would not move the snake. In the end it left of its own accord. Grace, had she heard, would have been annoyed by this superstitious nonsense, but Grace was not well. She had seen the doctor repeatedly, because her stomach pains had worsened. Now, almost a month later, although she was over it, she still slept badly. Once she was an early riser, now, everyone noticed, she found it difficult to get up at all. She looked so exhausted that Frieda and Myrtle had taken over the icing of the cake.

"'For the ornamentation, fancy forcing pipes are not absolutely necessary,'" said Myrtle.

It felt as though a thousand steel hammers banged inside Frieda's head. What was Myrtle saying?

"'This piping will not be easy for a beginner, but with patience and practice there is no reason why it should not be mastered.'"

Frieda imagined Robert. She saw his face reflected in the metal icing nozzle. The beautiful white icing reminded her of him. She wanted to write his name all over the cake. She wanted to write her own name next to it.

Soon the cake was finished, three tiers of it, all beautiful and porcelain – white, pristine and bridal. And then, on top of everything else, Frieda had developed another nagging worry. What was wrong with their mother? Was she sick with some terrible disease? In all her life Frieda had never known Grace to be ill.

'Have you noticed how quiet she is?' she asked Thornton, some time later. But Thornton too seemed preoccupied and answered only vaguely. Next, Frieda tried talking to Jacob.

'D'you think what happened to Christopher has upset her?'

'Christopher is an idiot,' Jacob said sternly. 'You must not encourage him to worry Mummy like this *ever* again. D'you understand?' He almost said, 'When I leave for England you will have to watch Christopher,' but he stopped himself. It was too soon to tell anyone of *his* plans.

Grace had changed. In the weeks that followed Christopher's escapade she stopped going into the city to visit the nuns and spent most of her time at home, sleeping. When she was awake, she seemed tired and short-tempered. Aloysius too was different. He seemed to have undergone a transformation, as far as Frieda could tell. He had stopped going to the club, played no poker at all and insisted Grace took her meals in bed. Frieda's worry grew.

'Alicia,' she said finally, 'have you noticed how exhausted Mummy is all the time?'

'Mmm,' said Alicia. 'How d'you mean?' She had just finished her practice and was staring at her list of things to do.

'Well,' Frieda continued, glad to have her sister's attention at last, 'yesterday, when Daddy finally went out, she got one of the servants to bring over a huge climbing jasmine. It was in full flower but someone had pulled it up by the roots. Now isn't that a strange thing to do? When I asked her where she got it from, she looked annoyed. She told me the nuns gave it to her as a present. I had a feeling she didn't want me to ask.'

'So?' asked Alicia, looking up briefly. What was Frieda talking about now? Was she wrong, or had her sister become a little dull of late?

'Well, isn't it a strange present to give her?' persisted Frieda. 'When we've got three jasmine bushes in the garden!'

Alicia shook her head, not knowing what to say.

'She got Christopher to plant it underneath her bedroom window,' Frieda continued. 'One of the branches accidentally broke and she started to *cry*! Can you imagine that? Mummy crying over a jasmine plant? And then, Christopher gave her a *hug*!'

Alicia had to admit, *that* was interesting. But then again she wasn't all that surprised.

'Weddings are emotional times,' she told her sister wisely. 'I read it in the *Book of Etiquette*.'

'Perhaps,' Frieda mused, 'the scare of nearly losing Christopher has affected her more than we realised.'

As she iced her sister's cake Frieda went over the sequences of events on that terrible night. Would any of them ever forget it? Even her father, Frieda noticed, had been affected by it. Her father was clearly very worried. At least Mummy has him, thought Frieda, wistfully, remembering again the way in which Robert had looked at Alicia. Lucky Alicia. Lucky everyone. Did no one care that *she* was suffering too? Staring at the expanse of white icing, thinking of her breaking heart, she listened to the rain. No, she reflected mournfully, no one cares. She was unaware that Myrtle watched her.

Myrtle of course, understood what Frieda's headaches were about. She had mentioned it in her diary, that morning.

October 31. Thank God the monsoons are here at last. I have not been able to write through lack of time. There are still two months left before this wretched wedding. G is too weak to be of much help. It looks as though Mr Basher was right although I had no idea her downfall would be through an illness. Well, it's as good as any other misfortune, if not better! She certainly looks pretty dreadful. A, of course, is full of such concern that it has become quite comical. I'd like to tell him that he should be looking forward to possible widowerhood! After all, I shall be there; I'll look after him. For the last couple of weeks, needless to say, I have been working like a coolie (with no acknowledgement). F remains uselessly slow and a complete misery, while our little Bride has her head in the clouds. Have an interesting theory about F. I have noticed she likes white boys!! If this isn't nipped in the bud soon there'll be trouble from that direction too. Like mother like daughter. Don't I know it! Anyway, G looks pretty terrible at the moment. There has been no need for me to do the thing Mr B suggested, as yet. Shall save it for the other event. Apparently the doctor thinks G's got dengue fever.

The month of November passed slowly. All across the capital the riots had temporarily destabilised the country. Everyone desperately wished to put it behind them. Christmas was around the corner to be followed swiftly by the wedding. The cake was ready, the invitations had been sent out. One evening Grace, appearing to be much better, came out to sit on the veranda. Everyone was pleased. Thornton pulled up a chair under her newly planted jasmine bush. Alicia began to play her mother's favourite piece of Schubert and Frieda went to tell the cook their mother would be joining them for dinner. Grace had been ill for nearly a month. She looked smaller, more delicate, infinitely more lovely, thought Aloysius, watching her, surreptitiously. He had grown cautious. On that first night, when she had been so distraught, turning to him for the first time in many years, Aloysius had not known what to do. She had begun to tell him something incoherently, and Aloysius had been afraid.

'Don't say anything,' he had told her. The less he knew the better. 'You don't need to tell me, darl.'

I don't want to know, he told himself, repeatedly. Whatever it was, it's enough that she's here, with us now. Afterwards, in the days and nights that had followed, when he had shielded her from the children's anxieties and protected her from Myrtle's curiosity, he had regretted stopping her. He had begun to wish she would confide in him. But as the days turned into weeks and Grace became aware once more of the need not to upset her family, Aloysius saw that the moment had passed. She regained control of herself and he intuited she would never turn to him in that way again. So Aloysius watched her struggle, talking with Christopher for long hours, pulling herself back to life, and refrained from comment.

'It's been too much for her,' he told Myrtle, fobbing her off, refusing to be drawn by her questions. 'What with losing Alicia soon, and Christopher's nonsense on top of that, she's not as strong as she likes to think she is.'

Myrtle raised her eyebrows.

'Of course,' agreed Frieda wistfully, 'it's the thought of losing Alicia that's upsetting Mummy so much! It's about the wedding, isn't it?'

They had all agreed. Then, as the wedding approached, Grace, with an enormous effort, did seem to pull herself together, so some, if not all, of their former pleasure appeared to return. Sunil was so much a part of their lives now it was hard to imagine a time when he was not present. After the riots he had won a small electoral victory with the UEP in the south.

'No one,' he told Alicia passionately, 'wants a civil war. This island has lived for centuries in perfect harmony, why can it not do so again?'

He had tried talking to Christopher, but here a door slammed heavily in his face. Sunil did not take offence. He continued his work with simple optimism, determined to walk the road of peace. There was still so much work to be done. His wedding was only a few weeks away. Then, after the Roman Catholic Mass, before they went upcountry for their honeymoon, there would be a brief blessing ceremony at the temple in St Andrew's Road. Sunil's mother had arranged it. For an auspicious time of day.

Somehow Jasper had escaped. He had always lived in a little room off the hall where the windows were covered with wire mesh. But at some point, due to the heavy rains, or perhaps his own feverish pecking, the mesh had worn out. Christopher, who in the past would have been the one to notice this, no longer either noticed or cared. Christopher was beyond all such childish interests. Silent and morose, he did not respond to Jasper's greetings. In fact, no one thought about the bird. Even the dog next door had disappeared and no longer provided sport for him. Bored and ignored, Jasper looked elsewhere for entertainment. Nobody bothered. Nobody missed him. The wedding and other events had more or less taken over the de Silva family. Several days went by. He flew gloriously out through one window and onto the jackfruit tree, then further on into the plantain tree. Swooping silently in through yet another window, pecking the kittens who mewed and hid under the furniture. For four days Jasper was mute, afraid, no doubt, of being caught. Then, having picked his victim, he descended on her.

Myrtle was not expecting this. After her morning ablutions she usually spent some time in her room. On this particular morning, she was in her room, a towel wrapped around her head, her dark body patched with talcum powder, wrapped in a vast multicoloured housecoat. She was holding a small metal object in her hand.

'Hello, sister,' said Jasper swooping down on her.

Myrtle jumped. And dropped the metal plate. Startled, she raised her arms above her face.

'Get out!' she screeched. 'Get out! Get out!'

Jasper watched her with interest.

'Atten-tion!' he said solemnly, imitating the army captain he had once seen.

'No! No!' yelled Myrtle, flaying her arms about in a vain attempt to drive him away. 'Get out! Get out!'

Jasper narrowed his eyes to thin bright slits. He perched on the top of her wardrobe, leaving a small deposit that ran easily down the smooth mahogany, landing on the back of the chair, close to Myrtle's neatly folded sari. He squawked imperfectly but with some satisfaction. He was still practising his devil-bird impersonation. Then he belched, as he had often heard Aloysius do.

'Easy!' he said. 'Easy, sister!' and he swooped down without warning on the metal plate on the floor. The light glinting on it had caught his attention. He began to peck it, cooing tenderly.

Myrtle went berserk. She had always hated Grace's pet. Now, confused by its presence in her room, she snatched up the metal plate, advancing towards him with gritted teeth.

'Bloody bastard, bloody nuisance,' she screamed. 'I'm going to kill you. I've wanted to kill you for a long time. Come here!' She chased him around the room, hitting out, almost catching him.

'Come here, you bugger,' she shouted, attempting to grab at his tail feathers.

Jasper was entranced. Never had he had so much success, so much flattering attention. Retreating to a point above the ceiling fan, he watched Myrtle. He sent down little presents that splattered onto the floor. He gave her his best saw-drill impersonation, he whistled the bit from *The Magic Flute*, he barked once or twice. By now Myrtle was weeping. Her room was wrecked. Grace and Aloysius, hearing the noise, came hurrying to her door. Quickly, hiding the plate, Myrtle let them in. The sight astonished them.

'Hello,' said Jasper, looking as pleased to see them as a mynah bird can. 'Good morning! Hello?' he asked, and he glided gracefully around the room. Grace, in spite of herself, felt her face twitch slightly.

'Jasper!' she said, adding weakly in case there was some mistake, 'It's Jasper. What's he doing here?'

'Enough!' screamed Myrtle. 'I have had enough of this family, *enough* of the way I am treated, enough of being used. Enough, enough, enough!' she shouted, shaking her head so her hair flew all over her face. 'Used and abused by everyone,' she screamed, unable to stop now, 'even the bloody bird. Look at me. *Just look at me!*' And she stood, arms outstretched magnificently, a crucifix with bird shit running down her face.

'The bird's a damn nuisance,' agreed Aloysius, wishing he could have a whisky. Life seemed to be one long crisis at the moment. His wife was depressed, his youngest son had almost been killed, his eldest daughter was leaving them, everything was changing. Nobody had any fun any more. Everyone made such a fuss about trivial things. He could *kill* for a drink. And after that he would willingly kill Jasper. Grace, however, would have none of it. She soothed her cousin, called for the servant to clean the room, encouraging Myrtle to have another shower, promising to catch Jasper.

'Shiny,' said Jasper helpfully. 'Hello, Shiny.'

'We should have him put down, darl,' said Aloysius, who was beginning to think the bloody bird would outwit all of them. Outlive them too, by the looks of it, God, did he need a drink!

'Shiny,' said Jasper again. 'Hello, Shiny.'

'Jasper!' said Grace softly, looking up at him, to Aloysius's utter astonishment, with a curious warmth to her voice, the first he had heard in months. Aloysius stared at her.

'Jasper,' she said again. 'You're a *very* naughty boy!'

Jasper, hearing the change in her voice, flew experimentally towards her and perched on the foot of Myrtle's bed.

'No,' he agreed. And making a whirling sound, like the grandfather clock being rewound, he sailed swiftly out of the window and into the plantain tree outside.

7

THEY CAME FROM AFAR TO THE WEDDING, like wise men bearing gifts. Uncle Innocent and Prayma, Auntie Angel-Face and the girls. Sarath and Mabel, Anthony and Coco with their own little bevy of children. There were others too, from Toronto and Perth, from Calcutta and Lahore, and Grace's old childhood friend from Glasgow. There were the Sisters of St Peter and St Paul who had come all the way from Stratford-upon-Avon, and there were the old white planters on their way to a World Trade Fair in Melbourne, stopping off to have a bit of light entertainment at Aloysius's daughter's wedding.

'Becoming something of a pianist!' they said.

'Quite famous, I hear.'

'How did the old boy manage it?'

'Healthy neglect. Or, more probably, it was the doing of that stunning wife of his, what's her name?'

It was worth a detour, they said, pleased to be asked. Aloysius always knew how to throw a party. There were other less colourful, more predictable guests, who came. Local people, neighbours, people who came to settle old scores, wanting to see how the de Silvas were faring. Drinking chums of Aloysius, friends of the children. But the most eccentric, the noisiest came from afar, with their huge suitcases laden with clothes for the big day, presents for the bride and groom, and of course whisky for the father of the bride. Depending on their relationship to the de Silvas they stayed either with them or in guest houses nearby. It was rumoured that the Prime Minister himself would be at the church service and maybe, for a little while, at the reception too. Aloysius was delighted.

'We'll need to buy much more champagne,' he informed Grace. 'I'll ask Sunil. He can get it on the black market. It won't be cheap, but only the best will do.' Grace did not disagree. Of late she went along with whatever he said. No one looked closely at Grace; they were all too busy. She seemed her old self at last, worrying about the catering and the guests. Had they *really* invited so many? What had Aloysius been thinking of? The cook was sulking because two new cooks from upcountry had been hired.

'If the Lady Grace wants coolies to cook for her then I am leaving,' she announced.

Myrtle, writing her diary, smirked. She was still smarting after Jasper's attack.

December 21. My best sari is completely ruined. No amount of cleaning can remove the stain of bird shit. Grace thought it was very funny. Oh I knew what she was thinking, she tried to be sympathetic, she tried her sweet voice on me, but I'm not fooled by it. Nor am I fooled by my dear cousin's jollity. I can see what no one else can. I can see that the preparations, the guests, the family, all of it is a huge effort for her. She's trying to hide it but there's no fooling me. I intend to get to the bottom of whatever it is that's the matter. Yesterday I spoke to Mr Basher who's suggested, as the results of the last card reading were

*inconclusive, I should get G's horoscope redrawn. Well, we shall
see. Meanwhile, I have to suffer all these wretched visitors; relatives I haven't seen for years and can't stand, especially that woman
Mabel.*

The relatives were not worried. It was true Grace looked a
little strained but they agreed this was perfectly understand-
able.

'She's losing her eldest daughter; she's losing little Alicia,'
they said affectionately.

'Of course she looks tired,' said Prayma. 'What d'you expect!'

'Besides, she *still* looks lovely.'

Some even thought, people like Uncle Innocent and Auntie
Angel-Face and Coco, that Grace actually looked *lovelier* than
ever. Yes, they argued, Grace looked more beautiful than on her
own wedding day, and they should know, they'd been there!
And off they went reminiscing about *that* wedding,

'Aloysius so handsome, he hadn't discovered the drink yet,'
remembered Auntie Angel-Face, screaming with laughter and
slapping Uncle Innocent on the back.

'Don't forget Benedict!' Coco remembered, smiling.

Ah, yes! How proud he had been of his motherless girl, cherished for so long, gliding on his arm. A vision, such a vision
of loveliness.

'Yes, a *vision*,' shouted Prayma, to Uncle Innocent who was
getting a little deaf. Those were the days, weren't they? When
Benedict's cooks produced the most wonderful Portuguese *broa*,
and *pente frito*, the likes of which had never been tasted since.

'Do you remember the shoe-flower sambals?' asked Coco,
starting up a whole hour of 'do-you-remembers'. Then it was
time to go to evening Mass. Did they have a Mass in the evening
here, darling?

The house party to the wedding meandered on. It was close

to Christmas, hot but not unbearable. The rains were still falling. The jasmine climber continued to bloom much to Myrtle's amazement, and Jasper still remained at large. Grace had given up trying to get him back into his room off the hallway.

'He has discovered the delights of independence!' said Uncle Innocent.

'With none of the responsibilities,' laughed Prayma.

'Well,' said Uncle Innocent, 'that will only come through a process of evolution and growth.'

'No, no, no, Innocent, you are wrong! The people in this country have not evolved for four hundred years. They have forgotten how,' said Auntie Angel-Face.

'Come on, Amma!' said Sarath, feigning despair. 'Jasper's just a bird, poor bugger.'

'But what a bird!' said Sunil, walking in just at that moment, smiling at his new relatives. A cry of delight went up among the aunts.

'Sunil!' shrieked Auntie Angel-Face, beaming at him. 'Where's your bride? How is she treating you today? Will she make a good wife? That's the question on all our lips!'

'I say, Sunil,' said Anthony seriously, 'shall we all go to the Galle Face Hotel tonight? You, me, Jacob, Thornton, Chris? No? What d'you say? Have a few drinks, men, meet some people?'

'Aiyo, yes!' said Auntie Angel-Face. 'Good idea. Why don't you boys all go out together? What fun.'

'Who are these fellows you are so keen to meet, Anthony?' Uncle Innocent asked.

'Well, who do you think, Innocent? Girls of course! These are Sunil's last days of freedom aren't they? He's allowed to roam like Jasper.'

They all roared with laughter, finding it hugely funny that sweet little Alicia, who they had last seen running around in a sundress and sandals, teasing her brothers, having her face pinched because she looked so delicious, should have gone and grown up and become so talented and now have this fully grown handsome fiancé. Clever, clever little Alicia to get such a handsome beau!

Myrtle watched the relatives from a safe distance. She found it astonishing that they could make such a fuss over the dark polecat Sunil, as she privately called him. She watched them teasing Alicia. Making her play Mozart, making her laugh, dancing around the piano, singing, until she begged for Thornton to rescue her. Hah! Thornton, thought Myrtle grimly, I'm watching *him*. Thornton, when he was in, became the life and soul of the group. But Thornton had often some mysterious errand, some urgent business that he hurried to attend to. So what was Golden Boy up to? wondered Myrtle.

'He's a busy man, you know,' said his cousins.

'Too busy to get a job,' said Jacob sarcastically.

Thornton smiled good-humouredly and played rock and roll on the piano. It was clear Mabel was smitten, and Thornton, charming them all as usual, picking up whenever Grace seemed to flag, played on. Even Jacob could see he had his uses on occasions like these. It let everyone else off the hook. The cousins had been away from the island for so long they wanted to do everything. Drink king coconuts, go for a swim, wander about the city having their horoscopes made, look for girls. Thornton was their man. He was their appointed guide, their chief entertainer. When he was there of course.

December 22, wrote Myrtle. *It is very curious that no one comments on Thornton's behaviour of late. I've noticed he makes a great deal of noise when he's in the house in order to cover up the fact that he's often out. I swear he's up to something. Yesterday I noticed he came home in a very great rush. Then he managed to exhaust everyone in ten minutes before he went out again, leaving them in a state of confusion. I've always thought that he's a clever devil underneath all that sweetness that G's so obsessed with. Just like the bloody bird that now flaps against my bedroom window all the time.*

Jasper, of course, was a nightmare. Aloysius had had mesh put up on Myrtle's window to keep him out because, for some unfathomable reason, Jasper was fascinated with her room. Neither Grace nor Thornton nor any of the younger children could get within striking distance of him. Somehow he evaded all attempts at capture.

'He always manages to slither out of trouble,' complained Aloysius, loudly, after a particularly difficult chase around the garden. 'I always said Jasper possessed native cunning,' he added, making Auntie Angel-Face hoot with laughter. 'Now you fellows can detect it for yourselves!'

The relatives found all this hugely entertaining. They were here to have a good time and would have been easily pleased no matter what, so Jasper was merely an added bonus.

'I say, Jasper,' said Uncle Innocent, 'come here, men, I want to tell you a secret.'

'No!' said Jasper from the middle of the plantain tree.

'Come on, men!' said Anthony. 'Come on, let's take some arrack together, hah?'

Jasper only narrowed his eyes, making his favourite saw-drill sound from the branch above their heads.

'He's a clever fellow, you know,' said Uncle Innocent. 'A bit like a terrorist. Cunning too.'

'Perhaps,' said Auntie Angel-Face, 'perhaps he is a bird card reader!' And they all dissolved into hysterical laughter.

'Hello, Shiny,' said Jasper solemnly, and Grace wondered if perhaps he was in fact disturbed by all the unusual activity.

Aloysius, seeing her smile, was heartened. Grace, though still suffering from frequent headaches, appeared much improved. The headaches, he informed everyone, were merely the aftermath of the dreadful fever she had contracted. Grace did not disagree. She was determined that Alicia's wedding should not be spoiled and whenever her migraines became overwhelming she simply slipped away to her darkened bedroom and waited until they passed. Aloysius made sure she was undisturbed whenever this happened. Everyone noticed with approval how Aloysius ministered to her needs. So that outwardly, at least, Grace was becoming her old self again.

Meanwhile Frieda struggled. It was no good; she would have to go to confession again. Her thoughts were treacherous, her heart was breaking, and nobody cared. She knew it was hopeless, she was wasting her time, but somehow her uncontrollable heart kept on longing. On Christmas Eve, before they went to midnight Mass, Robert had come over for the last time.

'To see you all,' he beamed, but Frieda, watching him stealthily, knew it was really Alicia he wanted to see. It was Alicia he wanted to kiss goodbye.

'I'm so sorry,' he said, in his soft English voice, making Frieda want to weep. 'I'm so sorry not to be here for the wedding.' He looked mournfully at Alicia. 'We'll be setting sail for England before the New Year, I'm afraid.'

Frieda was afraid too. She was afraid of her dark stormy thoughts. Was she turning into a monster? she wondered fearfully. Robert said his goodbyes. He wanted to say goodbye to Frieda too, although having arrived at the house and having met the relatives he was enchanted all over again by the others and did not notice Frieda's heart, lying broken and bleeding, at his feet. So Robert left, kissing the bride, wishing her luck, asking after Christopher who was nowhere to be seen, hurrying into the rain and out through the old part of the city where all the Christmas lights glittered in the trees.

Later, when the rain had stopped, the wedding party walked back from Mass. Everyone was unusually silent.

I will never see him again, thought Frieda sadly.

In a week I will be back here for my wedding, thought Alicia wonderingly.

In the New Year I will at last leave on a ship to England, thought Jacob with a small thrill of delight.

Grace, staring up at the sky, felt the darkness like a tight band around her; Thornton smiled in the darkness, his secret smile, thinking his own thoughts. Above them, huge tropical stars shone unblinking in the wide, night sky and, as they strolled slowly back in the balmy air, not one of them paused to question whether there would ever be another Christmas like this again.

8

WHEN IT DAWNED, THE DAY HELD ALL their expectations in
its clear unclouded sky. It was Alicia's day really, hers and Sunil's.
The others merely had walk-on parts. Frieda awoke and as usual
went into her sister's room. Only now it was for the last time.

'Come on,' said Alicia, pulling back the mosquito net. 'I
haven't slept all night, I've been so excited.'

Frieda burst into tears. The smell of milk rice drifted across
the house. Grace had ordered this most traditional of dishes
to begin the day. The aunts, having woken early, were bringing
in the flowers from the garden and the smell of jasmine filled
the air. Alicia hugged her sister. Suddenly long-forgotten childhood memories came rushing back to her.

'Oh, Frieda,' she said, 'do you remember when we climbed
in through the window, when we were late for Mass? The day
Sister Joan caught us and told Mummy how bad we were!'

But Frieda, ignoring Alicia, was crying in earnest now. For
of course she remembered the things they had shared. And now
she was crying for other, more complicated reasons, for which
there was no name.

Grace, coming in to wake Alicia, stood looking at them, her face unreadable. The recent past trembled before her. Last night she had lain awake looking at the evening star from her bedroom window. The year was nearly over, tomorrow night Alicia would be gone, life would move on. Since her despairing flight into Aloysius's arms Grace had not cried. The secret place within her had closed up, so that the shadows that had once been hidden, appeared now as faint lines across her life. She had known it would be so, she had expected it to happen, but the customs and unwritten laws of this place, the reality of living on this island, had at last been brought home to her. Since Vijay's death she saw that almost anything might be possible. Now that the lovely hope of youth had been disturbed, she understood that the dark shadows in her life could only increase. She was ready for anything, she told herself. But all night, in spite of these last two months, perhaps because of it, Grace had looked up at the sky and seen the stars. It was their light she had noticed. I still have my children, she thought. And she turned towards Aloysius, sleeping silently beside her. He had surprised her by his solicitude and his concern, watching over her with a long-forgotten tenderness, never questioning, never intruding. She had forgotten his generosity of spirit. She had been angry for so long that it had slipped her notice. But last night, when they had returned from midnight Mass, he had sat down at the piano.

'No, you fellows,' he had said, laughing at the others, 'it's my turn for a change. I'm tired of listening to Schubert and Gershwin. This one's for your mother.' And he had played 'When the Sun Says Goodbye to the Mountains', and sung it for her in his still beautiful tenor voice, in a way she had not heard for many years. Startled, Grace had laughed and applauded along with the others, but something, some particle of pain had shifted in her heart.

In the morning light standing beside Alicia's bed, watching her daughters, she felt a small ray of gladness touch her. The air was fragrant with frangipani and the sounds of preparation filled the air. Somewhere in the distance she heard the sigh of the sea. Sitting down on Alicia's bed, moving aside the mosquito net, Grace hugged both her daughters. Then, in order to distract Frieda, she told them about her own wedding day when, motherless, she had found her father picking her flowers early in the morning.

'He tied them with a piece of string, can you imagine! Auntie Angel-Face was so cross with us both. She had organised a magnificent bouquet and there we were collecting what she considered to be rubbish.'

'What did you do then?'

It was an old story but she told it again.

'Well, I couldn't hurt her feelings so I carried Angel-Face's bouquet all the way to the church in the valley.' Grace sighed. 'It weighed a ton!' she laughed.

They had heard it all before but now it had a new meaning. Grace talked on in this way until all three were laughing and then, hearing their voices, with a little flurry of feathers through the window, Jasper arrived.

'Hello, chaps!' he said.

Grace groaned. 'Oh, Jasper, you're not going to cause trouble today, are you?' she pleaded. 'I'm far too busy. I'm going to have you caught if you do. And caged!'

But Jasper, looking as though he had a new lease of life, was not listening. 'Hello, Shiny,' he said.

'What *does* he mean?' asked Grace. 'He keeps saying that. What d'you mean, Jasper?'

'Hello,' said Jasper, staring at Grace unblinkingly.

The girls laughed.

'Oh Jasper, Jasper, will you marry me?' begged Alicia. 'And tell me who Shiny is?'

'Maybe Shiny is his girlfriend,' giggled Frieda.

'Hello, Shiny,' said Jasper. 'Hindu bastards,' he added, sending them into peals of laughter.

'What's going on?' asked Mabel, coming in with Auntie Angel-Face. 'Is the bride awake? Hello, my darling Jasper.'

'Where's the witch?' asked Prayma, who did not like Myrtle.

When she had quietened them all down and sent them off to get ready, Grace went in search of Aloysius. He, like everyone else, needed close watching this morning.

Myrtle was busy writing her diary in her room. She had been up early this morning, before everyone else. With her black umbrella and handbag she had gone stealthily into the oldest part of the city. No one had seen her. No one except Jasper, whose new sleeping patterns remained mysterious. He had called out cheerily to her as she left the house but she had started to run at the sound of his voice. Always interested by her reaction, he flew swiftly from tree to tree whistling. She turned and hissed at him, shaking her umbrella. In any case, she was now beyond his new territory so, losing interest, he went back to his perch on the plantain tree. Myrtle was gone for nearly an hour. On her return, intent on slipping unnoticed into the house, she missed Thornton sliding quickly in through the back door. Jasper swooped down from the branches and gave a low wolf whistle. Thornton chortled joyfully. After the wedding, thought Myrtle, grimly, entering her room, I shall do something about Jasper. The situation was now insufferable. The creature waited constantly outside her room, scratching himself, barking, peering in. Spying on her. Shitting on her windowsill. Tomorrow, she fumed, tomorrow was Jasper's last day.

Inside, the house was humming with activity. Telegrams were arriving from absent well-wishers. The awning in the garden was opened and a servant began spraying the flowers to keep them cool. The catering staff had managed to soothe the cook's ruffled feathers and now food began to emerge slowly from the kitchen. Grace, dressed in a pink-and-gold sari, appeared amid cries of appreciation.

'Oh, just look at your mother,' said Auntie Angel-Face with pride.

'Mummy, you look so beautiful!' said Frieda.

'The bride! The bride!' cried Prayma, as Alicia appeared, trembling a little, wearing her mother's veil with small jasmine flowers in her hair.

Aloysius, about to have one for the road, caught sight of his wife and daughter and gave a shout of delight. But where was Thornton, why was he not ready yet? Ah! thought Grace rashly, here he was, the light of her life, the joy in her heart, devastating in morning dress. Thornton smiled at his mother, a sunbeam of a smile, and bells rang in her heart.

'Come on,' said Jacob, impatient, the formality of the clothes suiting his solemn air. 'We'll be late, better go now, Mummy.'

They stood all together for a photograph, her boys, Jacob, Thornton and Christopher, unfamiliar and silent in his new clothes, and Frieda the bridesmaid, trying not to cry again.

'Perfect, my darlings,' shouted Uncle Innocent. 'You all look perfect!'

So they left for the church, handing their mother carefully into the car, smiling, joking nervously, for this happy moment was the most perfect of all. The de Silva family. If only, thought Frieda later, if only it had stopped there. Could things have been any better than this moment? But had that happened no one would have seen Alicia smile meltingly as she walked up the aisle on the arm of the handsome, dashing, still debonair Aloysius de Silva. And all those future generations, all that life that shifted continents and changed the course of rivers would never have happened. So it was just as well that the momentarily stilled tableau jerked back into time and the car turned on the gravel and sped through the waiting sunshine, carrying Grace and her children to the church.

It was just as well that Aloysius, leading his elder daughter into the arms of Sunil Pereira, before taking his place beside his wife, had indulged in that drink for the road, for there were many people in the cathedral that day, not all of them expected. There was no time to think. Frieda was suddenly calm.

'Joined together in holy matrimony,' intoned Father Giovanni and the altar boys swung the censers high into the air, so that the smell of frankincense rose and hung in veils above them. Aloysius took out his handkerchief and blew noisily into it, indicating this to be a significant moment. Thereupon, everyone who wished to do so followed suit. And then it was over and the organist was playing the Bridal March, and Alicia and Sunil walked back down the aisle together, smiling and waving to them all, the relatives wiping their eyes, the friends, their nearest and dearest.

'Who's that woman talking to Thornton?' asked Grace.

The photographs were taken, the Prime Minister, who had come as he said he would, shook hands with the happy couple, and had his picture taken with them before speeding off in his limousine. The family went back to the house to welcome the guests for the reception.

'Now,' said Aloysius with a flourish, 'it's time for the champagne toast!'

In the square outside the church, not far from the sacred site of the temple trees and the almshouse, there were no glimpses of saffron robes today. All was quiet. The confetti, the rice and a blue ribbon fluttering in the breeze were all that remained of Alicia de Silva's wedding.

'Who's that person with Thornton?' asked Grace.

The reception was in full swing. After the food there had been the speeches and the toasts. The cake had been cut and a wish made by the newly-weds.

'Thornton,' whispered Alicia, 'come on, play something, quick. You promised!' So Thornton went over to the piano, followed by a round of applause and whistles of encourage-ment. He looked very handsome.

'This one's for the bride,' he announced, grinning. He began to play. It was the signal for everyone to dance. Sunil, unused to the kind of partying the de Silvas went in for, tried and failed to avoid it.

'Oh no you don't,' laughed Alicia, determined there would be no escape.

So Alicia taught her new husband to waltz, and then to foxtrot, and after that to tango, with many encouraging shouts from their audience. But she was laughing so much that it was an impossible task. Grace, not to be outdone, danced with Aloysius, but he soon lost her to all the others waiting for a turn. After that everyone joined in the dancing, and any barriers there might have been between the different groups of guests broke down.

'Now, let's get down to the real business,' said Aloysius, having watched his wife for a while.

The servants set up the card table and whisky and ice were brought out. Aloysius and his cronies retired to the veranda.

Before long it was time for the bride and groom to leave. They would spend the night at a guest house and in the morning would drive up to the tea country, near Alicia's old home. First, Sunil had promised his mother they would visit the temple where they would give alms to the monks and receive a blessing on their marriage. His mother watched them prepare to leave.

'You were right, putha,' she whispered to her son, kissing him goodbye. 'These people are no different from us.' She felt as if she had known the de Silva family all her life.

'You see.' Sunil beamed triumphantly. 'I told you, didn't I? There was nothing to worry about.'

They waved them off, then, with more laughter and shouts and good advice. Auntie Angel-Face threw a handful of rice and Frieda a shower of shoe-flower petals.

'It was perfect, you look beautiful, my darlings,' she said.

'No more looking at other girls, Sunil!'

'Don't forget us,' called Prayma, hugging Alicia, crying a little, for the moment required it.

'Give my love to the hills,' shouted Uncle Innocent, and they all paused for a moment, thinking of the blue-greenness of the slopes, the places where they had played as children, the sounds of the green bee-eater, their youth, *especially* their youth. Alicia and Sunil smiled at them all.

'Quick, someone take a photograph,' shouted Coco.

Standing back, fleetingly, Frieda imagined how it must have been, in the House of Many Balconies, their voices trapped forever in those hills. Alicia and Sunil were smiling. They had smiled all day long, thought Frieda. How happy they must be!

'We'll remember you to the hills,' they promised. And then, they were gone.

The sun was setting low on the horizon. In a moment it

would be dark. It had been an auspicious, radiant day, and now the full moon shone down on them. Tomorrow was New Year's Day.

But the party was not over yet. The fun had only just begun. The air of expectancy that hung over them all day was still present. Like a playful, soft-footed cat it prowled the edges of the day, waiting to pounce. The garden darkened, its murmuring and warnings muffled by the noise of the music. Someone turned up the gramophone and the serious dancing began. Jasper, masquerading as a bird of prey, flew smoothly across the moon.

'Hello, chaps!' he greeted the garden cheerily. 'Anyone for cricket?'

No one noticed him. Myrtle, his favourite, was nowhere to be seen. The night jasmine opened, pouring its scent into the darkness, glowing white against the foliage. There were no drums tonight, no police sirens, no screaming nightbirds. Yet the air trembled with expectation. Rushes of small sounds scurried along in the depths of the garden. No, the party was not over yet. It had a long way to go, unravelling itself, joining all the other events that made up the tapestry of their lives, giving it the colour it would otherwise lack. They would not see any of this just yet, but the soft-footed cat, the leopard in their lives, prowled quietly, closer and closer.

'Prayma, who's that woman dancing with Thornton?' asked Grace again.

'I don't know,' said Prayma. 'D'you know, Mabel?'

'No,' said Mabel. 'I'll ask Auntie Angel-Face.'

Auntie Angel-Face didn't know either. She was getting a little short-sighted, and deaf too if truth were known.

'She was at the church,' said one of the cousins.

'Well, let's ask him,' said Auntie Angel-Face, boisterously.

Grace would not do that. Her good manners would not allow herself the luxury of curiosity.

'She's white,' said Auntie Angel-Face, in a neutral sort of way.

'She's very pretty,' said Coco, uncertain.

'*So old,*' said the cousins.

'Innocent!' shrieked Auntie Angel-Face, being unable to stand the suspense any longer. 'I want to talk to you. Come here.'

Thornton was dancing with the So-Old-White-Woman. He was actually jiving. Rather well, so he thought.

'Who,' asked Auntie Angel-Face, 'who is *that*?' and she pointed a fat, nail-polished finger in the direction of the So-Old-White-Woman who was wriggling her hips and flapping her thighs together, and who suddenly took a leap into Thornton's arms, her bright red court shoes sticking out on either side of his slim hips, her head lower than his crotch, a suspicion of knickers for those who were looking. Uncle Innocent's eyes bulged out of his head. His jaw dropped. Cigar ash fell to his feet un-noticed. A slow, lascivious smile played on his lips. There were other changes too. He stood up straighter, cleared his throat of its customary phlegm, flicked imaginary ash off his shirt when in fact the ash was all over his shoes, and began to perspire heavily. Sensing an audience, Thornton turned, slowly, with a sensuous shake of his hips. The music stopped. He smiled broadly and walked towards them. Towards Uncle Innocent, Auntie Angel-Face, his cousins, his sister, towards his mother. He had been waiting for the right moment and here it was, presenting itself.

'This is Hildegard,' he beamed. 'Mummy, Hildegard and I were married this morning!'

'Hello, Mrs de Silva,' said Hildegard, holding out her pretty hand, filling the awkwardness of the moment. 'I am Hildegard.'

And then, as there didn't seem to be much response, 'May I call you Mother?'

No one spoke. Thornton looked at his mother. He saw with some surprise that the expression on her face was not as he expected. Because his mother, Thornton realised somewhat belatedly, was looking at him, the Light of Her Life, her Boy Who Could Tilt the World With a Smile, in a way that did not bode well for the immediate future. Thornton hesitated. The famous smile faltered. His mother's expression, he saw, would have to be dealt with.

Married this *morning*? thought Grace, disbelievingly.

'How *old* is she?' asked Auntie Angel-Face, and Prayma and Mabel and Uncle Innocent, stalling for time. And that was even before the uproar from Aloysius and Jacob. Jacob had a field day, years of accumulated resentment were aired that night, and the next, and for many nights after. In fact, Jacob had such a time of it that for a while he stopped thinking about his plans for the UK. Such was the disruption caused by that night. Such was the *drama*.

Only Christopher had no comment to make. It was debatable as to whether Christopher even knew what on earth was going on. He hovered on the periphery unnoticed. Alicia had tried dancing with him, the cousins had tried joking with him but Christopher would not be drawn. He had nothing to say. He wandered over to the servants' quarters where the cook's son was rolling betel and squatted down, belching loudly. Close by in the murunga tree Jasper kept watch.

'Here comes another idiot,' said Jasper.

'Hello,' said Christopher, rather unsteadily. 'What are you drinking?'

'Whisky, putha,' said Jasper from the depth of the tree, getting it right for once.

'Good idea,' muttered Christopher. 'That's the best suggestion I've heard all day.'

The servant boy offered him a bottle of arrack.

'Listen!' said Christopher, after he had taken a swig. He
stabbed at the air and swayed towards the servant boy. 'I'm
going to overthrow this government.'

The servant boy took the bottle back and Christopher glared
at him.

'It's no laughing matter,' he said loudly. 'D'you hear me?
You're going to help me.'

He belched and Jasper belched back, making him jump. Then
he laughed, high-pitched and strained. The servant boy stopped
rolling his betel and grinned. He pulled his sarong tighter and
nodded his head.

'Hello, Shiny?' asked Jasper suddenly from above.

Christopher collapsed in a fit of hysterics.

'Jasper!' he screeched. 'Jasper, I'm trying to organise a coup
and all you can do is talk about Shiny!'

The servant boy laughed. He had never seen Master
Christopher like this before.

'Bastards!' said Christopher, beginning to weep. The servant
boy held out the bottle again, but Christopher, having curled
himself up under the murunga tree, had suddenly fallen asleep.
In his tightly clenched fists was a small Perspex brooch in the
shape of a butterfly, the sort that was sold in the *kadés* that
lined the seafront. The servant boy picked up the arrack and
went inside, for he was certain he could hear shouting and
crying on a very grand scale.

He had known her for over a year. Her name was Hildegard
Rosenstall and she had travelled to the island from the Indian
subcontinent where she had been living for some years. She

was beautiful. And she was twenty years older than Thornton. Grace, looking as though she were on a saline drip, had the facts fed slowly to her.

'Now, Grace, take a deep breath. Slowly, breathe slowly,' said Auntie Angel-Face. 'Move away, everyone, she needs air!'

Frieda was crying because, well, because she was at an emotional point in her life, what with one thing and another. She felt incredibly sad and awfully tragic although she was not sure why. She hated atmosphere and there was certainly an atmosphere surrounding Thornton, and Grace. And almost everyone else. So Frieda was crying, buckets and buckets of tears.

'Will someone do something about Frieda, for God's sake?'

'Should we phone the newly-weds?'

'Innocent, don't just stand there!'

'Quick, get some ice.'

All was confusion.

After the wedding night came the morning after. Understandably, no one had slept. The combination of alcohol and angst kept them all awake. All except Christopher who stayed in his stupor unnoticed until the early-morning rain woke him, making him stumble, dry-throated, into bed.

'Poor boy,' reported Jasper without making it clear which boy he meant. No one took any notice of him. No one took a swipe at him. Even Myrtle, his favourite, seemed incapable of paying him any attention.

'Hello, Shiny,' he muttered, flying back into the trees.

Grace was still silent. Her anger was so great that it had rendered her speechless. The de Silva clan thought it was grief that robbed her of her voice. They had no idea that Grace had only two thoughts in her head. Should she kill Thornton? Or the Woman?

Thornton smiled quite a bit in those early hours. Beautiful, limpid smiles, but it was not working. He turned his eyes into dark pools of passion and sorrow. But that didn't work either. Jacob throbbed. He had turned into an engine of self-righteous speech. What on earth was it to do with him? wondered Thornton mildly. Not surprisingly Aloysius had reached for the bottle. This *was* a crisis. Uncle Innocent agreed, it was indeed a *crisis*. Uncle Innocent felt too many things, some of them to do with Hildegard herself, the hussy, but in the short term he felt he should show some solidarity with Aloysius and join him with the whisky and soda. The rest of them sided vociferously with Grace, whose beautiful teeth were clenched with rage.

Dawn came slowly. Rose-washed, delicate light, scented with the softness of rain. The heat of the day was slow to reveal itself, simmering, building up to its usual crescendo. Inside the de Silvas' house, outside on the veranda, and further back in the garden, however, the emotional temperature rose inexorably. Hildegard, her enormous eyes filling with tears, could stand it no longer. Thornton had begun to look like a little boy. He made her feel her age in ways hitherto unknown to her. There comes a time in a woman's life when her age begins to mean a great deal to her, and sadly this time had arrived for Hildegard. What could she have done? Her skin was still supple; her hair had no hint of grey. She had no children. Who would have thought this could have become a problem? Was every woman on this wretched island expected to be a sacred cow? Hildegard, her slim childless figure belying her age, wondered what she had done. They all clearly thought, as she had begun to feel herself, that she had seduced Thornton, instead of the reality, which was the other way round. Hildegard, whose eyes kept filling up, unaware of the effect it was having on Uncle Innocent, decided it was time to leave. She looked at Thornton for support but there was a vacant spot where Thornton's emotions should have been. So Hildegard left in a way that would be remembered afterwards, in silence and with dignified speed.

Thornton hardly noticed. He was feeling a little confused. Confused and with the beginnings of a serious headache coming on. He wished Frieda would stop weeping. It was getting on his nerves. He wished his mother would unlock her teeth. It was affecting the power of his smile. As for his eldest brother, he wondered again, what on earth *his* problem was? Still, he yawned, he was almost too tired to think. He had been certain he was in love but now, well, he couldn't be sure. His eyebrows shot up into a vulnerable position towards the top of his head. He felt tears of self-pity fill his eyes. Grace, noticing this, felt herself weaken. The family held their breath. And waited. It would be several days yet, but could the end be in sight?

'Quick,' said Auntie Angel-Face in command again. 'Prayma, tell the cook to make some food. Poor Grace has had nothing to eat.'

'It's lunchtime already,' noticed Mabel, surprised. 'How the time has flown!'

'I don't think we should disturb the newly-weds, do you, Auntie Angel? Let them have a little peace to enjoy their honeymoon.'

'Yes, yes, of course.'

'A telegram will only upset them,' shouted Uncle Innocent, wondering if he should catch up with Hildegard and offer her a lift somewhere.

Mabel took Frieda in hand and tried to staunch the tears, not in itself an easy operation, and Coco made some tea that no one drank. She had seen it done in the movies and thought she might try it herself. Jasper, feeling much better after a sleep, flew in and saw Myrtle more or less where he had last seen her.

'Hello, sister,' he greeted her cheerfully, whereupon Grace, to whom this was absolutely the last straw, arose majestically and hurled her slipper with such force and fury at him that she caught him by surprise, sending him squawking out of the window, knocking over Aloysius's empty bottle of whisky in the process.

It was midday. The heat had at last revealed its hand. The de Silva family, those that weren't asleep, sat down to a desultory lunch. It was, they realised, somewhat with surprise, New Year's Day.

'Happy New Year!' said Uncle Innocent, experimentally, seeing how the words sounded and how they all reacted to them. He was trying to keep any lustful thoughts of Hildegard to one side, in order not to cloud the issues at stake. But he kept forgetting what these were and all he could think of were those enormous blue eyes. Uncle Innocent was a sucker, as clearly Thornton had been, for blue eyes. All this passion, he thought feverishly, it was too much for him at his age. Besides, he was worried in case Auntie Angel-Face got wind of his thoughts. Grace was bad enough at the moment without Angel-Face at it too. He poured himself a glass of cold water, clear, cleansing, life-sustaining liquid that it was, and retired to his bed for an afternoon rest.

9

THE WINDS OF CHANGE COME SWIFTLY. Seldom is there warning. No darkening of the skies, no cockcrow. Instead, suddenly, there comes a stirring breeze, a spiralling dust cloud, a change in things forever. January was cooler. The rains still fell daily, soaking into the ground with the parched and insatiable lust of many months. The island could never seem to get enough wetness, never quite quench its thirst. It breathed in the rain then paused while the forests grew, waiting for the heat to continue.

Grace, appearing to cope with the shock of Thornton's escapade, headed for the church. The family held their breath.

'My child,' said Father Giovanni, 'have they had carnal knowledge of each other?'

'No, Father,' said Grace carefully. 'Not to my knowledge. My son is headstrong,' she ventured. 'He is deeply sorry. He wishes to confess.'

'Yes, yes, I understand,' murmured the priest, frowning. He mulled over the recent events. 'Would you say this young man was led astray? That he was gullible? That the woman was a corrupting influence, perhaps?'

Grace hesitated. Her anger with Thornton had not fully subsided. Where had she gone wrong? Should she have been firmer with him when he was a child? But he had been a wonderful child, thought Grace. She felt cornered.

Father Giovanni considered her. She was a fine-looking woman. An admirable woman, with an unfortunate, useless husband. More importantly, Kollupitiya Cathedral was heavily subsidised by the de Silvas. Christmas and Alicia's wedding had left a warm glow in the church. And there was little doubt: Grace had her fair share of troubles to bear. Looking at her face in the candlelight, he thought, The poor woman deserves a break.

'Well, now,' he said clearing his throat, making up his mind swiftly, 'he always was a headstrong boy, was your Thornton.' And he smiled at Grace. 'Tell him to come and see me in the mornin', will you?' he said. 'And we'll see what we can do to settle the matter.'

At home, the family held their breath, but they were confident. It was just a matter of time. Annulments came only from Rome and the Holy City worked in mysterious ways. It would not be hurried. There was nothing to do except wait. Twelfth night came and went. Myrtle noted the changes.

January 15. Well they never do things by halves here. Naturally we had to have two weddings! When the Golden Boy delivered his trump card the expression on G's face was so funny that I had to go out of the room because I was laughing so much. I had forgotten what a temper she has. Illness aside, she became her old self when it came to her darling son. A couple of pieces of her precious bone china went flying in the process. Aloysius tried restraint but there was no stopping G. I'm glad that everyone saw her true colours for once. Innocent looked as though he was having some sort of fit. He just stared and stared at the Woman! No one seems to know anything about this Hildegard, or where on earth Thornton found her. In some gutter somewhere no doubt, although why she wants to be married to him is a mystery to me. Can't she see how stupid he is? Well, anyway, she's not going to be Mrs de Silva for much longer by the looks of things. I knew Thornton was a fool but even I couldn't have anticipated such behaviour. They're all angry with him, even Jacob. If anything could kill G off it's this. If Mr B's horoscope is to be believed, there's more to come!

Grace appeared to have put aside her strange lethargy and depression. Uncle Innocent and Aloysius took to drowning their sorrows together, daily, Frieda was still crying intermittently despite all Mabel's efforts, and the bridegroom appeared to be in a state of confusion. He needed time to take stock, to confess to Father Giovanni. Had he thought about it, Thornton might have seen the desperation of Hildegard's love and the unsuitability of what he had done. But Thornton, as was becoming increasingly clear, had not been thinking clearly.

Everyone was preoccupied, leaving them unprepared for the next gust of wind. Quietly, unnoticed by anyone, except Grace, Christopher made plans to leave. Silently, without fuss, he went about his preparations. There was nothing to keep him here. No one noticed because what was there to notice? Only his mother, talking to him at odd, snatched moments, understood.

'What is there left for someone like me in this place?' he asked her bitterly.

He would be leaving in a few weeks. His ticket to the UK had arrived. He had confessed his plans to her.

'Things are getting worse here. I can't take any more,' he told his mother, flatly.

Grace looked at the ticket. Colombo, Cairo, Genoa,

Southampton. She handed him back his visa, his passport. He was exhausted by the effort of living. They both were.

'There's no justice of any sort,' Christopher said. He spoke quietly. There was no sign of his usual anger. Perhaps disillusion was a quieter thing. 'There's nothing left. The government is terrible. Wealth and religion and endless corruption have ruined my life,' he said. 'No one either notices or cares.'

His voice broke. Grace nodded silently. She could not deny any of it. She would not argue, even if she had the strength. Nevertheless, she asked him with infinite tenderness, 'What will there be in England for you, Christopher? What comfort will you find there? Away from your own people?'

'At least I'll find justice there!' he said. 'They have laws. Laws that work. They're English, aren't they? Decent English people. They care about the poor. They care about *their* people.'

She said no more after that. It broke her heart all over again. He is young, she thought, he has ideals. Who was she to question if he was right? She did not mention Kamala. There was no need to say her name. Kamala moved between them like a glimmer of light, in the untouchable layers of their conversation. Kamala and Vijay. The long years of her mothering stretched behind Grace. She could not have foreseen any of this. She could not have foreseen her pain. Finally, hesitantly, it was Christopher who spoke of Kamala.

'There will never be anyone else,' he said, so softly that she could barely hear him. He sounded lost and older than his years. 'All that sort of thing is finished for me.'

'You don't know that,' Grace told him, quietly. She too hesitated. 'One day, who knows? Don't talk in this way. Things happen. Unexpected things.'

Please God, she thought. She wanted to say more. She wanted to tell him to be different from her. She wanted to say, make something of your life, Christopher. Don't waste it. You are not like me, you have more possibilities. But she was silent, afraid of hurting him further. She knew the dark scorched places in his life could not be eased, and that the hurt he felt would not be spoken of again. Both of us, she thought, have learnt to control ourselves. The light had moved, evening was almost upon them, she could only dimly see his face. Her heart ached for her youngest son, for his aloneness and for his courage. England would change him further. He would grow a new self; wear it as though it were clothes. She wanted England to work for him and because of this she wanted to make his leaving as easy as she could.

'If it is truly what you want,' she said at last, her sense of hopelessness lengthening with the evening, 'then go. I can't say I don't mind, because I do. But if it will help, then go.'

She saw clearly what she must do. She saw that Christopher needed a last desperate leap in order to propel himself into his adult life and she acknowledged with sadness that her presence from this moment on could do no more than hold him back. This last act of her mothering was the most important. The time for *my* needs has passed, thought Grace. And she let him go.

The morning of Christopher's departure was dark and stormy. White-topped waves scurried outside the harbour bouncing against the small boats that took the passengers out to the big ocean liner. Christopher had one trunk labelled with the name of the ship. 'FAIRSEA', it said in blue and white letters. 'SYDNEY', 'COLOMBO', 'CAIRO', 'GENOA', SOUTHAMPTON', it declared. 'DECK THREE. CABIN 432.' Jacob stared at the ticket. 'Passengers are expected to embark at 1400 hours for departure at 1600 hours.'

Jacob was mesmerised. Never had he come so close to holding

a ticket. He blinked owlishly at Christopher as though seeing him for the first time. Christopher, the runt of the litter, was escaping first, Christopher, the unexpected one, chasing the monsoons across the seas, getting away. Jacob was stunned. It should have been him. Whenever he had imagined this moment of leave-taking, he had been in the leading role. He had imagined himself waiting to climb aboard the motor launch that would take him to the ship. Looking very tall and serious, impressing the other passengers, his family, everyone, with his quiet reserve. But here instead was Christopher, unfamiliar in his new suit, surrounded by the family.

'Have you only one trunk?' asked Thornton, surprised.

Loaded no doubt with party political leaflets, thought Jacob.

'He's got an ocean-liner carrying bag,' said Frieda. 'I packed it this morning. It has got your favourite sambals and chilli pickles, Christopher. There are some ambarella fruit as well and a couple of Jaffna mangoes. Any more than that and they will spoil before you have a chance to eat them.'

'I've put some rosary beads in a thambili, for you, darling,' said one of the aunts.

'And a picture of St Christopher as well,' said Frieda.

She knew Christopher would not want it but would keep it because it was from her. At the last moment she gave him a framed photograph of all the family at Alicia's wedding.

'Well,' said Jacob, trying to be magnanimous and show he did not care, 'you're about to become a travelling man and embark on *life*.'

Christopher, scowling and tense and with no sense of any new beginnings, suffered the wait while his family, together for the last time, solemnly wished him goodbye. First Thornton, his beautiful eyes filling with tears, no sign of Hildegard (where, wondered everyone, was she?), embraced him.

'Look after yourself, Christopher,' he said. 'I hope you'll be happy in England.' He felt sad for the brother he knew the least, the darkly raging one, the one who made life harder for himself by always going against the flow. 'I'll write to you. These are bad times we are going through,' he said, thinking of himself a little too, for wasn't his own life undergoing a stormy patch at the moment? 'I'll send you a poem of farewell!' he added.

Then Jacob embraced him and shook his hand as the English did. 'We'll be meeting soon,' he said cryptically.

Frieda demanded nothing, Frieda merely cried, making Thornton sigh heavily.

'When I have the schedule for my first concert tour I'll visit you,' said Alicia, wanting to be different from the rest of them in her new married state. 'I'll bring you some mangoes!'

Sunil had taken time off work. He alone looked relaxed and fresh. He kissed his brother-in-law on both cheeks with the genuine affection that touched everything he did, squeezing his shoulder, silently wishing him well. He knew the riots had affected Christopher deeply but he had never felt he could ask why. He hoped things would improve for him in England.

'I hope we'll meet again soon,' he said smiling. 'Take care of yourself.'

Myrtle watched them all. Today she wore her predictions like a tortoiseshell ornament in her hair. Christopher, she knew, was only the first to go.

Christopher waited, enveloped by the smell of hot diesel and his family's good wishes, passive for once, silent as always, alien already. Until at last, the great horn blasting them back onto the motor launch set them waving. Until Frieda's arm ached and his mother's small strained tearless face became one with the sea of faces below, until he could distinguish them no more. In this way Christopher watched them slipping away as easily as the island itself with its coconut-dense edges, sinking into the sea. Slowly the waving became ineffectual and the enormity of the water a reality. Beyond the haze of sunlight, the ship turned from the safety of the coral reef, sounding its long last farewell home, before heading for the open seas. For Christopher, the mist forming before his eyes confirmed only that there would be no new beginning, no wonderful future ahead, but simply the restless movement and the endless cycle of his karma.

So Christopher was gone, flown the de Silva nest while Rome worked slowly behind the scenes for Thornton. The de Silvas, with their network of contacts in the Catholic Church, were able to call in a favour from a distant relative in the Vatican. Just two months short of his twenty-first birthday Thornton's underaged marriage was ripe for annulment. Saved by a whisker, thought Jacob sourly. How did the boy do it? wondered Uncle Innocent, amazed.

'So *young*!' was on everyone's lips.

'What a waste! What a shame!'

Thornton the poet, the limpid-eyed heartbreaker, the lover of all the finer things in life, was left with no choice but to fall heavily and regretfully out of love with Hildegard. What a thing was this, thought Hildegard, weeping into the long hot nights. Packing her bags to return to a Europe she no longer had any taste for, running away as she had always run before. Vanishing (forgotten for the moment by all but Uncle Innocent), back to Europe where blue-eyed women cause less of a stir.

'Naughty boy,' said Jasper, quietly.

Jasper was growing old and no one heard him any more. The rains had finished for the moment, the tropical vegetation grew and the shuddering awfulness of the *karapoththas*, the cockroaches, seemed everywhere. The imaginary leopard cub that had prowled the edges of the garden during Alicia's wedding had grown unimportant. Aloysius, aware of the distant rumble of violence, of Grace's unspoken despair, was quieter, stayed closer to home, drinking less and seldom organising any card parties. Christopher's absence had made more of a difference that any of them expected. There was a dullness in the air. The gelatinous heat shrivelled up the once green and pleasant parks. Who cared if the elephants had left the jungles? Who cared if they were dying in the towns? Elephants could not provide a national identity. Only language could do that. Language mattered more than anything else now. This was the thing to provoke bloodshed.

The de Silva children were adults now. Frieda stayed close to home. After that first mad dash towards emotional freedom she seemed to shrivel, minding her father, whose liver was not as it should be, and her mother, whose silent indifference frightened her. No one noticed the flush of youth slowly fade from Frieda's face. Thornton too was more cautious these days. Aware of the change in his mother, he was careful. Jacob had reluctantly found him a job at his office in the hope of keeping him out of trouble. Only Alicia seemed really happy. Sunil was in the Cabinet now and his dream almost a reality.

'If only they would have a child,' Grace prayed, 'their life would be complete.'

Frieda, crying into her pillow at nights, dreaming of Robert Grant, thought, Alicia has everything except a child.

Alicia herself was puzzled by this absence.

'Why has it not happened yet?' she asked Sunil. 'After a thousand days, why not?'

Sunil was not worried.

'There is plenty of time,' he told her gently. 'We're both still young. Don't worry. It'll be all right. Next year, when the rains come, you'll see!'

He was busy in the run-up to the general election. Rumours of dissatisfaction among the Buddhist monks simmered beneath the surface, and in any case Alicia had her first concert tour ahead. There was work to be done. So he told her: 'There's plenty of time. Don't worry. Let's just enjoy our freedom while we can.'

In his letters home to Grace, Christopher painted a picture of England that was difficult to believe. His letters were full of the cold.

'What on earth's the matter with Christopher?' asked Thornton irritably when he read them. 'Why does he have to exaggerate everything?'

Christopher folded his disappointments in light blue aerogrammes, sending them home like small bullets of emotion.

Now that I am here I can see how wonderful it really is in Ceylon, he wrote. *Our country has so much to offer, its past is so rich and vibrant. All we do is destroy it. Believe me, there is nothing here for any of us. I don't belong here and never will. There is no point in any of you coming. Better to stay and fight for what is ours.*

He wrote with an inexplicable longing, saying he missed the heat and his home. He sounded confused.

Everyone here goes mad when the sun comes out. They talk of nothing else. They sit in parks eating tasteless food. They smile at the sun, yet their lives are ruled by the lack of it. And when it rains, which it does nearly all the time, they talk about the weather then too!

'Well,' said Thornton, 'Christopher has become like them. He too talks about nothing else.'

Jacob read the letters after everyone else had passed them

round, and was disbelieving. He did not want Christopher's
opinions.

'He's making most of it up. When has Christopher done
anything except complain? He's just showing off. It's fine for
him to go to England, but not us.'

Jacob had still not forgiven Christopher for leaving before
him, for doing what he had planned for himself. He could not
understand these furious and confusing communications. Soon
I'll find these things out for myself, he comforted himself.
Things won't stay this way forever.

It was true. Things don't stay the same, thought Thornton
joyously, coming home one afternoon.

'Look!' he cried, waving the newspaper noisily. 'Look,
everyone!'

Finally, he had had a poem accepted in the newspaper.

'Hurrah for Thornton, dazzling smiler, dreamer of dreams,
and now, *poet*,' said Frieda, seeing it. 'His poem on the fishermen has been published at last!'

'What he knows about fishermen could be written on a betel
leaf,' snorted Jacob.

'Still,' said their mother encouragingly, 'as everybody knows,
it is not what you know but how you say it.'

Thornton had indeed said it. Suddenly he had a whole new
crowd of admirers to join the old followers. Grace roused herself
and framed the poem.

'Good!' she said, determined to be cheerful. 'Now you must
write another.'

But before he could do so, one of his new fans, an intelligent, funny, dark young orphan girl from the south, arrived
like a laundry parcel tucked under his arm just as the new
moon was appearing. Where he had met her was unclear,
Thornton always being vague on these matters.

'Who cares anyway?' said Myrtle. 'It's an omen.'

'Oh no,' said Grace, belatedly alert, anxiety gathering on her brow, 'it's the End!'

'Good morning,' said Jasper solemnly, and the girl jumped. And laughed, delighted.

'Oh, Thornton!' she said, excitedly. 'I hope you've written a poem about him!'

Thornton looked at the girl with interest. A poem about Jasper? What a good idea. It's clear, decided Frieda, struggling with an instinctive hostility, and a heart that would not mend, this one is not good-looking enough for Thornton. It's clear, thought Myrtle, who could spot these things a mile away, that she is too clever for him. The girl's name was Savitha and she was always teasing Thornton.

'Oh please, smile at me,' she cried, clutching her heart and pretending to writhe in agony. 'I can't live without your smile. Your poems, yes, but not that smile!'

Thornton grinned. Grace, listening to them, glanced up in surprise. Jasper, watching them non-committally, barked loudly, sending Savitha into hysterics.

'Imagine Jasper with a tail!' she cried.

'Jasper's tale,' said Thornton, with a loud guffaw.

'Don't be rid-ic-ulous,' said Jasper, with his usual randomness, sending them into shrieks.

'Oh, don't you *see*?' said Savitha, hardly able to speak. 'That's the title of your next poem, "Jasper's Tale".'

Of course, thought Thornton, amazed. So amazed in fact that he bent over and kissed Savitha. They were both taken by surprise.

Savitha's interest in Thornton expanded imperceptibly. Her friendliness began to extend to the rest of the de Silva family. She found them as enchanting as characters from a fairy tale.

Fascinated, she looked a little closer and then she saw that all was not as it had first appeared. Thornton's mother was a very beautiful woman but something was definitely not quite right. There was an understated air of sadness to Grace that surprised Savitha. Ever since she had been a little orphan girl, dependent on her observational skills for survival, Savitha had taken a deep interest in other people. And, although she hid it well, she had the softest of hearts. So that now she asked herself, why was Thornton's mother so unhappy? Why did no one else notice? She's desperate, thought Savitha, her curiosity increasing with every visit to the house.

'Can't you see it?' she asked Thornton, serious for a moment.

Thornton was staggered. What did she mean? His mother was, well, she was just his mother, wasn't she?

'Hmm,' said Savitha. She wasn't so sure. 'I think she's depressed, don't you? Every time I see her I feel she's on the verge of tears. She's lonely, too.'

Thornton was both flabbergasted and silenced. He looked at his mother. She looked just as she always did. What was Savitha talking about?

'Perhaps,' he said, struggling with the idea, 'perhaps she misses Christopher. Although he did give her plenty of trouble.'

'Oh, Thornton!' Savitha said, laughing again. 'You're hopeless. You're *such* a dreamer. Then again,' she frowned, thinking her idea through, 'maybe, this country *needs* some dreamers.'

'How d'you mean?' asked Thornton, puzzled. He had thought they were talking about his mother. 'D'you want me to write political poems, or something? Be like Christopher? Is that what you mean?'

The idea wasn't appealing. Savitha suppressed a smile. Thornton with his air of confusion looked like a little boy. The sight brought out all Savitha's developing maternal instinct. But

143

being wise she waited. It was at this point that she noticed Myrtle properly, and for the first time.

'My God, Thornton. What's wrong with *her*?' she asked, truly shocked. What was the matter with the de Silvas that they could not see how much Myrtle disliked them?

'Myrtle does not like your family, one bit,' she announced. 'She shouldn't be living with you. Look how much she hates Alicia and Sunil. She's a jealous woman, isn't she?'

Once again Thornton was astonished. No one had asked him this sort of question, not his mother, nor Hildegard. Savitha made his family sound like a group of strangers. He had no idea how to respond.

Meanwhile, Savitha was indulging in a delightful little daydream of her own. The more she visited them, the more she was entranced by the de Silvas. She had never had a family in her life, let alone one as exotic as this. They were all so lovely to look at. Grace in particular looked as fragile as an orchid in a storm and Aloysius clearly adored her. Although, and here Savitha hesitated, puzzled, the other de Silva men were a different matter. Jacob's morose state was disturbing. He hardly responded when Savitha spoke to him. She didn't care much for him.

Three months passed. Savitha was a frequent visitor to the house. Thornton kept bringing her back. Frieda noticed and felt unhappy without knowing why. The two of them were always with their heads together, fooling about, and Frieda felt hostility bump against her every time she heard that laugh. What would Christopher make of these new developments? Myrtle noticed too and was uneasy.

What does this girl see in Thornton? she wrote in her diary.

Savitha was having a wonderful time. She felt as though she had strayed into a play. She wrote a funny article for the Sunday papers and it was published. She can write, thought Grace, rising from her trance, astonished in spite of herself. Savitha knew how to dig the knife into society. She had not got the orphanage school scholarship for nothing. The article was about the Westernised elite who had no love for their homeland. 'Our Troubled Isle' she called it and it was brilliant. Sunil was struck by it. Savitha had articulated everything he had always felt. She had stated boldly that the making of an empire had led inevitably to trouble. Several people wrote letters to the editor applauding it. Thornton was unprepared for this sudden catapulting into fame. He had only been mildly interested in Savitha until now. It had been *she* who had hung around, disturbing his tranquillity, worrying him with her questions, pushing against his contentment. Now, suddenly, Thornton began to see her clearly. He fixed her absent-mindedly with an altogether different smile and the world tilted once and for all for her. Even Savitha had her weaknesses.

Grace, watching this small girl with a stirring of interest, noticed her reaction to Thornton's smile and smiled, too, in spite of herself. Myrtle, watching, knew exactly what would happen next. She wanted to laugh out loud, but something about Savitha made her wary. Instead she wrote her comments in her diary.

March 18. This latest is unpredictable. I've caught her watching me. I fear she's here to stay. At first I thought she'd tire of our pretty idiot. Then I expected G to frighten her off, but the creature is clever, she seems to have won G over. Still, I have to admit, it's very, very funny. G, not to mention the darling boy, are getting drawn into something beyond them. Must be karma!

'All the troubles with Hildegard for *this*?' she remarked casually to Grace one evening after dinner. Grace was silent, not knowing what to think. Some instinct told her Savitha might not be such a bad thing for Thornton.

'She's not as pretty as the others,' she told Aloysius slowly.

145

'Yet there's something about her. She forces him to think about things. She's good for him. I think she's falling in love, don't you?'

Aloysius did not care. He just wanted a drink. He thought the girl insignificant. Only Myrtle knew: the girl was not. Meanwhile Thornton, in the throes of some new confusion, was hooked. Perhaps it was her sharp intelligence, perhaps it was her humour and her constant enthusiasm. It certainly isn't her looks, thought Myrtle nastily, but the idiot's mesmerised, like a chicken before a rattlesnake.

Thornton immobilised! wrote Myrtle, in her diary. *Quite a sight!*

'Hello, Sa-Sa!' said Jasper who had mistaken her name. No one corrected him.

Savitha laughed delightedly, and Thornton laughed hearing her. She's mad, he thought. He had never met anyone as ebullient as Savitha before. Laughing all the time they were, those two, in those early weeks, before they dropped the bombshell, when Thornton, taking even himself by surprise, brought his second bride home to his mother. He had done it again! Savitha's dark face glowed with an inner light. For all her liveliness she was not used to being so impulsive. Have I really been thinking straight? she asked herself, head in a whirl. Then, before any of them had time to decide, it was too late and Aloysius, it appeared, was about to get his wish.

'A grandson at last!' he crowed. 'A de Silva. A new generation on the way.'

'Fool!' said Jacob, who had booked a passage to England in two months' time.

'When?' asked Grace. But she spoke softly, and she looked closely at Thornton, who was much more alert these days, and had just announced he needed a better job.

146

'It's exactly what we need, darl,' Aloysius said delighted. 'To cheer us all up in this wretched country.' He glanced quickly at his wife, for still at the back of his mind was the residue of the old anxiety.

Frieda wrote to Christopher the very next morning, her tears (she was uncertain whether from joy or grief) smudging the words.

Thornton seems very happy about it, she wrote. *Can you imagine Thornton as a father? Mummy doesn't seem to mind too much. In fact, I think she's secretly glad. Savitha makes her laugh, something Mummy hasn't done much since you left.*

The night of the announcement, Aloysius celebrated with a new bottle of whisky. Hang his liver.

'A new generation is not announced every day, darl,' he said sheepishly when Grace glared at him. The father-to-be was missing. Where the devil is he? wondered Myrtle. Thornton returned triumphant with a new job offer. In his hand were the application forms for a passport.

'Idiot!' said Jacob angrily, unable to leave the subject alone. 'Throwing your life away. Saddling yourself with a wife is bad enough, but a child as well? What sort of job is it anyway? What makes you think they want you in England?'

Far away in Delhi, sandwiched between Schubert and Beethoven, Alicia heard the news of the coming of the new generation and she wept. For the smallpox Sunil had contracted as a child had left a hidden mark on him. There would be no new generation for Alicia. That night her music floated up towards the stars and her performance was filled with a yearning that had never been there before. Soon she would return home, in time for the general elections, to meet her sister-in-law.

*   *   *

147

Something was wrong with Myrtle. It was obvious to Grace, and to Frieda. But with Jacob's departure imminent there was no time to find out what it was.

'He's off his food,' said Jasper who seemed to have perked up with all the recent activities. 'Hello, Shiny?'

Myrtle was crying. No one knew whether it was the thought of the New Arrival or Jacob's departure. An exhausted Alicia, Sunil at her side, arrived to wish her brother goodbye. Frieda noticed their sorrow had bound them closer together. Myrtle, watching them, burst into tears.

'Good morning, Shiny,' observed Jasper helpfully and, when no one listened, made his now perfected devil-bird sound.

'Hey, Jasp!' said Thornton, who was in the best of moods these days. 'Hey, Jasper, what's shiny?'

Jasper barked loudly.

'Jasper!' said Savitha. 'Jasper, you are so cute! Oh, let's call the baby Jasper, Thornton!'

Jasper stared at her silently. He had no loyalties.

'What is the matter with everyone?' asked Uncle Innocent who had come down from the hills for Jacob's farewell.

'Silly old fool!' said Jasper, sailing out through the window, frightening the cook, sending her into a frenzy of waving and screaming so that Grace had to be called in to speak sternly to him. ·

'Stop it, Jasper,' said Jasper, enjoying himself hugely, running through his repertoire: barking dog, saw drill, crow caws, Mozart, all in quick succession. So that Grace could not help but laugh and Savitha clapped her hands with pleasure.

The line-up at the harbour was the same for Jacob's departure. Only Christopher was missing.

'We *will* visit you,' promised Frieda. 'When you're rich we'll come to see you and Christopher.'

'Get a big house,' said Thornton laughing. 'Because there will be a lot of us! Who knows, we might have twins.'

Jacob sighed. Would he never be free of his siblings?

'Well,' said Grace, taking comfort in the fact, 'don't forget Christopher will be there too. So you won't be alone.'

Why should I want to see *him*? Jacob was puzzled. We hardly spoke at home, what will be different in England? However, he did not say this. He was prepared to wait and see.

'Be good!' said Uncle Innocent. 'Or if not be careful!' he said chuckling with delight. He wondered briefly if Hildegard was in England before hastily squashing the thought. Myrtle watched Jacob go. She was crying again.

'What the devil is wrong with her?' muttered Aloysius, irritated. Really, the woman had lived with them for too long. He wished Grace would get rid of her. She was no use in the house now that the children were all grown up.

'Don't forget to send me some shirts, putha,' he told Jacob, 'and some good whisky, and some chocolate for your mother,' he added as an afterthought.

'Some bath salts too,' said Auntie Angel-Face. 'They put bath salts in the bath in the UK.'

'But we only have showers!' said Savitha, amused. She liked Angel-Face.

'Well, we can smell them instead,' said Angel-Face, confusing them with smelling salts. She was reading Jane Austen at the moment.

Looking at his mother's face, Jacob felt the stirrings of an old emotion from long ago. A leftover from those upcountry days. Savitha observed the family, her family now, and was silent; disturbed in a way she could not fully understand. Certain things, unclear as yet, mysterious and interesting, were beginning to reveal themselves. Veiled in morning sickness, part of

Savitha had begun to feel trapped. Sometimes, very occasionally, Thornton irritated her a little. His smile of course remained devastating, but certain things about him, certain *other* shortcomings had begun to annoy her. Still, she brushed these thoughts aside feeling the new generation turn restlessly inside her. Respect for the unborn subdued her for the moment. The harbour sounds were strangely haunting. Noises that spoke of unknown lands and other lives. Savitha shivered. What would it be like to leave? From the corner of her eye she saw Aloysius stub out his cigarette. He was looking edgy and uncomfortable. The smell of diesel made Savitha heave. Glancing at Grace she felt the moment stretch and magnify with unbearable poignancy. This is where Crown Rule has brought us, she thought. Dissipated by drink, full of suspicion, wanting to leave the country. Thornton was talking to Jacob, laughing at some joke of his own, ever-cheerful. In spite of herself Savitha felt her heart contract. She had married him impulsively, loving his beautiful face, his optimism. She had been right, she thought, this country needed dreamers like Thornton. What will we be like, she wondered, when we are old? Keeping her thoughts to herself, Savitha watched them all. Silence was soon to become her best tool.

There were twenty-one stormy days ahead before Jacob would leave behind the heat at the tip of the Bay of Biscay. Sweating in the coarse wool jacket of his UK-bound suit, wanting only to go, he had no clear memory of his departure. At last, was all he thought, at last. And then he was gone, with his two Jaffna mangoes and his packet of curry leaves, off to a *better life*. Following Jacob's departure Savitha wrote another article for the *Colombo Times*. It was an astringent little piece, cutting across social unrest and the looming elections. The article was about the rich stooges, as she called them, the nationalists who were forcing the Tamils to leave the country. They would go looking for a city paved with gold, taking all that was best in Ceylon with them. Savitha predicted there would be no rainbows, no golden treasures, and no happy ending, either abroad or on the island. It was a sharp piece on emigration, sending out a cry for island solidarity. The editor was struck again by the eloquence and wit of her prose. Grace, reading it, nodded. Once, long ago, she too had felt this way. Sunil read it and was amazed by her passion. He said nothing to Alicia, for Alicia, struggling with their joint sorrow, avoided Savitha of late. She was often at home, practising in between concerts, when Sunil was away canvassing for the elections.

It was July. The monsoons had broken again and the weather was tempestuous. Far out at sea, Jacob leaned over the side of the deck, looking out at the stormy inky water, longing for the voyage to end.

Which was where he was, on the morning of the general election in Ceylon. The island that was no longer even a speck on his horizon. The morning when Thornton, arriving at his parents' house for breakfast, leaving his wife still asleep in the one-bedroom flat that was their married home, looked down to find a gecko land on his shoulder.

'Thornton, master,' said the servant horrified, seeing him brush it off, 'that is very, very bad luck!'

Grace, irritated, shooed the servant away and laid another place for her son.

'How is Savitha this morning?'

'She's still tired, after Jacob's leaving party,' Thornton said. 'I thought I would let her rest.'

He was on his way to work but decided on the spur of the

151

moment that he would stop off at what he still thought of as home, for breakfast. It was almost like the old days only now Thornton had got a decent job thanks to Savitha's good influence. He sat down for a second breakfast and Grace smiled. She was pleased with the way things had turned out for him. Since the announcement of the new baby he had changed. Although they had all changed Thornton was the most altered.

'Your brother is so much more content,' she often remarked to Frieda. 'Less restless, happier, don't you think?'

And Frieda, agreeing, was glad it was Thornton who was the happy one.

On this morning of the election Alicia began her daily practice on the piano earlier than usual. She had slept at her parents' house because Sunil had been working through the night. It was an ordinary day with sunlight slanting down through the trees. Grace cut some flowers for the vases before the heat ruined them and entered the house just as Alicia began to play an old favourite, a Schubert sonata she rarely played any more. The slow, lilting second movement of the andante was one that Grace had always loved. Pausing, she listened. The sounds pierced her heart and stirred up her buried grief. Looking around the table where various members of her remaining family sat, she allowed herself to be overwhelmed by sadness. Once she had stood in this very spot listening to this same piece of music, unaware of all that lay ahead. Lately, she had begun to bring fragments of certain images out into the open. Lately, she had felt able to do this without falling apart. Memory flooded out with the music. Vijay! Yes, she could say his name to herself at last but she no longer could recall his face clearly. He had been but a moment in her life, a flicker of light, going out like a shooting star. Doomed to fall. Yet the essence of him remained strong.

Alicia had reached the tricky part of the music, the where she used always to go wrong, either stumbling over the chords or ruining the timing. Grace listened. How could C minor say so much? Today Alicia played with six years of experience, without smudging the notes, seamlessly shaping the phrases until it was no longer simply the melody they heard, but something more intrinsic, something more polished and complete than it had ever sounded before. Standing in the doorway, watching her elder daughter, seeing the young girl and now the woman absorbed into this slight figure, Grace closed her eyes. Even if she cannot have a child, she has her music. May it always see her through, prayed Grace, silently, as the andante was played out. No one heard the gate being unlatched. No one heard the knock on the door, or the simultaneous discordant ring of the telephone. No one bothered until a servant opened the front door and came looking for Aloysius.

'The police are here. They want the Master,' the servant called, alarmed.

Frieda, coming out from the cool interior of the house, saw the small crowd that had gathered outside, saw her father's face, ashen and crumpled, heard Myrtle's cry, calling for Grace.

'Oh my God, my God! Grace, Grace, I didn't mean it!'

Someone was screaming, over and over again. Frieda could not recognise her own voice, as she cried out for Grace, saying it was not true. For how could it be true, for there was Alicia sitting at the piano as she always did, calmly playing Schubert, dressed as she always was. There was Thornton, for all the world still a bachelor, eating his breakfast of hopper and jaggery before he went out. And there were the crimson gladioli that Grace had just cut for the vase in the hall, indeed there was Grace herself holding the flowers, about to plunge them in cold water, so how could it be true? This unknown part

messenger, telling them again and
not comprehend, things that made
it meaning. Frieda, rooted to the spot,
Grace, with her arms full of the dark
e piece of paper the policeman held out
shutters slammed against the sunlight
outside, stood, instantly, turning, blinded by her
understanding, towards her elder daughter. For as the last
notes were played, as they fell into the cool light of early
morning, she saw that Alicia had been widowed. Playing
Schubert. Widowed by a single stray bullet meant for someone
else.

Which was how it was that, watching flying fish on the high
seas and the dawn rising over the horizon, Jacob travelled
onwards in blissful ignorance of the bloodshed in his homeland. Twenty-one days is a long time for the dead to remain
unattended. There were so many in this latest massacre. A
prime minister with good intentions, a minister or two,
standing in the wrong place, what did they matter, a few civil
servants doing their jobs, counting ballots, perhaps if they
had counted faster they might have been spared. A chauffeur,
a servant boy bringing refreshments, another bringing a
marigold garland. A saffron-yellow robe splattered red,
strangely vibrant. Blue canvas chairs overturned, fallen onto
spilt rice, a begging bowl of smoothest ebony. What did any
of the flies care as they feasted in the sunshine, covering vast
tracts of unexpected pleasure? Twenty-one days is a long time
for the dead to lie unburied in such heat. By the time Jacob
heard the news from home, in his little bedsit in Brixton,
reading the letter in his father's beautiful handwriting, the
first letter he had ever received from him, by the time he
broke open the seal of the aerogramme, Alicia was already a

widow of several weeks. The lid of the coffin and her piano simultaneously closed forever. All her life summed up in these simple gestures.

The recording of Alicia de Silva playing Mozart's Piano Sonata in A minor, K310, was in the shops in time for Vesak. Sales were good, considering a state of emergency had been declared and a curfew was in operation. Her delicate, tender touch was instantly recognisable. A music critic on one of the English newspapers, who had followed Alicia's brief career, picked up a copy of the recording. He wrote a glowing review about this unknown young artist. He wrote of 'maturity and interpretation', 'virtuosity' and 'depth'. Would there be any other albums, he wondered, Liszt perhaps or Schubert? Uncle Innocent bought a copy of the record and played it in his house on the tea estate, listening to the familiar sounds of his childhood when Grace's mother used to play this very same piece. The elderly doctor in the old hill station who had long ago loved Grace, and who had delivered Alicia and her siblings, bought a copy and listened to it in silence. Jacob bought a copy with some difficulty and listened to the sound of his sister from across the seas, unaware that his face was wet with tears. Christopher, on the other side of the river in Finchley, listened to it. It was music, he realised, that had filled his life and formed his childhood. Lately, he had successfully suppressed all thoughts of home, hoping to close all that had hurt him. He had joined the newly formed Tamil Resistance Party in London and written to the newspapers in protest against what was happening in his country. But he had distanced himself emotionally. The rage that flared so violently on the night of the riots of '58 had very nearly finished him and ever since he had been living in this little corner of London, in his cramped bedsit, he had tried to see things differently. He had thought he had hardened his heart. He *had* hardened it. Until tonight. Tonight he was caught unawares. As he listened to his sister's music, he heard again the other sounds he had tried to block out, saw himself struggling as his mother held him. Heard his own despair.

'It's my fault!' he had shouted. 'She did nothing wrong. She was a Sinhalese!'

He heard his mother's voice, over and over again: 'No, Christopher, it isn't your fault. She was simply in the wrong place at the wrong time.'

Helplessly, for tonight he was defeated, Christopher rang Jacob. He hardly ever rang him but suddenly he needed the connection.

'Shall we meet up?'

Jacob sounded subdued. Christopher thought he could hear piano music in the background.

'OK,' he said, quietly. 'I'll come over to you. I'll bring some whisky.'

Later, as they sat without talking, their loneliness blunted by drink, an unfamiliar connection rose between them. Mutely they accepted it. It was as though Grace was in the room with them.

'How many more lives will be ruined before there is peace?' Christopher mumbled.

In the orange glow of the electric fire Jacob shook his head. 'I'll never go back,' he said, finally. 'I hate it there.'

Thinking of the house where they had once lived, and the tea-covered hills with their many waterfalls, he began to see how impossible his hopes had been. Greenwood could never have lasted. Their youth, he saw in hindsight, had been a hollow promise. That was all. Now he didn't even have that. Finishing his drink, he stood up. It was late; he had work in the morning.

'I had better go,' he said, reluctantly, 'or I'll miss the last train.'

Pulling on his coat he left. No, he thought, hurrying across the deserted street to the Underground station, he would never go back. He would never see his home again.

In his room, in the silence left by Jacob's departure, Christopher pulled out a battered suitcase from under his bed. Peering inside he found the cheap plastic butterfly brooch and the photograph, almost indistinguishable now, of a boy and a girl in the shadow of the sun. He placed the record carefully beside them; he would never play it again. Closing the suitcase, he fell onto the bed, clutching the handle, holding it tightly. It was his suitcase of lost hope. His life in pieces.

Alicia's pain sliced through the de Silva household, turning them mute. After the shock came a grief like no other. Then it retreated behind closed doors, horrifying glimpses, visible only occasionally. She was inconsolable. No one could have imagined such a complete disintegration. Like an injured animal she withdrew, leaving only echoes running through the house. Then one morning, almost twelve weeks after the funeral, a Buddhist monk arrived unannounced. After this latest massacre, and the involvement of the monks, the sight of an orange robe was enough to send most people into panic. The young Tamil servant girl, answering the knock, shrieked with fear. Myrtle, catching a glimpse of a shaven head, scurried into her room so that it was left to Grace to go to the door. The monk bowed respectfully.

'I have been sent here by a relative of Sunil Pereira,' he told Grace.

In the mahogany hallway his saffron robe was frighteningly bright. Frieda gasped. Aloysius, hearing the Sinhalese voice, came in swiftly.

'What the devil do you want?' he asked angrily, in English.

'We are Catholics, here,' he said. 'We have no need for your services, thank you.'

The monk bowed. He was a slight, youngish man, probably the same age as Sunil. Grace stared coldly at him.

'We are a house of mourning,' she said quietly. 'I'm sure you can understand. Our son-in-law is dead. Please, tell us what you want quickly.'

The monk placed his hands together in greeting. 'What happened was a tragedy,' he began.

'Yes, we know,' Aloysius said, sarcastically. 'We don't need a bloody Buddhist priest to tell us that.'

Grace laid a restraining hand on his arm. She did not want Alicia to hear him. The monk stood silent. Waiting.

'Why have you come here?' Grace asked.

'The man who is the uncle of Sunil Pereira sent me.' The monk spoke softly, in halting English. 'I have travelled up from Dondra. Mr Pereira, the uncle, has had a dream.'

Aloysius snorted and moved towards the front door. 'Oh, get out,' he said.

'No, wait,' Grace said, frowning at Aloysius.

'Mr Pereira insisted I came to visit you before any other misfortunes come.'

'What more can happen?' Grace said quietly. 'We just want to be left in peace.'

The monk held out his hands, palms upwards. 'Mrs de Silva,' he said, 'I understand how you feel but I have come only to help. There is some sort of obstruction in your garden. The dead man's uncle keeps seeing it in a dream. He has been having this same dream every night since the funeral. Please let me help you, Mrs de Silva. I have come with a boy to look for it, to dig behind the murunga tree. I have come to offer prayers. That's all.'

'What *is* this nonsense?' Aloysius said loudly. 'Clear off, men. We're not interested.' He turned angrily to Grace. 'He's just after money, darl,' he told her pointedly.

Grace opened her mouth to agree but it was Frieda who stopped her.

'Oh please, Mummy, please let him. I'm frightened. What harm will it do?'

Grace hesitated, uncertain.

'I am not here for money,' the monk said. He spoke firmly. 'Just let me take a look in your garden. Then I'll go.'

Grace looked at him; he's young, he doesn't look like an assassin, she thought. What harm can it do? Making up her mind swiftly, she nodded, and led the way into the garden.

The priest strode over to the murunga tree, as though he knew the garden well. Then, speaking in Sinhalese, he instructed the boy to dig under it. The de Silvas watched with a mixture of horror and fascination. By now the servants had come out and they too stood silently by the kitchen door, watching.

'Darl, he'll ruin the place,' Aloysius said. 'I'm going to stop this nonsense. We've had enough –'

Grace, her hand on his arm, mesmerised, held him back. A moment later the boy's spade appeared to strike against a root. Pushing him aside impatiently, the priest grabbed hold of the spade and continued to dig, then bending down, he hollowed out the soil with his hands. They could see him tug at something below the ground. The servants gasped, crowding round as the monk with a grunt pulled up a long metal sheet. There was soil everywhere. He wiped the plate with the palm of his hand and the cook, seeing what he held, let out a wail of fear. The monk ignored everyone, continuing to polish the metal until it shone. Grace could see it glinting in the bright sunlight.

'This is what I meant,' he said, walking towards her.

Even from this distance they could see the crude drawing of a man and a woman, etched on the plate, holding hands, garlanded by flowers, incised by lines.

'Here,' the monk said calmly, showing it to Aloysius. 'This is what Mr Pereira's uncle saw in his dream.'

No one spoke. Then the old cook who had been with the de Silva family for so long began to wring her hands.

'Oh missies, missies,' she cried. 'Who has done this terrible thing to this family?!'

'Someone put a curse on your house,' the monk told them quietly. 'On your daughter's marriage and on you. Only now can it be removed. I will bless this place with *pirith*. There will be no more deaths.'

'Hello, Shiny,' said Jasper, flying joyfully by, making them jump, seeing the metal plate glinting in the sunlight. 'Hello, Shiny,' he said again, before disappearing into the mango tree, heavy now with fruit.

'Mummy,' said Frieda, her eyes following Jasper, but Grace had turned and was walking swiftly towards the house.

'It's just a coincidence, darl,' Aloysius called after her. 'It's superstitious rubbish.' But he sounded uncertain.

Myrtle was laying out the tarot cards when Grace burst into her room.

'Have you given up knocking?' she asked sharply, but she looked frightened.

'Why?' asked Grace, through gritted teeth, grabbing her cousin's arm, scattering tarot cards on the floor. 'Why, after all I've done for you, do you hate us so much?'

'Grace,' Aloysius said, appearing beside her.

Grace shook him off.

'Have I not loved you as my own blood relative?' she cried.

'Did I not give you a home when you were homeless? Why have you wished my daughter, your niece, so much harm?'

'I don't know what you are talking about,' Myrtle said. Her oily skin looked pale.

'We are a Tamil family,' Grace continued. Her voice was beginning to rise. She hung on to Myrtle's arm, pushing her backwards and forwards. 'We are just another Tamil family. Trying desperately to exist in the midst of *so* much ugliness, so much violence and hatred. Have you *no* loyalty, whatsoever, towards your own people? That you can only wish us ill? Tamils fighting Tamils, is that what this is? Or is it because she chose to marry a Sinhalese? Is that it? Tell me which it is?'

She let go of Myrtle, pushing her away in disgust. Myrtle laughed. The sound was ugly.

'*You*, a Tamil?' she asked, in a voice that sent a shiver down Frieda's spine. '*You*, Grace?' Her voice rose to a high-pitched whine. 'No, no, no. Dear me, you're no Tamil!'

Frieda watched as Myrtle's face twisted and darkened. A nerve in her neck was pulsating. She looked as though she was about to strike Grace.

'You're a half-caste woman, my dear,' she said triumphantly. 'Your mother went off with a Burgher, didn't you know? Caused quite a scandal in the hills. Your father was so besotted with her that he took her back, pregnant and disgraced. Don't you know? You are no Tamil, my dear. You are the sort the Tamils need to be rid of.'

'So,' said Aloysius, advancing into the room. 'So, your private grievances have evolved into politics, have they?'

No one heard Alicia's door opening.

'What would you like?' he went on, easily. 'A pure Tamil state? Let's annihilate the others, shall we, keep the island for people like you and me? What d'you say? Let's get rid of these half-caste bastards, huh? Only trouble is the Sinhalese would like us out too. They want this place for themselves. There are more of them than us, so, what shall we do?'

He had moved close to Myrtle, his eyes fixed on her. With one swift gesture he swept the pots of powder, her diary, and everything on her dressing table, sending them crashing to the floor. Then, without taking his eyes off Myrtle, he put his arm around his wife.

'Get out,' he told her quietly. 'Pack your bags and get out. You are no different from the Sinhalese bastards. I can't have such a person in my house. I do not want you near my wife, soiling my home.' He paused and took a deep breath. 'I'm going to the club,' he said, more quietly. 'Pack your bags. When I return I want you gone, d'you understand?'

And without waiting for a reply, he walked out.

That evening, after Myrtle left and the Buddhist monk had gone, and the garden had been cleared up, Grace went to sit with Alicia in her room. She took a tray of food with her, to try to tempt her daughter to eat a little. She wanted to talk to her about all that had happened, to put the day and all its revelations into some context for both of them. But Alicia was not interested. Not in the food her mother had brought, nor in the events of the day. It had no bearing on her life. It could not assuage her pain.

'I had no idea,' Grace said, looking at Alicia's pale face. 'It was true. I did always feel different from Myrtle whenever we were together, but it was unimportant. I was so close to your grandfather, I used to feel sorry for Myrtle.'

Alicia pushed the tray away.

'Whenever any of the servants commented on how very

different we were from each other it would make your grandfather angry. I used to wonder why.'

'I'm tired,' Alicia said faintly. 'I want to sleep.'

She closed her eyes. She closed her mother out of sight.
Politely, she dismissed Grace.

Thornton and Savitha arrived for dinner. Aloysius, coming
in soon after, looked quickly at Grace.

'Has she gone?' he asked.

They told him that she had. He nodded.

'Good!' he said, pouring himself a glass of water.

Grace was astonished. Was that all he intended to say? There
were so many questions she wanted to ask. Why was Aloysius
not more surprised? Had he known about it all along? After
they had finished eating she decided to walk in the garden for
a bit. The day and all its implications lay heavily on her and
she felt as though she could not breathe. She needed to talk to
Aloysius but first she wanted to get her thoughts in order.

'I'm going to see if Alicia is all right,' Frieda said. She had
noticed that Savitha wanted to go into the garden too. She could
not face going out with her sister-in-law.

Leaving Thornton talking with Aloysius, Grace took her
daughter-in-law out into the garden to see the spot under the
murunga tree.

'You don't really believe in it, do you?' Savitha asked after
they had stared at the spot in silence.

Savitha was swollen with the child, for her time was nearing,
and she found walking difficult. So they sat on the garden seat
within view of the coconut grove. Beyond it was the sea. Grace
sighed. Although she felt exhausted, this moment in the cool-
ness of the evening was strangely peaceful. The garden appeared
transformed by the fading light, and the sound of the waves
came towards them, rising and falling very clearly. Savitha sat

quietly, her hands folded in her lap, carrying the new generation snugly within her. Thornton's child, thought Grace. Small fruit bats murmured quietly in the trees. Now and then they heard the rich, deep sound of a frog croaking in the undergrowth. A feeling of benevolence crept over Grace. Savitha seems so dependable, she thought. If I needed her help she would not fail me.

'No,' she said aloud. 'I don't believe in any of it. What hurts me is that anyone could have wanted to harm us so much. That one of our own, my own cousin, could feel this way about us, about Alicia.'

She needed to hold the pieces of Alicia's broken heart together. It was the thing that interested her now. Savitha placed her hands on her stomach and felt the baby kick. Looking at Grace, feeling the flutter of limbs, she thought, I am loved. At last I have my own family. At last I too belong. She wanted to tell Grace that it did not matter that Myrtle was a relative, that hatred was present in the most unlikely places. But she did not feel it was her place to say such things.

'Alicia is very, very beautiful,' she said instead. 'Someone will love her again, one day. Wait and see. You must not despair. We are here, Thornton, me, Frieda, Aloysius. You are not alone.'

In the quickening darkness, Grace looked at her daughter-in-law. In less than a month there would be a baby in the house. We *are* blessed, she thought, nodding. I love this dependable girl. My son will be safe with her.

Later when they were in bed, under cover of the darkness, she spoke to Aloysius.

'How long have you known?' she asked, hesitantly, staring into the night.

Outside, the frogs were croaking again and cicadas vibrated the air. He was silent for so long that she thought he had not heard her. Turning towards him she saw his face in profile. He was tired, she thought; wasted by drink. His hair was thinning. Grace hesitated, feeling her heart move. Then she did something she had not done for many years. She reached out and touched his face. Aloysius did not stir.

'I was never certain,' he said at last, very softly. 'There were rumours. A man at the factory told me some nonsense. I asked myself, who cares? Does the man whom she thinks is her father care? No. Well, neither do I. That's what I thought. Now go to sleep,' he said.

And he kissed her forehead.

In London, the ex-Governor, reading about the recent violence on Ceylon shook his head, saddened. He saw what no one else did: that a mantle of despair was settling like fine grey dust on the distant island, clogging the air, blotting out its brilliance and choking its people. And, as the dense rainforests turned slowly into pockets of ruins, and the last remnants of peace began to vanish, it seemed to those who loved the place that the dazzling colours of paradise would never be seen again.

10

IT WAS INTO THIS THAT THE new generation dropped. All un-suspecting, bawling its head off, uncaring of any grief except its own. Red-faced in the heat of its passion, full of unspeakable need, huge tears rolling down its face, letting the world know about its hunger, its tiredness, its discomfort. Eyes screwed against the sun, fists clenched already in the grip of a mysterious discourse of its own. Then when its shell-shocked parents realised that dawn and dusk could occur in the same twenty-four hours without their once having closed their eyes, it stopped as suddenly as it had begun. And it smiled; a smile of such magnitude that it tilted the world.

'My God!' said Thornton, taken aback to find himself looking in the mirror.

Ah! thought Savitha. Here lies trouble.

She was looking at her husband's face. He wore a look she recognised but could not immediately place. Then she realised. It was exactly the way Grace looked at Thornton.

'Hmm,' said Savitha, cryptically. 'One in the family is quite enough.'

In spite of the fact that she was hallucinating most of the time through lack of sleep, Savitha was maturing nicely.

'Yes!' Grace told Aloysius, with mild surprise. 'I see the family resemblance!' She felt a little detached from the event. 'Almost like Thornton.'

For the new generation, that milestone for which Aloysius had waited with such eagerness, hiding a special bottle of Scotch to wet its head, was not quite as he had imagined. Benedict Aloysius de Silva (as he was meant to be called) had not behaved according to plan. He was, in fact, a girl. Yes, yes, fooled you, fooled you, bawled Anna-Meeka de Silva, berating her exhausted parents, the visitors to the cradle, and anyone in fact who dared look at her.

'My God!' said Thornton again, having given in to his wife's fanciful choice of names, feeling the weight of parenthood press down sharply on him.

'My God! I've got a daughter!' Something stirred within him, some vaguely familiar feeling. Fragile and unexpected, it rushed towards him. Was this how his mother felt about them all? Rousing himself from the terrible events that had occurred, he found his carefree youth had vanished.

Perhaps, reflected Frieda, with amazement, he had been changing anyway. They had all changed, she realised sadly. While they were grappling with their sorrow, time had moved on. Frieda knew from his brief letters that Christopher had hardened his heart towards his homeland. She knew he would never return. What's left? thought Frieda. She was still lonely. Nothing had changed for *her*. Alicia was reduced to a ghostly presence in the house while Grace had become slower these days and easily confused. Their mother was growing old. The thought brought tears to Frieda's eyes. Myrtle of course had gone. Myrtle, who used at least to talk to Frieda, had moved back upcountry.

No one kept in touch. Neither Aloysius nor Grace talked of what had happened and no one ever mentioned her name. The revelations of that day were buried once more. Often at night, after writing to one of her brothers or returning from Mass, having checked on her sister and her parents, Frieda would lie on her bed and return to her hopeless fantasies of Robert Grant. Their first meeting remained as fresh for her as though it had occurred yesterday. Distance had inscribed it with an unreal substance. She no longer cared about reality, she saw only what might have been. And now she added Catholic guilt to this. Remembering her past jealousy, Frieda chided herself inwardly. Alicia has nothing either. It must be my fault, my life is my punishment, she argued silently, grappling with her burden of guilt.

Thornton had no guilt. Guilt had never been his problem. His problems were different. His new daughter was barely six weeks old. Her smile pierced his heart, and when she cried he found he was paralysed with love and anxiety. He wondered if Savitha was up to the task of bringing the child up. Then he noticed something else.

'Savitha!' he said excitedly. 'She is going to be really very clever!'

'Not the way she's going,' said his wife, who planned to kill the child if she did not sleep tonight.

'How on earth will we give her the education she needs?' Thornton wondered. 'She must be educated in *English*!'

Grace looked at the child; Thornton's child, her first grand-child. Things had not worked out in the way she had expected. There was no longer any music in the house. All that she had once hoped for, all that she had longed so ardently for, had gone its own way, the family she had nurtured was slowly being torn apart. Alicia hardly ventured from her room, and since

Sunil's funeral, Aloysius had begun to drink again. There should have been no hope left. But somehow she felt closer to Aloysius than she had ever been before. Knowing what he had kept hidden for years had impressed her far more than the illegitimacy of her birth and a new gentleness crept into her voice when she spoke to him. Slowly beneath the surface, invisibly, the house was stirring. It had new life in it, vigorous and noisy. Grace felt it move impatiently. She felt it tug and pull at her and urge her to smile. It refused to take no for an answer. Grace looked again at Thornton. She felt a glimmer of amusement at the sight of her son's new life. Responsibility had settled on Thornton like thick tropical dust.

Unknown to his mother, other changes were occurring in Thornton. Sunil's death had affected him more than he realised. It had taken on a different, more sinister meaning. For Thornton, never having shown the slightest anxiety about the race riots, now began to listen daily to the news. How safe was this country for his daughter to grow up in? Should they too leave the island? Politics were pressing in on Thornton's life in a way it had never done before.

'Well,' remarked Jacob, reading the news from home, and ringing up Christopher, 'he's got his comeuppance. Time he joined the real world. He should try living here.'

Christopher made no comment. He seldom wrote home. He had nothing more to say. Since Sunil's death he felt as though all ties with his family had been severed. It had happened slowly, but he felt there was no point in dwelling on the past. He saw it as a hostile place of no return. Only when he thought of his mother was he was filled with an unbearable anguish. Her grief still communicated itself to him subliminally even though Christopher no longer had the capacity to deal with it. She had let him go; she would always be with him but having learned to hide his hurt Christopher wanted no reminders. It had become easier for him to go to the pub than to write home. His only concessions were the occasional phone calls and spasmodic meetings with Jacob.

Thornton began planning. Panic had made him active.

'We can't bring Anna-Meeka up in *this* country,' he declared, realising what Frieda had already seen coming. 'Not with all that's going on. What on earth will her life be like?' It was clear, even at this stage, that nothing was too good for his tiny daughter. 'We *must* go to England,' he decided. 'Anna-Meeka can have a good education there. She is clever. She might become a doctor. Who knows?'

'Clever like her father, then,' said Savitha who, having discovered the delights of sarcasm during the long sleepless nights, was beginning to sharpen her teeth. It seemed there might be a shift in their lives. For a moment it seemed as though there might even be a little hope.

'Hello?' said Jasper with what appeared to be false jollity, ruffling his feathers and preening himself.

He loathed the baby. She was larger than all the cats put together, and commanded more attention. Her screams confused him.

'Be quiet!' he said querulously.

Grace smiled. She had taken to waiting eagerly for their visits.

'You know,' she told Frieda, 'Savitha is exactly what Thornton needed. She is what we *all* need.'

And she gently picked up the yelling child and carried her out into the great garden where Jasper sat sleepily in the murunga tree.

'Oh no!' said Jasper turning his back to them, but the baby stopped crying and began to laugh.

Savitha looked closely at Grace. Through her exhaustion (for the new generation had energy on its side), she turned her clever eyes on Grace. She watched as the baby was introduced to the servants, noticed how they carried her when she cried and listened as they talked to her in Sinhalese and in Tamil. Seeing the unshakeable affection for their mistress spill over and envelop Anna-Meeka, Savitha's admiration for her beautiful mother-in-law increased. Slowly, hesitantly, in the moments when the baby slept, and Jasper approached the house with caution, she talked to Grace.

'There are so many things that have to change,' Grace told her. 'The government should be focusing on these things, instead of being obsessed with eradicating the English language. There is so much superstition everywhere, crippling our lives.'

'Oh, that's just ignorance,' Savitha said, 'that's what *that's* all about!'

'Take Myrtle, for instance,' Grace continued, casually. 'She should have known better.'

Savitha hesitated. 'Why was she so jealous?' she asked, at last.

'It's an old story,' Grace said lightly. 'From when we were young! She loved Aloysius once, you know.' She paused, on the brink of saying more. 'If we are ever to move forward, we must rid ourselves of all this useless superstition,' she said, finally.

Savitha nodded, absent-mindedly.

'Do you remember the eclipse?' Grace asked. 'Everyone was frightened by it. People thought it was the cause of the riots!' She laughed, softly, her face sad.

'I remember,' Savitha said.

'Someone I knew was killed on that night,' Grace said.

She spoke faintly and Savitha, who had been daydreaming, glanced sharply at her. Grace's eyes were full of unshed tears.

'It was all such nonsense,' she was saying. 'But you couldn't convince anyone, even –' And she stopped speaking abruptly.

'Only education will sweep those devils out,' Savitha agreed. She didn't know what else to say. Averting her gaze she waited. At last Grace nodded, smiling gently. A light breeze had sprung up, shaking some blossom to the ground.

'It needs to be offered to everyone or it simply won't work,' Grace said.

Savitha was at a loss for words. She had lived most of her life with only her sharpness of mind and her passionate desire for the truth as her companions. She had lived for so long without love or family affection, without encouragement or good looks and she was unaccustomed to such intimacy. Her mother-in-law astonished her. We think in the same way, she told herself, basking in this unexpected affection.

'How wonderful to hear you say that,' she told Grace.

'We were very privileged, you know,' Grace said. 'When Thornton was growing up, we had everything we wanted. My father always used to say we should put some of it back into the country. The country is like a garden. It has to be tended, he used to say.'

It was dark now. The evening star was out. Savitha felt as though some danger had passed.

'It wasn't easy for Aloysius,' Grace continued. 'He was very handsome when I first met him. Like Thornton. But the British kept him in their pockets, you know. He used to tell me he was just their puppy, everything was fine if he did what they wanted. It wasn't any life for a man like him.'

Savitha listened intently. She was slowly beginning to under-stand.

'In the end . . . all that eternal gambling, endlessly trying to prove himself . . . it was such a mess. Vijay . . . someone I knew, a long time ago . . . said it was because Aloysius had lost his way. He is a clever man. He could have done anything he wanted.' She sighed. 'It was all wasted. Then after Sunil's death . . .'

Her voice tailed off. One generation forever trying to put right the mistakes of another. All of them ground down and exhausted.

Later, when she was alone with her daughter, back in their little annexe, when Thornton had gone to meet a contact for the UK, Savitha mulled over the conversation with Grace.

'You must not be like them, Anna-Meeka,' she told the sleeping infant, seriously. 'You must be the one to change your family's history.'

Perhaps, after all, Thornton was right and they should go to England. With the future here so uncertain, England might save them. Her daughter must learn to be resilient, Savitha sighed. That was what was important. The child stirred and sucked her thumb. Savitha gazed at the tiny dark lashes sweeping down from closed eyes.

'Your father is a handsome man, Anna-Meeka,' she told the baby. 'But he doesn't always know what's best. He's making plans for your future; he's full of ambitions. He wants you to be a doctor, to be famous, to be rich, God knows what he wants. Your Dada is bursting with love for you, but . . .' and she paused. She folded her lips together as though they were a paper bag, looking disapprovingly at the framed photo of her husband, hanging on the wall.

'You must do what suits *you* best,' she said out loud, firmly to the sleeping baby. 'I don't care what it is,' she added, tenderly rocking the cot, 'so long as you do it well.'

Anna-Meeka grew rapidly. In no time at all she began to talk.

'Jasper!' she said as soon as she could. Both her mother and grandmother were delighted. Cautiously, for he was still un-certain, Jasper approached the house. Softly, fearful of the response, he made a whirling noise like the grandfather clock. Then, because the hideous screaming seemed to have stopped, he began to whistle his favourite bar from *The Magic Flute*.

'Look!' said Savitha to her daughter. 'Jasper wants to be friends with you.'

And indeed Jasper, whose affection had been only for Grace until now, began to follow the child around.

When she was two, Anna-Meeka began to sing. Savitha and Grace listened entranced. Their friendship was growing, un-noticed by anyone. Something tender and unspoken, a thread of kinship, invincible and unexpected, surfaced and became stronger. Immeasurably and powerfully it arose. Effortlessly it linked them, for here were two generations of women springing from the same nation, their love for their family enduring and certain. Feeling some impermanence in the air, Savitha brought the child almost daily to the house in Station Road while Grace lived moment by moment, a hostage to fortune.

Thornton made his application to leave the island. The troubles had worsened and many Tamils were leaving Colombo. Thornton wanted to leave while they still could.

'Oh, not yet!' cried Grace, before she could stop herself. She hoped the little girl would have a few more years of sun, some time to grow with them, as a talisman for the future.

As her daughter grew, the change in Savitha became more visible. She had started out with fixed ideas but motherhood had begun its rich transformation. The sharpness in her face had softened and her passionately held values became more complex. These days she felt the insistent stirrings of some other inexplicable and complicated emotion. It gathered strength within her, glowing softly, as though being stored for what lay ahead. It coursed through her tenderly, drawing from the air what fragrance it could find, collecting up those everyday sounds, of bicycle bells and barking dogs, and shouts and bangs, and the sudden dull thud of a coconut falling in the grove nearby. And all the time, as the bright colours fixed themselves unconsciously on her mind, as the monsoons came and went, Jasper sat somewhere in the plantain tree, whistling small snatches of *The Magic Flute*, reminding them of a slowly receding era.

That year the rainy season was late. When it arrived the daily downpour seemed relentless. The child had grown like a plant. Looking at her daughter, Savitha knew she would resemble Grace; she would be beautiful. With unaccountable sadness, she knew that some day others would see this too and would remember Grace. At five, Anna-Meeka started school in the little convent next door to the cathedral where her silent aunt Alicia had been married. The nuns knew the de Silvas. They remembered Frieda, and they knew Grace. When Anna-Meeka began to learn to play the piano they were not surprised by her talent. They had all heard her aunt on the radio. Savitha was delighted; here were the signs of the family talent. Only Thornton was uneasy. Sunil's death and the change in his sister had affected him. He too had not touched the piano since that day and although he was pleased to let Anna-Meeka learn he informed his wife it would be bad luck for her to follow in his sister's footsteps. Savitha was puzzled. She had not realised Thornton was so superstitious. She saw with amazement that many things had begun to frighten him. History frightened him. He did not want it to repeat itself. He did not want Anna-Meeka to go down that particular road. Thornton was no longer happy as he once was. The changes in him were imperceptible.

It touched the luminosity in his eyes, dampening the glow of youth. He stopped dreaming and became anxious. As the hatred for the Tamil people grew he wanted only to leave. His brothers received the news of the family's unease in the thin blue-paper letters that arrived with regularity, difficult to comprehend and, very soon, impossible to connect with. What was there to say about the shortage of food, the lootings, the random destruction of property? How to explain that a pint of Guinness and a pie spelt happiness at the end of a long grey London day, when the thick fleece of clouds left no room for the sun?

As two more years went by, Thornton made his preparations. Civil unrest was no longer a rumour. It was a fact. Tamil youths were set upon in the street, a bus carrying Tamil students was fire-bombed, a sweep seller lynched because of his name. Trouble erupted at unexpected moments. An exodus to Jaffna was under way. Some Tamil families applied to leave for Australia. In just over five years, as predicted, the jungle had crept into the towns. Grace could do no more than accept the inevitable. Alicia's arpeggios were a phantom presence; the bone china in the glass-fronted cupboards remained unused. Few people visited them these days.

At seven, Anna-Meeka was enchanting. Whenever Savitha brought her to see her grandmother the silent house at Station Road became filled with noise and laughter. She followed her aunt Frieda like a shadow; she loved it when her grandfather teased her. Grace's letters to her sons were full of all of this. They were interspersed with other disconnected things from long ago, from her memories of the House of Many Balconies with its faded water-lily gardens, for lately she longed to see the place again. She wrote telling them of the deaths of Uncle Innocent and Auntie Angel-Face. Did they remember Mabel? Her son had been born deformed, her husband taken by the rebels into the jungle. He was never seen again. Someone, a relative, found a bundle of his clothes, torn and mangled, left by the Mahaweli River. Jacob and Christopher receiving this information did not know how to reply.

Months went by. When Thornton received his visa for entry into the UK departure became a certainty. Seeing this, stirring herself, Grace began to give Savitha some of her precious china. She gave her the blue-and-white bowls, the tureens, some delicately painted teacups, a dinner service.

'It's for you,' she said, pressing them on Savitha. 'Keep it in memory of us.' She wanted her little granddaughter to enjoy them in her new life in Britain. It was a gesture of acceptance of their impending separation; a torch to be held by Savitha in all the long lonely years of their coming exile, until Anna-Meeka would be old enough to receive her legacy. Then, with their departure hanging over them, with civil unrest reaching boiling point, Grace decided to visit her childhood home one last time. To show Anna-Meeka where her father had been born. Late in June, when the heat in Colombo was unbearable once more, and the sea breeze no longer strong enough to keep them cool, Grace and Aloysius, with Thornton and Savitha, with Anna-Meeka (now nearly nine), made the trip upcountry on the grand black-and-red steam train.

They left at night and travelled inland. They had booked a sleeper but Anna-Meeka was too excited to sleep. As the train climbed higher and higher hooting its smoke along the narrow-gauge track, she sat humming to herself, first with Thornton and then Savitha, watching the dark ravines rush by, catching glimpses of the many waterfalls flash past in a gush of white foam. Towards dawn, the air cooled and all of them slept, exhausted. They did not wake again until the smell of tea assailed their noses. Hurrying to open the blinds, they saw to their delight and astonishment the bright green tea-covered hills, just as they had left them, swathed in veils of mist, rising softly all around.

'We're home,' murmured Grace. 'At last!'

'Oh, Jacob should be here!' Thornton cried.

Aloysius chuckled. 'Look, darl,' he said, 'that's the place where they used to have the tennis tournaments, remember?'

'Meeka,' Thornton said, excitedly, 'I used to walk to school along this valley. Look! There's a cloud of butterflies. I used to try and catch them.'

Grace nodded. Her eyes were shining. She remembered.

'Let's have lunch at the tennis club, first,' she suggested. 'Anna-Meeka, you'll be able to eat wild strawberries now, because they grow here.'

Savitha watched mesmerised. She had never been upcountry before.

'We'll take a taxi to the house,' Aloysius cried. He was laughing with delight.

'Well, let's put our bags at the rest house, first,' Grace decided. 'And have a wash.'

The air was thin and fragrant as they stepped off the train. Kingfishers darted through the trees.

'There must be a lake nearby,' Thornton said. 'Oh, I wish Jacob was here. And Alicia –' He stopped, abruptly. No one said anything. Grace glanced uneasily at Savitha.

'Come,' she said firmly. 'Let's get to the rest house first. Then we'll go up to the house.'

'I hope it's how we left it,' said Thornton, uneasily. 'D'you remember how it was screened by the trees? I hope they haven't cut them down.'

What had prompted them to look back? Jacob and Christopher, receiving a letter sent jointly to them weeks later, read it from their great impassable distance and were nonplussed. How could they feel the heat now, except as a distant memory? A strange paralysis had descended on these two brothers. Survival in this urban jungle with its cold wind tunnels and its incomprehensible communication took up most of their energy. How could they explain this to the mother who could not even see their greying hair? Their thoughts of the past were vague these days, insubstantial as breath on a cold morning on the way to work. They sat reading, brought together by the letter, somewhere in a cold winter pub. The task ahead, this thing called the *new life*, had not yet opened up. When it did, they would be unable to see its possibilities; they would notice only its limitations. So they sat, in their ill-fitting suits, holding their newly fractured lives, uncomprehending. They were in need of cherishing but this too was no longer available, and the likelihood of their recovery from such a brutal uprooting was a sad illusion. Somewhere in that pub, sitting close to the coal fire, the brothers read their mother's letter and struggled to imagine the rooms where they had once slept, with the painted walls scraped and broken by bullet holes, the polished green and pink glass smashed, the ropes swinging from light fittings, the chipped and dark-stained marble floors. It was time for another round of Guinness before reading the rest of the letter. Then, drink in hand, they learned about Jasper. Jasper, who should have lived to a ripe old age, shot for shouting at an armed soldier, while they were all away upcountry.

'Hello, sister!' he had shouted as, too late, the servant girl tried to stop the man from raping her.

Tucked away in the cosy pub, on that wintry evening, somewhere in the Borough of Southwark, halfway into their second round of Guinness, the brothers, reading of Jasper's fate, remembered and could drink no more.

Errors

11

August was mercilessly hot. It brought a rancid stench from dustcarts that mixed with the cloying sweetness of roadside shrine-flowers. Faded black umbrellas and orange robes walked the streets. Danger hovered in every alleyway. Fear hung oppressively around the city, turning what had once been lively and festive into dark suspicion. Gone were the days when the rich moved upcountry, opening their houses and their tennis courts, while their servants served soft drinks in tall bead-covered jugs. Gone were the days when the sound of rickshaw bells and horns and whistles and *baila* music from transistor radios filled the air. Once August had been the month of the Perahera, when shadow-dancers on the high trapeze pointed their elbows at the neon sky. But now all that was over. Carelessness was a thing of the past. Conversation in public was a dangerous thing, for language had become an identity card. No one was to be trusted. No one knew who might be listening. Anger filled the streets where once the shadow-dancers had walked. Anger was everywhere, simmering like the heat, unquenchable, taut, tar black and desperate.

This August was Grace's undoing. As she lay awake in the stifling heat, in a house grown empty, with a life that had shrunk to a husk, she listened to the night swelling in the darkness. Wherever Thornton and his family were, she knew it to be some other hour. What were they doing? Was it daytime in the place they were? Was the sun shining on them? They had left her. Now at last she understood what this meant. Before they left she had held herself together, wanting to be strong. Wanting to hold together these last precious moments so that later, when she was alone and Aloysius and Alicia and Frieda slept, and the sprawling house was silent, she could bring out the images of their departure. And look again at the faint imprints that were all that remained of the sad slow ebb of her life. It had been Savitha, almost completely silent for days, who had broken down with astonishing grief. Savitha, and then Thornton. Anna-Meeka had merely hopped from foot to foot, anxious to be gone, hoping that if they went quickly then no one would cry. Solemnly she promised Grace that she would look after her parents. Chattering brightly, on and on, wriggling and jumping up and down with suppressed excitement and worry, promising not to forget them all, to write often, and yes, yes, she would be good too.

'You won't cry, Granny, will you?' she had begged anxiously.

Grace had promised. No, she would not cry.

Now, staring into the unbroken darkness, the thin whine of mosquitoes just beyond the net, she heard a piano. The girl in the next house was playing a nocturne. Slowly the notes dropped like polished glass into the balmy air. Alicia slept in a room further down the hall, locked away, silent, impenetrable. Grace pictured her small form, crumpled among the white sheets, dark hair covering her face, sleeping just as she had as a child. Alicia had shown no sadness when Thornton left. No, thought

Grace, recalling her daughter standing at the harbour in her widow's white, Alicia had nothing to say. She had witnessed too much. She was no longer reachable. Only Frieda, simple uncomplicated Frieda, with her abundance of tears, had hugged Anna-Meeka who, oblivious to the effect of her smile, talked on, telling her aunt kindly that they would be back soon, making it sound as though she was going to the market with her mother. In spite of herself Grace had smiled, even as she kissed her son goodbye, wondering if it was for the last time, remembering the small boy who used to walk home from school along the valley with its waterfalls, its blue-green tea-covered hills and its storms of butterflies. Remembering how he had played jazz late at night, his foot jammed on the loud pedal, until his sisters shouted at him, fearing he would break the piano, while Jasper, turning round and round on his perch, also shouted at him.

'Turn it down, old chap!' Jasper had shouted. 'Be quiet!' he had said, making them all laugh.

And now, thought Grace, as the night jasmine uncurled itself, now what shall I do? Four thousand years of peace and an ancient god were no longer enough for a country brimming with violence. A sacred tree, a thin white thread around Savitha's wrist, what use were any of these things? The night was filled with doubts. Her son's discarded hat in the hall, Savitha's parcel of chillies, forgotten in her haste, Anna-Meeka's plastic doll, its blue eyes staring at the sky, all of these things with their touch still warm on them were more than reminders of her own grief. Seeing it from this great, terrible distance she knew it was a loss for the country itself. Other losses would follow. Irretrievably. But tonight was hers alone.

The sound of the piano had stopped, the lights had gone out, the garden was steeped in darkness for it was a moonless night. Small rustling noises, soft murmurings filled the air. Frogs croaked intermittently. All these noises, thought Grace hearing them afresh, turning her despair against the wall, would never be heard by them again. Far away, as though in answer, in a distant part of Colombo, came the sound of heavy gunfire, muffling the constant rhythm of the sea.

Thornton looked out of the window and shifted his legs. Opposite him, Savitha talked quietly to Anna-Meeka. They were all exhausted. High banks of grassy slopes, scattered with butter-cups flanked the railway line; late summer in all its glory. Railway dust, golden and abundant in the wonderful morning sunlight obscured the view. The sky was a cloudless blue. Looking up, Thornton could see a small glider rising up with the thermals. He watched it until it disappeared from view. Every now and then a neat patchwork of wheat-combed fields flashed by.

'Mama, I'm thirsty!' said Anna-Meeka in her sing-song voice, waggling her head from side to side. She stared at the man sitting opposite until he looked away.

'Why can't I have a drink, Mama?' she asked.

She scratched her head with an enthusiasm and a single-mindedness that did not seem quite possible. The sound of the train was different from the sounds she was used to. She swung her legs in time to its beat.

'My head is scratchy,' she said, adding in a voice that carried clearly across the compartment, 'Do you think I've got head lice? Or have they died because it's cold in England?'

The man opposite looked at her again and Meeka scowled at him. Someone else further along the carriage sniggered. Savitha spoke, aware of the man's glances, knowing he was listening. She spoke softly in Sinhalese. Anna-Meeka, ignoring her, continued to scratch her head. Thornton bent his hand-some profile towards his daughter. He smiled at her.

'Leave your head alone, Meeka,' he said softly. 'Your mama will wash it with soap when we get to our place in London.'

'Why is that man looking at me?' asked Meeka, losing interest momentarily in her head, fixing the man with a limpid unblinking stare.

'Anna-Meeka,' said Thornton sternly, 'don't speak so loud. These people *all* understand English here! We're not at home now.'

He turned back to the window and the boat train, hooting at a level crossing, passed swiftly through the sunlit country-side with its black-and-white cows, its green public footpath signs, its small farm outbuildings, hurrying and clattering into a small tunnel, speeding onwards to London's Waterloo.

In the taxi, sandwiched between her parents and the small amount of luggage they had brought, Meeka caught her first glimpses of the city. London encased in summer, lit by the after-noon sun, washing the embankment and the pineapples on Lambeth Bridge with its golden glow. London, that place her parents had talked about so much, bringing her here, they said, because here they could give her all the things no longer possible to give her at home. London, thought Meeka enchanted by what she saw, was beautiful! Huge buildings, their tops dipped in light, their sides covered in grime, were everywhere. The traffic swished richly, silently, on thick rubber tyres, on roads without the smallest pothole.

Traffic that behaved, thought Thornton in amazement. No bullock carts, no horns, no open-topped vehicles with radios blasting or vegetables spilling out. Why had Jacob not written about the silence? It was hard to imagine his brothers here, in this huge city. He had not seen Jacob for thirteen years, longer in the case of Christopher.

Too big, thought Savitha, shivering a little, and too fast. She had been frightened for days. She felt beaten.

187

They were over the bridge now, passing Lambeth Palace.

'Where're yer from then, mate?' asked the taxi driver sliding back the hatch, addressing Thornton looking at him in the mirror.

Thornton started. What had the man said? Was he talking to them?

So Meeka told him, in her clear sing-song voice, liking the man instantly, liking his funny way of talking, jumbling all his words up together, wanting to make him talk some more, wishing she could talk like him.

'We're off the boat train, mate!' she said copying him, liking the sound of his laugh.

'Blimey, you're a caution, ain't yer, luv? Mum an' dad'll 'ave ter watch it. Ye'll 'ave ter watch 'er, guv!' he said addressing Thornton through the mirror, winking at him.

'Yes,' said Thornton not knowing what on earth this man was talking about, but willing, very willing to be helpful.

'Yes. We have just spent twenty-one days at sea so my daughter is a little tired. We are all looking forward to a rest on dry land tonight.'

And he nodded his head politely. His wife, clutching her bags, frowned nervously and whispered something in the child's ear. The black cab, symbol of all they had anticipated for so long, crossed and recrossed the river in a cunning dodge of the one-way system, drove past the school where Meeka would be going, before depositing them at last at their front door. They had travelled seven thousand miles.

Then this is what they found. A little ground-floor flat (the estate agent had called it a garden flat) in a block of dirty Victorian houses, on a wide tree-lined street close to the cricket ground. Thornton brightened a little when he saw this.

'Aiyo! There is no veranda,' said Savitha, struggling to keep the tears from her voice. She wanted to go home.

'Carpets!' said Meeka, dancing down the hallway having kicked off her shoes and socks. She did not like wearing socks.

The rooms were gloomy, for the house faced west and although it was only four in the afternoon darkness threatened. The de Silvas prowled around the flat, released from the captivity of twenty-one days, uncertain what to do next. The beds had piles of thick blankets folded neatly, waiting to be made up. Heavy fusty curtains lined the windows, ready to be drawn, ready to block out anything that passed for light. Dotted around were small metal stoves that Meeka's Uncle Jacob had warned them about. He had found them the flat, and put in Aladdin paraffin heaters for when it got cold.

'It's cold now,' said Meeka laughing, throwing herself on the unmade bed in what was to be her bedroom, waving her thin legs up in the air, banging them against the wall. The cold was exciting, it made the air smell of all sorts of foreign exciting things, things she did not know about but wanted to investigate. It muffled the sounds around her. The silence had a texture to it that made her wish she had a piano to play.

'There's a note here from Jacob,' shouted Thornton from the kitchen. 'He's coming over tomorrow with Christopher and he's left some food in the fridge.'

'Yes,' said Savitha pursing her lips together, showing the first spontaneous emotion since they had embarked on their journey, so that Meeka, sensing some interesting drama, put her legs down and sat up.

'Hmm, that bastard! Couldn't he have met us at the docks?'

She spoke softly and Thornton, not hearing, replied, 'Come and see what he has left in the fridge! All sorts of things. Butter wrapped in paper and fresh milk! Come here, Meeka, putha.'

Curiously, Meeka went to see the strange cheeses, bread and something called liver pâté. Thornton set the yellow Formica table, found an old teapot and pulled out the packet of tea they had packed. It was, he noticed, with a stab of quickly suppressed homesickness, from the valley where he had been born. For a moment Thornton struggled. The distance seemed infinite. His mother was no longer a bus ride away. How had the past arrived so quickly? Grief, unexpected and sharp, tightened around him. There was a bottle of milk with a shiny gold lid on it, a box of dark chocolate. A feast.

'No, wait,' said Savitha suddenly, 'wait, I'll get one of our teapots.'

She unpacked one of their boxes, pulling at everything, so that the smells of sandalwood and ginger tumbled out and moved around the room. The sun had vanished. Had there really been sunlight when they were on the train? Or had they imagined it? Anna-Meeka shivered. The tune in her head had gone. It was suddenly too cold and her mother looked small and pinched. Her mother looked as though she was about to cry.

'Can I have some rice?' Anna-Meeka asked firmly. 'Rice with *malu* curry?'

The brothers arrived the next day. Memories followed them into the room. Distance framed their childhood, sharpening its focus. Sentiments rushed in like warm air, for the moment anyway. Then Thornton smiled. No surprises here of course, nothing to write home about, thought Jacob, wryly. Everything was as it always was, in that respect at least. There were other shocks. In that swift first greeting, Jacob and Christopher saw their mother sharply defined in Thornton's face. Had he always looked like her? wondered Christopher, momentarily taken aback. He felt the angry stirring of emotions he thought he had left behind. Home tugged insistently. For a moment no one could speak. Savitha had been cooking, it was not much, but the smells were of home. Even twenty-one days and an expanse of water had not altered the smells they once knew. Christopher looked closely at his sister-in-law. The last time he had seen Thornton he had been in the thralls of Hildegard. Savitha seemed very different from *her*. Well, well, well, thought Christopher, so the film star played it safe in the end. I wonder what this one's like. His lips twitched. Savitha, serving them tea in their mother's bone china, realised that no one noticed or cared.

'Here,' said Thornton, 'have some of the *vadi* Frieda made.'

Somehow the sight of Frieda's present, prepared for this exact moment, made him unable to say more. Anna-Meeka looked at her father curiously. He was behaving in a very odd way. Was he going to cry? She helped herself to the *vadi* ignoring Savitha's frown. Christopher was the first to recover. He considered Thornton with satisfaction. He's much blacker than me, he thought, trying not to laugh.

Thornton was thinking too. He's fat, he thought, mildly surprised, and not so black! And there's something different about him. What is it? Christopher, noticing the look, patted his stomach and grinned. He *was* indeed fatter. The lean hurt look had left him, vanished into an unattainable past; the despair so transparent at Kamala's death had hardened into something else entirely.

'Hmm,' muttered Savitha, folding her lips. She had just noticed a bottle of whisky in her brother-in-law's coat pocket. But Christopher, giving her a challenging look, burst out laughing. It seemed Thornton had found himself a conventional woman. It was only to be expected. The old spark of jealousy, never fully dampened, flared up momentarily. Thornton *always* managed to get everything he wanted: an education, a wife, a child.

'I need a drink,' Christopher said out loud. 'I need a drink to get through this bloody reunion.'

Thornton frowned but Christopher, ignoring him, turned to Savitha.

'I say,' he said, 'give me a glass, will you? I want to drink to your arrival!'

And he took the bottle out of his pocket and offered it to his sister-in-law with a mocking bow. In spite of himself Thornton was surprised. How had Christopher, always so silent at home, become this confident?

'Can I have another *vadi*?' asked Meeka, getting bored with the atmosphere. She helped herself to three.

'Anna-Meeka!' said Savitha. She spoke more sharply than she meant because she was embarrassed. 'Don't take *three*. What's the matter with you, child?'

'I'm hungry,' said Meeka, stuffing *vadi* into her mouth quickly.

Hmm, thought Jacob who had been observing it all from a point of some detachment, I can see there's going to be trouble here. He blinked owlishly, hoping the new arrivals would not cause him any headaches. He knew what Thornton was like. Did Savitha know about Hildegard?

'Do I look like my photographs, Uncle Christopher?' asked Meeka suddenly, smiling up at him, sensing her mother's dislike.

'More tea, Jacob?' asked Savitha sweetly, holding out her hand for his cup.

Looking around at his family Thornton was confused. They seemed strangers. It made him weary. Jacob looked disapproving. Thornton hoped they would not start any unsuitable stories from his past. There was the child to think about now. What did any of his brothers understand about family life? Christopher was not listening to any of them. He was looking at Anna-Meeka, seeing her properly for the first time. But she's wonderful, he thought with delight. How on earth did these two idiots produce her? She should be *mine*!

'How many years is it since you three met?' asked Savitha for something to say, as if she didn't know.

There was nothing impressive about the de Silva men, she decided. There were too many of them, in her opinion, crowding into this small sitting room, standing all together, just like a clan. Savitha wrinkled her nose with distaste. It was clear they needed their mother to keep them in order. Silently, Savitha gave them more tea.

'I love London! I can't wait to go to school here,' said Meeka. And she danced between them and their long shadows.

They tried to pick up where their letters had left off.

'So poor Jasper's dead,' Christopher observed.

'Jasper!' cried Meeka, delighted, wanting to talk about him.

Yes, that's it! thought Jacob, who had been puzzling over it. The child reminded him of Jasper. Something about the way she fixed them with her eye, something about her darting movements. It was worrying. They would have to be careful, speak guardedly if necessary.

But something had changed overnight. Summer had moved swiftly, even as they slept, into a landscape chilled at the edges and tinted with the subtle unmistakable smell of autumn. The early-morning sunlight on the grass looked damp. Surely it was not possible? Thornton ventured timidly out into this cataclysmic change. The breeze was sharp and unwelcoming. He walked on the neat grey paving slabs carpeted by golden plane leaves that fell at his feet. His feet, too, seemed to belong in some strange land, clad in unfamiliar shoes, walking on unfamiliar missions.

'How do I get to South Walk?' he asked the girl in the library. The girl's hair fell like a curtain of gold, ramrod straight, silky as the cashmere sari his wife had worn on their wedding day. Tossing it back from her face, moving threads of it from her mouth, she laughed a little.

'South Walk? Do you mean Southwark?' she said.

She was unprepared for his smile. Lighting up the corners of her desk, alighting on her card indexes, softly tinting the long high windows until it seemed as though strains of some unidentifiable music filtered through them.

Why, it was sheer poetry, thought the girl confused, watching as the smile hovered over the bunch of ochre-pink chrysanthemums. She had bought them on impulse, at the tube station that morning, never knowing how the day, this ordinary day, would present itself to her, like a bunch of glorious late-summer flowers. Exactly like the flowers, changed by the light, so too was her day altered by that smile. Sensing this, Thornton felt gladness flutter faintly, a small bird of continuity, the feathery down of hope, in his heart. Clearing a path through the leaves he headed for the river and his interview.

Later, returning home in the gloom, marvelling at how swiftly the night descended, he told Savitha he had got the job.

'Now at least we will have a proper income,' he said proudly.

Savitha did not answer. She was preoccupied with the jar of seeni sambals from home, a casualty of the journey, covered in white inedible fur. She had been saving it for this very occasion and now she had no contribution to the celebration. So she was silent. The journey had left her disorientated and defeated. She had not expected to feel this way. In the short time that they

had been here her homesickness had increased rather than less-
ened. She carried it heavily in her jacket, bound tightly in place
by her sari, wrapped close against her breast, out of sight from
the rapidly cooling air. The kitchen smelt of paraffin.

'I must trim the wick,' said Thornton, thinking over his day,
remembering the girl with ramrod hair, smiling so that Anna-
Meeka, watching him curiously asked, 'What are you smiling
about, Daddy?'

Tomorrow was the beginning of the new school term. Meeka
had already visited her school. It was nice. There was a carpet
in the headmaster's office but nowhere else.

'Because of the mud,' the headmaster had said. 'It would be
too difficult to keep a carpet clean.'

Meeka knew about mud. Mud came with the monsoon. But
then the rains went away, and so did the mud. Was it going to
rain here all the time? Was it going to rain and be cold at the
same time? When? When was this going to happen? The headmaster had smiled.

'Her English is very fluent,' he said to Meeka's mother. 'We'll
try her in the top class to start with.' Then he had turned to
Meeka. 'The weather is wonderful this year in England, Meeka.
It is what we call an Indian summer.'

He had gazed gently at the child seeing the brightness within
her face. He hoped she would settle but he could see it would
not be easy. She was rather exotic for this part of Brixton, he
thought. And so he chose her class with care.

The night before her school term started the brothers called
round. Anna-Meeka had gone to bed, much to Christopher's
disappointment. She was still exhausted from the journey.

'Here,' said Christopher, pushing some money into Savitha's
hand. 'Buy her some chocolates from me.'

'Now, you must be firm with her,' Jacob began when they sat down to eat. 'You know Brixton is a dangerous place. The area is full of working-class people. You'll see what I mean after a while.'

'What's wrong with working-class people, ah?' asked Christopher challengingly, helping himself to Savitha's excellent fish curry. At least the conventional woman could cook, he thought. He paused and glared at Jacob.

'Don't start, men,' Jacob said hastily, catching Savitha's eye. 'I'm talking about the child's education. It's important that she only mixes with the right people.'

Christopher opened his mouth to speak, then changed his mind and laughed instead. Without waiting to be asked, he helped himself to more rice. Once again Thornton was struck by his brother's lack of manners. At home they had waited to be served. But Christopher seemed to have forgotten his upbringing. It made Thornton uneasy. And added to his homesickness.

'I say, Anna-Meeka is very clever,' he told them, changing the subject. 'Ask Savitha. She's a little difficult, you know, but clever all the same.'

They ate in silence.

'She will probably study medicine one day,' he added casually.

Jacob glanced up. He had heard all about his niece from Frieda's letters. He could tell they all thought the child was some sort of genius.

'I've lived here longer than you,' he said, at last, finishing his food and taking a gulp of water. He had not eaten anything so spicy for a long time and it was burning his mouth. 'This isn't Colombo, you know.' He hesitated, wanting to find the right words, trying to make Thornton understand. 'Don't have too many hopes, men. In *this* country ambition alone isn't enough. You need much more than ambition here.'

Unable to say what was needed he paused. 'You have no idea what being a foreigner in Britain is like, men,' he said, adding confusingly, 'Even going to the moon means nothing here in Brixton. Have you heard of the Swinging Sixties, for instance? Hah?'

Thornton looked at him blankly and Jacob nodded at him grimly. It was patently clear that the Swinging Sixties had not entered Thornton's consciousness yet, much less Meeka's. As far as Jacob could see, hell was merely in abeyance.

'Wait, men, I tell you, things aren't that easy,' he advised.

It was perfectly clear to Jacob, from the little he had seen, the child would need a firm hand. Well, he decided, conscious of unspoken hostilities, he would say no more. He had given them fair warning and in any case it was only marginally his business. Christopher stretched his legs and yawned. Then he gave a small whistle of admiration. He had enjoyed eating the chilli-hot curry. Thornton scowled at him.

'Look –' he began angrily, but Jacob held up his hands. He had not meant to start any arguments.

'I'm only here in an advisory capacity, men,' he said, backing off. 'I promised Mummy I'd keep an eye on things. Until you settle down, that's all.'

It was time to leave. He hoped he would not be needed too often. For Jacob was a busy man. His time was strictly limited as, unknown to any of them, he had recently acquired a girl-friend and therefore had various plans of his own.

When they left Savitha cleared the dishes.

'At least they liked the food,' she said finally.

Twenty-one days at sea had left her longing to cook with ingredients from home. But she felt exhausted and confused

197

with the effort. She felt utterly tired in a way she never had before. And worse, she felt an alien among the de Silva brothers. Struggling with these emotions she told Thornton crossly, 'In future, don't start talking about Meeka to them.' Adding, 'What do they know about children?'

Thornton grunted. Although he agreed with her he would not admit it. The discussion over Anna-Meeka's future worried him more than he was prepared to say.

'We are here because the predictions of war have become an actuality,' he reminded Savitha. 'Anna-Meeka will have every opportunity in this country. She *will* become a doctor, I tell you.'

Savitha folded her lips. Worry buzzed around her head, moving pointlessly, like flies. Had they taken so momentous a step too lightly? Should they have waited a little longer? Surely only time could tell how clever Anna-Meeka *really* was. Time was what they all needed.

'It's too early to say what she'll become. We're from another culture; we have to settle first,' she told Thornton. She did not ask how long this might take. She did not want to think of that. 'I want her to be happy,' she said slowly. 'That's what's important. I can't bear it, if all we've done is bring her to an unhappy place.' She struggled to express her own hopes for Anna-Meeka in the face of Thornton's confusion. 'I want her to sing again,' she said abruptly, feeling her eyes prick with unexpected tears. 'She used to sing all the time. I don't know if you've noticed but she stopped as soon as we were on the boat.'

'Sing?' asked Thornton, looking at her amazed. 'Why of course she won't stop singing! What are you talking about? And if she studies hard and becomes a doctor, of course she'll be happy.' He frowned, feeling both annoyed and uneasy. Savitha had a knack of unnerving him.

'Perhaps she'll want to do music,' Savitha said tentatively.

She knew nothing about music. All she knew was that the nuns in Ceylon had said her daughter was musical. They had told Grace that Meeka had a very good ear and could play any tune she heard. Savitha had caught the tail end of Alicia's performances, in the days when music had still filled the house in Station Road. Now she hesitated.

'She may be as musical as Alicia, you know?' she said.

But at this Thornton shook his head vehemently and stood up.

'No, no,' he said firmly. 'Not music, men. Let's not talk about that. Think of my poor sister's life now, will you? She has nothing now the music's gone. Not music, Savitha. For enjoyment, yes, but not in any other way. If Alicia had had another profession, if she had been a doctor, she would be working now, going out, meeting people. She would be able to —'

He broke off and clamped his mouth shut. Savitha fell silent. She had never understood why Thornton connected Sunil's death with Alicia's music.

It was not the time to argue. It was up to the child, to show them what she really wanted. So thought Savitha as she embroidered her daughter's name on her socks and her PE clothes. So thought Savitha as she checked on the sleeping child, removing the new school tie from her hand, only to have it tucked under the pillow again by Thornton when he looked in on her later.

It took nearly three weeks to reach them. The servant brought in the post while they were having breakfast. There were four letters. The sight of them filled the day with translucent light. Which one should they open first?

'Thornton's,' said Frieda.

'No, let's see what the little one makes of the place,' chuckled Aloysius.

I start my new school TOMORROW! Anna-Meeka had written. *And I'm going to make lots and lots of English friends. Please could Auntie Frieda send some more* vadi *so I can give some to them.*

The child seems a bit of a handful, wrote Jacob. *Thornton is right to be worried. I told him he'd need to be firm with her. This isn't Ceylon. Things are different here.*

'Nonsense!' laughed Frieda. 'Thornton will never be able to refuse her anything.'

'Savitha will have to keep them all in order,' chuckled Grace.

'Why are they so worried? She's in England,' Aloysius said. 'It's the children in this country who we should worry about. What's the matter with that boy?'

The little one is an absolute delight, wrote Christopher. *So clever, so inquisitive, so funny, so like Jasper really! As for Thornton and his wife, I can't imagine what they have in common of course. Meeka is certainly the best thing this family's ever had! She'll be the one to succeed in life, where all of us failed. She should have all the opportunities we did not. As far as I can, I shall make sure of that.*

Christopher has changed, wrote Thornton rather non-committally. *I've no idea what has happened to him but he is very strange. He seems fond of Meeka, which is worrying too. I hope he won't start talking politics with her.*

'Oh listen to this,' read Frieda laughing, 'they're squabbling over Anna-Meeka already!'

I haven't heard Frieda laugh for such a long time, thought Grace, glancing at the empty place set for Alicia. Her elder daughter seldom arose before the afternoon.

'She'll shake them all up,' said Aloysius, enjoying the conversation hugely, glad to see Grace look so happy.

He misses them too, thought Grace. Aloysius looked frail.

200

He had developed a persistent cough and was easily tired. After Sunil's death his hair had whitened dramatically. These days, he drank less and because of the intermittent curfew seldom went out.

'D'you remember how we used to be?' she asked them both, smiling a little. 'All together, in this house, milling around, coming and going, talking, arguing. Remember how this place was filled with music?'

They nodded, remembering. It was hard to believe.

'No one could keep the boys in for long,' Frieda said, wistfully.

'And then Thornton went and married that woman, Hildegard,' Aloysius reminded them, shaking his head.

They burst out laughing. They could laugh about it now.

'Mummy, you were so angry,' Frieda told her. 'We thought you'd be angry forever!'

'Poor Hildegard,' agreed Grace. 'I wonder what became of her.'

What's become of any of us? she thought later when she was alone. How have we come to this? What would you make of me now, Vijay, if you were here, if you could see me? Could you have predicted any of this on that terrible night before the eclipse? Now you are all gone, Sunil, my sons, and Alicia too, in her way.

Outside a few monkeys chattered angrily in the trees. They had taken up residence in the small coconut grove nearby. The owners of the grove had tried and failed to have them caught. The monkeys were raw-faced and defiant. They were outlaws. There was a rumour they had a fever-carrying disease and the owners of the coconut grove were frantic to have them caught before they bit someone. But the monkeys did not care. They laughed and pulled faces at the passers-by. A man had been sent from the army barracks to scare them away. He had fired a shot but they had simply raced off, swinging across the branches as they ran. The army man had lost his temper. Not wanting to be beaten by monkeys, he had fired away at them all morning but with no success. All morning he stood in the raging heat firing into the horizon, unable to see the pointlessness of it. Those who saw him dared not laugh for he might have turned the gun on them.

'Fools,' said Grace, closing the shutters against the noise.

'I will write to them,' decided Frieda. 'I will tell them about the monkeys.'

She would not tell them about the Tamil boy who had died yesterday in the centre of Colombo. He had strapped some explosives to his chest and blown himself up at the Fort. Six other people had died with him. The boy had been the same age as Anna-Meeka.

'I'm ready!' said Meeka, coming into her parents' bedroom in her school uniform. White shirt, navy blue pleated skirt, sweater, long white socks, new polished shoes. A huge chorus of birds had woken her. The sounds were very different from the birds she knew; softer, insistent in a different way. She hummed quietly to herself.

'I can't do my tie,' she said holding it out.

It was five thirty in the morning. A chink of light showed through the dull mustard curtains. Thornton woke with a start. The street lights had not been turned off yet. He waited for the barrage of sounds to assail his ears, the crows, the servant girl using her coconut scrapers, discarding the shells one by one hollowly on the ground, the sound of the fisherman crying '*malu, malu*', dogs barking, bicycle bells, whistles. He waited for the lurking heat outside the darkened room to come in, ready to pounce at the merest hint of movement, making itself felt, flooding the room with sweat. He waited, his heart pounding, but all he could feel, all he could hear was the sound of his daughter's humming. Close by, Savitha was snoring gently. Thornton had been dreaming of the girl with the ramrod hair. She had been smiling at him, moving threads of gold away from her mouth. He had been showing her around the Fort before the curfew, they were eating *thosai* and drinking king coconut. The girl kept smiling, telling him how wonderful his poems were, and Thornton was just reaching out to touch that great shining mane of cashmere gold with his long sensitive fingers, when Anna-Meeka woke him. He groaned, pulling the eiderdown away from his chin. Could a man not have a bit of peace, even in his own bed?

'Can you do my tie,' said Meeka firmly, tugging at the bed covers, soaking him in cold air, determined.

The dawn chorus had got louder and she hummed louder too.

'It's five thirty in the morning!' said Thornton, squinting at his watch.

Regretfully, promising to return at a later date, he put Miss Ramrod away. You understand, he told her, it's nothing personal, nothing to do with how I feel, but it is just not possible to have any conversation when my daughter is around. She is a fearsome presence, you know, a barrier to all carnal pleasure. Miss Ramrod smiled, still removing hair from her mouth (how much hair did the girl have? Thornton wondered fleetingly), and swiftly faded. She knew when she was beaten.

Later, even Meeka could smell the change in the air; a subtle shift here and there, some traces of dew on the uncovered earth, soft mist on the horizon. Thornton, walking her to the new school, bleary-eyed from his early start, felt it and was

203

pierced with a sharp longing for the hills of his childhood. Meeka felt it and associated it forever with the first day of term, new pencils, ruler, rubber, resolutions. All across the street were children walking to school, calling out to their friends, laughing, chewing bubblegum. Meeka was entranced by them. She skipped along beside her father, singing softly to herself. At the gate her father kissed her goodbye. He smiled, a tall handsome man, waving to his daughter as she disappeared into the crowd. Several mothers noticed him and would look for him again in vain. Tomorrow Meeka would walk to school alone.

But, in spite of the early start, in spite of all the eager anticipation, the day did not go well. She could not remember when it began to go wrong. Was it during break when she could not drink the cold milk they were given? Was it the awful lunch, which for some reason was called 'dinner', or perhaps it was when she called the 'dinner ladies' the servants and everyone shouted at her? They had offered her something they called pineapple but it had borne no resemblance to any fruit she knew. Clearly the pineapples that grew in England were a different kind. Perhaps it was simply the fact that she had no one to talk to all day, no one to have as a best friend that had made the day go so badly. This very first day at her new school in England, which she had longed and waited for, from as far back as she could remember. In the afternoon she wondered what her granny might be doing, in her beautiful house by the sea. She had wanted to tell someone about her granny, but there was no one to tell. The tune she had been humming repeated itself over and over again in her head. It reminded her of the sea she had left behind.

When the bell finally rang, she was lost in thought staring at the floor, watching it dissolve before her eyes, for something was wrong. No, thought Anna-Meeka, *everything* was wrong, from the way she spoke, to what she said, and how she looked. It dawned on her at that moment, in a flash of piercing insight, with belated astonishment coming from the morning's solitude, that she was very different from these large, fair-skinned children.

Savitha was waiting at the gate. Anna-Meeka could see her sari, tea-green and yellow, through the railings. She was standing alone, away from the other parents. She looked cold. Meeka swallowed. Her mother looked wrong too, as well as unhappy.

'Did you enjoy your day?' asked Savitha.

'Yes,' said Meeka, walking hurriedly on, pulling her by the hand, moving as fast as she could from the school building, the teacher on playground duty and all the throngs of children.

'I'm hungry,' she said. 'Can I have some rice when we get back?'

She had nearly said 'get back home', but somehow, what with one thing and another, the word 'home' was beginning to confuse her too.

12

THERE WAS NOTHING TO BE SAID. They were here to stay. Having finally unpacked all their luggage, Savitha threw away the things that had mould on them or were broken or stained by all the blood-red spices. The moment the trunks were opened, great clouds of powdery smells were released into the air, leaving traces of pungent condiments. She sat with the old newspapers that lined the trunks, reading about events from months ago. Already the paper was torn and yellowed. Here was a photograph of the murdered Prime Minister; there was another of a saffron robe splattered with blood. A review of a piano recital said the air conditioning had failed that night but the Beethoven was unbelievably beautiful. A report of the New Year festivities stated they were subdued. Like us, thought Savitha.

She felt desperate. Her loneliness frightened her. Being on her own in the house for many hours, with nothing to do and no one to talk to until Meeka returned from school, her thoughts circled around the past. She had often been lonely in the orphanage, but she had been younger and in those days she had been fearless. This feeling was different. Ceylon appeared to belong in another life. Savitha felt as though she had been cast adrift, abandoned in ways she had not thought possible. All that she had lost appeared before her, vast and incommunicable. Anna-Meeka no longer wanted Savitha to walk her back from school and Thornton, when he returned from work, was too exhausted to speak much. Savitha watched as her once cheerful family became slowly more preoccupied and withdrawn. She was bewildered and wanted only to spend her days dreaming of the time when she used to pick her daughter up from school in Colombo, returning home after a hot dusty train journey with Meeka in her white school uniform, a hard white hat keeping out the sun. In that other, extinct life.

'Mama!' Anna-Meeka would yell as soon as she came into view at the school gate. 'Can we go to Elephant House, and have a Lanka lime?'

They would walk towards the station, Savitha holding her sari high above the filth on the road, Meeka begging for some ambarella, or mango rolled in chilli powder and salt, from some filthy fruit sellers. Why had her daughter always wanted to eat from the dirtiest stall? wondered Savitha, smiling at the memory. How impossibly difficult it had been to drag the complaining Anna-Meeka onto the hot crowded train, to even find a seat.

But then, thought Savitha, dreamily, sitting on the carpet, watching the flames from the paraffin heater, the train would begin to move and there below them, a little way from the rocks, would be the sea. Miles and miles of endless golden sand, miles and miles of blistering beach. Only mad dogs would be out on it. And the sea would swish and the cool breeze would waft in through the carriage and Meeka would stop scowling and grin and sit there, with the sweat trickling down from under her hat, her sweet small face streaked with dirt, demanding to know when Thornton would be home to take her for a swim. Thus remembered Savitha, feeling the salty spray against her face, and the sense of bereavement all around.

Nevertheless, Savitha was nothing if not resourceful. She had not lived all her life in that convent orphanage without a strong feeling of self-preservation. She had, after all, that famously sharp mind of hers and she realised dimly that it was time to use it. One morning she came to a decision. She had, with some difficulty, made a cake. She had begun to understand that the Cambridge Certificate in English and those brilliant pieces to the newspapers back home were as nothing here in Brixton. Shopping for the sugar and the flour, the eggs, the butter, and then afterwards negotiating the unexpectedly well-trained traffic (would it suddenly lunge out at her, would a bullock cart appear from nowhere to knock her down and break her eggs?), all needed care and concentration. She was exhausted by the effort of venturing forth, of contact with people, even before she started baking. While she had been buying the ingredients at the corner shop, she had caught sight of a notice in the window. It said: 'WANTED. SEAMSTRESS FOR PIECEWORK. SMALL FACTORY. FLEXIBLE HOURS. 195 RAILTON ROAD, SW9.'

Later on, in the afternoon, and before Meeka came home from school (why *did* she insist on walking home alone?), she was going for a job interview. She had told no one. For who was there to tell? In any case her husband lived in a mysterious world of his own, and the child could not be counted on.

Sewing was something Savitha could do. Often during those Cambridge Certificate years sewing had been her recreation, her right arm occasionally turning the wheel of her Singer, her foot pedalling furiously. It was what she did when she had a lot to think about, and, without a doubt, she had much on her mind at the moment. Changing into her brightest red-and-orange sari, she left the house, caught a bus (so like the ones back home, but smarter, newer), and headed in the direction of Brixton. The bus drove past the arcade and a crockery stall caught her eye. It was piled high with a wonderful array of blue and white, willow-patterned china. Another stall flashed by. It had trousers hanging up all over it, flapping in the breeze. Savitha wondered curiously what it would be like to wear a pair. The bus passed under the bridge. The stalls here were run by black people. Savitha watched them curiously. They sold a confusion of interesting vegetables. A streak of red, a splash of dark green leaves, the sun-baked saffron insides of fruit, all flashed past her, jostling happily alongside stalls of apples piled high, and tight pale cabbages. Savitha's heart missed a beat. These black people appeared to be conversing easily with the white people on the nearby stalls. Even from a distance she could see their ease of manner. The experiences of the past weeks had almost overwhelmed her, shutting down the desire for analytical thought, but sitting here on the bus, lulled by its rocking movement and without the fear of bombs or gunfire, Savitha felt a sudden unexpected interest in her surroundings. The bus stopped at the terminus and she walked, A–Z in hand, towards Railton Road. So many closed faces. Here oppression descended once again so that it was something of a relief to climb the narrow stairs of 195, past the dingy passageway with 'Dora's Place' and 'Sally' on the doors until at last she reached the door marked 'Rosenberg's Retail Studio'.

He's Jewish, thought Savitha, looking at the man, shaking his hand and looking at the rows and rows of women, mostly pale, one or two of them black. Fleetingly she thought of Hildegard. The room was huge and high-ceilinged with large windows divided into many panes of glass. The lower ones were covered over in white paint.

'We don't want distractions, do we!' said Mr Rosenberg heartily, seeing her look at them.

'Come into my office,' he said, shouting above the noise of the sewing machines, eyeing her up, taking in her sari, her open-toed shoes, her feet without any stockings. Clearly this would not do. He made a clucking noise.

'One o'clock until four p.m. Starting tomorrow, promptly,' he said, standing legs apart, tilting backwards so as to balance the weight of his stomach. 'You will have to wear trousers. D'you have any? Well, you'll have to get some. We can't have all this.' He waved his hand in the direction of her sari. 'It wouldn't be safe with all the machinery. Besides,' he added jovially, almost as an afterthought, 'there's no heating here in the winter so you will get a trifle cold!'

And he laughed a long, long laugh that followed her back all the way down the stairs, echoing out onto the street, ringing in her ears all the way to her front door.

Full of energy she put some rice on to boil. Next she scraped two carrots and one of those peculiar things called parsnips. She fried some coriander and some cumin from her precious spice jar and then, as a treat, she added a little of the fast-diminishing dried Maldive fish, bought specially from Wallisinga & Sons in Pettah. The hot smell hissed and spluttered, filling the kitchen and swarming out through the extractor fan. Out it went through the communal garden, over Mr Smith's vegetable patch and through his wife's kitchen window so that Mrs Smith, sniffing the air, could not think what on earth to make of these new neighbours with all their curious smells. Savitha stirred the saucepan vigorously, adding onions, garlic and small chillies sliced diagonally, a dollop of tomato sauce, some chopped lamb, coconut milk and then the vegetables. There, it was done. She lifted the lid off the rice, fluffing it with a fork so each grain gleamed white, and the hot fragrant steam rose, engulfing her with a wonderful sense of comfort like no other. Meeka would be home soon. She would be pleased to have a bowl of hot rice.

While she waited she decided to reorganise the cupboard that held her collection of bone china, miraculously unharmed by the journey. But when she opened the cupboard, hidden memories tumbled out, competing with each other. In the flurry of leaving, Savitha had not paid much attention and only now did she see the extent of Grace's generosity. Her mother-in-law had given her the best, most treasured pieces of her china. Savitha gazed at them, unexpected tears springing up. Some of the china was much older than the rest. All of it would need protecting from Thornton who, unused to the task, was clumsy with the washing-up.

'I want you to keep them for Anna-Meeka,' Grace had said. It had been late afternoon, everyone, even the servants, had been resting. Savitha could still hear her mother-in-law's voice clearly, could see her standing in the shuttered dining room.

'It's all I can give her,' Grace had said. She had smiled, but her eyes were unfathomable. 'Everything else, the house, the land, all of it was sold off years ago, you know, Savitha. All I have of any value is the china.'

And Savitha had answered, 'It is enough. I will keep it safe, I promise. I am its custodian!' With new admiration she recognised Grace's courage. Dimly she saw what these treasures, taken for granted by her children, meant to her mother-in-law. Things of beauty in a hostile land.

'In my safe keeping,' she murmured to the empty room. 'Until Anna-Meeka is old enough to have them.'

Loss scattered like drops of rain around her. She imagined the grand old house in the hills, not as she had witnessed it on that terrible trip, but as it must have been long ago, in its heyday. When the de Silva women, wearing gorgeous cashmere saris, ate Tamil sweetmeats piled on these Hartley Green plates, and drank tea from W.T. Copeland cups. Lost in her daydream, Savitha stared at the flamboyant Royal Doulton dinner service, the pale Wedgwood. Silent receptacles of memory; witnesses to a vanished way of life. Here were the tea plates on which Sunil had been served petits fours. The touch of his hands remaining long after he had gone. Here in the cupboard in Brixton. Who could have imagined such a journey? Holding the tea-rose cups high up to the light, Savitha felt as though she was cradling her own fragile existence. Fiercely, stacking the lily-of-the-valley tureens, she decided, I will *never* stop using them. I will *never* allow Meeka to forget her home. A faint scent of straw from the ship's packaging filled the air, engulfing her in a terrible wave of sadness. As if in response, the sun broke through a cloud, exposing the dirt on the windows from many years of winter neglect, now unreachably high.

She did not tell Thornton about her job until the next morning. If she had wanted to surprise him she did. She wore her new slacks and made the breakfast. It was a brave decision and at first Thornton did not even notice. He was looking very handsome in his new work suit. The table was set; all seemed normal. An English breakfast, with toast, marmalade, string hoppers, last night's lamb curry, tomato ketchup and a kettle of water for the tea. There were his mother's pink-and-white cups and saucers, gold-rimmed and delicate. As far as Thornton could see everything was as usual. Why should he suddenly look more closely? Why should he have to keep an eye on everybody *all* the time? He knocked loudly on the wall of his daughter's bedroom.

'Meeka,' he said, 'Meeka, get up. You'll be late for school.'

Letting out a small sound of fury, Anna-Meeka thumped out of bed and shot straight out of her room. She glared at her father who was about to bang on her wall again. Then she stopped, and stared at her mother. Thornton went back to his toast with its coating of thick-cut marmalade. He was reading the newspaper.

'There's something here about Ceylon,' he said to his wife. 'You know, you should start writing for the papers here.' And he held out his cup for more tea.

'What are you wearing?' asked Meeka dubiously.

Savitha eyed her daughter. The good thing about Anna-Meeka, she decided with satisfaction, was that she *always* noticed everything. But she did not say this.

'Hmm?' asked Thornton, not looking up. 'I'm wearing my new suit of course, for work. Now hurry up and get ready.'

He picked up another of the newspapers he had bought that morning. He was trying to decide which paper to take regularly. Christopher had said he should only buy the *Guardian* but Thornton had no intention of taking his advice untested. He wanted to check out all the possibilities for his future poems. It would be a pity to lose the momentum he had almost gained back home. Meeka stared at her mother.

'Mama!' she shrieked, suddenly wide awake and horrified to see her mother's legs evident in this way. 'You can't go out like that.'

'Aha!' said Savitha triumphantly, waggling her head from side to side. 'Good morning, everyone. So finally someone speaks! My husband is blind but thankfully my daughter has inherited her sight from me. Well, I'm exceedingly sorry, men,' she said, addressing the dining room in general, 'in case you're interested, I have got a job!'

And she went back to pouring the tea into their lovely bone-china cups. But it was not that simple. Whatever made her think it would be? Later on, even though she was busy, there was plenty of time for her homesickness to return. Mr Rosenberg had put her in the corner of the room, a little away from the rising and the falling of machines, the movement of the pedals beating the air like wings and the sound of scissors against cloth. She sat working, her own rhythm out of step with the rest of them. A small exotic seabird, stranded on a narrow spit of land, her wings closed. Sewing together this thing called denim: piece against piece, raw edge against raw edge. She wore black slacks.

Outside, the last fragments of a late-October sunshine gathered together for one final salute, one last display of warmth of the Indian summer, turning the afternoon, pivoting slowly, lifting up the edges of the plane leaves so they gave the appearance of being young and tender.

The green is so different here, thought Savitha, raising her face to the last of the sun. Soft sap green, lacking the sharpness of tropical colour. Muted just like the birds in this place, she thought. Caught below the tideline of the whitewashed windowpane, Savitha could see very little, working silently, bent over the cloth, words running like music through her head. An idea for an article was taking shape but it was too early to say where it might lead. To a random harvest maybe, or nowhere perhaps?

In the beginning the women she worked with had tried to be friendly, but after she had overcome the business of understanding their speech she could find no point of common reference between them. She had been coming to the sweatshop for nearly a month now. When they were not working furiously, racing against the clock, the women gathered together in groups for their break, going outside for a cigarette, catching the last of the glorious autumn light, chatting, laughing even. Savitha was astonished, what was there to laugh about?

In the end they left her alone, thinking her stuck-up, having their breaks without her, cigarettes and mugs of tea in hand. Their conversation drifted backwards and forwards and again Savitha noticed how easily the black women fitted in. They were always teasing Mr Rosenberg. Savitha did not know what to make of this either and, with no one to confide in, began every evening at home to write some notes of her own. Thornton, pretending to read the newspapers, eyed her slyly and was relieved. He hated her working in the factory. It made him ashamed and angry.

'What would my mother say if she knew?' he was always asking her. 'What would Frieda think?'

Savitha refused to comment. Privately Thornton felt very unhappy. The woman he had married was changing. We no longer laugh together as we used to, he thought, puzzled, feeling helpless in the face of Savitha's stubbornness. So that every evening, hiding behind his newspaper, he watched her as she scribbled furiously. Clearly she was going back to writing. With any luck she would leave this stupid job, get out of these completely unsuitable clothes, and go back to behaving as a wife and mother should. This flat is too small, fretted Thornton. We're all on top of each other here.

Savitha, unaware of any of this, continued to work out her own confusions. Yesterday afternoon, during one of the short and difficult-to-negotiate tea breaks, two new recruits were introduced to them. Indian women both of them, wearing baggy red silk trousers, their hair was heavily oiled with ghee and plaited along the length of their backs. Looped gold earrings and startling fluorescent bangles moved discordantly on their arms. Mr Rosenberg introduced them first to the group and then singled out Savitha.

'There you go, Savinta,' he said. 'I've got a couple of your countrymen so you can be 'appy. Don't say I don't give you nuffin!' He laughed a little nervously. For 'Savinta', as he mistakenly called her, was not like his usual ladies. With her silent efficiency, her fluent (though heavily accented) English and her inscrutable stare, she was a mystery to Rosenberg.

'She's a bleedin' snob, ain't she!' observed Doris, his longest-standing employee and foreman by default.

Rosenberg was inclined to agree with her. 'Savinta' unnerved him.

'What's she got to be a snob about, then? She's no better than the others.'

Having hired the other Asians with the hope they were as efficient as Savitha, he herded them together in a little bunch, away from everyone else.

'All together, keep you 'appy,' he told Savitha, smiling with a heartiness he did not feel.

Savitha stared at him with astonishment. The women were *Indian*. What did Rosenberg mean? They were Indian coolies, probably from a plantation rather like the ones the de Silvas once owned. On that last trip upcountry Aloysius had talked about the ancient rulers who once lived in the palaces. Grace and Thornton had shown her the lakes where Grace's mother had grown the flamingo-pink lotus flowers. They had stayed at a wonderful rest house and listened to the roar of a nearby waterfall. The air had smelt of soft rainwater and tea.

'All this,' Aloysius had told her, proudly sweeping his hand across the view, 'all this belonged to us once, you know, Savitha.'

The younger, idealistic Savitha had stared at the old filigree carvings, the sacred statues softened by lichen and daily offerings of flowers, and had argued hotly over the injustice of such privilege existing hand in hand with the coolies working on the hillside. But now, *now* she felt torn. Now she was no longer certain of those beliefs. Something puzzling was happening to her principles. More and more since her entry into this country, she found herself being crushed between her old socialist tendencies and a new uncertain alliance with the de Silvas' past. The women beside her were Indian peasants hardly able to speak English, staring at Savitha with unabashed curiosity, talking to each other in their own language, cocooned in a strange world of their own. Refusing, thought Savitha, furiously, *refusing* to speak in English! Who did they think they were, refusing to learn this beautiful language? Why weren't they trying to integrate? Hadn't the British been criticised for this very thing? She glared at them.

During their break the two newcomers sat huddled on the landing eating from their tiffin boxes. Savitha's mouth watered but still she refused their overtures of friendliness. Was she a snob then? Was this her secret weakness? She felt she had become like the people she had once despised in Sri Lanka. She had hated them for their airs and graces, their useless pride, their snobbishness. And here she was behaving in the same way. It distressed her that it seemed no longer possible to live up to her ideals. But I am not like them, she wanted to cry, confused and upset without knowing why. How do I make myself interested in what interests them? There is something wrong with me, she decided, finally, filled with a different kind of despair as she continued to drink the weak dishwatery tea provided by the establishment, concentrating, instead, on reading George Bernard Shaw's *The Intelligent Woman's Guide to Socialism and Capitalism*.

13

COMING BACK LATE ONE EVENING, on a night with a full moon, Grace smelt the lime trees growing beside the house. The rain had washed away the dust and crushed the leaves, releasing their scent into the air. The monsoon was almost over, but the heat had not become oppressive yet. She had been to evensong at the cathedral. Small flecks of light hovered around the statue of the Virgin. It was the first time she had ventured out in months; Frieda and Aloysius had not wanted her to go but the curfew had been lifted temporarily. She would have gone anyway, but they did not know this. She no longer cared about her own safety. There had been another letter from Savitha. Included with it was a piece of paper covered in badly drawn musical notations from Meeka. Thornton had scribbled a note at the bottom of the letter, saying he would be writing separately.

Savitha was lonely; Grace felt the loneliness struggle through the thin blue paper.

Winter will soon be here, wrote Savitha, *the light has almost vanished. You can't think what that means until you are threatened with its loss. I listen to the sound of sewing machines all day. They remind me of the wings of small birds. My thoughts are continuously of home. I think of you all the time. When will it be safe for us to return?*

'She has a job?' Grace said to Frieda, puzzled. 'Sewing? But she can write so vividly, with such passion. Why isn't she writing her articles?'

Frieda was nonplussed. Savitha had always been a mystery.

Thornton has become very quiet. He misses you and he worries all the time about Meeka.

From this Grace deduced Savitha was worried about him. And little Anna-Meeka, what news of her?

She's grown a lot, wrote Savitha, proudly. Grace was thrilled.

She's changing fast, wrote Savitha.

Must be the better food, thought Grace.

I forgot to mention Thornton has managed to buy a piano. You knew how much Meeka wanted one? Well, now she's very happy. She plays it all the time, listening to the records we have and copying the tunes. She can play anything just by hearing it once! A few weeks ago we found a piano teacher as well. A Polish woman, called Mrs Kay. Thornton asked her to put Meeka in for her Grade 4 exam. He thinks it will be a good thing if she could do some exams. But Meeka doesn't want to do exams, she says. Mrs Kay says she only wants to improve on the Beethoven! Mrs Kay says it's not such a bad thing, and it shows where her interest lies, whatever that means, but Thornton is furious. He thinks we are wasting our money and wants to find another teacher. Anyway Mrs Kay has been teaching Meeka to write music (see enclosed) and she's been writing down all sorts of things. D'you remember how she used to suddenly make up little tunes when she was at the convent? Well, she's still doing that. Her teacher told us that perhaps Meeka should study music theory instead. Thornton was disappointed, although he tried to hide it. You know he would hate her to try to be a concert pianist, but still, I think he would have liked her to show some sign of her aunt's talent. Anyway, yesterday Meeka was playing some of these 'tunes' when Thornton came in. She told him, 'This one is for Granny and Auntie Frieda. It's about the sea and about Jasper.' Thornton didn't say anything, he just stood watching her and then he told her to go back to practising her exam piece.

'Hmm,' mumbled Aloysius, jerking his head in the direction of Alicia's room. 'That's different. *She* never did that!'

So you see how she remembers Sri Lanka, continued Savitha. *And every day*, she added in her postscript, *every single day we drink our tea from your beautiful bone china!*

Thornton's letter had arrived a few days later. Grace stared at the well-loved handwriting for a long time before she opened it. But then, in spite of everything she felt, somehow the letter had made her laugh, for Thornton was unable to hide his irritation with the world, especially his beloved daughter.

Anna-Meeka, he told his mother, *is trying to talk like the white children in her school! She has a piano now but she's very stubborn and she keeps changing the notes in the exam pieces she's supposed to be learning. I hope this isn't going to be the pattern with her other lessons because she has the eleven-plus exams to take soon. Christopher makes matters worse. He's forever encouraging her to do whatever she wants, telling her stories about me from the past, simply to annoy me. As for Jacob*, continued Thornton, his irritation gathering momentum, *I just don't understand him. We meet up but he has nothing to say of any interest. He's become very withdrawn since he left home.*

Walking in the garden that evening, when the heat had died down a little, Grace thought about her letters. Even after all this time some things did not change. Thornton and

Christopher were no closer to each other. Their squabbles and their worries continued, regardless. She could see no problem with Anna-Meeka though. It was Thornton and Savitha who were the ones in need of attention. Yesterday Aloysius had written to his granddaughter, his hand moving shakily across the paper, telling the child things about their daily life in Sri Lanka, reminding her of her home, aware that he was unlikely to see her again. Watching him, Grace had felt bereft. A fatal gap had opened up between them all. The ship that had carried them away had left a space too wide, and impossible to cross.

Two nights previously the curfew had been lifted and there was life back on the streets, giving it a deceptive air of normality. But it would not last. Thin rice-paper clouds moved silently in the sky. The crescent moon glided through them. Beyond the lime trees a performance of Kathakali dancing was taking place. Grace could hear temple drums. Last week there had been another suicide bomb in the capital outside the Central Bank. It had killed fifteen people including the child who had carried it. There had been a piece in the paper by Amnesty International protesting against the use of children in war.

As she walked across the moonlit garden, Grace noticed the lights in Alicia's room were on. Turning, she looked at the gate, half expecting to hear the sound of Thornton returning. Of all the pointless things civil war is the most pointless, she thought. Tonight she had knelt in the candlelit church and prayed for the country to unite, hoping that when it was all over there might be something left to unify. Through the branches of the trees she caught glimpses of her elder daughter moving in her room. There was no longer any trace of the girl she once had been. Christopher had called this place a poisoned paradise, and Grace, with Vijay so recently murdered, had agreed.

'But we cannot blame the land,' she murmured to herself, as the garden shifted and settled into the night. The land in all its beauty was not at fault.

Like the garden, her thoughts moved restlessly. It would take five days for a letter to reach her children. Lately, a soft film seemed to be passing before her eyes, making writing difficult. Before long her father's blindness would be hers.

'Are my sons happy?' she had asked feverishly, when she prayed. Always, she came back to this single unanswerable question. Could they be happy having cut their connections with their homeland as though they were the ribbons that had stretched from the ship? Could they be happy at such a price?

A servant hurried through the trees. He wanted to warn her he had seen a snake in the grass where Grace stood. 'The moon was nearly gone,' he said, shaking his head. 'It's a time for serpents. Did you notice an offering to the gods was left outside the gate earlier?' The servant was frightened. It was not an auspicious thing to happen.

'Ignore it,' said Grace. 'Why worry about the serpents and devils when all the time the real enemy walks, unmasked, within our midst?'

Above her, the luminescent moon slipped silently behind the clouds.

'Well,' asked Christopher, 'what d'you think then?'

He placed two pints of Guinness on their table and sat down, pushing some loose change towards Jacob. Then he raised his glass to his lips with a smile of satisfaction. He had not had a drink since lunchtime. Jacob frowned. Somehow, since Thornton's arrival, he seemed to have got sucked into the habit of meeting his brothers for a drink at the pub. It was Christopher's fault.

'Let's introduce him to pub life,' he had said.

Why do I always end up paying? thought Jacob irritably. What do they need me for?

'Haven't you been paid yet?' he asked.

'No, men, not yet. I'll buy a round next time. Don't fuss.'

'That's what you always say,' said Jacob.

'Yes, OK. Don't be such a bloody capitalist. I'll pay next time. Now then,' he leaned towards Jacob, his eyes bright, 'tell me what you think of our sister-in-law.'

'Oh!' Jacob was not interested in Savitha. 'She's all right, I suppose. At least she keeps Thornton in his place.' He yawned. Then he remembered something else. 'Are you seeing that woman in the leopard-skin coat?'

'What?' asked Christopher startled. 'What d'you mean? Has Thornton been spying on me again?'

'Calm down, Christopher. Thornton will be here in a minute. It was the barman who asked me, actually. I hope you're not entertaining a call girl?'

Christopher stared at his eldest brother disbelievingly. Then he burst out laughing.

'You know your problem, Jacob,' he said conversationally. 'This country has turned you into one of the bourgeoisie. You were halfway there before you left Sri Lanka and this country has simply completed the job. Soon you'll marry someone safe, just like our dear brother, and that will be that.' He paused for a second to take a great gulp of his drink. 'And if *I* want to be seen with a prostitute,' he continued challengingly, looking around for the barman, 'that's up to me, no?'

Jacob winced. 'Keep your voice down,' he said wearily. 'I'm sorry, Christopher, but you worry me. You're drinking far too much. What will they say at home? What will Mummy say?'

Christopher snorted. 'You don't know what Mummy thinks?

Let me tell you, she's not the person you think she is. Let me tell you –'

Jacob held up his hand. 'Don't start getting excited about everything I say.'

They both fell silent. Sipping their drinks.

'We have nothing in common,' Christopher said finally, flatly. 'You and I and Thornton.' He spoke without heat, his face expressionless. 'That's the truth of it.'

'Whose idea was it to meet?' Jacob said, defensively.

'Mine,' Christopher said, suddenly serious. 'It's what Mummy would have liked. I suggested it for her sake. Not my own.'

Jacob was surprised. England had changed his youngest brother almost beyond recognition. He had become confident. Or maybe he always was, thought Jacob, but we never noticed. Christopher drank too much and when he was drunk it made him want to pick a fight. Just like Daddy, Jacob sighed. Why was it that every time he had any dealings with his family it was always unpleasant?

'The only good thing about *him*,' remarked Christopher catching sight of Thornton, 'is Anna-Meeka. She should be my daughter!'

Thornton had told Savitha he would be late back. He had a feeling Savitha did not want Christopher getting drunk in their house. He also suspected Anna-Meeka listened in on their conversation. So he was happy to meet his brothers in the pub. Tonight he had come straight from work where, as usual, his day as a clerk at the Central Office of Information had been both confusing and tiring. He had not told anyone, but he would never like the job. He had not made friends but he did not tell his family this either. Picking up his glass, he went over to his brothers.

'Aha!' Christopher said immediately, in a combative sort of way. He looked alert and full of energy.

'God, Christopher,' Thornton said mildly, sipping his beer, 'where do you get your energy from?'

'How's my niece?'

'She's been asked to join the school choir,' Thornton said, brightening up.

'Really? I say! This calls for a present.' Christopher leapt up and went over to the bar to buy some chocolate.

'He told me he didn't have any money,' Jacob said.

'Oh, he's mad,' said Thornton. 'Take no notice. I'm so cold,' he added, distractedly.

Jacob considered him. Thornton looked unbelievably oppressed, weighed down and unhappy. The speed with which he had saddled himself with a wife so unlike him still amazed Jacob. A wife now working in a sweatshop, no less!

'How's Savitha's job?' he asked.

Thornton groaned.

'Tell her to give it up, men. How can you let her work there?'

'Shh!' said Thornton, for Christopher was returning. 'Don't start *him* off, for God's sake.'

Jacob shook his head. His family was a complete mystery. Thank goodness his new girlfriend was nothing like any of them. Christopher threw the bar of chocolate down on the table next to Thornton.

'For Meeka,' he said. 'Ask her if she's written another tune yet.' He gave a short laugh. His brothers both looked like a couple of stuffed cats. 'Cheer up,' he said, 'it might never happen!'

Half-term arrived. Meeka seemed a little happier at her school. Savitha noticed she had some friends, now. There was a girl called Gillian and another called Susan. Meeka talked earnestly about them and Savitha listened, suppressing a smile. Thornton did not think it significant but *she* could see her daughter looked more confident, and had begun to sing to herself again. Thornton only wanted Meeka to work hard. Soon she would be taking her eleven plus and he wanted her to stop wasting time playing piano and get into the grammar school. He noticed Meeka was still adding bits to the sonatas she was supposed to be learning, trying to improve on Beethoven he called it, disapprovingly. He noticed she was trying to talk in the peculiar way of the white children. He was not happy about this either. Nor was he pleased when she told him one evening that from now on she would be calling him *Dad* because Daddy was too babyish. All this added to Thornton's irritation. Only Savitha was simply glad her daughter was settling down. Once or twice she suggested Meeka bring a child home for a meal but Meeka mumbled something about the children not eating spicy food.

'What d'you mean?' demanded Savitha. 'I can make them a cake. You like my cake, don't you?'

But no one came and eventually she forgot about it.

Savitha had decided to stay on at the sweatshop until she found a better job. They needed the money, and besides, the article she had been writing was developing nicely. She planned to polish it up and send it to a newspaper back home. Until then she would stay with Rosenberg. On the first morning of the holidays, she left Meeka alone in the house while she went to work the early shift. There was plenty of rice for lunch and there were two curries. She showed her daughter how to warm them. There were some sweetmeats and apples. On no account was Meeka to open the door to anyone. She could go down the road to the children's library to change her books but she was to come straight back. No dawdling, no going into shops, no buying sweets. Meeka nodded, keeping the gleam out of her eyes. Her mother wrote the phone number of her father's office, and Rosenberg's too. She then went to the bathroom and fussed around, changing her slacks, redoing her hair, looking at herself in the mirror, admiring her new coat. Meeka groaned inwardly. Would her mother *never* leave?

'I'm off now, Meeka,' she called out finally.

Meeka, lying on her bed, legs waving in the air, put them down hastily. Savitha came into the room and gave her a kiss. She hesitated. A feeling of unease was beginning to form at the back of her mind. There was something a little unsleepy about the child. Savitha could not put her finger on it, but there was a tension, a feeling of excitement, running along the length of Meeka's sleek little body as she hugged her mother with slightly too much enthusiasm. Savitha looked at her.

'Are you sure you'll be all right?' she asked again, anxiously, feeling her way around the dark corners of doubt lodged in her suspicious mind.

'Yes, Mum,' said Meeka obediently and she sighed, and she yawned and then she slumped back into bed for all the world as though she were dog-tired.

Savitha hesitated again. She looked at her watch. If she did not leave now she would be late for Rosenberg's. After all, there was not much that Meeka could get up to. Finally, satisfied, she picked up her umbrella, saying she would be back at two. And out she went, shutting the front door with a brisk little tug. A small slam, the sweetest of slams, the most beautiful sound in the world, thought Anna-Meeka, pausing a moment. Which was just as well because Savitha was back a moment later having forgotten her lunch. But then finally she left, trailing a string of instructions behind her, unable to linger any longer.

'Yes,' said Meeka. 'Yes, yes, yes!' She went on saying it for a few moments after this second wonderful closing of the door. Just in case.

She counted to ten. (She had overheard someone saying there was safety in numbers.) Then, in a flash, she dressed. She forgot to do her teeth or wash her face, but still, she was dressed and her hair hastily combed. There was no time to waste. Her mother would be back by two. Pulling out a paper bag from under her bed, she went into the dining room to set the table for lunch.

It was quite chilly in the dining room. She had learned that you said 'chilly' when it was cold and 'cold' when it was freezing, unlike her father who said it was cold even when the sun was shining. So far, she noticed, no one at school said it was cold yet. Clearly it would get a lot chillier. It was from the dinner ladies, now her firm friends, that she got much of her information. All those bits that Gillian and the others failed to tell her, all the filler-in bits that were needed for daily life, came from these wonderful ladies. They told her she was a little horror, and, holding this new applauded status to her chest like a shield, she hoped finally to be accepted by the *boys* and get into the rounders team. It was a modest ambition but one that, so far, she had been unable to fulfil. When she asked Geoff why this was so, he had grinned and tweaked her hair. Then, making a noise like a motorbike, working the imaginary handlebars with his hands, he told her.

'Titch!' he said succinctly. 'Everyone thinks you're a titch. Won't catch the ball, will yer. That's wot. Won't run fast enough!'

He grinned, not unkindly, for Geoff was the sort of boy who was nice to his cat. Later, he offered Meeka some Maltesers, but this was not enough for her. She took the Maltesers of course, but she loathed and hated Geoff-the-messenger. For a while she could barely talk to him. Luckily Geoff did not notice.

One evening Meeka had asked her father if she was a 'titch'?

'What is that you are saying?' asked Thornton suspiciously,

looking up from one of his newspapers (tonight it was *The Times* and the *New Statesman*).

'What is that word?'

Meeka wished he did not talk so loud. Get so excited every time she opened her mouth.

'Of course you are not small!' her father had said, outraged. 'You are my daughter. You are *beautiful*!' Having given his final word on the subject, Thornton went back to his reading.

After some time Meeka decided to change tactics with Geoff and the other boys. Suspecting rightly that he was the most powerful one in the class, she decided to be nicer to him. Since Geoff had never noticed she hated him in the first place, this too was lost on him. The subject of rounders never came up again but Meeka was merely biding her time. And that was when she had her good idea.

Today, at twelve o'clock, she was having a party. She had invited her whole class for lunch. She had given them invitations telling them it was her birthday. It was not her birthday, but still, that was a small point. Her stepmother, she told them, was a frightening woman. They would not want to meet her. But thankfully, Meeka assured them, she would be out. So would her father. They had left her to have her party in peace. Unfortunately the party would have to finish at two o'clock promptly, as her stepmother wanted the house tidied up for when she came home. The children were agog. Never had there been such interesting goings-on in their class.

Meeka began getting ready. First she stood on a chair and got Savitha's new cookery book from the bookcase. The *Good Housekeeping Book of Dinner Parties*. Prawn Cocktail, she was going to make prawn cocktail, without the prawn. Then she was going to heat last night's leftover rice. Last night's curries would also be reheated. There were crisps and fish fingers, which had been defrosting nicely under her bed for a couple of days but, because the money was running out, only a few chocolates. She had been saving her pocket money for weeks, ever since she had first had the idea of the birthday party, to spend on bits of food from the shop at the end of her street on her way home from school. There was nothing to drink, only water. She had, however, noticed her mother buying some limes last Saturday, and Meeka planned to squeeze these into water to make Lanka lime. It was all decided in her mind. She had two hours to get everything ready. It was a race against the clock.

Carefully, so as not to break it, she took out the special china. There was a lot to choose from. The cupboard gleamed with the most beautiful things: pink-and-white plates covered in rosebuds, blue-and-white dishes, small bowls, jugs and teapots. But it was at the back of the cupboard that she found the real treasures. At the back, tucked away behind the Whitefriars crystal glass, were small neat stacks of the oldest pieces. There were tureens with worn patterns, cups and saucers, a whole dinner service with delicate figures, dense foliage, ivy, ferns, passion flowers. Meeka picked out her especial favourites. Side plates, sugar bowls for the jelly that she was about to make, serving dishes for the curries, a tureen for the rice. She spread them around on the floor, vague memories like the music that lived constantly in her head, rose up to greet her. Here was a dish that her granny used to serve *bolo de coco* on; here was another that always had *pente frito* in them whenever she visited her grandparents in their beautiful house in Station Road. For a moment she longed to taste some *vadi* or some *thosai*. To smell again the rose water and cinnamon in Auntie Frieda's kitchen. Her aunt always had something sweet for her to eat whenever she visited and when she hugged Meeka she always smelt of rulang and cochineal. Meeka had loved visiting them, her grandparents and her aunt, in their house by the sea. In the excitement of being in England she had forgotten how much she loved the island.

Suddenly, with unexpected force, she heard the rhythmic sweep of the sea and her father's laughter as they ran the length of the beach together. She could almost taste the fried prawns they used to buy. The texture within the sounds in her head changed becoming slower and more intense and she heard her younger self, screaming with excitement, as her father chased her under a wave. Droplets of spray sparkled in the sunlight as she swam through the water. When they returned to the house in Station Road, Aunt Frieda used to dry Meeka off with a soft towel and then serve a delicious meal on the old pink-and-white plates. On one occasion, when Meeka was sitting on the veranda, a crow had flown down from the murunga tree, knocking over a dish and breaking it. Auntie Frieda had said that was exactly what Jasper used to do when he was young. Meeka had loved the stories of Jasper. Thinking of him, after so long, she wished suddenly that he were still alive. Her father, who used to tell her lots of funny stories about him, still found it difficult to talk about the way he had died.

The memory of Jasper made the music in Meeka's head shift subtly, getting faster. Forgetting about her preparations, going into the sitting room, she lifted the lid of the piano. Then frowning with concentration she began to play. It was not quite right. She played the G minor scales adding six extra notes. Then she went back to her piece of music and added the bit in Debussy to the end of it. Her music sounded a bit better, but was still not quite right. Perhaps it was the scale that was wrong? Her mother, who always encouraged her, had said, 'Practice makes perfect, Meeka.'

At the thought of those folded lips, a sudden twinge of unease gripped Anna-Meeka. Hastily, so as not to spoil the day in any way, she put the thought firmly out of her mind and went back into the kitchen. There was still an awful lot to do.

She set the table with the special white damask tablecloth, lemonade glasses, dishes, side plates. Then she made the jelly. When she poured the boiling water over the ruby-red gelatine the bowl cracked and coloured water began seeping onto the draining board. Hurriedly she took some Tupperware from under the sink, hiding the cracked dish at the back of the cupboard. Again the feeling of unease washed over her, only this time it was much stronger. But it was too late to start worrying now, she told herself sensibly.

Soon the jelly was setting nicely in the fridge. The prawn-less cocktails were done, arranged in long crystal glasses. Unfortunately there were only four. The children would have to share. Or have a teaspoonful each, so it would all go round. The recipe book asked for something called cayenne pepper. Meeka did not know what this was. It looked red and the book said it was hot. So she sprinkled some chilli from her mother's spice jar. It looked so nice that she sprinkled a bit more on top. Gillian was bringing a birthday cake with candles. Meeka had told her there would be no cake because her stepmother would not bake her one. It was against her religion, she said. When Gillian's mother heard this her eyes filled with tears.

'Poor little mite!' she said to Gillian's dad. 'Don't you fret, Gilly luv, we'll make her one. You can help me mix a Victoria sponge.'

So Gillian was bringing the cake. Soon the table began to look wonderful. True, the jelly did not seem to want to jell and the fish fingers smelt funny and had crumbled but the curries were magnificent. Meeka had heated them as her mother had taught her, with a tiny bit of water on a low heat, scraping the non-stick saucepan with a fork, until the familiar smell rose invitingly. The rice too had reheated successfully. All that remained was the mess from the limes she had squeezed rather vigorously. It was a quarter to twelve. She felt excitement rise up like the smell of paraffin from the heaters in the house. The telephone rang. It was her father, checking she was all right, checking she wasn't lonely, checking she would take his library books back.

'And don't waste time on the piano before you finish your homework. Understand? You *must* do well, Meeka. Playing the piano all day isn't going to get you into the grammar school, huh?'

'Yes,' agreed Meeka, hopping from one foot to another nervously. 'Yes, yes, yes. Bye-bye, Dad.'

Again she felt unease creep up behind her, trying, but not quite succeeding, to stifle her excitement. Then, just as she wondered, what if no one came, the doorbell rang.

By the time they got to it, the jelly was almost set.

'Oh good!' said Meeka taking it out of the fridge, bringing it to the table with a flourish, all semi-wobbly and red.

'Now,' she said firmly, 'if you eat some of this your mouth will stop burning.'

The curries had proved too hot for the children, and the prawnless cocktail was too full of chilli. But there was cake, Gillian reminded her, when she had become crestfallen. There was still the cake. Meeka brightened up and it was then, as Gillian and Jennifer and Susan began to stack the plates and the dishes and the cutlery in a great clattering heap in the sink, that she had remembered the jelly, jammed at the back of the fridge, against a jar of seeni sambal and jaggery. So it'll be all right, thought Meeka.

'Sweet things always take away the burning of a hot curry,' she said, unconsciously quoting her mother.

The boys tucked in, jostling each other in their greed. Meeka's presents were piled on the floor. She would look at them later. Two girls had locked themselves in the bathroom and she could hear them giggling and flushing the toilet. Gillian opened the back door letting in a thin stream of cold air. It was raining a little.

'Let's play murder in the dark,' said Geoff, having had enough of the food. He was trying not to think about it, but he felt a little sick.

'No,' said Gillian firmly. 'We have to sing "Happy Birthday" now, you idiot. The grown-ups will be here soon and we'll have to go home.'

And she swept the remaining crockery into the sink, unfortunately dropping two cups on the hard linoleum floor. They broke into perfect halves and lay there, two generations of use, resting neatly by the plastic waste-paper basket.

'Oh whoops!' said Gillian, smiling apologetically at Meeka.

'It doesn't matter,' said Meeka. Being her parents' daughter she was polite. Her granny and her mother had always said if a servant broke something one should never get angry. It was bad manners. 'I'll clear it up later,' she said airily.

She ignored the strange feeling in the pit of her stomach and the knowledge that somewhere in the distance, waiting at some traffic light, crossing some road, were her mother's feet marching determinedly home. An advancing army. She would have to work fast to get the place cleaned up. The truth was she wanted the children to go home. They had played pass the parcel. They had played musical chairs. Meeka had a feeling they might have scratched her father's record of a Mozart opera, but that at least could be hidden. It had been difficult playing musical chairs to Mozart, and even harder to play it to a Beethoven sonata.

'Don't you have any singles?' Marion asked her. 'Any Beatles?'

''Ow abowt the Monkees?'

Meeka had none of these wonderful, exotic things, none of this forbidden fruit. The questions served only to highlight her inadequacies. Old-fashioned music was all that was on offer.

'Cor! Yer mum 'n' dad are different, 'nt they?' Geoff observed.

'Thas cos they're foreign,' said Gillian, loyally.

In that moment of careless innocence Anna-Meeka felt a great longing not to be foreign. What would she have to do to stand with these children and be counted as one of them? She paused for a moment, wondering about her choices. Change her parents? Stop them listening to this old-fashioned music? Never. Her father would never stop listening to it and going on and on about Auntie Alicia. He could be surprisingly stubborn. Even if, by some miracle, she worked on him, what good was that, there was still the matter of the funny way they talked. That will never change, thought Meeka sadly.

She played dead lions with the children, but now she was desperate for them to leave. She was tired and hot. There was so much clearing up to do. And all the time the army was nearing. Geoff was being very friendly. Sam seemed to like her too. Susan wanted her to be best friends, annoying Gillian, who felt, quite rightly, that it was she, after all, who had *discovered* Meeka. Meeka listened to this talk as from a great distance, thinking about the Hartley Green pieces of bone china on the kitchen floor, and suddenly, she was certain. She wanted them all to go.

But there was still the cake to cut and the candles to blow out. Gillian was calling them to the table. Meeka had never noticed it before but Gillian was really very bossy, and large. She had the beginnings of breasts. As if reading her thoughts, Geoff grinned.

'Bossyboots!' he said, and he winked at Meeka.

'When we get back to school,' he said, 'I'll pick you for the rounders team.'

Meeka grinned. Her grin did not reach her eyes, but no one could tell. Only her mother would have known that it wasn't her usual smile, but her mother was not there, thank God. Not yet. Gillian lit the candles and they all sang 'Happy Birthday' and Meeka grinned again, this time because Jennifer had emerged from the bathroom with a pair of Savitha's knickers on her head and was singing the loudest. She blew out all the eleven candles with one huge whoosh while the children screamed, 'Make a wish, make a wish and it will come true!' before cutting deep into the soft sponge covered in butter icing and thick strawberry jam. And it was like this, caught in the stream of cold air from the open back door, caught like a rabbit in the beam of a headlight, so too was Meeka caught in the icy rays of her mother's astounded stare.

It was clear she had died and gone to hell. Such was the power emanating from that glowing, red-ringed stare that when the front doorbell rang a moment later, signalling the arrival of the parents, Gillian's mother and Geoff's older brother, Marion's dad, Meeka was still standing at the Mouth of Hell. She would stand there for a long time.

'*Lasciate ogni speranza, voi ch'entrate!*' intoned Jacob solemnly when he heard the story. 'Abandon all hope, you who enter.'

He savoured the words slowly, rolling the sounds around his

mouth, delighting in the movement of his lips as he spoke. It was as musical as the warm Irish brogue of Geraldine, his new girlfriend. The richness of her voice was what had first drawn him to her, thick and sleepy as a morning under the crumpled covers on her bed, with him beside her. Geraldine was the best thing to have happened to him and the key to his future success. She was his inspiration, the person who for the first time encouraged him to do what he wanted. She was *the one*. With her beside him his business idea seemed almost a reality. It was almost time for her to meet his family. Although so far he had hesitated, had been unable to mention her name to any of the de Silvas. Partly, he supposed, this was because he needed to be certain this warm, hoarse-voiced relationship was going in the right direction. Although *mostly* he knew it was because his family were so peculiar. He never knew from one minute to the next what their individual or collective responses might be. He never knew what major crisis might be taking place among them. What *drama* was going on that might suck him in. A point perfectly illustrated tonight at this meeting in the White Hart pub.

It was an Emergency. Thornton had been the one to ring him up on this occasion, and Christopher, finding it highly entertaining, was laughing now. Thornton finished his account of Meeka's behaviour and Christopher was still laughing in huge phlegm-gathering shouts, his whole body rocking from side to side. He slapped his thighs, he clung to the table. When Thornton came to the part where Savitha, walking into the house, found her underwear on some white child's head, Christopher seemed to have a seizure. Thornton wrinkled his nose in distaste.

'Holy shit, men!' said Christopher wiping his eyes. 'Holy shit! I'm going to buy the girl a birthday present!' And off he went again hooting like the Capital Express that travelled across the island twice a day. It was not *that* funny.

'*Lasciate ogni speranza, voi ch'entrate!*' said Jacob again, loving the music in the words. 'Do you remember the language teacher we had, Thornton? Back home? What was his name, men?'

Thornton could not remember. There was a crisis in his immediate home, never mind 'back home'. His wife and daughter stood with horns locked, his mother's priceless china was broken, there was mess all over the kitchen and birthday presents that needed to be given back. It was not easy. His head ached.

'If you don't stop making such a noise,' he told Christopher with uncharacteristic fury, 'I'm walking out of this place.'

He had come here for some peace, for a drink with Jacob, not to be laughed at. Why is this jackass here, he thought, resentfully, forgetting he had rung Christopher in the first place. Why is he poking his nose in my family affairs? Thornton glanced at Jacob for support but Jacob was not listening. Is he going off his head too? wondered Thornton, amazed.

'What do you care about some teacher at Greenwood School?' he asked, crossly. 'How many years ago was Greenwood for God's sake?' Thornton shook his head in disbelief, lowering it into the foam of his Guinness. 'Greenwood belongs in another life,' he said abruptly.

A life that had contained his mother and had order in it. This life, thought Thornton raging inwardly, is filled with worry from morning to night.

But Jacob continued to stare into space dreamily.

'I can *still* remember that last afternoon as if it were yesterday,' he told them both, proudly. 'You and I walking along the valley towards the house. There were cream butterflies everywhere, d'you remember, Thornton? They were everywhere, streaming through the sunlight, in between the trees. You said the sunlight was dappled and you were going to write a poem about it! Then you picked some of the azaleas, even though I told you not to. You said they were for Mummy. Now what on earth was the name of the language teacher?'

A great longing, an unbearable sadness brushed lightly against Jacob. All at once, and with piercing sharpness, his forgotten ambitions, and Dante, and his teacher's name came back to him.

'Hugh Wallace-Smith!' he said triumphantly. 'That's it!'

Thornton ignored him. Living too long in the UK had obviously made Jacob soft in the head. I am alone, he thought. Alone, among aliens and fools. And he too felt the gentle hand of the past brush against him.

Christopher, seeing his brother's face, tried to control himself. The old childhood grievances quivered within him. What use were Thornton's good looks here in this country? Back home his looks had got him almost everything he wanted. Here they were all third-class citizens, good looks or not. Here they were nobodies.

But all he said was: 'The girl is a rebel, men. She is courageous! I predict great things for her. Not your medical-school rubbish,' he said scornfully. 'My advice, dear brother, is tell your wife to stop her weeping and wailing. Tell her to stop her bloody shouting and throw her crockery in the bin. Then you must encourage the girl with her music. Let her write down those tunes in her head. She is the future, men. Let her do what she wants, otherwise, mark my words, you'll have trouble on your hands.'

He laughed again in spite of himself, a wild rasping laugh full of admiration for Anna-Meeka, who should by rights have been his and not his pretty brother's at all. And he thought

how strange it was, this feeling of kinship, this sweet tenderness he felt for his small firebrand niece, fighting her way
through the jungle of her new life. How unexpected it was that,
having folded away his old emotions, having given up on his
passions, he should be reminded of them once more by this
child. He had never thought he would feel this way again.

14

FRIEDA BROUGHT THE PHOTOGRAPH IN TO show Alicia. She had no interest but Frieda pretended not to notice. Sometimes Alicia wondered why her sister didn't just give up.

'Look,' Frieda said. 'Alicia, do look. It's a photo of Anna-Meeka, in her new school uniform. She looks just like those photos of Mummy when she was little!'

Alicia did not care. The child was a stranger. She had been born in the most terrible year of her life. The child meant nothing to her.

'I was imagining how wonderful it would be to see them again,' Frieda said, wistfully.

Alicia made no response. She was stretched on her bed, reading. That was all she ever did.

'Alicia, don't you want to do *something*?' Frieda asked, her voice strained. She did not say, 'Don't just sit here reading, day in and day out, hardly going out, never showing any interest in anyone.' She did not say, 'At least you were loved, unlike me.' She could not be so disloyal. But they had these non-conversations regularly.

Alicia waited patiently. Eventually Frieda would go off to finish some job or other. Eventually she would leave her alone. She knew they had expected her to 'pull herself together' long ago. She knew they were at a loss, uncertain how to cope with her. Maybe they had hoped she would find someone else. The thought always angered her. Years had passed, his name was no longer mentioned. She no longer went into the room where the piano was. It was true, she did not go out much but that was because she hated crowds. The problem was she had nothing to say to anyone any more. They thought she was *still* thinking of him. Of course she thought of him, but not in the way they imagined. He had simply become part of her flesh and bones, her skin, her hair. He was in the air that she breathed. Everything was overcast because of it. Most of the last few years had been spent in a colourless vacuum. They did not understand this and so they were frightened of saying the wrong thing. How could she tell them all she felt?

'I'm going to Mass later,' she said instead.

Mass was the only other thing she actually took pleasure in. It was the only music she could stand. But she did not tell Frieda this either. Nor did she invite her to accompany her.

'There's no service tonight,' Frieda warned. 'Don't forget there's a curfew. There was a suicide bomber in Kollupitiya.'

Today was a bad day. Her sister was lost in another world, an unreachable, untouchable world. Frieda sighed. When Alicia had first been widowed she had blamed herself.

'I was jealous,' she had cried in confession. 'I wanted what Alicia had.'

Afterwards, she had vowed to devote her life to helping her in every way she could. But Alicia did not want any of it. She doubted if Alicia even noticed her any more. Slowly, as the years had passed, and her own desires changed, her guilt faded, replaced instead by an uncomplicated sadness for her sister. She looked after her parents. She talked to her mother; for the first time she had her mother's undivided attention, and she found that she was strangely content. In spite of all the trouble around her, in spite of missing her brothers and her niece, she was happier than she had ever been. For the first time in her life she felt more confident than Alicia.

Frieda gazed at the picture of her niece. Anna-Meeka had an air of determination about her. Frieda suspected she was not easy.

'I bet she's stubborn,' she said, laughing a little. Then, when there was still no response, she went out, gently closing the door.

Anna-Meeka did not pass her examination. She did not get a place at the grammar school. Thornton was speechless. Jacob shook his head; things had come to a sorry pass. Christopher laughed his phlegm-choked laugh and offered Meeka gainful employment with the Socialist Party. Savitha said nothing. What was there to say? She had only just recovered from the birthday party. She needed to get her strength back before she could comment, plan a course of action, prepare for battle. Her batteries were flat. She had sent her article to Wickrem Fernando at the *Times* back home only to have it rejected by that island stooge, that corrupt man who was not prepared to stick his neck out and blow the whistle on Life in the Kingdom of the United. Well, that was that. Her writing was rejected, her crockery was broken and she had had enough of Rosenberg and his damn sweatshop. Discarding her slacks forever in favour of her national dress (she should never have succumbed to such a betrayal), clutching her Cambridge Certificate and her newspaper cuttings, she marched on those now famous feet over the bridge to Millbank and into the Department of Environment, in search of a new job. If Thornton could do it then so too could she. Anna-Meeka, listening to those marching feet, that army of discipline moving off, kept silent, having only recently returned from the Mouth of Hell. Common sense told her to lie low for a bit. Instinct made her discreet.

Every afternoon after school, she went to the library, where a beautiful girl with ramrod hair and blue eyes worked.

'Is your dad called Thornton de Silva?' asked Miss Ramrod.

Meeka was wary. Was this a trap? Was her mother having her watched? These days she could not be certain. Only this morning at break she had said as much to Susan (they were going to be in the same class at the new school). So Miss Ramrod mentioning her father was understandably a little unnerving. Miss Ramrod smiled. Her hair smelt of hyacinths and winter.

'It's just that you reminded me of someone who comes in quite often. I thought maybe he was your father.'

'Yes,' said Meeka, deciding to take a chance. 'Yes, he's my dad!'

And she loved the way she said it, like everyone else in her class. Just like Susan or Gillian or Jennifer, straight out and uncomplicated.

'He's my dad!'

Miss Ramrod smiled again. She moved strands of hair away from her mouth, and stamped Meeka's books.

'He's nice, your dad,' she said softly.

Meeka was a little taken aback. Then she too smiled, throwing Miss Ramrod into an alarming confusion. The world tilted. Seeing a sliver of a possibility, the chance of an experiment, unable to resist, Meeka took it.

'We live alone,' she said sadly, nodding her head, 'me dad and me.'

'Ever since me mum died, we've lived alone. That's why I'm often out on my own.'

She smiled once more at Miss Ramrod, picking up her library books, ready to flee, congratulating herself on her performance. Then she noticed Miss Ramrod's eyes fill with tears. Was she that good? Obviously she was going to become an actress. Meeka couldn't wait to tell Susan and the others. Miss Ramrod was speaking again, so softly that Meeka had to bend forward to hear her, and again she smelt the hyacinths.

'Oh, poor man!' said Miss Ramrod. 'Poor, poor man. He must be so lonely.' She looked at Meeka; the smile had vanished as quickly as it appeared. Poor little thing, thought Miss Ramrod, probably the child is lonely too.

'Give him my love,' she said. 'Tell him it's Cynthia from the library. He'll know me. You'd better go home now,' she added, for the little girl was hopping from one foot to another.

Meeka nodded. She was going to become an actress. Definitely.

Dinner that night was unusually silent. Everyone was preoccupied with their own thoughts. Savitha had got the job. Much to her surprise, her interview had been outstanding. Her future boss did not speak in the tongues of the local people but in the kind of English Savitha understood. He had quoted Kipling and welcomed her to the department. Savitha had squirmed with delight; at last, she had found an intelligent person to talk to. Someone she could share her love of poetry with. As she served up the food thinking about her boss, Mr Wilson, the quintessential English gentleman (so different from that rat Rosenberg), she smiled silently to herself. They had talked about Swinburne at teatime and Mr Wilson had offered her a biscuit from his biscuit tin.

Meeka watched her mother peering into the pot of lamb

curry, delving into the rich umber juices, the curry leaves and the potatoes, smiling lopsidedly with concentration. Meeka watched closely; her large eyes were curiously bright and sharply focused. Had Jacob been there, he would have noted the resemblance; Grace certainly would have recognised it at once and Christopher would have been delighted. It was as though Jasper was in the room perched above them, watching with interest. Every time Savitha moved, her smile broadened in a peculiar way. Meeka glanced at her father but he was helping himself to dahl and raw coconut.

Thornton was busy thinking about *his* day. The office girl had come in, looking so thin, so pink-and-white and panty-hoseish, that everyone had commented. Thornton, never having registered her before, was startled. Belatedly he had realised she was looking straight at him. The boldness of the women in this country compared to those back home fascinated Thornton. Savitha was speaking and with a small jolt Thornton realised where he was. He glanced hastily around the room. Then he looked at Anna-Meeka. She was eating quietly, not talking too much for once. It occurred to Thornton that he was still very disappointed with her for not doing well in her exams. The headmaster had told them at the parents' evening how well she had made the transition to her new life.

'She's a perfect example of integration,' he had said.

But he had not talked about her eleven-plus results. When Thornton grumbled to Jacob later all his brother did was shake his head.

'Find the money for a private school, men,' had been his best suggestion.

Meeka, helping herself to a little more rice, tried to gauge the situation. A new tune circled around in her head. She wanted to play it on the piano after dinner. She knew she had been in the bad books for a long time, what with one thing and another, but she had an important announcement to make. Her father was quiet tonight. Even though he never said so, Meeka knew he missed her granny. She knew her mother did too. In fact, she was sure they did not like it here in Brixton. If only her granny lived in Brixton she was sure her parents would not fuss so much. Tonight, however, everything seemed fairly calm. Her father was not shouting or waving his hands about and her mother was smiling in a most peculiar way. Meeka wondered if her face would get stuck if the wind changed. She giggled. Instantly, both pairs of eyes were upon her, her father's suspicious, her mother's watchful. Oh Gawd! thought Meeka.

Thankfully, she did not say it. Instead she said what she had been waiting to say all evening.

'I'm going to be an actress,' she announced, 'when I grow up. I'm going to be like Julie Christie, and I'm going to dye my hair blonde!' She smiled her father's sweet smile, looking straight at them, piercing their hearts with love and fear and a longing to end this nightmare, leave it all right here on the Formica table and go back home. To take their darling daughter back to safety. Civil war or not.

'I think I have talent,' she added, being her father's daughter and therefore certain. 'And looks!'

Savitha gave a hollow laugh.

'We are going to put you in a private school to give you a proper education,' Thornton said pompously. 'Your mother and I are somehow going to find the money. Do you hear me?'

He had not meant it to come out like that, but there, it was out in the open. All his cards on the table. Meeka looked at her mother, but her mother's smile had vanished and she was frowning at her father.

'I went to the library today,' she said, hoping to distract them.

247

'After school. Cynthia said to say hello to you, Dad. She said you were nice. She's got blonde hair and you like her, so why can't I have it too?'

Afterwards, she could not understand what all the fuss was about. Why, for instance, her mother turned her mouth into a dark wrinkled prune and her father banged his fists on the table shouting in the 'back-home' language that Meeka was beginning to forget. Would Cynthia, smelling as she did of hyacinths and winter, like the way her father had curry stains on his nice white shirt? she wondered. Anyway, she had one last thing to tell them. They were not in the mood at the moment. She would make it clear at some later date, when they were less excited. She was *not* going to any private school. There was no way this was going to happen. She would run away and live with Susan, or Jennifer or Geoff. Whatever happened, Meeka was quite clear about one thing. She was going to the local comprehensive school with her friends. In September.

September, however, was still a long way off. There was the summer to get through first. Their first summer in London; a slow, gentle summer of days that would be etched on their minds forever. They had been in the UK for nearly a year. All that angst, all that planning to get here, and now a whole year had gone so swiftly. Thornton looked out from his office window at the tube station with its stack of *Evening Standard*s and its buckets of scentless, forced carnations. He watched the red London buses sailing close to the tops of the huge plane trees and he remembered the glimpses of sea that used to be his view. He sat dreaming of the early-morning swims with Meeka, the walk along the beach towards the crab seller and the snacks in greasy cones that burnt their hands. It seemed only yesterday that his small daughter in her checked cotton dress, a gap in her front teeth, would pull his arm as he nodded off on a rattan chair on his mother's veranda.

'Come on, Daddy, I'm bored. Let's go to the beach,' she would pester.

And all the while his mother had watched them, standing in the doorway smiling, as luminescent tropical light slanted through the green glass of the skylight, gathering in iridescent patches, spreading on the cool marble floor. Alone in the office Thornton shook his head. Everything has changed, he thought, his beautiful face taking on the softness of loss.

They had come here for safety, to give their small daughter an education, a better life. But other things were happening to them instead. He was not prepared for any of it. Having grasped this thing called 'The New Life' with both hands, his beloved daughter was now turning it into something he had not anticipated. I can see it, thought Thornton staring out of the window, they all think I'm a fool, but I can see where it's going. Straight to the dogs, that's what.

Yesterday he had finished early at work. He had forgotten to tell either Savitha or Meeka. He had intended to surprise them by being in the house when they returned, making one of his salads or doing the washing-up. With this in mind he had taken the tube, walked quickly past the park in Kennington, past the new corner shop just opened by an Indian family, past the library (it grieved him now that he had not even stopped here), such was his desire to get back before anyone else. As he turned into the street where he lived, he saw a group of children walking back from school, shouting and screaming, in that terrible unintelligible way he hated. One of the children was a girl with a skirt so short as to be almost indecent and hair like a bird's nest. She was throwing her school bag up in the air, dancing about, screaming louder than the others (singing quite beautifully, Thornton observed), making the other children laugh. It was only as she broke away from the group, taking her key out of her bag, that he registered who she was.

'Bye,' said Meeka, waving at the little group, laughing so much that she could hardly get her key in the lock. 'Bye, see yer tomorra.'

Thornton hung back, skulking behind a plane tree. For a moment he felt ashamed to be stooping so low. It was early afternoon. The roses were just beginning to bloom. Thornton was shocked. Was this screaming harridan he had seen really Anna-Meeka? She had done something to her school uniform, turned it into a miniskirt. And there was something different about her face too, he thought, puzzled. She looked older, somehow. Why had her mother let her go to school like this? What sort of mother *was* Savitha? His own mother would be horrified if she could see the child of her favourite son looking this way. Thornton's anger rippled through the summer leaves of the plane trees. Unable to stop himself, he went to the main road in search of a phone box and some change.

'Hah! It's me!' he said as soon as the phone was answered. 'What sort of woman are you, letting my daughter go to school dressed like a white child? Hah?'

Mr Wilson, who had picked up the shared telephone, listened for a moment and handed it to Savitha.

'I think it's for you,' he said with a small courteous bow.

'Yes?' Savitha. 'Oh yes, what can I do for you?'

'What *is* wrong with you?' fumed Thornton, unstoppable now. 'You have no standards. Money, money, money, that's all you think of. Why don't you stay at home and look after our daughter, huh? She has turned into a slummer!'

'Yes,' said Savitha. She nodded earnestly. 'I quite agree. You'll need to look into the source of it. Try finding the original file.

It's probably in the archives somewhere. Go back to the beginning, I think.'

She put the phone down with a firm little click,

'I'm sorry,' she said to Mr Wilson who, being the perfect gentleman, would never have dreamed of asking her a single question. 'We have some trouble with our plumbing.'

And off she went, to wash her hands in the ladies' lavatory.

Thornton's eyes bulged. What was he to do? His wife did not seem capable of a coherent conversation. His immediate worry, however, was his daughter. All he had wanted to do was to come home early and surprise them both by being there, clean the house, wash the bloody china, read a newspaper or two. Now here he was, a wreck, outside the phone box on the Vassal Road. He searched his pockets in vain for some change, wondering if the pubs were open yet or whether to go back and confront Meeka, or phone that idiot wife of his again.

This was how Cynthia found him. Fortunately she had finished work early, ramrod hair swinging, short exquisite miniskirt that showed off a pair of gorgeous long, long legs, pretty pink lips, pretty handbag, pretty everything it would seem. That's how Thornton saw her.

'You have arrived at a moment of crisis,' he said, going towards her.

Having played rounders all afternoon Anna-Meeka was starving. She heated some leftover chicken curry. Then she made a sandwich, adding some sliced raw green chilli, some tomato ketchup and some crisps. But before she ate it, just in case her mother came home early, she rolled her skirt down from the waistband, combed her hair and plaited it just as she had done before going to school that morning. One thing Anna-Meeka de Silva had learned over the months was the golden rule of not cutting it too fine. Since the fateful day of her disastrous birthday party she knew always to leave plenty of time for clearing up. She removed the traces of the day from her appearance, washed the eyeliner from her lashes and cleaned her teeth for good measure. Then, and only then, did she eat her sandwich. There were two letters on the mat, both blue aerogrammes. One was for her parents and the other was addressed to her in her grandmother's frail handwriting. Meeka opened it slowly. She had not written to her grandparents for ages. Somehow there was never enough time.

Her grandmother's face rose clearly from the paper. Guiltily, she wished she had kept in touch more. She had promised never to forget them all, never to forget her home, but she had forgotten. Her grandmother did not reproach her.

My darling Anna-Meeka, she had written. *I have been thinking about you a great deal, as have your grandpa and your aunties. We've all been wondering how your music is coming along, whether you are still making up your tunes or whether you are busy with exams. I long to hear you play. There is no music here.*

Yesterday I walked to the end of the garden to the bench (near the coconut grove, d'you remember where I mean?).

Meeka paused. Of course she remembered.

You can hear the waves from there, although you can't quite see them. I tried to pretend you were down there on that little stretch of beach, with your daddy. That soon you would both walk up the hill, laughing and shouting, being starving hungry! D'you remember how Auntie Frieda used to scold your daddy for not wiping the sand off your legs? My darling Anna-Meeka, how I miss you all.

Grace's voice came over the seas to her, carrying with it the traces of coconut polish and heat. It brought with it the memory of an almost forgotten language. She made it clear she thought

Anna-Meeka was wonderful. Once when Meeka had told her she wanted to be famous her granny had nodded in agreement. She hadn't laughed, or folded her lips, as Meeka's mother would have done. She had not knitted her eyebrows together like her father. She had simply looked delighted, saying she was *sure* Anna-Meeka could do whatever she wanted to. Thinking about her now, wishing also that she had made another sandwich for she was still hungry, Meeka vowed to write more often to her.

It is late afternoon now, Grace continued. *The servant is out in the yard at the back shaking out some mats. I can hear the coconut man throwing the coconuts to the ground. Do you remember the thambili you used to love? And the coconut sambals?*

Meeka stopped reading for a moment. A strain of music ran through her head, borne on a distant sea breeze. It mingled with the harsh staccato of the crows, cawing in the afternoon as she fell asleep. Grace's loving voice rippled softly. The voice drifted on, telling her of her aunt Frieda and her grandpa. More trouble was brewing on the island.

It is a good thing, she wrote, *your parents have taken you to England. You will be safe there, safe from the terrible violence and corruption of our own people. In England,* she continued, *there is justice. Still, no matter what, Ceylon is still your home, the place where you were born. There is something magical in that because it's where you will always belong. One day, Anna-Meeka,* wrote Grace in her tired handwriting, *I hope you'll be able to return home safely.*

Meeka read swiftly, skipping these boring parts of the letter. She agreed with her grandmother (dare she call her 'Nan' as Gillian and Susan did?), England was fab. Then she saw that Grace had saved the most interesting bit of news for the last.

Your Auntie Alicia is coming to England. I have written to your mummy and daddy separately. We have been able to buy her a ticket at last.

Meeka gave a shriek of excitement. Her memory of her aunt was vague, but because of her tragic past she remained an exotic figure in Meeka's imagination. There was the music and the fame of course, and then there were the shootings.

Tomorrow, thought Meeka, I'll tell them about it at school. She frowned, thinking furiously. It would go something like this: 'The gunman entered my nan's house. He overturned the grand piano, killed a few servants in the process and smashed all the bone china. Then . . .' Meeka paused, her mind racing, 'he shot the mynah bird and shot my uncle Sunil too. Everyone screamed; there was blood everywhere. My dad came in like the man from U.N.C.L.E. and wrestled the gun from the man's hand, but he killed my mum by accident. All this happened long before he married my stepmother Savitha, of course.'

Such was the drama of her story that Anna-Meeka's eyes shone with emotion. It was how Savitha, opening the front door just then, coming in cautiously after work, fearing God knows what in this madhouse, found her daughter. Standing in the kitchen talking to herself.

'What?' demanded Savitha, her eyes darting swiftly around the room, searching for the hidden children, the broken crockery, the mess, the God-knows-what. But all she could see was Anna-Meeka, standing alone, looking very sweet, her hair plaited, her uniform immaculate, and a few crumbs of food on the table. Savitha, shuddering, peered suspiciously at her daughter.

'Where's your father?' she asked.

Meeka shrugged. How was she to know where her father was? Didn't her mother know she had been at school? Was she keeping tabs on her father too? Perhaps he had been having a party. The thought struck Meeka as funny. She opened her mouth to say something and then she remembered the *news*.

'Mum! Mum!' she said. 'Auntie Alicia is coming. She'll be here soon.'

God, thought Savitha in a panic, I better start cleaning this filthy house now! But all she said was: 'Has she got a visa, then?'

Thornton lit a cigarette. Then, with a gesture of exquisite courtesy, he placed it gently between the pretty lips of the stunning Cynthia Flowers.

They were sitting in the White Hart and Thornton was watching Cynthia Flowers sip her Babycham in its delicate glass. The frisky fawn, etched on the side of the glass, looked so much like her that he felt a poem coming on. A feeling of well-being drifted over him. It had been some time since he had felt the urge to write any poetry. Cynthia Flowers, frisky as her Babycham Bambi, saw the light in his eyes and the glow surrounding his beautiful face. It had all been her doing, she thought later, the poor man had been in such a state when she happened upon him. What could she do but take him to the pub? It had taken her some time, to find what the problem was. It was his daughter of course. How he loved her! Heavens, thought Cynthia, he must have really loved his wife. The child was probably a daily reminder of this lost love. Cynthia Flowers was too sensitive a person to ask him exactly how his wife had died. How could she ask when the man was in such pain? She had not yet begun to feel jealous of the dead woman. Not yet. So she did what she was very good at. She listened.

'In Ceylon,' Thornton said, angrily, 'girls don't behave this way.'

Cynthia Flowers, her rosebud mouth very pink and kissable, asked, 'Where is Ceylon?'

'It's a little island,' Thornton said, used now to explaining where it was to the English. 'A small piece of the world, shaped like a teardrop.'

'Oh!' exclaimed Cynthia, covering her kissable mouth with her hand, giggling. 'Is it that bit of land joined to India?'

Thornton sighed and shook his head, momentarily distracted.

'No, men. If it was, the world might take more notice of what's happening there.'

He went back to the problem in hand. The child did sound a *bit* of a handful, thought Cynthia. With the wisdom of her twenty-two years she decided she probably just needed a little mothering. Having listened carefully, Cynthia suggested Meeka come to the library to see her after school. Perhaps she could get her interested in reading the children's classics.

'You are so wonderful!' said Thornton draining his pint, looking thin and interesting. 'You have given me hope again. That I might save my child from these slummers!'

Cynthia gave a small gurgle. 'I just want to help,' she said, downing her Babycham with such speed that all the bubbles went down the wrong way making her laugh some more. She really could not help it. The early-spring evening glowed with promise. Dappled sunlight fell across the empty pub tables even though there had been no sun a moment before. It lifted the smoke in the air in shafts across the room and out through the windows which seemed high and majestic and wonderful.

Walking home, full of Guinness and largesse, thinking about the sonnet he would write, Thornton realised it was getting late. Letting himself into the house he felt a sudden urgency for the lavatory. Savitha, hearing this, thought, Yes, he's been to the pub again. Meeka, also hearing the sound of the flush being pulled, thought, Oh good, he'll be in a happy mood now. Then she remembered the *news*.

'Auntie Alicia is coming to England! She'll be here soon.'

Thornton sat down heavily at the table. He was hungry.

'What's to eat?' he asked Savitha, feeling suddenly exhausted.

'Drunk!' said Savitha triumphantly, as though she had scored a hit. 'I suppose you've been drinking with those brothers of yours? Like father like sons, is it?'

'I am not drunk!' bellowed Thornton, glaring at Savitha's retreating back and at his daughter's grinning face.

'What's wrong with you?'

Then he looked at his daughter again. She seemed normal enough.

'What are you wearing?' he demanded, confused.

Meeka, still in her school uniform, was doing her homework.

'What do you think she is wearing, you stupid man?' asked Savitha. 'They don't wear saris to school in this country, you know.'

Thornton's eyes bulged. He wondered again if his wife was going mad. For the first time in his life he wished he had had a son.

'My father was right,' he informed Savitha. 'Only now do I understand him. A man should have sons.'

Anna-Meeka giggled.

'Respect,' declared Thornton. 'Without sons you cannot get respect.'

He glared at Savitha who looked as though she was trying not to laugh. Here he was in a household of bloody woman all laughing, all completely mad. The feeling of well-being had vanished, along with the inspiration for his new sonnet. There it was. He sighed again and began to eat the rice, the fried green beans and chilli Savitha had put in front of him.

15

AFTER THE REBELLION, NEARLY A HUNDRED THOUSAND people were thought to be dead or 'disappeared'. A stillness fell over the island. It was the lethargy that only follows great violence. The heat in the south had intensified. There was no sign of rain. Everywhere, buildings were deserted, looted, burnt. Those who dared ventured onto the streets. There they found the bloodied remains of unidentified corpses, strewn at the crossroads. In the sprawling white house on Station Road the shutters were closed against the heat and the gunfire. Someone had thrown a brick against one of them and now and then a hinge creaked in the slight breeze. A thin sliver of light knifed through the gap, streaking across the floor inside. Otherwise all was quiet.

The manservant who had been a mere boy on the night of Alicia's wedding came to see Grace. Word had come to him, he said, that someone had been murdered in his village. Murdered and strung high on a tamarind tree. The murdered man was young. He had swung for hours. No one dared touch him or take him down. No one dared even come out of the houses. The shadow of the dead man moved slowly across the ground. Backwards and forwards, backwards and forwards it swung. Carrion crows circled overhead. Silent, at the ready, waiting to swoop, in one graceful spread of talons and wings. Finally a woman, holding a blanket, screaming, inconsolable, racked with grief, had run out. Others followed; they had taken the body down for her. It was her son.

'I don't know if the victim is my brother,' the manservant said. 'We have not seen each other for nearly a year. After I left home we drifted apart,' he told Grace. 'Once we lived together, sleeping close to each other.' The murdered man's mother had gone mad, it was rumoured. 'I need to go to my village, to see if it is my mother. If it is my brother,' the manservant said.

Grace watched him go. He took nothing with him, no clothes, just himself. Grace watched his slim figure in its flapping white sarong walk out into the blinding heat, a fluidity of light around him. He looked like the distant figure from her past, a symbol of all she had tried to protect and all she had lost. Her thoughts moved slowly, backwards and forwards, like the shadow of the dead man. The many aspects of her life no longer surprised her. Only her capacity for loving remained constant. Untainted by time.

'Imagine that poor woman!' she told Aloysius later, visibly upset by the manservant's story.

'Her son's age is immaterial. He remains her child, you know. Her feelings for him will be as strong as they were on the day he was born.'

Aloysius listened without comment, head bowed. He looked defeated.

'However old she is, she is still his mother.'

Aloysius nodded. He went over to check the telephone but it wasn't working. It hadn't been working all day. Sometimes they would go for days with no phone. The last letter from

England had been delivered over two months ago. Savitha would still be writing. She always wrote regularly, especially as she was so much happier in her new job. It was the fault of the post they had had no letters. There was a rumour circulating that it was censored. Other things were happening. Often the generator was broken, often they could not even tune into the World Service. They were cut off from the rest of the world, with only each other for company.

'There is nothing more we can do,' Grace told Aloysius.

'Savitha will be Thornton's rock,' Aloysius reassured her. 'His and Anna-Meeka's. And the boys will have each other.'

This was how they comforted themselves. Outside, the sun was like a drum beating in a cloudless sky. The heat stretched tautly over the skin of the drought-ridden garden. The cook, scraping coconuts in the yard, saw something tossed over the wall; it landed among the hibiscus bushes and fell with a soft thud onto the ground. It was a woman's arm, severed at the elbow, charred at the edges, congealed and black.

'We can't go on like this,' cried Grace. She sounded hysterical. 'It isn't safe here for the girls,' she told Aloysius. 'They must leave.'

'I'm not going anywhere,' Frieda said instantly. 'I'm not leaving you. We are in this together.'

But Grace could not rest. 'They must go to England. I cannot bear it,' she begged Aloysius. You must do something. Alicia has suffered enough; Frieda, you must have some sort of life.'

It was not that easy. The smell of human flesh burning through the night filled the streets, and here and there across the city pyres, piled high with bodies, were openly set fire to. The elephants were not just out of the jungle, the elephants hardly existed any more. Aloysius, silent for so long, found a link from the past. Dodging the curfew he went out. Someone he knew, he told Grace, returning late that night, owed him a favour.

'I've managed to buy a passage to England,' he said. 'But it is only one ticket. What shall we do?'

'Send Alicia,' said Frieda instantly. 'Send her. It might be what she needs. I don't want to go. I will never leave. Don't waste time asking me.'

Who would have said it of Frieda? No one had seen the colour of her stubbornness before. It encircled them like steel cables.

'She is the strongest of us all,' Aloysius said when they were in bed at last. 'All these years, we hardly noticed her in the business of our lives, but Frieda is *our* anchor.'

Alicia did not want to go either, but Grace gave her no choice. A week later, they bundled her up and sent her out onto the harsh indigo sea. Sailing out towards safety. This time, Grace was dry-eyed.

Their second summer was hotter. London sweltered in a heatwave. The garden at the back of the flat in Brixton was a mess of builders' rubble and years of weeds. In July Thornton began to clear it; the sun had given him heart. He would grow a lawn, he decided, and pomegranates, he told his wife. It would be a welcome for his sister.

'How long do you think this weather will last?' asked Savitha, surprised to find herself laughing. 'Haven't you noticed they don't have pomegranates in this country?'

Still Thornton worked on the garden, after he finished at the office and at the weekends. It was light now, long into the evening, a soft violet light, mellow and very beautiful. They had not noticed this before. Last year they had only been aware of the cold. Now, already, they saw shades of colours and splashes of loveliness in this place. One evening, after Savitha had washed her soft-paste porcelain, her blue-and-white willow-patterned dishes, she stood watching her husband turning the soil and clearing the ground as though he had been a gardener all his life. Afterwards, sitting at the kitchen table, with the sound of Meeka playing the piano, she wrote her weekly letter home to Grace.

It is astonishing, she wrote, her admiration reluctant, but growing daily. *Here is a man who had not polished his own shoes until a year ago and now he talks of growing potatoes. Here is man who, in spite of all the odds, is trying to adapt.*

She paused, watching Thornton moving between his rose bushes. Since their marriage she had grown to understand him better. Once, this handsome husband of hers had wanted for nothing. And in those halcyon days the world had fallen at his feet when he smiled. The careless abundance in his life had attracted her. Now, without his family, Thornton had grown smaller and needier. His good humour was fading, he felt diminished. This move had affected them all but *his* unhappiness was the most apparent. She did not tell Grace any of this, but she let her admiration show.

Watching him as he gardens, she wrote, instead, *I see he has inherited your green fingers, your ability to make something of chaos. I wish you could see it!*

Savitha stared at what she had written. She knew now, in the face of Thornton's unhappiness, what she had been uncertain of before. She knew she loved him, but she knew also that he was flawed. Raising her face to the soft summer warmth, feeling how her skin had aged since only a year ago, she thought, And I am the stronger of the two of us.

He's looking forward to Alicia's arrival, she continued. *As we all are.* And she sealed up the letter.

Privately, Savitha wondered how Alicia would cope away from her mother. She had never been close to Alicia. There had never been the time or inclination on either of their parts. Perhaps, she thought, the time had come for that now. The sound of the piano stopped. Meeka had finished practising. Thornton came in with a handful of runner beans.

'If only she did her homework as well as she played the piano,' he said disapprovingly, 'she would be the best in her class.'

'Perhaps we should be encouraging the music instead of all these other subjects she has no interest in?' Savitha said, risking his annoyance.

'Don't start,' Thornton said, his good mood evaporating. 'There's absolutely no future in it. She'll never make a concert pianist, she's not good enough.'

Savitha sighed. She heard Meeka heading towards the kitchen, looking for food. How her daughter was changing. These days she seemed to be eating all the time.

'I'm starving!' announced Meeka, coming in in a great hurry. 'We had roast beef, mashed potatoes and gravy for school dinner today.'

'What's all this school dinner?' growled Thornton. 'It's called lunch.' He washed his hands. 'I'm just going to the library before it closes,' he added. 'I want to get a book on potatoes.'

And off he went, escaping with a splash of aftershave before his daughter could question him more closely or, worse still, insist on coming with him.

Savitha watched him go. Who would have thought it possible a year ago? Who would recognise them now? They were carving a little path for themselves, cutting a small road of near contentment. Bravely. Things are not so bad, she told herself. Many times in the past months she had badly wanted to go back. At nights, often after reading Grace's letters, knowing Thornton's unhappiness, she had wanted to admit defeat, return. Her homesickness had not disappeared, she doubted it ever would, but she knew now that they would stay. Besides, even if they could, there was no life in Sri Lanka for them. Something had gone terribly wrong. Their own people had changed beyond recognition. Their easy-going, gentle temperament had been transformed into an unscrupulous cunning. Some implacable force had taken root within them.

That July Mrs Smith next door began to speak to Savitha. First they had smiled at one another and then slowly, when she saw the de Silvas in the garden, she had come over with little gifts. A few plant cuttings, a packet of seeds, some radishes from her husband's allotment. Shyly, for she was on uncertain ground, Savitha accepted. One day Mrs Smith made a remark about Mr Smith. Spontaneously, understanding the grumble, Savitha laughed. They had become friendly after that, the two of them, with caution acting as a fence between them.

At the end of July, as the summer holidays began, Meeka was once more left alone in the house. Thornton and Savitha gave her instructions on what she could and could not do.

'I'll just keep an eye open,' said Mrs Smith to Savitha. And she winked knowingly. She did not call Savitha by name. She was not sure that she could say it right. Also, as she told her husband, it seemed disrespectful somehow. Savitha was a proper lady in Mrs Smith's eyes. Savitha, liking this small formality between them, felt glad of Mrs Smith's eye.

Meeka did not care. She knew her mother and Mrs Smith were friendly but, well, Mrs Smith could not stand at her window all day, could she? So Anna-Meeka joined forces with Gillian and Susan and Jennifer, and roamed the streets of London whenever she could. It was 1966. It was still possible to dodge the ticket collector and ride the tube, round and round the Circle Line, on a ten-pence ticket. They went with Jennifer's gramps to the old pie and mash shop on Coldharbour Lane and ate jellied eels washed down with cider when no one was looking. They walked along the embankment eating ice creams, and they ran amok in the British Museum. All in all they had a wonderful time. It was in this way that Anna-Meeka began to understand the city, this adopted home of hers. She was certain she would never love another place in quite this way. The smell of the Underground soot and the sight of the river from the top of a double-decker bus were part and parcel of her life now. Sri Lanka was nothing to do with her. It belonged to some other life.

By the time her parents returned home in the evenings she was lying on her bed with the huge sash window open, reading. The librarian had taken a great interest in her and was forever finding her more and more books to read. When she was not reading, the thing she enjoyed the most was the piano. She played it endlessly, her head constantly filled with the sounds of the sea. Sometimes these textures were stormy and full of tempo, sometimes intense and melodious, but always at the very heart of her music was the sea, in all its endless vast expense of water. She played with great concentration. Mrs Kay, her piano teacher, had left before the school holidays. She had moved out of London. Before she left she quarrelled with Thornton.

'Your daughter is very musical,' she had told him. 'She needs nurturing. Music isn't about mechanically sitting exams.'

Meeka, listening outside the door, could tell Mrs Kay was angry.

'Thank you very much,' Thornton said. He was polite but firm. 'My daughter's music is a hobby.'

Mrs Kay gave up. She had taught Meeka to transcribe the short pieces of music she was always making up and she had taught her how to see the sounds as notation. She had refused to allow Meeka to play only her examination pieces, insisting she learned other pieces, tackled more challenging music as well. She did all this with an air of furtiveness.

'Get rid of the scaffolding, Anna-Meeka,' she would say. 'Just show me how you build your musical house! You don't need so many notes to do that.'

Meeka had enjoyed those lessons. She had enjoyed the way Mrs Kay listened so seriously to what she played, her head tilted on one side. Mrs Kay never called these snatches of sounds 'tunes'. She gave then names like 'Study' or 'Scherzo'. And now she was leaving, Meeka didn't want another teacher.

'I don't need any lessons,' she told her parents. 'I can teach myself.'

She mastered the B minor scales. She was learning harmonics, and the results for her theory exam when it came showed she had got a distinction. Uncle Christopher bought her a wad of manuscript paper so that she could write down her pieces. The slow shift, the modulated harmonics and tender tones that she sometimes, accidentally, achieved were what she loved most of all. Thornton, returning from work on these warm summer evenings, hearing these tunes from afar, paused for a moment. Savitha listened as she opened the front door.

Then, as the summer turned a corner, Alicia arrived. Thin, beautiful Alicia, frail as the stalk of a lotus flower, silent and unhappy. She came with letters from home, and dust in her heart, shaken by so many days at sea, disorientated and utterly alone. The brothers were shocked. Savitha felt as though she had brought the island with her.

Jacob found her a bedsit in Highgate and Christopher bought

his sister a record player and some records of her favourite pianists, some orchestral pieces, some opera. Savitha made her new curtains and Thornton had picked all the roses from his garden for her. They greeted her helplessly, for what could they offer Alicia from their own robust lives, what could they say that would give her comfort?

From the very first moment Savitha could see that it was not going to work.

'Alicia doesn't want to be crowded by all of us,' she told Thornton.

What she meant was that her sister-in-law did not want to be friendly towards her. Well, that's that, thought Savitha, folding her lips. She doesn't like me. She shrugged her shoulders. Savitha did not like to waste energy. But she was sorry for Alicia all the same.

'She needs more inner resources,' she told Thornton, firmly. 'It's now eleven, nearly twelve, years since Sunil died. Someone should start talking to Alicia about him.'

Thornton looked uncomfortable.

'She needs to move on,' Savitha added earnestly, wishing only to help. 'Perhaps London will give her some distraction.'

Thornton refused to be drawn. Alicia's grief frightened him.

'Why don't you take Anna-Meeka with you to see her?' Savitha persisted. 'It might cheer her up.'

But Anna-Meeka, too, was strangely reluctant to visit her aunt. She hated the closed windows, the drawn blinds, the hot radiators. The summer days beckoned. Outside were children's voices, a ball being kicked, an aeroplane droning. What was the matter with her aunt that she always had the heating on? It isn't cold, thought Meeka, astonished. It's absolutely sweltering! Savitha noticed her daughter trying to wriggle out of these visits and wished there was something she could do that would help Alicia. Thornton, disturbed without knowing why, made no comment. Weeks went by. Christopher's record player remained untouched.

'You must try to help her,' Savitha said, again. 'Her grief has become stuck. He would not have wanted this for her.'

'I can't,' said Thornton, fearfully.

Then one afternoon, almost a month after her arrival, as Thornton and Meeka walked up the stairs to Alicia's room, they heard the sounds of Mozart's Sonata in A. It cascaded towards them. Thornton, caught unawares, lost his footing on the step.

'Who's playing it?' he asked, shocked.

Meeka paused too, and held her breath; the notes seemed to catch in her throat, crystal clear and bell-like. She was transfixed.

'Is it Auntie Alicia?' she whispered.

Thornton shook his head. 'It's a recording,' he murmured. 'I didn't know she still had it. Your aunt's recording. Before Uncle Sunil died.'

They stood outside listening. The music ran on, lifting this ordinary summer's day, turning it into something suffused with light. The sound resonated in their ears. It wrapped itself around their limbs. It poured from the high, bleak window on the landing, seeped out from the cracks under Alicia's door, it propelled Anna-Meeka forward so that she felt as though she were flying, until at last, looking at her father with astonishment, she cried, 'She plays wonderfully!'

16

AND THEN, WITHOUT ANY WARNING, JACOB, the eldest de Silva, the circumspect man, that dependable custodian of all their moral dilemmas, found he had a small problem of his own. Just when he had thought life could have no more surprises, suddenly he saw he was wrong. Thinking of this delicate matter was enough to bring the blood surging to his face. Jacob's problem showed no sign of going away. If anything it seemed to be getting bigger. He went to see Thornton, wanting to discuss it with him, but the child was always present, listening. Snooping around, smirking just like her father used to, unaware, like her father, of her capacity to create havoc. And in any case, thought Jacob unhappily, if it wasn't the child, it was the mother. Prowling around the kitchen, sharp eyes on the alert. Thornton's family, thought Jacob shuddering, was a nightmare. So he arranged to see both his brothers in the pub instead. Not that *that* made it any easier.

'I don't know how it all happened,' he said when they were settled in their usual corner by the window at the White Hart. It was Christopher's turn to buy a round, which for once he did without a murmur. Jacob was sweating, whether it was because of the heat or the thing he was about to tell them was difficult to gauge. Christopher was unusually solicitous; perhaps he too was affected by the potency of the moment? He hoped Jacob did not disappoint. So often his family made a drama when there was no drama to be found.

'Wait, wait, men,' he said. 'Wait till I get the drinks. Same again?'

'Yes, yes,' said Thornton expectantly. He wished Jacob would get on with whatever it was.

'I don't know how it happened,' said Jacob when they were all settled again.

'Shit, men!' said Christopher losing patience. 'Get on with it!'

'Shut up!' said Thornton, but Jacob was not listening to them. He was thinking back to the beginning.

Was it that night when she had nibbled his ear? Which night was that precisely? She nibbled his ears most nights. That was, he supposed, the problem. No, the problem was, well, in truth the problem was . . .

'She's in the family way,' he said, being unable to think of a better way to put it.

'*Who?*' asked Thornton and Christopher in unison.

'Geraldine,' said Jacob, forgetting they had never heard of her before.

'Who the fuck is Geraldine?' asked Christopher.

Such was Jacob's state of mind that he let this go.

'We'll have to get married,' he said, demonstrating his resourcefulness.

'Have you got someone pregnant?' asked Thornton, catching on.

Christopher, who had been staring incredulously, burst out

laughing. Both his brothers were at it now, breeding like rabbits! Mr Enoch Powell had better watch it, he thought. There seemed an army in the making, with the de Silva family alone.

But he didn't say that. Thank God. Although he did think it was hugely funny.

'You need a whisky, men! A celebration whisky! Unless you are thinking of an abortion?' he paused, interested.

'Sit down for God's sake, men, and stop shouting,' said Jacob nervously, looking about. 'You don't understand. She's Irish!'

'*Irish!*' said Christopher loudly. '*Irish?*' This was getting funnier and funnier. 'In that case you've had it, men. No chance there.' He clutched his neck and made choking noises. 'Better accept fatherhood graciously. I believe it's not too bad,' he added, glancing slyly at Thornton.

Thornton could not understand what all the fuss was.

'Now listen,' said Jacob, rousing himself, 'this is the plan. We'll announce the wedding first. Write home; tell everyone, her people too. Then we'll say she is pregnant. So the baby can be born early. You know what I mean?'

He appealed to Thornton. Thornton knew exactly what he meant, but Christopher was annoying him. Why couldn't the silly bugger stop sniggering like a smutty schoolboy?

Unfortunately there was more to come.

'But why on earth do you want to get married? That's for the bourgeoisie. What's the matter with you, Jacob? Why are you so spineless? This is the age of free love. What's wrong with you, men? You're like an old woman from back home. Stand up for freedom!'

Christopher would have gone on longer but luckily he needed a pee.

'So,' said Jacob with some relief when he had gone, 'that's settled then. We're getting married. Now you must bring Savitha and Meeka to my place to meet her. Meeka can be the brides-maid,' he added, regretting this almost the instance he had said it.

Tonight, he would write to his parents. 'I won't say anything about the baby just yet, so I don't want you to breathe a word to Mummy either.'

'What?' said Christopher, coming back after his pee. Unfortunately his flies were only half done up. 'Mummy won't care, men. Don't you know she isn't like that? Don't you know she doesn't give a damn for stupid bourgeois conventions? Don't you understand? Don't you know? . . .' He stopped. It was clear they did not.

'What?' said Savitha when she heard. '*What!*' and she laughed.

'Yes,' nodded Thornton, 'I promise you, it's true. She's called Geraldine and she's in the family way.'

'Blimey!' said Savitha, forgetting herself entirely and using the favourite word of the messenger boy at work. She couldn't stop laughing.

Thornton's eyes bulged. Meeka, standing on one leg outside the door eavesdropping, was amazed. Her mother was being surprisingly *with it*. Meeka was bursting with a hundred ques-tions. What was this Geraldine like? And why, if she was in the family's way, did she not simply get out of it?

Meeka herself was always getting in the way, always being told, 'Get out of the way, Meeka.' She would like to meet Geraldine. But even more she couldn't wait to see Gillian, Jennifer and Susan. She could hear herself tomorrow recounting the develop-ments when they all went for a wander on the District Line.

'My uncle is marrying an Irishwoman called Geraldine,' she would say. 'Unfortunately she is in her family's way but I am going to be the bridesmaid and I will be telling her what to do about keeping out of it.'

That's what she would say tomorrow, when they were out on their jaunt, and as always everyone would be impressed.

When it finally occurred, the meeting had all the ingredients of failure. Had he been a betting man Jacob would have recognised this. Savitha and Geraldine entered the ring slowly with lowered heads and Meeka entered at a trot. Christopher came along for amusement only. Alicia came but only stayed for a few minutes. She had discovered some small solace in the long walks she went on daily and wanted to be somewhere else entirely. Outdoors, not cooped up in the bare-boarded, damp house that Jacob rented along the Finchley Road. She left to go walking on Hampstead Heath.

It was a Saturday afternoon, a good opportunity for high tea, thought Savitha who was rereading Jane Austen. She knew what *she* would have done in the circumstances. She would have made a cake of spectacular, unbearable lightness. All eggs, fresh lemons and air (imagine, she thought, they have three different sizes of eggs here, even the hens do as they are told!), and then she would have iced it, pink and white. Out would come the bone china, the pale green Copeland perhaps, as it was a special occasion, or even the Spode, for the rosebud teapot was so lovely. Anyway the point was she would have made an *effort*. She would have put on a *good show*. Here was the soon to be married Geraldine, born in the land of Yeats, lucky thing to have such a famous countryman, unlike Savitha who came from the land of peasants. But what did they find when they arrived, thought Savitha afterwards, what did they find? Only Irish filth!

'It's the best I could do!' said Geraldine apologetically. 'You see, I feel sick all the time.'

Shameless Geraldine, admitting the obvious within minutes of their meeting, throwing her large husky voice around, giving out private information then producing a Lyons Corner House cake, serving it on ghastly Swedish-style plates, producing some 'fizzy' for Meeka in a tangerine bark-textured glass. Savitha wrinkled up her nose, declining the cake. Thornton ate some, nervous as a foal, forgetting to smile. Jacob ate a slice; well, he had to, didn't he? Meeka ate huge pieces of the rubbish; it looks so stale and flat, thought Savitha. Have any eggs been used at all?

Meeka didn't care; she just wolfed it all down, swinging her legs.

Poor little mite, thought Geraldine, bet the bitch doesn't feed her properly. Only Christopher was enjoying himself. Who would have said his family could be such fun?

'I say, Meeka,' he said, 'what d'you think of this cake?'

''S good,' said Meeka with her mouth full, helping herself to some more.

'Meeka,' said Savitha warningly, 'that's enough now. You've had six pieces.' And she wrinkled her nose.

'But Mum,' wailed Meeka, 'I'm starving.'

Christopher drank mug after mug of weak tea (there were not enough hideous teacups to go round). It's clear Geraldine doesn't know how to make tea either, thought Savitha. What's Grace going to make of her new daughter-in-law?

'We're planning to go home after the baby arrives,' said Jacob, looking self-conscious. Geraldine dimpled and patted her stomach archly.

'Baby? What baby?' asked Meeka between mouthfuls, wriggling on her chair.

Everyone ignored her. The talk turned inevitably to what was happening back home. A general election was coming up. Christopher had no faith in it and argued hotly.

'It will take more than a bloody general election to stop this war now. That damn Sinhala government is completely corrupt. There'll never be socialism in that bloody country with those Western boot-licking bastards.'

Does he have to swear? thought Savitha with distaste. Though she agreed with him she was not prepared to say so.

Christopher helped himself to a swig from his hip flask.

'Can I try some, Uncle Christopher?' asked Meeka idly, sending him into a spasm of laughter.

'Not on this occasion, putha,' he said, winking at Geraldine. 'This is mother's ruin!'

'*Christopher!*' said Thornton and Jacob.

Meeka, opening her mouth to ask another question, caught her mother's eye and changed her mind. Geraldine stood up. She'd had enough.

'I'll make a fresh brew,' she smiled.

That's just what it is, thought Savitha.

'You look like your daddy,' said Geraldine, smiling at Meeka. The child was on to her seventh piece of cake; did her mother never feed her?

'Mum doesn't like interfering with nature,' Meeka said suddenly.

Geraldine was taken aback. She looked at Anna-Meeka with narrowing eyes. What was the child trying to say? Had her sister-in-law-to-be been talking about abortion? How dare she, thought Geraldine hotly. The child shouldn't be here, listening to adult conversations, repeating things. It wasn't right. Jacko had warned her to be careful. Look out for trouble, was what he had actually said, watch what you say to her and watch your back, she's like her mother.

'She doesn't want me to have a brace,' added Meeka, but no one heard her.

'More tea, Thorn?' Geraldine asked, coldly.

What's all this 'Jacko' and 'Thorn'? wondered Savitha, annoyed, wanting to go home immediately. Who *was* this impostor from the Isle of Poets?

On the tube home, for once, they were in agreement: the afternoon had not been a success. United in the face of change they considered Geraldine.

'What does he see in her?' asked Savitha. 'What on earth will your mother make of her?'

Thornton shook his head. He made a hissing noise through his teeth. 'Of all the women in this country!'

'Did you notice, there wasn't a single book of Yeats poetry in the house?' When she got home Savitha intended to look up her favourite Yeats poem.

Thornton the poet did not mind about Yeats. He had other doubts.

'Her ears are pasted to her neck. It's an old Tamil saying. Never trust a person with pasted lobes. And she's dirty,' he pronounced fastidiously, as the tube passed from Belsize Park to Chalk Farm. 'Why couldn't she comb her hair?'

He was thinking most specifically of Cynthia Flowers and the curtain-of-gold. The lovely Cynthia, who probably awoke each morning, rising like Venus, majestically with her perfect hair. All over her mouth, thought Thornton, remembering her mouth. Yes, yes, he thought, imagining her sleepy mouth, imagining her first thing in the morning. He went into a small delicious daydream. So, no, Geraldine was not a bit like Cynthia Flowers.

Meeka watched her father. He had his silly look, all soft and furry at the edges. She wondered what he was thinking. She opened her mouth to ask him when she caught sight of her mother's reflection in the tube window. Her mother had folded her lips again. It was a good sign, Meeka knew. Her mother was thinking furiously and was displeased with someone other than Meeka for a change. As far as Anna-Meeka could see, this was as good a moment as any.

'Is she going to have the baby before they get married?' she asked. Loudly.

September came in with heavy rain. What had started out as a desperate bid for freedom was now filled with dissatisfaction. When her aunt Alicia had arrived trailing her sorrow like a thin chiffon scarf, the summer had seemed full of possibilities, but now it was over. Anna-Meeka had her way and was accepted into the comprehensive school. She was not unhappy, but you could not say she was particularly happy either. She no longer had any piano lessons and the music lessons in school were useless too. The teacher was often absent and supply teachers, who had little interest in music, took the classes. There was not even a piano in the classroom. Soon after Christmas her aunt Geraldine had had the twins.

'Cousins!' Uncle Jacob had said, expecting everyone to be as proud as clearly he was.

'What a riot!' Meeka muttered with the cynical onset of adolescence, not wanting to visit.

Two identical boys, screaming shrilly. Michael and Patrick, fair as their mother, blue-eyed like her.

'What a waste,' was Savitha's only comment. 'Why waste blue eyes on boys!' She said nothing of this in her letters to Grace to whom she still wrote regularly.

More and more it was Frieda who replied. Grace was having trouble with her eyes, and found it difficult to write.

We are trying to get her to see a specialist, Frieda wrote. *But she keeps saying she doesn't need to, or she will when the war is over. She walks into things around the house all the time. I fear her sight is getting worse. Anyway, I have made an appointment for next week without telling her, so I will let you know what happens. She has become much frailer since Alicia left. Almost as though she was holding on for Alicia's sake. She hardly goes out any more.*

They had been shocked when they heard, unable to imagine what Grace must be like now. Thornton tried phoning. His mother sounded just the same in the few minutes' conversation before the lines went down.

In the end Jacob did not go back with the twins. They were so small and the Foreign Office had issued warnings of the dangers of the war, so they sent photographs instead. Jacob looked haggard and overworked. The twins were a handful and Geraldine was bad-tempered and depressed after the birth. Although she still had her hoarse Irish brogue, his wife was almost unrecognisable. She no longer nibbled his ears under the covers. In any case, no sooner had his head touched the pillow than it was time to get up again.

'At my time of life fatherhood is hard work,' he admitted to Thornton, adding, somewhat reluctantly, 'Maybe you did the right thing, men, by having Anna-Meeka when you were young.'

Anna-Meeka had become quieter. She too had changed. School and her friends absorbed all her attention. Her grandmother, her aunt Frieda and the island seemed a long way away. The war was remote from her daily battles over her schoolwork, her hair and the length of her skirt. Soon her parents' curfew was far more important than any news from back home. Besides, her relatives got on her nerves.

'Moan, moan, moan,' she told Gillian wearily. 'We're *here*, aren't we? What's the use of thinking about a place we can't live in any longer? Why do they go on and on about Sri Lanka?' she groaned.

Gillian was mystified. Meeka's family had always puzzled her.

'Every single time they get together that's all they talk about,' Meeka told her. 'They are so unbelievably boring, so utterly predictable!'

Gillian was forced to agree.

Even Aunt Frieda's letters, thought Meeka, are no longer interesting. Feeling uncomfortable and guilty, without even realising it, her own letters to her grandmother gradually petered out.

One evening, Jacob, in his new busy life as a family man, rang to say he had some news.

'He's coming over at the weekend to tell us,' announced Thornton.

'What now?' asked Savitha, laughing. 'Let me guess, the Impostor's pregnant again?'

'Oh, Mum,' wailed Meeka, 'they're not bringing the bloody twins, are they?'

'*Anna-Meeka!*' said Thornton shocked. 'Anna-Meeka, don't let me hear you use language like that again. They are your *cousins*! This is Christopher's doing, men,' he said, turning to Savitha. 'He's always trying to undermine me, d'you see?'

'Dad!' said Meeka, wishing her uncle Christopher was here. He was the only one of her relatives she could stand.

Jacob and Geraldine arrived with their news. Geraldine carried one twin and her rolls of new baby-fat. Jacob carried the other.

'We've been saving up for the lease of a corner shop,' Geraldine told them proudly. 'Your brother is about to become a businessman!'

'My God!' said Thornton, his voice edged with what sounded dangerously close to envy. 'An Asian businessman. You'll be rich.'

'Well,' said Christopher when he heard, 'he always had a tendency towards being a capitalist bastard!'

Christopher refused to get excited about Jacob. His whole family was a disappointment. All, that is, except his delightful niece. In any case, he was off to Trafalgar Square to join a huge Amnesty International demonstration. Did anyone want to go with him?

The twins were crawling now and Anna-Meeka loathed them. She had been the only child for so long that there was no room in her life for these large bawling infants. One twin crawled up to her when she was playing the piano and bit her leg, making Geraldine laugh her belly-rumbling emerald laugh. Meeka was silent, rubbing her leg, her smile not quite reaching her eyes, swearing silently to herself, saying nothing.

Watching her daughter, wryly, Savitha noticed that she no longer said everything that came into her head. Lately she had begun keeping her thoughts to herself. She is growing up, thought Savitha with a twinge of fear.

It was the end of the decade.

17

ONE MORNING, BEFORE HE WENT TO WORK, Thornton received a letter. It landed gently on the mat.

'Nice stamp,' said Meeka glancing at it. 'Who do we know in Lausanne?' She was late for school.

'Have you seen this?' her mother called out from the kitchen. She was reading a copy of a newspaper over breakfast. The paper was still called *The Colombo Times* but Ceylon was now renamed Sri Lanka. 'The news is terrible! Those bastards in the government are reducing the numbers of Tamils going to the universities now.'

Meeka winced, wishing her mother would not shout so much. Thornton shook his head.

'I saw it,' he said, surreptitiously pocketing the letter, thinking no one had seen it. He was not expecting any letters, but instinct made him secretive. 'There'll be rioting again,' he said.

'It's odd,' Savitha continued. 'We haven't heard from Frieda for a while. D'you think we should phone them? See if your mother is all right?'

'Leave it till the weekend. She gets alarmed when the phone

rings. Anyway, I think it's just the usual story of the post not getting through. We'll phone on Saturday.'

'Don't forget, it's parents' evening tonight.'

'I haven't,' said Thornton. 'Tonight we decide the future!' he added, trying in vain to raise a smile from his daughter.

Anna-Meeka scowled at them both and, picking up her lunch, went out. Thornton followed her. He often walked part of the way to her school before branching off to catch the tube. It was a situation that annoyed Meeka intensely. She would have preferred to walk by herself. She would have liked to wander across Durand Gardens alone, taking in the early-morning mist over the little park, peering in through the lighted windows of the big tall houses, dawdling. Another school year was under way. September was over and October was here again. This time it was not the Indian summer of their arrival. Looking back, Meeka remembered her younger self with embarrassment. She remembered wanting to feel the cold. Now it was cold all the bloody time. And she had nothing to look forward to any more.

They passed Philippa Davidson's house. Philippa was in Anna-Meeka's class. Mr Davidson was standing by his bright red two-seater. He was laughing with Mrs Davidson. Oh yes, very funny, thought Meeka sarcastically. What a bloody funny morning. She imagined the Davidson family, from the time they woke up. Laughing while they cleaned their teeth, laughing as they dressed. Oh my God, how they laughed as they had their breakfast! She could just imagine it. Mr Davidson did not spill his tea all over his jumper or eat too fast and dribble marmalade on the tablecloth, and Mrs Davidson did not shout at him about some bastard in the government. She was sure Mrs Davidson didn't even know the word 'bastard'. And Philippa? She probably had her head in a school book, shining hair tucked behind her ears, a dimple flashing on her cheek as she looked through her homework.

Seeing Meeka as she passed, Philippa turned and waved. In a friendly way.

'Hello, Meeka!' she said. 'Hello, Mr de Silva.'

Meeka scowled, mumbling reluctantly.

'Pretty girl,' observed Thornton as the two-seater drove off. 'Why don't you make friends with her?'

Meeka scowled harder.

'Don't walk so fast,' Thornton said mildly. 'You're not late.'

They parted at the top of the Clapham Road, Meeka turning with a sigh towards school, her father heading towards the tube station.

The tube was crowded and Thornton could not read his letter. Then when he got to work his boss was waiting for him, her face thunderous. Now what have I done? wondered Thornton wearily.

When he had sorted out the problem and apologised again, it was almost time for his tea break. The women in the next office fussed over him, plying him with chocolate biscuits and tea. It was nearly lunchtime before he next remembered the letter, but then Savitha rang.

'Alicia phoned after you left,' Savitha said, sounding harassed. 'I didn't have time to talk to her. The sink is blocked, and Meeka's forgotten her maths homework, again.'

Thornton opened his mouth to speak. Savitha's voice buzzed angrily in his ear.

'What was I supposed to do? I was already late. I couldn't take it in. She had to hand it in today or she'll be given detention. We've got a parents' evening. I hope you haven't forgotten. I hope you're not planning to meet your brothers?'

Thornton's head was beginning to ache. Savitha was like his boss. She could stretch a single complaint into a thesis.

'No, no,' he said, wearily, 'I haven't forgotten. I'll get back early, and I'll ring Alicia, see if everything's all right.'

Alicia had been to a concert the night before at the Royal Albert Hall. The first concert she had been to in fifteen years.

'It was so wonderful,' she told Thornton, astonished.

As they spoke he could hear music in the background. Alicia was playing another record.

'I sat in the front row listening to the Berlin Philharmonic! The choral part was unbelievable,' Alicia told him.

Thornton was taken aback. Alicia sounded animated. He made a mental note to tell his mother.

'We're ringing home this weekend,' he told her tentatively. 'Why don't you come over?'

After he had finished talking to Alicia he rang Jacob to tell him their sister had finally gone to a concert. But Jacob was busy and could not talk. Then he tried ringing Christopher at work. Christopher had taken a few days off to go to a Communist Party meeting in Paris. He remembered his letter, suddenly, sitting snugly in his pocket, but by now his boss was hovering and, although he wanted to read it, he decided to wait. At lunchtime the office boy came to collect his pools money and stayed chatting to Thornton and before he knew it the hour was over. Although mildly curious he decided to save the letter for later.

The afternoon was long and tedious, an in-between afternoon, not quite summer, not quite autumn, not quite anything. Dampness hung around the trees. Thornton stared out of his window rearranging his pens and sharpening his pencils, threading a new ribbon into his typewriter.

Of such moments, he thought, was his life made up. Trivial markers for the minutes, the hours, and all the days of what was left to him. In three weeks it would be the end of the month and he would get his payslip. Briefly, vistas would open up, things of beauty and pleasure, things that were the stuff of dreams. Like the bright two-seater convertible he had seen this morning. Last night, when they had gone to bed, he had asked Savitha, 'Would we have come to England had we known what it really was like?'

Savitha had not answered and he realised she was asleep.

'I am tired,' he had said, softly, into the darkness. 'This endless to-ing and fro-ing every day to my prison in Euston Tower is killing me. What will happen to people like us, so far from home?' he had asked. But Savitha had slept on peacefully.

Looking out of his window he saw thin misty rain break into a shower, sending people scuttling across the street below. In a few short years Meeka would leave them. Already she was an alien being beyond Thornton's understanding, struggling through a private war of her own, wearing ridiculous clothes, speaking with that ridiculous accent, trying to be someone else. Staring at the heavy rain clouds, Thornton shook his head. I will grow old and useless in this tower, he thought, sadly. He still missed his mother. The truth was he had never really got over leaving her or his home. Her presence had given substance to his life; his old home had been his anchor. Without them he belonged nowhere.

I don't want Meeka to have the same fate, thought Thornton, watching the rain dislodge the dying leaves. He glanced at his watch. They had a parents' evening tonight. If only his daughter could have a respectable profession, become a doctor, earn a good salary, *then* she would be safe. It was the reason they had brought her here. It was his goal. Placing a piece of paper in his typewriter, he opened his shorthand notebook and began to work with renewed vigour.

He did not think of the letter again until he was on the tube, caught in the rush hour coming home. It was still raining when he arrived at the Oval and he stood for a moment in the draughty entrance taking the letter out of his pocket, but apart from being postmarked 'Lausanne', there were no other clues. The space for 'sender' remained blank. Something familiar about the handwriting puzzled him and made him nip quickly round the corner to a pub. It was five o'clock on a wet Monday in October. He would have to hurry if he was to get to Anna-Meeka's school in time for the meeting. Savitha would be waiting impatiently for him. Meeka would most likely be playing the piano. Thornton opened his letter.

It has taken me a long while to pluck up the courage to find you again, he read. *So much water has passed under the bridge. But I never forgot you. Then last year, I met a friend of your family and I found out you were living in London and had been for a few years.*

Outside the rain intensified. Thick banks of clouds gathered, darkening the sky. A huge lorry had drawn up by the pub. The driver began depositing barrels of beer, rolling them along the pavement. Someone had left the front door open and a sharp wind rushed in, curling itself around the tables, bringing in the sounds from the busy road outside. A taxi, its engine running, stopped by the traffic lights, an ambulance sounded plaintively far away. Fragments of voices hurried past, rushing out of the wetness. Thornton heard none of this. He did not notice the people coming into the bar shaking themselves free of the rain, he did not hear them ordering drinks or see the pub fill up with voices and smoke. His drink remained untouched as he read Hildegard's letter.

For Thornton was suddenly back on the dance floor. All around, the lights were twinkling in the trees. His father's shouts of triumph as he won a round of Ajoutha, drifted across the veranda. He saw his mother, her head thrown back, laughing, while his sister tossed away her bridal bouquet, as her new husband helped her tenderly into the car. And then, thought Thornton remembering, there was the serious dancing with the curly-haired girl beside him. How they had outdanced everyone, laughing all the way into the garden across the lawn and under the tree where Jasper watched them curiously. While the first moon of the New Year rose and shone all over her golden hair. Uncle Innocent had been unable to take his eyes off her. And Thornton, that younger, dark-haired Thornton, dangling his cigarette from his mouth, ignoring her protests, had thrown her up in the air. Laughing and jiving.

I understand if you find this letter distasteful. I know you have a very different life now, a wife, a child, how old is she? Does she look like you, Thornton?

Again he heard the music. How they had laughed, thinking it a joke, marrying on the same day as Alicia. How careless of the consequences he had been. Where had that life gone? It had vanished without warning and he had never noticed. Every part of that foolish marriage had been his idea, but he had let her take the blame. Never once had he tried to contact her, never once had he said he was sorry.

If there is any chance of seeing you again, for the sake of old times, such a terrible cliché, I know, please tell me. I only want an hour with you, to see you one last time. I shall be in London next summer. I should be glad of that chance.

Thornton looked up from the letter. London, the pub, the evening, everything, seemed strangers to him. He had no attachment here, no relation. Anything might happen, his link with reality seemed suddenly to have been cut like a balloon at a birthday party; it had broken off and was flying free. He looked at his empty glass; he had drunk what was in it without realising. Somehow he was still here. How had he come from that life to this, crossing time zones, sailing past the equator, never questioning where it would all lead, never quite understanding his choices?

Outside the sky had been swallowed by the night. At home, Savitha would be wondering where he was. If he did not hurry, they would be late for the parents' evening. Buttoning his coat against the wind, he walked out, noticing the paleness of the faces around him, as though for the first time. Young and old, hurrying past. A longing so great, a need suppressed for years, rose up and engulfed him. At this moment he wanted nothing more than to go back to where he belonged. To the place where the sun, when it vanished from the day, left its warmth on the land, and the people walking on the street, the *ordinary* people, were of the same colour as him.

This is what I am now, thought Thornton, overwhelmed by sadness. This is what I will be always, no matter what, no matter how long I live. The old cries for home will stay with me forever. They can never leave me now. I will simply live with them. And yes, he told himself, I *will* see her. Digging his hands deep in his pocket, clutching his letter, he thought, I will see her one last time, as she asked. It's the least I owe her.

They were late and her mother was cross. Anna-Meeka stalked ahead not wanting to be part of their argument. The Head of Year was waiting. He was smiling thinly. They were the last parents.

'Fantastic!' muttered Meeka. 'Just wonderful! I'm really looking forward to this.'

'Science,' said her father grimly, as soon as they sat down. 'She must do science.'

There were here to choose her examination options. Meeka

could see he was still fixed on medical school. She stifled a yawn.

Thornton looked at his daughter. Still reeling with the shock of his letter, he scowled. Then he took a deep breath and forced himself to concentrate on the matter in hand. Since he had first sat on the end of his wife's hospital bed holding the newborn Anna-Meeka, gazing with delight at his responsibilities, none of his ambitions had wavered. Many generations of responsibility were in that gaze; many past histories of love passed down at that point; a father's to a daughter, a mother's to a son. It had been this way for Thornton as little Anna-Meeka lay gently sleeping in his arms. So Thornton's determination was not to be meddled with. He could not be budged from his resolution. Not after all this history.

'She must do science,' he said again.

'Well, her test results throughout the last year are not good,' said the Head of Year puzzled, running his finger down the list of names.

'No, no, no. She has to do science to become a doctor.' He had planned her future, step by slow step. Didn't this man know?

The Head of Year was taken aback. He looked at Thornton. In all fairness to him he had no idea what he was taking on here. He thought this was a simple parents' evening. He thought that in a few minutes they would be done and he would be able to go home. How was he to know that he was taking on a whole valley covered in mist and tea and an ancient family home with a lake and God knows what? How was he to know he was taking on Thornton's lost education? He had never even heard of Grace de Silva for heaven's sake. How would anyone in this school, not far from the Brixton Road (he told his wife later as he drank a glass of Eno's to clear his stomach), how could anyone have known what this man wanted?

'They usually want their girls married off quickly, and sent back home to have babies.'

Well, this one was different and it took a while before the Head of Year realised.

Savitha spoke next. 'I don't care if she becomes a doctor or not,' she said slowly, 'but she must have some secretarial skills. Should everything else fail, you know, she doesn't make it to medical school, et cetera,' Savitha waved her hand, 'well, then I want her to be able to get another job. Perhaps she could do music as well.'

'Well,' the Head of Year said, looking doubtfully at the timetable, 'she can't do both music and chemistry. They're on at the same time. So she'll have to choose. If she wants to do music at university we recommend she does one foreign language at least. Possibly two. Does she play an instrument?'

'What?' interrupted her husband, startled. 'No, no, no. Nothing of the kind. We are going to fix private tuition in maths, physics and chemistry. No? So don't you worry about that, men. She will be fine. Just put her into the right classes. That's all we want from you.'

Savitha folded her lips. She was not about to have a public argument with Thornton in front of a schoolteacher. Later on, when they were back in the house, that would be a different matter.

Where, for example, did he intend to find the money? How he was going to pin Meeka down for these private lessons, had he thought of that? The girl was only interested in playing the piano. It was the only thing she did when she was at home. Shouldn't she be allowed to study it?

Savitha glanced across at her daughter. Their arguments had increased with the onset of adolescence. It both puzzled and saddened Savitha. What a sight the girl looked. With her maxi-coat and her eye make-up, her nail polish and her dark hair all over her face. Straight out of the jungle, thought Savitha, half in despair, half inclined to laugh. What were they going to do with her? Here she sat, slumped on a chair, sulking as usual, trouble written all across her brow. Of course Thornton might be right. Anything was possible, but from where she was sitting she doubted there was a future in medical school for Anna-Meeka. Sex, thought Savitha, *sex* was what she saw. Sex would be the next problem. Undoubtedly. Which teacher would they consult then?

The Head of Year was an optimistic man. It was why the job suited him so well. He believed, for every problem there was a solution. Savitha could see he had no concept of the misty hills, those tea-covered valleys or the boys' school her husband had once attended. She doubted if he ever drank his tea from delicate porcelain cups placed on fragile saucers. No, Savitha could see he did not have a clue. So she let him get on with it. Sitting back on the loose-weave blue office chair, crossing her saried legs, she waited.

'Anna-Meeka,' said the Head of Year kindly, a smile crinkling the corners of his eyes, 'we've done all this talking but we haven't asked the most important person what *she* wants from these next two years. Given that your parents want you to stay on, which subjects would you like to take?'

'Dunno,' said Meeka, glancing across at her parents.

There was a silence. In that moment, unexpectedly and without warning, she saw them as if for the first time, from a great distance. They looked so small and defenceless sitting bolt upright in this unfamiliar place. Her father was wearing his psychedelic tie but the expression on his face did not match it. His face, she saw with surprise, looked closed, stubborn. And sad, somehow. Her mother wore open-toed sandals and socks under her sari. She too looked wrong. Like the time outside the school gate long ago, Anna-Meeka saw, her mother looked cold and confused. How *old* they looked. How unhappy. She had not noticed this before. They had changed, she thought, in slow revelation. Suddenly, with blinding clarity she saw them as she never had before, their faces dark and troubled, and in this colourless room, their love for her so utterly transparent, so desperately clear.

A piece of music lodged in her head played over and over again. All day long the sounds had run on in this way, like slow-moving water, gathering and growing within her. She could think of nothing else. It engulfed her, flooding her senses, leaving no room for anything else. It seemed to hold all the colours from their discarded life, all the dazzling brightness they had once taken for granted. It was filled with the sound of the sea. She wanted to get home quickly, to write it down on the manuscript paper her uncle Christopher had given her. She wanted to play it in order to understand more clearly the subtle shifts and changes, and what difference these enharmonics made to the whole. She needed to sit quietly at the piano and let the sounds come to her, flow through her fingers, correcting themselves as they fell into the early-evening air.

'Dunno,' she told the Head of Year. 'I want the science option, I s'pose. Like my dad says.'

18

'THERE'S A VISITOR HERE TO SEE YOU!' Frieda said, unable to keep the pleasure from her voice.

Her mother was sitting by the window looking out towards the garden, waiting for Aloysius to arrive with the newspapers. Every morning he insisted on going across the street to the hotel where he had a glass of whisky. Then he brought back the newspaper to read aloud to her. Grace never complained, although Frieda was aware she worried about her father's safety. Slowly, over the last few years her parents had grown closer. Aloysius had changed after Grace's glaucoma had been diagnosed. These days he gambled and drank only moderately. Although physically much frailer than his wife, he did what he could to ease her path into the darkness, reading endlessly to her, writing her letters and taking over whenever Frieda went out. In the years since Alicia had left the three of them had become a tightly knit unit.

'Guess who's here, Mummy?'

Grace turned towards her daughter's voice. When she spoke her own voice was strong and full of life. Her face remained beautiful. Only her sight, realised Ranjith Pieris, shocked, only that has gone.

'Hello, Mrs de Silva,' he said, taking her outstretched hand, 'd'you remember me?' adding, as she struggled to rise, 'Please, don't get up. I'll sit here by the window with you.'

'Of course I remember you,' Grace said, radiant with delight. 'Of course!' And she clung to his hand.

'You were Sunil's best man. How could I forget you! Where have you been all these years?'

'I've been in Canada, until just two weeks ago, and now I'm on my way to the embassy in the UK. I couldn't leave until I'd seen you all once more.' He would not let go of her hand. 'How are you? How's . . .' he hesitated, 'Alicia?'

So they told him. Over tea, on Aloysius's return, they told him all the news.

'She stopped talking,' Grace said quietly. 'D'you remember how she cried? How she could hardly stand up at the funeral?'

Ranjith nodded. He had been one of the pall-bearers.

'We could hardly hold her down,' Frieda murmured. 'We thought she would hurt herself.' She shuddered. The monsoon rain had fallen, soaking into their grief.

'Afterwards the doctor had to sedate her for days,' Grace said. 'Only it wasn't much good. Her pain broke through.' Black, terrible, rain. 'And then, after that, only silence.'

Ranjith nodded. He could guess how it must have been. He had been about to leave the country when Sunil had been killed.

'I stayed because of the funeral.'

He had visited the house, again and again. But Alicia had been unable to speak. He had gone then, as planned, moving from embassy to embassy. Wandering the world, not wanting to come home. They had not seen him for years.

'I'm going to England now,' he told them. 'For four years.'

'Oh, but you *must* meet them all,' Grace said joyously. 'Can we send gifts with you?'

'Of course, of course. No problem!' Ranjith said, delighted. 'You don't know how much I have thought of everyone here, over the years.' He hesitated. 'I was at the ballot counting when it happened, you know,' he said very softly. 'I *saw* Sunil being machine-gunned down.' He shook his head, unable to go on. They had known that it had been Ranjith who called the ambulance. 'When I accompanied the policeman back here, I could hear the piano.'

'She was practising,' Frieda said. 'I remember it too.'

Schubert, thought Grace. But she didn't say so. She remembered the Schubert, even now. But she had not known it was Ranjith who brought the news.

'How could you,' Ranjith said. 'You were too distraught.'

He had lived with the guilt of being the one that survived, he told them. All these years, he had lived with this thought. They were silent. They had not spoken so openly for years.

'If Alicia will see me,' he said, 'of course I'll visit her.'

'She still won't say his name,' Frieda told him. 'But she is happier in England. Strange, Thornton says she likes being left alone. There's nothing to remind her, I suppose.'

'Maybe we should have sent her away long ago. Soon after it happened,' Aloysius said.

'No.' Grace shook her head. She was certain of it. 'No, no. She was not ready for that. We sent her at the right time.'

They talked late into the afternoon. Many things, previously unsaid, were uncovered. Frieda watched her mother's face brighten and become animated. The sun moved slowly across the sky and the servant brought in lunch. They ate rice, seer fish and murunga curry, followed by fresh pineapple and a slice of Frieda's cake. It was while they were drinking tea that a dull thud was heard. The house shook briefly. There was a harsh crackle of breaking glass followed by a moment's silence.

'It's another bomb,' Aloysius said. 'Another suicide.'

The sky was a hard cut-glass blue; the afternoon's heat merciless. In a moment the air filled with sirens and distant screams.

'They'll put the curfew on again,' Aloysius observed. 'You'd better go, Ranjith, while you can.'

'We'll write our letters tonight,' Frieda promised. 'And get a parcel of things together for you to take. I'll see if I can get some ambarella for Savitha.'

In the four years she had spent in Highgate Alicia had made no friends. She kept away from Savitha. Savitha was the one who had had the child, the husband. She was the one with a life. They had never been close. Thornton, once her favourite brother, was greatly changed, preoccupied with concerns of his own and often bad-tempered. Alicia referred to this change in her letters home.

They are very different now, she wrote. *You would hardly recognise them, Mummy. I feel as though I will never have anything in common with this new generation of de Silvas. I can't even tell the twins apart and as for Anna-Meeka I have the strong feeling she doesn't like me much. I don't blame the child; she used to remind me of things I'd rather not think about.*

It was the closest she had ever come to speaking of the past. Regret lurked in the letter.

Thornton seldom brings Meeka to visit me any more, she continued. *I think he's embarrassed by her sulkiness. Last Saturday I went over there to deliver your latest parcel. I could hear Anna-Meeka playing the piano. I didn't recognise the music so I stood outside their front door for ages without ringing the bell. I suppose it was one of the pieces of music she makes up. It was strange but also very beautiful, and quite complicated. Not at all the sort of thing I'd expect her to be capable of, given her limited musical knowledge. I was reminded of Elgar and also Benjamin Britten and it made me feel bad that I'd never shown any interest in her. Still, it's too late now. When I rang the doorbell she stopped playing immediately and when I went in there was no sign of her. Savitha told me she had gone to finish her homework but I think she didn't want to see me.*

Apart from her solitary walks and occasional visits to concerts, Alicia's letters to her mother had become the only other regular feature in her life. As usual it was Frieda who wrote back, answering for the three of them, sending the news. Then, one day, Frieda's letter had news of a different kind.

Guess who's going to London? she had written excitedly. *It's someone you know! He's a big shot in the government. Can you guess?* Frieda had chosen her words carefully. *He was Sunil's closest friend.*

Alicia stared, her throat constricting. The name sat on the page branding itself into the flimsy blue paper, the 'S' and the 'u' and all the other letters falling into their place, making up his name, with such a sense of rightness, such a sense of loss that time itself stood still again. Somewhere in her head were the harsh sounds of weeping. Beyond this, she knew, terrified to read any further, were all the memories she dared not look at. She paused. Her hands were shaking. Often in the past she had wanted to end her life. When she first arrived in England she had come close to doing so. No one had known and, somehow, she had not. But her depression rarely lifted. The endless years of her widowhood stretched before her.

On an impulse, later that day she wrote back to Frieda. Yes, she would meet Ranjith.

*   *   *

Yes, she thought, that's him.

And she turned to the waitress and ordered a pot of tea for two. Ranjith Pieris had not changed much. He was a little greyer, perhaps, smaller than she remembered, but he still had the same smile, the same round face. There was an air of careful-ness about him, a hint of authority, revealing itself as he threaded his way across the room. He was looking for her. She had suggested they meet in the British Museum for tea among the potted palms, behind the Sphinxes. Alicia loved the Sphinxes, the great dark obelisks, the ancient gods. Often before a concert she would while away an hour or two in their enigmatic pres-ence. Like them she too waited for the end of time. The women in the café knew her now, knew all she wanted was a pot of tea, or at most an egg-and-cress sandwich. She looked as though she might have been somebody once, they decided. It was hard to say why. Perhaps it was in her face, perhaps it was the way she moved, or maybe it was simply that she never seemed to notice anything: their glances, the glances of others, the occa-sional smiles of curiosity.

She must have been lovely too, they remarked, this enigma-of-the-café.

'She's *still* lovely,' said the chef. 'With those large eyes, those high noble cheekbones!' he said, half in love with her.

But Alicia never smiled. She always looked cold, even in summer. Like some small bird, a sparrow who had strayed in for a crumb, a sliver of something, but who knew it could not settle here, she came and went. They watched her before going to take her order, gazing at the soft fineness of her faded sari. She was so unlike the other Asians that came in. Their resident sparrow. Belonging to the museum, coming early, staying late and always, so the invigilators reported, always wandering through Egypt.

Today seemed at first to be no different. She came in quietly.

'Ah,' the waitress murmured, 'she'll be wanting egg and cress, a glass of water, and then her tea.'

She had her book with her; it fell open at the page she wanted, marked out by a blue aerogramme. Today, although she opened her book, she seemed restless, searching the room, her eyes a great beam of light moving up and around, first to one side and then another, pausing always by the entrance to the café. From this, they deduced, she was waiting for someone.

Ranjith Pieris saw her a second after she had ordered the tea and broke into a smile. She's aged, he thought, shocked, moving towards her. And he folded her in his arms tenderly, with something of the love for them both, Alicia and his dead friend.

'Alicia!' was all he could say; too much clamoured for attention between them. They stood, their hands tightly clasped as they once had when he visited her backstage after a particularly fine performance. It had been on the occasion of Alicia's engagement. Ranjith had come with Sunil, bringing flowers. She had teased him then, saying it was his fault for introducing Sunil to music. Their children would blame him, she said, when they were old and quarrelling with each other. Now he knew they were both remembering these words as they stood among the tables, with the china clattering and the tea urn bubbling, and the voices of tired children clamouring for a drink.

'Let's have some tea,' said Alicia. Agreeing to this meeting had shaken her but it was nothing to how she felt on coming face to face with Ranjith Pieris. Knowing this, Ranjith sat down with her holding her hand, and drank the tea and talked of other things easily, letting it run on, about the troubles on the island.

'How's Jacob?' he asked. 'And Thornton? What's Christopher up to?'

Alicia smiled and shook her head. 'Where do I start! How long are you in England for?'

'Four years,' Ranjith said. 'Plenty of time to meet up. I'm staying with Robert Grant in Canfield for a while, just until I find my own place. D'you remember Robert Grant?'

'Ah,' said the café staff to each other, 'the little sparrow has found love!' They meant no harm; it was just the way it looked from where they stood serving teas.

'Who?' asked Alicia gratefully, for he was pressing on her wound and the floodgates trembled. They could spring open of their own accord at any moment she knew. 'I don't know the name.'

'Yes,' said Ranjith, still holding her hand, giving the café staff hope. 'Yes, you played at the party for his father at the Governor's house. Remember? The night of the riots that Christopher was involved in?'

'Oh! Yes,' she said too quickly. Now she remembered. 'Robert Grant, was that his name? Didn't he use to be Thornton's friend?'

'Everyone was Thornton's friend,' Ranjith said, smiling broadly.

'Well, you should see Thornton now,' Alicia warned. 'I don't think he has any friends. He married,' she hesitated, not knowing how to describe Savitha. 'He has a beautiful wayward daughter,' she said instead.

'Remember Hildegard?' Ranjith said.

'Oh Hildegard! Mummy saw her off pretty quickly!' and Alicia laughed softly, thinking, yes, there were other, good things she could talk about after all.

'Thornton is very different, now,' she said. 'His daughter's changed him. He's very serious. Bringing up Anna-Meeka is a serious business!'

Ranjith looked at her with amazement.

'It's true,' Alicia said.

'Oh, I want to meet all of them again,' Ranjith said delightedly. 'And the wives, tell me about the *Irish* one. She's had twins, hasn't she?'

He looked at Alicia, searching her face for the clear-sighted girl he had once known. Wondering, fleetingly, what had happened to the music.

They talked and talked. About Grace and Aloysius and Frieda. And the light coming in from the high windows, curved and elegant, faded to a thin rosy glimmer until the bell heralding closing time rang, and rang again. The staff in the tea room clattered away the cups, and saucers and plates, until, at the third and final ring of the bell the huge fluorescent lights flickered off. They left through the side entrance. Maybe the sparrow will be happy now, the staff said again, taking off their aprons, hoping it was so. And the Sphinx slept, and the obelisk slept, and all the ancient gods from the Middle Kingdom slept, while the tiny magic eye of the security system kept watch over all of history and its memories trapped like so much dust in the fine midsummer air.

'She seemed diminished,' Ranjith told Robert Grant later that evening. He had arrived at the Grants' country home in Canfield by train after saying goodbye to Alicia. Dinner had been served in the elegant candlelit dining room, for Robert now lived in grand style, although traces of the boyish youth still remained, nurtured by his wife, Sylvie, even as he rose up the political ladder. During the week he stayed at a flat in London, working, dining afterwards at the Athenaeum Club, rarely coming home.

Tonight, however, was an exception. Tonight he was home in honour of Ranjith, the new Undersecretary of State for the Sri Lankan government.

'Tinpot Undersecretary!' Robert had greeted Ranjith teasingly. He was fond of Ranjith, having spent some happy times in Sri Lanka with him when he was not with the de Silva family.

'I had no idea any of them were here,' he said as they paused over the port and the golden bowl of summer fruit. 'Why on earth didn't they contact me?'

Ranjith shrugged. How to explain the fierce pride of the island's elite, their sense of loss since war broke out?

'You must understand, Robert, Sri Lankans are complex. You fellows on the outside see Sri Lanka as an appendage of India, but you know, it has a legal code introduced by the Dutch. And then of course it had the British.' He sighed. 'Two thousand years of Buddhism interfered with, gone wrong. God, what a mess! There's a lot of despair among the old, wealthy Tamils. Shame too, over the way things went when the British left.' He paused, searching for the right words. 'The personal tragedies of the de Silvas are mirrored all over the island, you know,' he said, at last. 'There's been a huge loss of dignity, a sense of alienation. Everyone there is depressed to a greater or lesser degree. It wouldn't have occurred to any of them to look you up. They were too busy surviving.'

The telephone rang and Sylvie went to answer it. Robert poured more port into Ranjith's glass.

'Is anybody taking care of Alicia?' he asked.

Ranjith looked at him sharply. Sometimes Robert had no imagination.

'She has everything except the one thing she can never have again, Robert.'

Robert was silent. He remembered how beautiful he had thought her.

'Schubert,' he murmured. 'I remember her playing Schubert.'

'Yes.'

'One of the sonatas? Which was it?'

'She was very talented,' Ranjith said.

They were both silent.

'What about the other sister, what was her name?'

'Frieda? Oh, Frieda's wonderful,' said Ranjith warmly.

'Ah yes. Frieda. I remember!' Robert smiled. 'I met her first, did you know?' He would like to meet them all again. 'And Thornton, beautiful, charming Thornton. I can't imagine him with a daughter!'

Ranjith laughed. Neither could he.

'Look, I'd like to see them again,' Robert said. 'Can you organise something?' He thought for a moment.

'The garden parties will be starting up soon. Your embassy people will be invited, I expect. Why don't you bring the de Silvas? Come to supper afterwards. Sylvie would love to arrange it, wouldn't you?' he said, turning to his wife who had walked back in.

'Yes, of course,' agreed Sylvie. She was happy for Robert to indulge in a little flash of nostalgia. Theirs was a marriage of great good sense.

So it was decided. Those de Silvas who wished it would come as Ranjith's guests. Which was how Alicia, Christopher, Jacob, Thornton and their families received invitations to attend a garden party at Buckingham Palace.

19

'GARDEN PARTY?' ASKED GERALDINE, PAUSING AS she strapped the twins into their pushchair. 'To be sure, I'll not be going to any garden party.' She snorted. 'The very idea of it! What in the world are you thinking of, Jacko?'

She had been unable to find any smart clothes to fit her since the twins were born and they were three now. Besides, why should she have anything to do with that stuck-up bloody de Silva family?

'Not your little brother Thornton of course,' she added dimpling. 'Ah sure, he's sweet. And not Christopher, he's just like a naughty boy.' No, it was Savitha she could not stand. 'Little bitch,' she said richly. And the daughter was no better.

'Stuck-up cow. With her "*music*"!' said Geraldine. 'I know the girl hates m'darling boys.'

So, no, Geraldine was not going to any feckin' garden party.

'Good!' said Savitha satisfied. 'Then I'll go.'

It would be a chance for her to see how the rich lived. She wasn't clear whether she meant Ranjith and those from the embassy, or the British aristocracy. She asked her boss for time off.

'We're going to a garden party at Buckingham Palace,' she said, as though taking time off for the dentist.

Her boss, that delightfully old-fashioned Mr Wilson, bowed low and called her Lady Savitha.

'You're all damn hypocrites, men,' Christopher sneered. 'Of course I'm not going. Who d'you think I am? That idiot Ranjith *knows* I'm a Marxist, a man for the underdog, a man of the people. Anyway,' he continued loudly, 'as it so happens I shall be selling the *Socialist Worker* in Trafalgar Square on that afternoon.' He grinned at Thornton's surprised look. 'No, men, the short answer is I'm not going. You couldn't lend me ten pounds, could you? I'll pay you back next week?'

'All right, if I must,' said Alicia, reluctantly.

'Oh no,' said Meeka in despair, 'what on earth shall I wear?'

It was all very well for Thornton; he just went down to Burton's and pointed. Then he came home again and had a shower. With his looks, all he needed was a shower.

'Who's paying for all this?' asked Savitha, whose own wardrobe was proving problematic.

Every time she decided on something to wear she was met with shrieks of horror from Anna-Meeka. Really, they're both a pain, thought Savitha, groaning inwardly. What was *wrong* with a yellow sari, red jacket and a yellow cardigan? Was she meant to freeze? Did the Queen freeze? No, of course not. Neither would Savitha then. What was wrong with this family?

'I'm beginning to wish I hadn't been so eager to go,' she said out loud.

But what could she do now? Everyone at work knew. They wanted a daily progress report on the state of her wardrobe.

Her nickname, Lady Savitha, seemed to have stuck. Secretly she was enjoying all the attention.

Meeka began sorting her clothes out. There was her long patchwork skirt, her skimpy cheesecloth shirt and a fringed shawl. Thornton's eyes bulged at the sight.

'Are you planning on seeing the Queen dressed like that? Are you planning on completely disgracing your father then?'

Savitha waited until he had finished shouting. Then she spoke, quietly.

'You're wearing a sari,' she declared. 'It is time to begin wearing your national dress. You're a Sri Lankan girl and you're old enough now. What better occasion than this? We'll go to Soho to choose one.'

She spoke firmly. Meeka opened her mouth to protest but no protest emerged. It seemed she knew when she was beaten. Thornton looked at his wife with amazement. She had turned her lips into a folded paper bag again.

Ranjith sent them personal invitations. Included were two stickers with large yellow crosses on them, to be placed on the windscreen (both front and back) of the car. It would allow them through the traffic lights at Trafalgar Square, and through Admiralty Arch, and on into Birdcage Walk. Meeka stared at the stickers.

'Where's the car?' she asked, aghast.

'Where's your bloody CD number plate, men?' laughed Christopher, when he was told.

Thank God *he's* not coming, thought Thornton distastefully. But there was still the matter of the car. Meeka in wild despair (they simply *must* go now, how was she to face her friends if they didn't?) suggested her father learn to drive.

'Don't be foolish, child,' said Thornton forgetting himself. He was already under too much pressure from Savitha.

Geraldine, taking the twins to playgroup, hearing of the latest crisis, was glad *she* wasn't going. The zip from the last pair of jeans she would ever wear had finally given up the ghost and broken today.

'It's the end of an era,' Geraldine told the boys with a flourish of her hand. Tomorrow she and Jacko would be signing a contract for the lease on a newsagent's shop along the Finchley Road. One door closes, another opens, she sighed throwing her jeans away. What did she need a garden party for? She would be stocking her shop with important things like Andrex while the rest of the de Silvas were wasting their money on a stupid fantasy.

In the end Thornton resolved the problem by walking into the taxi rank along the Brixton Road and ordering a taxi for the great day.

'Where to, mate?' asked the man in the office.

'I beg your pardon?' said Thornton, confused.

'Where to? Where do you want the cab to take you?'

'Oh, I see,' said Thornton, relieved. 'Buckingham Palace please.'

'Did you 'ear that, Steve? This coloured bloke who's just came in ordered a cab for next Thursday to take 'im to Buckingham Palace!'

'Yeah?'

'Yes,' said Thornton, looking worried.

'Perhaps 'e's going to see the Queen, Bill. Charge 'im double!'

The de Silvas handed their invitations to the footman.

'Dr and Mrs de Silva, and Miss de Silva,' announced the footman. 'Mrs Alicia Pereira.'

Thornton was thrilled. He did not show it but he was. The footman had called him *Doctor*. He walked along the red carpet looking down at his feet, veiling the pleasure in his eyes.

'Where are you going?' hissed Savitha, pulling at his arm as he veered slightly off to the left.

'Dad!' said Meeka, and she giggled. 'Now you're a doctor I don't have to become one!'

Savitha's lips twitched.

Outside a small group of musicians were playing something she recognised. Meeka began tapping her foot. She felt uncomfortable in her sari; it threatened to unravel at any minute, all six yards of it. Serve her mother right if it did. What a fright she must look. Even Uncle Christopher had given her a funny look. Luckily none of her friends had seen her. There had been another almighty struggle this morning over her mother's cardigan. Meeka had ranted and raved.

'Like mother, like daughter,' Thornton had complained, wearily.

Glancing at him, Savitha noticed a piece of paper sticking out of the back of his collar.

'Go and check your father,' she whispered urgently to Meeka. 'I think he's got the label hanging from his collar! Quickly, Meeka, go, before anyone sees him!'

Anna-Meeka went over to where her father stood gazing at the lawns that sloped down to the water. She tried to walk like her mother and her auntie Alicia, without tripping up.

It was in this way that Ranjith Pieris first saw them. Father and daughter, arm in arm beside the lake in the grounds of Buckingham Palace. Meeka, her head thrown back, laughing at Thornton for wearing a price tag when he went to see the Queen. All around them was the gentle murmur, the subdued hum of voices. A pair of swans flew smoothly overhead. Women in pastel silks, the ribbons on their hats fluttering gently, stood tall as beanpoles. Men in morning dress, their laughter deep-throated and benign, balanced delicate cups of tea and plates of tiny cucumber sandwiches or bowls of strawberries and cream. Music played.

'So, Thornton,' said Ranjith, coming up unnoticed, placing a hand lightly on his old friend's shoulder, 'we meet again. After how long? Now tell me, who's this beautiful woman you are with?'

Meeka grinned. She looked around for her mother but her mother was staring at her cup of tea. Savitha turned the saucer over and peered at it and then she held it up to the light.

'Look at Mum!' Meeka said suddenly, tugging at her father's arm. 'Any minute she'll turn the cup over and the tea will spill all down her sari!'

Thornton frowned, ignoring her.

'Chi, Ranjith!' he said.

And he smiled his old smile, reminding Alicia of those distant days. The music changed tempo. Visitors queued in the marquees for another cup of delicious Fortnum & Mason's tea.

Crown Rule! thought Savitha, looking at the royal crest. Somehow the thought had lost its sting in the face of so much elegance. Grace had sold a dinner service with the de Silva crest on it to pay for Alicia's passage to England.

'This is my daughter, Ranjith,' said Thornton, barely managing to keep the pride out of his voice. 'Meeka, this is an old friend of our family.'

Meeka looked at the man. 'I'm sorry,' she said giggling, 'but I think my bloody sari is about to fall off!'

'Chi!' said Thornton, annoyed, losing his feeling of pride. And forgetting for a moment where he was, he glared at Meeka. Why did the child have to *say* such things? He looked around for Savitha to take her off his hands, hissing at her, but Savitha, deep in a blissful dream, was ignoring him. Ranjith Pieris was entranced. He could not take his eyes off Anna-Meeka.

'Goodness me,' he said admiringly, 'she's a younger version of Grace!'

Thornton took a deep breath. He wanted to tell Ranjith that having a daughter was not an easy business. No one, he wanted to say, not even Savitha, understood the things that could go wrong.

'I'm starving,' said Meeka, interrupting his complaints and smiling his smile. 'I'm going to get a sandwich, with Auntie Alicia.' Picking up her sari with the unconscious elegance of many generations, she walked away.

'Yes,' Ranjith agreed watching her go, puzzled by Thornton's new capacity to worry. 'Of course there'll be problems, but still, what an extraordinary thing it is, to see your mother, in such an unexpected place!'

He laughed with sudden joy at the thought of Grace here in the grounds of this quintessentially English garden, with its skylarks, its delicate flowers and its understated beauty.

She's lovely, thought Robert Grant, and no, Ranjith was wrong, Alicia was not diminished at all, just a little lost, and *still* so lovely. Feeling his heart constrict with pity, he went towards her. She was standing with her niece and for a split second Robert was taken aback. Turning, Alicia saw his mistake and she too smiled.

'Yes,' she greeted him, before he could speak, 'she looks like Mummy, doesn't she? Meeka, this is an old friend of our family, Robert Grant. Robert, my niece.'

Meeka gave an exaggerated sigh. The place was crawling with 'old' family friends and she didn't want to speak to any of them. Her aunt had been telling her about a recent concert she had been to. It had been a rare moment of connection but the old man had interrupted them. Bloody nuisance, thought Meeka, peevishly.

Savitha, watching from a safe distance, could see exactly what was going on in her daughter's mind. She folded her lips. It was safest to keep well away. She was having a wonderful time and planned to buy some new china tomorrow. Would the woman in the arcade know where she might get some Wedgwood like this? Savitha would be quite happy with seconds provided they were papery thin. She wondered if anyone would notice if she turned her plate over again and had another look at the mark.

The afternoon wore gently on. At some point the music stopped and the sound of clapping rose in the air. It floated across the lawns, delicate as willow on leather, overlaying the distant hum of London traffic. Then, magically from nowhere, the royal party entered. Meeka watched, mesmerised. But the Queen was so small, she thought, amazed. And was that *really* Prince Philip looking exactly like his photograph? The guests with green tickets joined a privileged curtsying queue. A small Asian woman, the High Commissioner's wife, was talking to Princess Anne.

'She has done a lot for the Girl Guides,' whispered Ranjith.

'Look, the Queen Mother has a plaster on the back of her calf,' Meeka said, delighted without quite knowing why.

'Will you have dinner with me?' Robert was saying to Alicia, hoping she would not refuse.

'Yes,' said Alicia, breathlessly.

Ranjith turned to look at Thornton's daughter again.

But she's beautiful, he thought with wonder. Really, he chided himself, what is wrong with me?

Everything seemed a little flat after the garden party, like a calm sea, but without the sun on it. Thornton went back to work, travelling the lift to the top of his glass tower. In a few weeks he had agreed to meet Hildegard. They had been in contact several times by letter and had planned to meet at Liverpool Street station. There were other things on Thornton's mind too. Ever since the garden party several people had remarked on Anna-Meeka's appearance. Even Jacob had brought up the subject.

'Isn't it time the girl was introduced to a suitable young man?' Jacob had asked. Adding caustically, 'Before she finds something unsuitable herself' (knowing Meeka it *would* be unsuitable), 'bringing it into the house of her own accord?'

Thornton groaned. 'What am I supposed to do?' he asked. 'She needs to pass her exams and get to medical school. I can't think about a suitable boy just yet.' This child of his had been nothing but trouble. 'Why can't she show some interest in her schoolwork? In physics and chemistry? Why is the only thing that interests her the piano?' He was working himself up into a fury. 'You're good at giving advice,' he said, bitterly. 'Send her to private school, find her a husband. Make sure she has a career.'

'But Thornton, the two things are not incompatible,' Jacob told him, earnestly. 'Women can have a career and marry, you know. Look at Geraldine, she more or less runs the shop, you know.'

Thornton had no wish to look at Geraldine. The idea of broaching the subject of a suitable boy with his daughter filled him with fear. He imagined Meeka with that big mouth of hers, hooting with laughter at the very idea. Popping a Rennie into his mouth he hurried home to see what Savitha would say.

'I know we didn't have an arranged marriage,' he began, sitting in the kitchen, watching Savitha prepare the food. 'But we were living at home then. Here you don't know what sorts of fellows there are.' He paused and cleared his throat.

'So, what are you planning then?' asked Savitha, when he recounted the conversation.

'Planning, planning?' Thornton said, instantly furious. 'I'm not planning anything, I'm *asking*. Can't you tell the difference?'

Savitha folded her lips. Years ago, when they were still living in Sri Lanka and Anna-Meeka was a baby, she had had a discussion with Grace. Long before the subject had even entered Thornton's head, her mother-in-law had told Savitha something she had never repeated to anyone else. She had never forgotten the story. It had made a deep impression on the romantic Savitha who wanted a love match for her only daughter. Something complete and perfect, something everlasting, was what she wanted for Anna-Meeka. She had decided this many years before. She did not want a marriage chosen by horoscopes or planetary influence. She did not want a marriage founded on superstition or the time of her birth. It was all such nonsense; she wanted her daughter to marry for *love*. One day she hoped Meeka would find happiness with a person of her own choosing. Savitha had no intention of voicing any of this and there was little use telling her besotted husband anything at the moment. In any case, she knew, he was simply frightened; he did not want Meeka to get hurt. Well, there's nothing we can do to stop that, thought Savitha. So instead, to take his mind off his worries, she said experimentally, 'Well, she has been menstruating for two years now, so you better start looking straight away!'

Thornton spluttered. He turned red. Who would have thought he would develop a temper in early middle age?

'Aiyo!' he shouted, with disgust. 'When did you become so coarse, woman! You're just like Christopher.'

Savitha turned her back to him. Her shoulders shook with silent laughter.

'What's the problem?' she asked. 'Do you think it's not about sex then?'

Anna-Meeka walking into the room just at that moment confused Thornton further. He glared at her. Meeka raised an eyebrow.

'Mum, he's flipped,' she cried. 'Being called "*Doctor*" by that footman in Buckingham Palace has affected him!'

Savitha burst out laughing. Oh good, thought Meeka, at least we've got a happy mood in the kitchen. She wondered if this was the time to talk about the skirt she wanted to buy. Increasingly she was becoming interested in the differences between her parents' wishes and her own desires.

But the moment was not right. The garden party had had a profoundly disturbing effect on Savitha. She had gone to the arcade in search of the papery bone china she had seen at Buckingham Palace, but instead all she found was a crude imitation of the real thing. She would find nothing like it ever again. The day itself and all its luxury had vanished but the feeling of elegance was still with her. It lingered elusively in her mind in the weeks that followed, surrounding her like a mist of fireflies. Everything seemed to be touched with this new discovery. Nothing was real any longer; all was insubstantial. For on that afternoon, in the palace grounds, Savitha had caught a glimpse of something different, something that had been completely invisible until now. It gave context to this thing they called Empire and to the people who once had ruled their country. With a shock she realised that only by leaving her home could she have seen any of it. For distance, thought Savitha, was what had been needed, distance had sharpened her perspective, revealing many hidden truths. Distance had brought her to this point. Here it was then, unchanged by the centuries, distilled down and concentrated. On a perfect June afternoon, with the roar of traffic a faint smudge beyond the palace walls, with the sun so gentle, and the flutter of well-pressed linen all around, here, in this privileged corner of England, was the thing she had until now only intuited. Forcefully, she glimpsed it; effortlessly, she understood. Never had she had this capacity to connect in such a way before. Never would she see it so clearly again. For history, thought Savitha, *history* was what made you what you are. History was what made you feel at ease with yourself. History gave you a solidity, a certainty, in everything you did. She had thought they were escaping to a place they could call their own, but now, she saw, this could never be.

In that moment, all her ideals, all her hopes for their life on foreign soil, seemed as nothing. We are nobody, she thought with silent pain. It was so simple. We are displaced people. *They* had no history left, for carelessly they had lost it along the way. Escaping with their passionate ideals, they had arrived here. Hoping. Hoping for what? Acknowledgement perhaps? Understanding, maybe? But she saw it was for *them* to understand. We belong nowhere, thought Savitha in despair. No longer certain, she hesitated, wondering what she might do. She was halfway through the journey that was her life, middle age beckoned; the monsoon heat was seven thousand miles away. Suddenly she felt a great longing for the connections they had shed so lightly, the old certainties of her youth, the simplicity of it all. Looking at her daughter's young face, seeing the struggle ahead, saddened, Savitha kept her own counsel.

The summer wore on but it was disappointing; low clouds crossed the Atlantic, the sky was overcast. The promise of June would not be delivered. On the news it was reported that suicide bombing continued in Sri Lanka. Two British journalists, sent to cover the war, had been captured and were reported missing. Outside in Thornton's garden, rain splattered the roses to the ground. Late one evening, a telegram arrived. Grace had died peacefully in her sleep.

20

FROM THE BEDROOM WINDOW THE VIEW into the garden was mysterious. Overgrown honeysuckle and roses tangled with each other, forming a rough, dark tunnel. Thornton had not engineered this; it had just grown that way. As he glanced out while straightening his tie, combing his hair, brushing his jacket, he thought, I must cut it back. I must clear the space. But he did nothing. So the tangle of roses and honeysuckles flourished, mixing and knotting across the kitchen wall, scrambling the sash window, making it almost impossible to open. Overnight Thornton had aged. Everywhere he looked he saw his mother's face, heard her voice, felt the loving touch of her hand on his life. Like rivulets joining a stream, her presence threaded through everything he had ever done. Instead of growing closer to the others, Jacob, Christopher, Alicia, he retreated into a private grief. Like a man with third-degree burns, any bandage, any sign of containment was too painful to bear.

None of the de Silvas could go back for the funeral, none of them could organise their papers in time. There was also a nagging fear they might not be allowed re-entry into Britain. Instead they gathered at the Catholic Church in Highgate for a Mass, loosely together in spirit, bereft and silent, each with memories of their own. Sons, daughters, grandchildren, they were all present. Jacob, remembering his mother's face as he waved goodbye, felt his alienation with piercing sorrow. He had always felt he was the one on the outside, emotionally absent from his family. In the end his mother had never seen his wife or his sons. It had always been this way, thought Jacob, genuflecting. When the telegram had come, he had cried out to Geraldine, 'What more could I have done?'

Standing with his head bent, listening to the words of a discarded liturgy, Jacob recalled his last walk across the tea-covered valley towards the House of Many Balconies. It was always the last day at Greenwood School that he remembered. 'Everything finished that day,' he had cried, when the telegram came.

He saw now, with the clarity brought on by her death, that he had blamed her for the loss of his hopes of a university education. But he had loved her, he told Geraldine. For all that he never showed it, he had loved her. And he had always done whatever she wanted, whatever was needed, without complaint.

'She was lonely,' he said. 'Like me, she was lonely.' One of the aunts, he told Geraldine, had said their mother had loved a man from a lower caste. 'If it was true we never saw any sign of it. The main problem was always my drunken father.'

'It's not your fault,' Geraldine had consoled him. '*They* were the ones who stopped you going to school. It wasn't fair, what they did. You were clever.'

He had got away, although he did not belong here either. He would spend his days sitting forever behind the till of his corner shop. Looking around the church at his family, he felt a great weariness descend upon him. His youth had gone. Until this moment he had hardly noticed it. Jacob was not a political man. He was not like Christopher. All he had wanted was to study, to live and to die in the place where he had been born.

Alicia knelt in the pew behind Jacob. She had thought she had no tears left but she had been wrong. With her mother went the last of her youth. The incense in the church reminded her of the radiant day when she had married. The church in Highgate was a modern one; the stained-glass windows were not as beautiful as the one in Kollupitiya. But the sun still filtered in through them. They stood for the Creed. Sunil. She could say his name, at last. On this day of her mother's funeral, something that had been stuck in Alicia for years seemed to loosen. Like grit it was falling away. She had done nothing with her life. How her mother had worried over her. Sunil would not have wanted her to live like this. Earlier that day Alicia had spoken to Savitha and a small barrier had come down for the first time.

'I never considered her feelings, once,' she had cried.

Savitha had held on to her, saying nothing, comforting her with silence. A strange peace descended. Savitha had astonished Alicia. It was time to bury the dead. Next week Robert Grant was taking her to dinner. She was not certain why she had agreed. Suddenly, Alicia was aware of the need for connection. It was now nine o'clock in the morning. Across the world, in the afternoon sunlight, her mother's body was being placed in the ground. 'Dust to dust,' Father Giovanni would be saying.

Looking around the church, seeing the stunned faces of her family, Alicia was overwhelmed with love. It was many years since she had felt this way.

Christopher, shuffling his feet, did not weep. He was damned if he would weep in front of Thornton. Late last night, after all the others had made their phone calls, after all of them had done their weeping and wailing, Christopher had rung Frieda. Privately. His grief had always been a private thing. He had declined staying for the meal Savitha had cooked, declined talking on the phone with the rest of them. Instead he had walked home across London and made his own phone call.

'It's me,' he had said, offhand, not wanting to say much.

'Christopher?' Frieda had asked.

Her voice had come across the ocean, faintly and somehow young. She sounded strained and bereft. It had caught Christopher off guard, reminding him of his mother's voice. She had even said his name in the way his mother used to. With a questioning lilt. It had been Christopher's undoing.

'Don't worry,' he had said. 'I know how you suffered. I was there. I knew about Vijay.'

Frieda had talked over him, trying to comfort him, not understanding a word he said.

'Your secret is safe with me, forever,' he had said. 'I *saw* what happened to you. It was the same for me.' Then he had mumbled something about being the son most like her. 'Not like Thornton,' he had told Frieda. 'Not like that idiot.'

Taking Communion in Highgate, he remembered planting the jasmine bush, silently keeping his mother's secret, never uttering a word when the others had talked about the change in her.

'The body of Christ,' the priest said.

I have only ever loved two women in my life, thought Christopher. There will never be another one.

Meeka, dressed in a pale sari, knelt in the pew opposite, her long hair falling across her face. She moved slightly, pulling at the silk, struggling with its length, wishing she had never agreed to wear it, wishing she had resisted her father's insistence.

Turning, she caught Christopher's eye and hesitated, uncertain, not knowing if she should smile at him, her face unusually solemn.

But she's here, thought Christopher, astonished. Couldn't they see? Their mother was here with them, in this church. By some miracle she had come back. And she was young again. He stared at his niece. This is the one who will carry the de Silva name forward, he thought, clenching his fists. It must all come right with this child.

Anna-Meeka felt guilty. She remembered her grandmother of course, but time had blunted her memories. So many years had passed since she had lived that other life. She wished she could shake it off. Why on earth did her parents keep looking back? It only brought endless misery. She was here to support her father. *His* grief frightened her. Fear tightened her chest, made her hands cold. It made her feel a child, just when she had decided she would never be a child again. Maybe, she thought, waiting for the priest to clean the chalice, she should work harder at school, try to become the doctor her father wanted her so passionately to be. At this moment she was prepared to do anything for him to stop this grief. She fidgeted, distress crawling across her back, black-beetled and slow. Feeling disconnected, glancing at her mother, she noticed Savitha had a peculiar expression on her face. Meeka pressed her lips together. It was too much. Her mother looked so funny that tears of hysterical laughter filled Meeka's eyes.

Savitha felt apart from the de Silvas; she was not a Christian, she was a Buddhist. Churches gave her no comfort. She understood more than any of the de Silvas about karma and the cycle of cause and effect. The link that joined all their lives would exist through Anna-Meeka. While the de Silvas were only just beginning to see this Savitha had known it long ago. It was her job to anchor her daughter until she grew up. I am the custodian of their history, she thought, listening to but not understanding the Mass.

Ranjith could not take his eyes off Anna-Meeka. So much life in the midst of all this sorrow, so astonishingly beautiful. What was a man like him to a girl like this? He doubted she so much as noticed him. Watching, he saw her determination, mistaking it for certainty, forgetting the difference, forgetting his own youth. Watching her, Christopher felt her struggle and was filled with love.

Aloysius and Frieda simply waited for the day to be over. It was the longest day of their lives. There had been more bombs in the centre of the city and another member of the Cabinet had been assassinated. Frieda prepared the food silently. She needed something to do. In the middle of the preparations, unannounced, Myrtle had arrived. Frieda, trying to stay calm for Aloysius's sake, had been thrown. Myrtle had not brought a suitcase with her.

'Don't worry, I won't be staying,' she said before Frieda could speak.

Frieda looked around wildly. Her father was resting.

'I'll go, if you want,' Myrtle said, looking uncertain. 'I had to try to get here. I wanted to speak to Aloysius. I wanted to tell him that I'm sorry.'

She looked about to cry. Frieda was shocked.

'I know, I know, I'm the Devil from Hell, but she was my only relative. I tried to write to her afterwards but I never managed it. Don't think things have been easy for me either. I just wanted to say goodbye. But I'll go if you want.' She managed to sound both upset and belligerent.

'Would you like a cup of tea,' Frieda asked, helplessly, not knowing what to do. Her mother, she knew, would not have borne a grudge, but her father was a different matter.

'I'll see if he's awake,' she suggested, uncertain.

Myrtle looked terrible. Her skin had darkened, her hair was white and she looked as if she had not slept for days. Aloysius was not asleep. He had been lying in the shuttered room watching the sunlight flicker through a gap in the wood. A bee-eater chirped in the trees outside. Everything around him looked as it always had. Only he had changed forever.

'Let her stay,' he said heavily, when Frieda told him. 'If she wants evidence of what I feel about your mother, then she'll get it. If not, she should not have come. I don't care either way.'

Frieda's eyes filled with tears. She had been crying on and off during the last few days and she was exhausted. Her face was swollen with grief. She missed Alicia and Thornton desperately. She wanted Jacob with his sense of duty to help her to carry this new burden. She had never felt so alone in her life. Her father had been unable to eat or sleep. She was frightened that he too might suffer a heart attack. She had summoned the doctor several times in the last few days to sedate him. Frieda gave him another pill and tried to make him go to bed but she knew he would not sleep until later. Then she went back to talk to Myrtle.

'Please,' she said, 'have some tea.'

Myrtle stared at her vacantly. 'How are you?' she murmured. And then when Frieda remained silent, continued, 'It's so strange. I half expect to see her come in.'

Frieda's face quivered. She didn't have the strength to deal with her aunt. But after that one remark, Myrtle seemed more interested in telling Frieda about her own life in the years since she had left Station Road.

'They are playing merry hell in Jaffna. No one here has any idea of the things going on there.'

She told Frieda about the shortage of food and the people who disappeared suddenly in the night, children plucked from their beds, boys on their way to school, old men who had connections with the Sinhalese.

'People are suffering,' Myrtle said. 'Your mother would have been shocked.'

She paused and neither of them spoke. In a few hours they would have to leave for the church. Frieda felt faint with the strain.

'She was better than me, you know,' Myrtle said at last. 'Your mother.'

The sound of distant gunfire added to the unreality of the moment.

Then, quicker than she could have anticipated, it was over. The cars arrived and Frieda brought Aloysius out into the bright, terrible heat. A peacock cried plaintively in the garden next door. The air was still; even the branches of the coconut trees were motionless against the dazzling, weightless sky. A few neighbours had come out onto the road to watch as Grace's coffin, surrounded by flowers, was borne swiftly away.

Afterwards, because of the curfew, those mourners who had come from afar left hurriedly. All that remained in the soft, sad, afternoon light was the scent of jasmine. Evening approached and the sea sighed.

'Nothing has changed,' said Aloysius, 'except me. And for me everything has finished.'

After he had thrown the first handful of earth he had spoken briefly to Myrtle. 'Thank you for coming,' he had said, simply. 'She would have been glad of it.'

Myrtle had cried, embracing them both. She had given Aloysius a small photograph, taken many years ago, of a young and happy Grace, standing with her father in the garden at the House of Many Balconies, smiling into the sun.

Towards nightfall, the others rang again. Thornton had been unable to say much. Frieda had dreaded speaking to him, aware that he would be the worst of all. Incoherent in the end, he had handed the phone to Savitha. In all their lives together, Frieda had never known him be like this.

'Is he going to be all right?' she asked, frightened.

'Yes, yes.' Savitha's voice came back to her with its own echo. 'Don't worry, he is strong. As long as he has Meeka he will be all right.'

Anna-Meeka, sounding restrained and distant with her strange English voice, spoke next. 'Hello, Auntie Frieda,' she said. 'How is Grandpa?'

I no longer know her at all, thought Frieda. She has become someone else entirely.

Christopher didn't ring until much later.

'Meeka looks very much like Mummy, men,' he said, awkwardly.

He spoke first to his father and then to Frieda. But when he heard Frieda's voice he had begun to cry. He had cried and cried for so long that she began to worry about the cost of the call. Then Frieda asked him something she had vowed never to ask any of them.

'Please come home one day,' she asked. 'When this war is over, come home.'

And Christopher had cried, wretchedly, 'I will, I will.'

After the phone call, Aloysius went to bed. He was beyond speech and his eyes were bloodshot with exhaustion. Frieda gave him something to help him sleep. He had been drinking all day and she was worried about him. She closed up the house and moved some of the flowers into the hall where it was cooler.

Glancing around, she caught sight of Jasper's old perch. It stood motionless against the skylight. No one had thought of removing it in all these years. Hesitating a moment, she went into her mother's study. Everything was as usual. Her diaries were stacked on shelves; photographs lined the walls, Thornton's published poems, Alicia's press cuttings, books and papers. Grace's glasses lay uselessly on her desk. Through a blur Frieda saw her mother's inner life spread out as though she might return to it in a moment. Grief struck her forcefully, sending her hurrying out to pour herself a glass of whisky, the first in her life. Tomorrow, she thought, tomorrow was time enough to start going through her mother's papers.

Distance distorted their grief. Thornton placed his sorrows out of sight, pressed like flowers within a book. Meeka, racing through her scales with impatience, reminded him of all that was best in his misspent youth. He had begun to understand that Grace would be with him forever. She was a collection of perfect things in his imperfect life. He closed his mind and refused to speak of any of it. He had almost forgotten he was to meet Hildegard. Cutting three roses, telling Savitha he was visiting Alicia, he left the house.

Summer was almost over. It was an unremarkable day of the palest blue, with a touch of autumn in the air. Catching sight of his reflection in the tube, he saw a man reaching early middle age carrying roses. How strange it was, he reflected sadly, to be travelling across London clutching yellow roses on his way to meet Hildegard after all these years. He could not remember the last time he had carried flowers for anyone. Idly, he wondered what she was like. They had corresponded a little since that first letter and he had told her of Grace's death. There was, he felt, a certain reluctance on his part to put too much down on paper, in case it might be misconstrued. Better to say whatever they wanted when they were face to face.

The train lurched and rattled, emptied of almost all its passengers, carrying Thornton with his reflections and his roses and all the uncertainties working in him as though he was a young man again and his mother in the house in Station Road waited for him to come home.

He did not see her. He was too deep in his melancholia, lost somewhere in the scent of the flowers that rested beside his cup of tea. The station café was a transient place of unhappiness and filth. Platform announcements cross-hatched his thoughts. The tea was watery. It smelt of detergent. Thornton sat as though he were resting after a great journey. Exhausted. Nearby sat an old, very large woman with thinning grey hair. A tramp. She coughed once or twice raspingly and Thornton glanced up only to look away again. The waiter began to sweep away the rubbish under the tables. A train rattled past, the café filled and emptied of people. Thornton sighed, staring into space.

Just like a ghost couple, thought Hildegard, sadly. Here, then, was her heart's desire, while she was changed beyond recognition.

'Look!' she tried to say. 'It's *me*, Hildegard. Can't you see?'

He could not see. Hildegard sat, stunned, her throat constricted. Like quicksilver, like the music his sister made, her passion had always run too fast. I was always out of step, she thought with despair, willing him to look at her again and see the woman he had once loved. Wanting him to recognise her. And even then, she thought, although my body was lithe and supple, and I could dance with the best of them, outdance him even, although I was pretty and golden-haired and Uncle Innocent loved me at first sight, it was never any use. I could never be one of them.

After a while, having looked at his watch several times, when the tea was cold and undrinkable, and the sound of rain on the high wrought-iron roof rattled like a thousand grains of rice, Thornton grew increasingly restless. Meeka was having a private lesson in physics at six o'clock and he wanted to be back to check she didn't miss it. Savitha, who took a dim view of the lessons, would not fuss if Meeka stayed at her friend's house. Where was Hildegard? he wondered, irritated. She might have rung him at work if she had changed her mind. Pushing his half-drunk tea away in distaste, he rose.

Well, he thought, frowning, glancing at his watch again, I at least have kept the appointment.

He had wanted to make his peace with her; he had been willing to talk. But she had changed her mind obviously. Enough, he had waited long enough. Pushing the flowers into the rubbish bin he strode hurriedly away.

Robert Grant stared at the ceiling. A thread of light from the street lamp moulded itself against the cornices, sharply defined in the darkness. A slight breeze moved the curtain and the thin line changed and swelled. It was raining again. The leaves were singed with brown. Autumn was on the march. With the children back at school he would be able to spend more time at work. Sylvie would busy herself waiting patiently until he finished work and came home. Now you can relax, supper will be ready in a minute, she would say, turning the side lamps on in the large drawing room, humming to herself as she moved plates and glasses about, lifting the casserole out of the Aga, pleased he was back. Sylvie asked so little. And here he was betraying her in this old-fashioned way.

Beside him Alicia slept. Soundlessly, hardly stirring, limbs curled towards him, dark hair covering her face. If he moved his head and lifted it slightly towards her, took in the faint perfume of her long hair and listened, he could hear her even breathing, could see her small body rising and falling underneath the covers. Robert stared at the line of light across the ceiling. Every night this is what he saw.

Every night, he thought wryly. Every night! If only it was. He loved her. It was the simplest feeling in the world, and yet unbearable. He would have thrown everything away for her. Every last thing he had worked for, his children, his work, everything he possessed was a pale shadow beside Alicia. Had he loved her all those years ago, when he had first heard her play the piano at the Governor's house? Since meeting her again the constant restlessness that had dogged his life had gone.

It seemed such a short while ago that he had taken his leave of her in Sri Lanka, dodging the monsoon, laughing as he went, putting the de Silvas out of his life. The trees in their garden had been strung with coloured lights in preparation for the wedding. He had been vaguely aware of Grace's watchful eyes and he had told himself firmly that he was glad to be sailing away. He had not dared to think of what might have been had Alicia met him first. And now, there was no one he could ask, no one he could share this love with.

She did not want it. She took from it only the barest crumb. There is nothing of me left, she had said candidly, lifting her small face towards him. Not wishing to deceive him, not once, not even for a moment. Such was her honesty. He had only himself to blame. He glanced at her as she slept. Though no longer young, her skin was silky to the touch, glowing against the whiteness of his hand.

Anyone who knew him would have thought him crazy. Risking all he had, not thinking about his children, his reputation? If the papers got hold of the story it would be the end of his career. Caught by his conflicting desires, his thoughts circled round and round his head, like the endless wheels of a train, the street lamps kept on shining, and his heart kept on beating and Alicia went on sleeping, while the thread of light on the cornice marked the hours and the minutes ticking relentlessly towards the dawn.

21

No one had seen it coming. In one stroke, all that had been established lay shattered at their feet. They would never find it again. Time moved slowly for the de Silvas. Their last great realisation had shocked them. Life would not be what they had dreamed. Since his mother's death, since his failed attempt to meet Hildegard, Thornton had withdrawn quietly. Savitha watched him tending the garden. She served him hot rice in his mother's tureens, gave him cups of tea in her bone china, but there was nothing else she could do. She could see what she had always suspected: without their mother's influence the de Silva family was disintegrating. In spite of a drunken husband, in spite of the war, Grace had kept them together, while she, Savitha, could not even control her daughter. One end-of-summer evening, soon after the funeral, while Thornton cut the grass, Savitha sat at the kitchen table and began writing a letter to Frieda. All letters home were now written entirely by Savitha; Thornton simply sent his love.

He's all right, Savitha wrote, knowing Frieda worried about her brother. *We talk less but I expect that would have happened anyway. When you have been married for as long as we have, silence hardly matters. I know what he's thinking, anyway! You mustn't worry. Of course your mother's death was a shock, but living here has made him strong. I've been having dreams about the day we left Sri Lanka. You have no idea how frightened we were that morning when we said goodbye. Everything frightened us then, leaving you was terrible of course but the huge ship frightened us and the sea was so enormous. I thought we would drown. We were terrified! So we talked more. We are no longer like that, we are resilient. We have lost something else. Perhaps it's our innocence.*

She paused, not knowing how to go on. Not knowing how much Frieda would understand. It had taken the garden party to mark their dislocation. *You see, Frieda*, she continued, struggling to explain herself simply, *I have discovered that being part of an empire means you lose your individual and collective identity.*

Savitha stared at what she had written. Frieda would think her mad. Meeka had begun to play the piano. It was something she had been tinkering with for days. Recognising it, Savitha raised her head absent-mindedly and listened. The music travelled under the closed doors, reminding her of something familiar yet elusive. It drifted softly across the house, very sweetly and melodiously. Meeka played a chord and then a series of arpeggio. Her hands ran across the keys, pausing and the music changed texture, its modulation rising slowly. Savitha held her breath without understanding why. Thornton, pausing as he cut some roses, heard it faintly and hummed absent-mindedly. The piano needs tuning, he thought. Frowning, Savitha went back to her letter.

We no longer know who we are, or what we want. Our sight is impaired and our anger too great.

She sighed. What was the point? Frieda would not see beyond her grief and the civil war that had taken her family away. With Grace gone there was no one else Savitha could speak of such things to. But she did mention Christopher. She had begun to understand Christopher better, she told Frieda.

He saw what the war would do long before anyone else. How it would destroy everything of value and wrench us apart. It has taken too many people away, dispersing the richness in the place, robbing it of its talent. Christopher saw that. And because he can't do anything, because he is a man, he drinks to forget this betrayal.

We are from the same place after all, she decided, pausing, thinking about Christopher, remembering Sunil, the other person who had tried to do the impossible alone. The piano music had changed into a minor key.

Things will only change slowly, she continued, hoping Frieda would understand, *and probably not in our lifetime. Fairer societies do not come overnight.*

'Is that Frieda you're writing to?' asked Thornton, coming in with some vegetables from his plot. He went over to the sink and turned on the tap. The scent of newly cut grass wafted in through the kitchen door.

'Close the door,' said Savitha. 'It's getting cold.' Autumn was heading towards winter.

'Send my love, will you?' Thornton said. 'Say I'll write as soon as I can.'

His face was silhouetted against the fading light. He looks tired, she thought. His mouth was stern, disapproving. Pity clutched at Savitha's heart. She saw clearly what Grace had always known. I have come all the way from the orphanage in Dondra to this place, she thought, but I am so much stronger than he is. Sighing, she added Thornton's love and sealed her letter. Then she stood up. It was time to cook the evening meal.

The piano music was reaching its end. For the moment, the green of the island retreated from Savitha's mind and instead the twilight of the late evening was filled with the tender sound of swallows.

It had started with her clearing Grace's room. Tidying up the papers, putting them in order. There were still letters to be answered. For a long time Frieda had been reluctant to do anything. Every time she went into her mother's room she simply cried. She was too apathetic to care. In this way eighteen months passed before she could face it. Then, one afternoon when Aloysius went for his walk to the hotel and she was a little stronger, she forced herself to begin sorting out Grace's things. Aloysius would not look at them. He was very frail now but he remained stubborn on the subject. Frieda let him do as he pleased, staying out even when she felt it was not safe, and drinking. It was all that was left and she had not the heart to stop him. She had given up worrying about the curfew and the bombs. They were part of daily life.

It was while she was sorting out the photographs, making them into piles, some for Thornton, some for Alicia, others for Jacob, that she found the photograph. Sitting back on her heels, Frieda glanced at it. She did not recognise the tall, slight man in the sarong. A few, yellowed jasmine flowers fell out of the envelope along with it. Idly she turned the photograph over.

My dearest love, Vijay, Grace had written. *October 8, 1950*.

Frieda looked at the picture, puzzled. Vijay? She did not know anyone called Vijay. She put the photograph aside, meaning to ask her father when he came in, but then something made her reach for Grace's diary. What had they been doing in October 1950?

Today is June 23, Grace had written. *Three years and one day*

334

since Vijay died and I have been unable to write until now. A thousand days and nights have passed since that terrible night. Somehow I lived through all of them. Smiling on Alicia's wedding day. Dealing with the family, Thornton's crazy marriage. It's a small miracle that I managed to survive. Through the skin of my teeth and in spite of Myrtle's inquisitive stare, I have survived.

Frieda read swiftly.

Only two of them know what I have been going through. Christopher and Aloysius. Who would have thought it possible, that my drunken husband, the man who wasted my money, who gambled away my home, should have kept me sane through these terrible days! Even though I have betrayed him with another man.

Frieda gasped. In an instant her world seemed to have turned upside down.

Nothing will bring Vijay back, nothing can change the past and yet, in spite of everything he knows, Aloysius does not judge me. How can this be? All he wants, he tells me, over and over again, is that I can be happy again. Poor Aloysius. I never knew how much he loves me. I will never leave him, never, never. We have both suffered enough.

The sound of her father returning made Frieda jump. Shutting the diary, she hid it quickly. The palms of her hands were sweating and she was breathing rapidly. It was the servant's day off and Aloysius would want a cup of tea.

Later on, after they had finished their evening meal, she read to Aloysius from *A Tale of Two Cities*. But all the time she was distracted by the words she had read about a man whose existence she had not known of until this afternoon. *My mother?* she thought incredulously. The past rolled like thunder. She sensed a passion she had never experienced in her own life. I always lagged behind, she thought, behind Alicia, behind Thornton, behind all of them. Life has passed me by. There had been the business of Robert Grant but she could no longer even remember his face. She was impatient to get back to the diary.

Aloysius had had enough of Dickens. Frieda switched on the radio so he could catch the evening news. The Sinhalese newsreader warned the fighting was very bad in the Batticaloa area. The Tamils were bearing the brunt, being stopped suddenly and hauled away at roadblocks, never to be seen again. The sky had begun to darken; the evening was over.

'Look,' Aloysius said, with pleasure. 'Your mother's jasmine bush is opening its flowers. She must be thinking of us!'

The air was fragrant with perfume as Frieda stared out into the garden, seeing it with her mother's eyes. Her mother as she had never known her. A sentence repeated itself in Frieda's head.

Until everyone can have the same opportunities, Grace had written, *until we stop this cruel caste system, until everyone is given the same chances, my dearest Vijay will have died in vain.*

Tomorrow, Frieda decided, I will go to the orphanage and offer my help. I will see what I can do to give some Tamil child another chance.

Anna-Meeka failed her physics, her maths and her chemistry A levels. Biology was a borderline pass.

Her father, sounding like a reversing lorry, shouted, 'Retake! Retake!'

But in the end even Thornton could see it was useless. Anna-Meeka did not have the makings of a doctor. Savitha, watching her daughter slowly turn into a bad-tempered beauty, was at a loss as to what they might do for the best.

'Perhaps you're right,' she conceded reluctantly. 'We should think about introducing her to someone from Sri Lanka.'

It was Saturday afternoon and as usual Meeka had gone to

her friend Gillian's house. She was meant to be revising for the retakes. Thornton gave the grass its last cut for the year and came in for his cup of tea.

'I can't do any work,' he said, abruptly. 'I'm too upset by her results. After all our hard work, after the struggle we had to get to this country, she's ended her schooling with no career. She won't become a doctor now, men.'

He sat at the kitchen table, defeated. Savitha said nothing. She too was upset, but for different reasons. Anna-Meeka's wanton behaviour was what confused her.

'How's she going to manage when we die?' Thornton asked belligerently. He waggled his finger at Savitha. 'She has no brothers, no sisters. She can't go back home. So who will look after her? At least if she had become a doctor she could have got a job anywhere in the world.'

Savitha closed her eyes. She was tired of listening to Thornton and worrying about their daughter.

'Well, you're not a doctor and we managed,' she ventured. 'I told you, you should have let her do her music. Maybe she could have become a music teacher.'

Thornton snorted. 'How much money d'you think she'll make as a music teacher, for God's sake?'

'Stop shouting, she'll be back in a minute.'

If Anna-Meeka were to hear them there would be another one of their eternal arguments. Savitha was sick of them. Gone were the days when they could tell Meeka what to do. Gone was that sweet smile. These days Meeka was eager to pick them up on more or less anything they said.

'She has no respect,' Thornton fumed. 'In Sri Lanka, girls have respect for their elders.'

What d'you know about the girls in Sri Lanka? thought Savitha, wearily. But she didn't say this. Nor did she tell him that only the other day she had noticed Ranjith Pieris staring at Meeka a little more intently than he needed to.

Meanwhile, the subject of their concern was standing on the corner of the street talking to a group of teenagers from school. She was carrying a pile of books.

'Where's you been, Meeka?' one of them asked her.

'None of your business,' said Meeka, tossing her long mane of hair and laughing. 'I've been revising for my retakes.'

The group gave a disbelieving guffaw. 'That's what you tell your parents, Meeka, not us!'

Meeka smiled demurely. 'Must go,' she said, 'talking of parents! I'm late and they'll kill me.'

'Oy, Meeka, what's that on your neck? You got a love bite, or 'ave you been bit by a snake?'

Anna-Meeka, ignoring them, was running towards her house. Her father was sitting drinking his tea. He looked nervous and her mother looked cross. She guessed they had been having an argument. She took a deep breath. There was simply no easy way to do this.

'I've got a job,' she said, bending her head low for the shrapnel which would soon be whizzing around the small kitchen. 'It's at the hairdresser's. They're going to train me while I work. Then when I'm older I can set up a salon. So you don't have to worry about my future any more.'

She had expected disapproval, but to her surprise Thornton had looked merely crushed, and although her mother had glared at her and folded her lips, she too had said very little. This silent disapproval had been unnerving but the relief of leaving school was so great she didn't care. She had given up trying to please her parents. When she was not learning how to cut or shampoo hair, she spent her time daydreaming. Music continued to fill her head. The sounds followed her everywhere, faint echoes that haunted her waking moments and sometimes also her sleep. She listened to Elgar and to Vaughan Williams and she listened to Benjamin Britten's *Curlew River* until she knew it by heart. She spent all her money on cassette tapes which she listened to on a pair of headphones. It made it impossible to hear her parents' complaints.

One evening, on her way home from work, she bumped into Philippa Davidson. Why did she have to meet her when she smelt of shampoo and hairspray, looking her worst with nothing to say? Oddly enough Philippa did not seem to notice. She appeared really friendly. Meeka listened curiously as Philippa Davidson told her she was going to university. Of course, thought Meeka a trifle sourly. Clever, sorted-out Philippa was going to read English at Oxford. Meeka could not think of anything to say in response, but Philippa, hardly noticing, promised she would not lose touch.

That winter Meeka began to write a new piece of music. Every evening after work she would sit at the piano and work on it. Occasionally Savitha would stop what she was doing and listen. Her daughter's music was strangely beautiful. It always reminded her of home, fleeting images and snatches of conversations, memories from that distant life, all just out of Savitha's grasp. When she tried to talk about this to Thornton he would shake his head and refuse to be drawn. His daughter was eighteen; he had given up.

A new pattern began to emerge. Most evenings, after Meeka had spent some time at the piano, the three of them would eat their meal of rice and curry. They no longer laughed or argued as they used to. Then when the plates were cleared and if it wasn't too late, Meeka would go round the corner to Gillian's house. No one stopped this new-found freedom. No one dared.

'Don't be too long,' her mother would say.

Her father would look at his watch, pointedly. 'Shall I come and meet you?' he would ask tentatively each time.

And each time, Meeka would tell him, easily, 'There's no need, Dad. Gillian always walks me back.'

She was never very late and they knew Gillian, so they said no more.

One night after dinner Jacob phoned unexpectedly and Thornton went to meet him at the White Hart. It was the first time in months that Thornton had seen him.

'Don't drink too much,' Savitha warned, but she spoke mildly.

'No, no,' Thornton said. And he went out.

It was with a sense of relief that he began to recount the changes in his daughter to Jacob.

'She's always out,' he said, 'visiting that friend of hers, Gillian. She's completely dropped her studies. Even Savitha can't understand it. Can you believe it, a de Silva working as a hairdresser? After all we've been through to get her to this country.'

'Forget it, Thornton,' Jacob said, shaking his head. 'Haven't you noticed? Everything's changed. All the old values are slowly being lost. The young people from our country just want to integrate with these white fellows.'

He looked at his brother not unsympathetically, for he knew how ambitious he had been for Anna-Meeka. Coming here had been a gamble, they had always known that. Jacob himself was not without troubles of his own.

'It isn't any easier for me,' he said. 'The twins are fighting with next-door's children. Aiyo, they're all ready to start a war! Geraldine just laughs and says boys will be boys, but I'm worried about where it will lead.' Really, Jacob was appalled. 'I've got the Irish situation right on my doorstep, you know, men.'

Lately, now that he saw less of Thornton, Jacob had come

to feel a lingering affection for his brother. Looking at Thornton's whitening hair, he felt as though he was watching the tide go out. Helplessly, unable to stop it. He himself was completely bald.

'Meeka has grown up here, Thornton,' he said consolingly. 'You can't expect her to obey you as though we were back in Sri Lanka. She is part of this system. I told you long ago, women here are different. They do what they want. Look at Savitha. Does she listen to you? Remember when she got that job in the factory?'

Thornton could not deny it. His brief sense of relief had passed. He moved restlessly, wanting to get back and check that Meeka had returned home safely. They finished their drinks and parted. Walking back, crossing Vassall Road in the moonlight, Thornton passed a young couple caught in an embrace. Dimly as he passed, he registered the girl's slender form and her long dark hair. Thornton sighed deeply and continued quickly down Southey Road, towards home.

At the end of January the weather got colder and snow threatened. Ranjith Pieris came to say goodbye. He was returning home. Savitha gave him some parcels to take back for Frieda and Aloysius. Meeka was nowhere to be seen. Later that evening, not long after he had left, Anna-Meeka came home from the hairdressing salon to find her mother cooking a chicken curry. Her father was reading the *New Statesman* and did not immediately look up. Meeka did not mind. She went over to the newly installed radiator and began warming her hands.

'I'm cold,' she said.

'Well, why don't you wear something warmer?' Savitha told her, bringing a bowl of rice to the table.

Meeka gave her mother an odd look. Savitha brought a dish

of ladies' fingers to the table. Seeing it, Thornton gave a sigh of pleasure.

'Ah, *bandaka*,' he said. 'Good!'

Meeka grinned. The grin did not quite reach her eyes.

'I've got some news,' she said.

'Don't tell me you're leaving that bloody hairdresser's at last?' Thornton said, mildly.

Savitha looked sharply at her daughter. Some strange premonition made her heart miss a beat. Meeka was shivering with suppressed excitement.

'Mum, Dad,' she announced, hardly managing to contain herself, 'guess what? I'm getting married in the summer!' She held up her hand, anticipating their questions. 'He's from Calcutta,' she said. 'And his name is Naringer Gupta. He's a *doctor* and he's dying to meet you!'

Alicia opened her letters over breakfast. Robert poured her some fresh orange juice and signalled the waiter for more coffee while watching her surreptitiously. She looked relaxed. It was the first holiday they had had together. The last few years had been very difficult for him. He was absent as often as he dared but sometimes he suspected Sylvie knew what was going on. He had wanted to confess and leave but Alicia would have none of it. She did not want Robert to hurt Sylvie more than they already did. Every time Robert brought up the subject of his wife, Alicia appeared on the verge of flight. So this was how they had lived for nearly four years. He did not like it but he did not want to lose Alicia either.

A week ago they had arrived by water taxi from the airport. Alicia had never been to Venice. Robert wanted to show her his favourite city. Sipping his coffee he reflected on the previous day. They had had an astonishing night. He had booked tickets for *La Clemenza di Tito* at La Fenice. It had been a wonderful performance. On their return to the hotel, whether as a result of the music or not, Alicia had gone to the grand piano in the reception area and without any warning played Mozart. Robert had been speechless. Alicia had stumbled a little but the receptionist and a few Americans who were present had burst into spontaneous applause. Afterwards, without a word, she had taken Robert's hand and led him upstairs to their room. They had made passionate love to the soft sounds of the water lapping outside. This morning the Grand Canal sparkled and shone as though studded with diamonds. Robert felt a lightness in his heart. A change had occurred. It made him afraid to breathe. The day stretched before him. He felt full of optimism and youth.

Alicia was frowning as she read Frieda's letter.

'Now what?' said Robert.

The de Silvas had such colourful lives compared with his own.

'Frieda is thinking of adopting a Tamil orphan.' Alicia said. She began reading aloud from her letter.

'*I've decided to try to help a Tamil child. They are in a desperate state. If they go back to the North they will simply get sucked back into the insurgent movement, which will mean certain death. I've been visiting the convent for some time. The nuns are very grateful for any help they can get. Of course I haven't said anything to Daddy as yet. He's very frail and I don't want to upset him unnecessarily. I wanted to ask you what you thought about the idea. This house is too large for the two of us. Mummy would have approved, don't you think? Remember how she used to help the nuns?*'

'Well,' said Robert. 'Why not? She is a remarkable woman. Why not?'

'Mmm,' Alicia said uncertainly, 'I suppose so. She was wonderful with Anna-Meeka when they lived there. She was wonderful with me too,' she added softly.

Robert nodded. He wondered how much Alicia had told Frieda about him. For all their differences, he knew the sisters were closer than was at first apparent. There was only so much Alicia divulged to him and there were some places where he felt unable to intrude, but he was certain Frieda knew. Alicia was opening her other letter.

'It's from Thornton,' she said, surprised.

The waiter brought them more coffee. Outside, coins of sunlight danced a ballet on the water. A *traghetto* packed with businessmen was crossing the canal. Robert felt impatient to show off the city to Alicia.

'Does he know you are with me?' he ventured.

Alicia shook her head, briefly. Then she began to read her letter.

'Oh no,' she said suddenly. 'Oh my God, *no!*' She looked at Robert horrified, her mouth moving soundlessly. Then she threw her head back and began to laugh.

'Now what?' Robert asked again.

'Oh, Robert,' said Alicia. 'Oh my goodness, Robert, you're not going to believe this!'

Robert smiled. It was good to hear Alicia laugh.

'Honestly, that *girl!*' Alicia continued, barely able to speak for laughing. 'Would you believe, Anna-Meeka has just announced she is getting *married*. To an Indian! Thornton is beside himself!'

So that was that. She was getting married and the de Silvas were in uproar. The telephone lines were almost on fire.

'Well,' said Jacob when he heard, 'why are you so surprised?

344

At least she told you before she did it!' Try as he might, he could not resist the dig.

'Has Princess Meeka blotted her copybook then?' asked Geraldine, picking up one of the twins and kissing him.

'*An Indian!* But why an Indian?' asked Savitha flabbergasted.

Her daughter's foolishness amazed her. Meeka glared at her mother and self-righteous rage kicked in.

'Mum,' she shouted, belligerently. 'He's a doctor! What's the matter with you? He's *not* English. What's your problem? I thought you'd be pleased.'

Savitha was speechless in the face of this new development. She stared at Anna-Meeka helplessly.

'You better get used to it, Mum,' Meeka was saying. 'We're getting married *anyway*.'

What was wrong with her parents? she asked Gillian in despair. 'They've spent my whole life telling me how they hated *all* my white friends. Now I'm marrying someone like them but they're still not happy. And he's a doctor, for God's sake! You'd think my dad would be happy, wouldn't you? What the hell *do* they want?'

Gillian had no idea. Meeka's family had always been a mystery. 'What will you do?' she asked.

'Get married, of course,' Meeka said, shortly. She wished for the umpteenth time she had parents like Gillian's. Nice, quiet English people. The sort of parents she deserved. 'I'm worried Naringer will think they're freaks. He hasn't even met them yet. God knows what sort of a wedding we'll have at this rate.'

'We'll help,' Gillian said, consolingly. 'Mum and I'll help.'

Meeka nodded her thanks absent-mindedly, remembering her birthday party.

'Did they really know nothing about Naringer?' Gillian asked admiringly, unable to let the subject alone. Her friend always lived so *dangerously*.

Anna-Meeka shook her head again. 'D'you like him?' she asked, suddenly.

Gillian nodded, cautiously. Her own boyfriend seemed dull by comparison. 'Yeah. A bit quiet, but, yeah.'

They were both silent.

'What's happened to Geoff?' Gillian asked, offhandedly.

Meeka swallowed. Tears of self-pity pricked her eyes. Geoff was English. He was training to be a plumber. *He* was not a doctor. Couldn't her parents *see* she had made the best possible choice?

'All I ever do is try to please them and this is the thanks I get.' She looked at her watch. 'I gotta go,' she said. 'I'm meeting Naringer at the tube station.'

Naringer was sheltering from the rain. He was tall, and from a distance he looked handsome. Only on closer inspection, however, was it was possible to see the scars left by a heavy crop of chickenpox scabs. He had been born on a barge that glided along one of the many canals towards the Hooghly River. His family had been better off than most. Their barge was top-heavy with bamboo. They had poled it inch by inch through a mass of purple water hyacinths. The humidity, the factory smoke and most of all the rains were part of Naringer's memories. His mother had nine of them to feed and never enough money. His father existed on rice with chilli and onion for flavour, followed by strong tea. But somehow Naringer had attended school. His mother, unlike others, had not sent for him halfway through his school day. Most of the boys left early to help with the business of making a living. Naringer had his mother to thank for a different fate.

When he was seventeen he moved into the centre of the city where he worked running a rickshaw from the arcades of Chowringhee along the length of the Lower Circular Road. At night they choked on the acrid fumes from the street campers that flickered among the filthy bodies. Somehow, call it karma or luck, Naringer managed to escape. By the time he had got a scholarship for the university he was much older than the other students. Introverted and hard-working, intensely proud of all he had achieved, Naringer shed his relatives. All except his mother. He would not forget his mother. He had never told Meeka this but one day he intended to take her back to Calcutta to look after his mother and to live among the purple hyacinths.

Anna-Meeka approached him with a frown.

'What, no is-smile?' he asked mildly. 'I have been waiting at this is-station for ten minutes and you can't is-smile?'

'Shh!' Meeka said. 'Don't talk so loudly, and don't say is-station. It's *station*.'

'Ah! Fine mood, fine mood,' Naringer said humourlessly, waggling his head, drawing her towards him in a tight embrace.

The rain increased, forcing them further back into the station.

'You are very beautiful woman,' Naringer told her seriously, pinching her cheeks together with his hands. *Grammar*, thought Meeka, but she said nothing. She wondered if Naringer was too tall for her. He began to kiss her neck, pushing her hair back. Meeka shivered. Naringer's hands were everywhere, like an octopus. Standing in the shadows of the tube, she wriggled uneasily. Supposing someone she knew saw them?

'So?' he said finally, disentangling himself from her. He rolled a cigarette. 'How's the father?'

Meeka didn't answer and Naringer glanced at her indulgently. He hoped the parents weren't going to cause trouble. He had never met any Sri Lankans before. When he had first met Meeka, coming in again and again to have his hair cut, he had thought she was from north India.

'North Indian girls are very good-looking,' he had told the blonde girl who had first cut his hair.

The girl had giggled and passed the compliment on.

'I'm Sri Lankan,' Meeka had said with her posh accent.

'Where all the fighting is taking place? *That* place?' Naringer had said, surprised. They were difficult people, he suspected, small-built, unlike Indians, he thought wryly. Nothing special.

Meeka was smoothing her hair. She looked at Naringer. In spite of her edginess her good mood was almost restored. Seeing this, Naringer took her hand and planted another kiss on her head.

'Come on,' he said, 'why don't I just call on your parents now?'

He was unprepared for her screech of horror.

'Are you crazy?' shouted Meeka. 'Don't even suggest it. Oh my God! Are you *mad*? You've no idea what they're like. I've got to prepare them first. It could take weeks.'

'You stupid bastard,' Christopher told Thornton, when he was told the news. This had all happened when he was away in France. 'I knew it, I knew it. It's all your doing. *She*'s trying to please *you*, you idiot.'

Thornton did not hear. The shock had affected his hearing.

'Your mother must have felt like this,' Savitha said.

Thornton did not care. He was not interested in anything anyone said, or felt. He was beyond mere speech.

'I'm worried about him,' Savitha said, ringing Jacob up for a rare conversation, wishing she had not said that about his mother. 'He went out to the off-licence earlier and now he's drinking, whisky.'

348

Meeka, coming in just at that moment, put an end to this conversation.

'Hello!' she called. 'Anyone home?'

It felt as though this was a war zone. No one spoke. Savitha folded her lips and waited.

'I want to talk to you, Anna-Meeka,' Thornton called hollowly from the sitting room.

Having got himself into a state, having had all his dreams shattered, having declared war on his only daughter, Thornton was torn. Love and rage combined to form a lethal cocktail. He glared at Meeka. She was wearing black stilettos and a pale green dress. Around her neck was the gold chain her grandmother had given her long ago. Her hair gleamed (she had presumably done something to it at work), and Thornton stared at her as though seeing her for the first time. He had no idea where she had come from. The sleek young woman in front of him was a total stranger. He realised she was talking.

'What?' asked Meeka, again.

She kicked off her shoes and faced him patiently. With a great effort Thornton pulled himself together. I must be calm, he thought.

'When are we to see this man, then?' he bellowed.

He could not bring himself to say his name. Savitha, hovering behind the door, came in quickly. Thornton had not slept for days. It's too much, Savitha thought in alarm. An old feeling, some long-forgotten emotion attacked her. Her husband looked terrible.

'You need something nice to eat tonight,' she said.

Going back into the kitchen, she took out her spices and roasted a tablespoon of coriander. She rinsed the Venetian glasses. Then, glad that the arguments seemed to have ceased for the moment, she went shopping. It was a Saturday after-noon. I'll make a crab curry, she thought, slipping out quietly.

Outside on the street, Mrs Smith from next door was posting a letter into the pillar box. Mrs Smith hesitated. She did not want to look as though she was spying. Savitha smiled un-certainly; neither knew what to do.

'You all right, luv?' Mrs Smith asked, plucking up courage.

'He's an Indian,' Savitha blurted out, before she could stop herself.

Her voice wobbled dangerously. Mrs Smith nodded, kindly; she had heard everything of course, through the wall.

'We know nothing about Indians,' Savitha said, trying not to cry.

Having started, the relief was enormous. Mrs Smith nodded again. It was as she suspected. Swiftly she decided to take a chance.

'Why don't you come in and have a cuppa?' she asked.

Mrs Smith's kitchen was nothing like anything Savitha had ever seen. It was filled with clutter. Even though she was upset, Savitha could not fail to notice the dresser filled with crockery. They were the sort of thing Geraldine bought and Savitha disliked. Somehow, in Mrs Smith's cosy kitchen, they didn't look so bad. There were newspapers and knitting patterns strewn about. And balls of wool. A half-finished child's pullover lay on a chair.

'For our grandson,' said Mrs Smith apologetically, scooping it up. 'Sorry about the mess.'

Savitha was shocked. In all the years they had lived next door she had not even known Mrs Smith had grandchildren. In the corner of the room, facing the window, was a large white seagull. Catching sight of Savitha, it opened its beak and gave an ear-splitting screech. Savitha jumped.

'Don't mind Jonathan,' Mrs Smith chuckled. 'He's recovering from a broken leg.'

In spite of her own state of shock, Savitha was astonished. Over a pot of tea, hardly aware of what she was doing, Savitha began to tell Mrs Smith what was happening.

'If only we had consulted the horoscopes and found a decent Sri Lankan man,' she said. 'You know, my husband and I don't really believe in that sort of thing, but you know, we're in a foreign country. We should have protected ourselves. I think that was where we went wrong.'

Mrs Smith's eyes were round with wonder.

'He's a Hindu,' Savitha continued. 'And Meeka says he's a doctor.'

Mrs Smith nodded sympathetically. 'It's nice for us,' she said suddenly, 'having you living here. But I can see, it can't be easy for any of you. You've got two places in your head to deal with, luv. See, my husband came from Bournemouth and he finds it hard enough! I always tells him, think how hard it must be for them.'

Savitha was lost in thought. Mrs Smith stirred her tea.

'She's beautiful, your Meeka,' she ventured. 'She could have anyone!'

'What's the use, being beautiful,' Savitha reflected sadly, 'if she behaves in this terrible way? It was the way she deceived her father, that's upset him, more than anything else. All those lies about visiting Gillian, keeping it secret. For four whole months!' Savitha folded her lips, tightly. 'We know nothing of this man, other than he's a doctor.'

She paused and they drank their tea in silence.

'She's a difficult girl, you know,' she continued. 'She gets obsessions. Sometimes she plays the piano for hours and hours, forgetting to eat, forgetting the time. What kind of wife will she make?'

'We love hearing her play that piano,' Mrs Smith smiled. 'Mr Smith always switches the radio off to listen to her.'

'I don't know what to do,' Savitha confessed.

Mrs Smith poured out another cup of tea for her exotic guest. She was having a wonderful time. Then, boldly, she put her hand over Savitha's.

'Get her to bring him over,' she said confidentially. 'Get the lad in the house, take a look at him. He mightn't be so bad. She's a clever girl, your Meeka, I'm sure she's not doing anything stupid. And she loves you all right, don't forget that. My Mr Smith always says there's no knowing how things will work out.'

Savitha was startled. Mrs Smith sounded as though she really cared and Savitha felt her eyes brim with tears. She had held herself together for so long, she had tried to be strong, but the effort had made her terribly tired. Sipping her tea, staring at the worn linoleum floor, she felt an unexpected sense of belonging, here, in this messy kitchen. Mrs Smith was not like Savitha's boss. She could not quote Yeats or Tennyson, nor did she have any exquisite bone china, but there was something very sweet about her nevertheless.

'Thank you,' she said, standing up with quiet dignity. 'Thank you for the tea, and for being so kind to me. You're absolutely right. We must see him.'

'Righto,' said Mrs Smith cheerfully. 'Good luck, ducks,' she added, forgetting herself. 'All is not lost!'

And she let Savitha out.

Naringer planned his visit. It had taken two weeks but at last the invitation had come.

'Will I have to discuss my thesis with your father?' he asked.

Meeka looked at him sharply but he was not joking. She wanted to laugh. Naringer's visit coincided with the return of Alicia from Italy. Alicia wanted to see her niece to congratulate her on her news and, she told Thornton firmly, she was not prepared to judge Anna-Meeka.

'Let's give it a chance, at least,' she told him calmly.

Savitha was taken aback by such decisiveness. 'What?' she asked, momentarily distracted.

Alicia, when she arrived by taxi, had an air of well-being about her. Thornton wore his new suit, causing Meeka to stare at him with irritation.

'What's the matter with you, Dad? Why d'you need to dress up?'

Thornton said nothing. He was no longer shouting but his silence was worse. It made Savitha even more nervous.

'He's in a hell of a rage,' she confided to Alicia. 'I've never seen him like this.'

'I'll tell you what's wrong with him. He's feeling ashamed,' said Alicia, shrewdly. 'Never having had an education, he finds, on top of everything else, he's going to have a son-in-law who's a doctor and this worries him. If only Daddy had educated them, Thornton wouldn't have become so obsessed with Meeka's education.'

Naturally Savitha knew exactly what Thornton was thinking. *She* knew how his mind worked, but she had not expected Alicia to be so astute. She looked at her sister-in-law with new respect.

'You know he asked me if he should send for the Greenwood crest, so he could wear it on a blazer for the wedding!'

'Oh, poor Thornton,' said Alicia, laughing lightly.

Naringer arrived for lunch and, for once, Meeka helped her mother with the preparations. She *looks* nice, anyway, thought

Savitha, hiding her unease. Alicia joined them in the kitchen and an unusual calm fell on the household as the three women worked together preparing the food. Only Thornton continued to look terrible. He had started early on the bottle of whisky and Meeka, cautiously calling a truce, waited on him, filling his glass with ice. In spite of her own rage, her father's expression made her want to cry. Naringer declined any whisky and asked for some soda water. Thornton, keeping his face neutral, poured him some.

'You're a doctor, Meeka tells me,' he said casually, not noticing his daughter's grin.

'Yes. I've just finished my is-studies at Imperial College,' Naringer told him.

Meeka scowled.

'After we get marriage I'm going to is-start a job in Oxford. That's why we wanted to get married this is-summer.'

Thornton swallowed hard and loosened his tie. Then he poured himself another whisky. Over lunch Naringer talked about things Thornton could not understand. He talked about drugs and chemical formulae, using words Thornton had never heard before.

'Are you going to be a GP?' Thornton asked him, looking important. 'Or a hospital doctor?'

Naringer looked blankly at him.

'No, no, no,' he said, understanding. 'I'm not a *medical* doctor! I'm a Doctor of Philosophy.'

There was a short disconnected silence while Thornton digested this.

'So you're *not* a doctor, then?' he asked, finally, his face bleak.

'Yes, I *am*!'

No one said anything. Alicia offered Naringer some more iced water. Savitha served her husband more rice. Naringer was eating heartily; Thornton hardly at all. After a while the conversation resumed and Naringer continued to talk about his research. Meeka, watching her father nod his head wisely, knowing he didn't have a clue, suppressed a giggle.

'I wish he'd stop being so stuffy and make a joke,' she whispered to her aunt, when they were making the tea together. 'I wish he'd say something funny like. "Has anyone noticed Naringer's ears are pasted?"'

Alicia flashed her a smile and squeezed her hand, encouragingly.

'Give him time,' she said. 'Your father's a shy man, Anna-Meeka.'

After lunch Alicia had a surprise for Meeka. She smiled at Naringer, handing her niece an envelope.

'It's your wedding present,' she told her. 'Go on, open it!'

Inside was a small key tied with a pink ribbon.

'I'm having it delivered to your new home,' Alicia said, delighted by Anna-Meeka's expression. 'I know it's totally impractical, *but* that's what wedding presents should be. Your grandmother would have wanted it for you. She believed wedding presents should be fun!'

Meeka stared. No one spoke. Never had her sister-in law looked so radiant, thought Savitha.

'Well?' said Alicia. 'Aren't you going to say anything? Don't you know what it is?'

But Meeka, already having guessed, flew to her aunt, crushing her in an embrace.

'What is it?' asked Naringer, mildly interested.

'It's a piano!' shrieked Meeka, coming alive, dancing around the room.

'But you have one already,' Naringer said puzzled, pointing to the one in front of them.

'Ah, Naringer,' said Alicia, 'this one isn't any old piano. *This* is a Bechstein Baby!'

'Yes,' sang Meeka, 'yes, yes!' and all the tension of the past weeks, her father's expression, the sunshine outside, all these things, made her eyes shine with unshed tears.

Well, well, well, thought Savitha, with the faintest flutter of hope.

The wedding took place at Our Lady of the Rosary, along the Brixton Road. There was no nuptial Mass because Naringer was a Hindu. Suddenly, it became a jolly affair. Everyone rallied round. Gillian and Susan, Jennifer married now and pregnant, even Philippa Davidson, down for the weekend from Oxford, came. So it was a big wedding after all, not by back-home standards, not like his sister's wedding, thought Jacob, but huge for Lambeth.

Christopher came, shaking his head with anger. 'Just look what she's gone and done,' he said to Alicia. 'Thanks to her stupid father.'

Christopher would not have come if he did not love the girl so much. 'What the hell do I want with weddings?' he asked, loudly.

He had spotted the groom. 'Weddings are a state-organised form of capitalism suitable only for the bourgeois bastards,' he told Naringer, pointedly.

He started handing out Socialist Party leaflets until the priest told him to stop. Christopher let out a short barking laugh and went outside for a cigarette. The truth was he was deeply upset by his niece's choice of husband.

'She's my niece,' he told the photographer waiting for the bridal car. 'She could have made something of her life, but no, she has to marry a doctor, to please her bloody father!'

The photographer smiled thinly.

'She's very talented. I used to hope there was a chance she would escape from drudgery. I told them to encourage her music, but no one listens to me.'

In the distance coming slowly towards them with a streaming ribbon was the wedding car. Nodding hastily, the photographer went to meet it.

On the morning of her niece's marriage Frieda was tending her mother's grave, taking fresh flowers to it, talking to her of what was happening so far away.

'She has grown up,' said Frieda. 'Imagine! Alicia says she looks *just* like you, Mummy. She must be so beautiful. Thornton's broken-hearted. No one will be good enough for Anna-Meeka.'

It was the hot season and the air was very still and golden. A large lizard darted jerkily across the ground, reappearing against the white marble of Grace's headstone. Frieda stood, head bowed, thinking of her niece and her brother's broken heart, imagining her mother's voice chiding them. Anna-Meeka was still young; she had time on her side. Wait, her mother's voice seemed to say. Wait. And it seemed to Frieda that the jasmine bush she had planted waited, and the crows perched on the telegraph poles waited, and the land, war-torn and exhausted, waited for the rains to come, as Anna-Meeka de Silva was married on that summer's day in the church on the Brixton Road.

Savitha sat in the front row with an enormous orchid caught in her hair, hoping her sewing of Meeka's jacket would not unravel. Christopher, drinking from his hip flask, glared at anyone who looked at him. Thornton walked his daughter up the aisle. How lovely she looks, thought Robert Grant. He was looking at Alicia. The lightness in her face was his doing; *he* had given her something. Alicia was looking at her niece, remembering that other wedding long ago. Only now could she face the memory of it without flinching.

Thornton took his place next to Savitha. He felt defeated. The church was full of family friends, far more than they had expected. Mr and Mrs Smith from next door, smiling broadly and nodding their approval, the office girl from Thornton's office now married with two children, all the girls from the typing pool, little Cynthia Flowers no longer so little (she had found another sort of love, less exciting, more stable and the baby was due in a month) and Mr Wilson, Savitha's boss, standing at the back. Savitha had worn the orchid specially to impress him. Then, before they knew it, it was over.

'You look great, Meeka!' shouted her friends.

'Be happy, darling,' cried Alicia wiping her eyes.

'Well, what happens now?' asked Geraldine.

Time was money; the twins had been babysat for nearly four hours already. Silly cow, thought Savitha, looking at Geraldine, why can't she wash properly? But then her daughter was gone, with a quick flurry of hugs and confetti, in her father's arms fleetingly, all those years of goodnight kisses distilled into this public moment, and Savitha, glancing at her husband, thought with shock, How frail he looks.

22

IT HAD NOT WORKED OUT AS FRIEDA hoped. Perhaps it was too late for a new beginning. The Tamil boy did not want what she could offer. He had seen his father's throat slit and their sub-post office in Jaffina burnt to the ground. His sister had been raped and shot, together with his mother. One by one he watched them die. Frieda's kindness had no real bearing on his life. Kindness was like chocolate. It could not satisfy hunger. Kindness only made him rage. The Tamil boy tore through the house like a hand grenade. Frieda saw that the laws governing his small life could only work if he had his own victim. The Tamil boy was eight, but he had lived several lives already. He went back to the orphanage. It was the best solution. The Devil was the best painkiller. The Devil danced inside him, telling him that love was safer at a distance.

Aloysius began to complain of stomach pains and the doctor had him admitted into hospital. Frieda rang Thornton and Savitha. She heard their desolation even before she gave them the news. It matched her own. Aloysius was eighty-four. His liver had finally given up. In the early hours of that morning, at the beginning of a rose-pink dawn, surrounded by the sounds of police sirens, he had died. Only his younger daughter and an empty glass were at his side.

'No,' Frieda told them. 'I am not leaving. Not now. This is where I belong.'

She found it difficult to express her feelings. She had never been good at that. But she felt one of them should remain and, she saw, with exceptional insight, she was that one.

After the wedding the Guptas moved out of London, into a suburb of Oxford where Naringer had a job. He had fallen in love (he supposed it was love) with Meeka swiftly. She was beautiful in the way privileged Asians were, although of late he was beginning to see how odd her family was, full of inexplicable habits, full of pride in the things they might have achieved rather than what they actually had. They talked constantly about Meeka's grandmother as though she was a legend, as if she was still among them. He could not understand this. They were all uneducated, without a single university degree between them, but even though he had married Meeka, he sensed his father-in-law disapproved of him.

The move out of London had come as a shock for Anna-Meeka too. She got a job in a hairdresser's salon but the women she met there were not like the Londoners she had grown up with. She gave up the job and found she was both lonely and bored. The de Silvas came to visit. Christopher was the first, a bottle of whisky in each pocket and a carrier bag filled with books and flyers. Meeka was overjoyed to see him. Ah yes, thought Christopher, I'm not surprised.

Naringer was at work.

'Good!' said Christopher.

That settled it. He opened one of his bottles of whisky and poured himself a celebration drink.

'Uncle Christopher,' said Meeka laughing. 'It's not lunchtime yet!'

'Now don't turn into your bloody parents, please, putha!'

Meeka played the piano for him. She had just written another piece of music. 'Listen to this one, Uncle Christopher.' She had no one to play to since her marriage. Naringer did not like music. 'Listen to the tone of this piano. Isn't it beautiful?'

Christopher closed his eyes enjoying the smoothness of the whisky as it slipped down his throat. You are too, he thought grimly. *And* talented, and you had your whole life in front of you. So why the hell did you marry this cloth-eared, humourless man? For once, Christopher refrained from comment. Instead, he suggested they go for a walk.

It was cold and windswept outside. Once this village must have been small and pretty and well planned. Now it had grown like a weed into a long shapeless sprawl, full of sixties houses and ugly estates. There was a supermarket, a petrol station and a row of indifferent shops. Women with pushchairs bent double in the cold sharp wind, red-and-blue plastic bunting flapped unhappily over the car showroom. A few of the shops had started putting up Christmas decorations. Seeing this, Christopher snorted.

'Capitalist bastards,' he muttered.

Meeka slipped her arm through his and hugged him. She was surprised at how glad she was to see him.

'Is that a library?' asked Christopher, suddenly alert.

And he darted in. Pulling out some Socialist Party leaflets from his pocket, he began to pin them on the public noticeboard. Then he went over to the desk and placed some on the counter. An elderly man was having his books stamped.

Christopher gave him a leaflet, winking at the girl behind the desk at the same time.

'Uncle Christopher,' said Meeka tugging at his arm, laughing a little, 'Uncle Christopher, what are you *doing*? Come on, let's go. Dad would be mad as hell with you if he could see you now!'

'Your father is an idiot, putha,' said Christopher, belching loudly. 'Don't talk to me about him.'

The librarian was approaching. 'Shh!' she said loudly.

'I'm sorry,' Meeka apologised, suppressing a giggle. 'We're just going.' And she dragged her uncle out before he could reply.

Outside it had begun to drizzle. The sky was an opaque impenetrable layer of clouds. Nothing except the bunting and a few sticklike trees moved. No birdsong, no flowers, nothing.

'Oh God,' said Christopher, unhappily, 'I hate this weather. I hate this bloody place. I want to go home. Come on, let's find a pub.'

Naringer hated the visits from his wife's relatives. Coming home late, hoping for a quiet end to the day, his heart would sink at the sight of the lighted windows and the strains of music. Always the damn music. He knew that if the visitor was Christopher, he would probably be drunk. He would give Naringer a book on the political crisis in Sri Lanka or the theory of socialism or some other rubbish. Then, although he said it was a gift, Christopher always somehow managed to extract money from him for it.

'Why does he think I want these books?' Naringer would ask irritably afterwards, when Christopher had gone. 'What's the matter with him? Doesn't he know the East is always in crisis? It's a Third bloody World, innit?'

At first Meeka tried reasoning with him. Christopher, she told him, was only being friendly.

'Then why does he charge me for them?'

Meeka laughed. 'He's probably short of cash!' she said.

Thankfully, Meeka's parents preferred the Guptas to visit them. In the early days she only went with Naringer, but it was soon clear he was bored.

'They are all is-snobs,' he told Meeka.

Meeka made no comment. She began going home alone. Christopher, turning up, watched with interest.

'That husband of hers is a bloody cold fish!' he remarked to Jacob. 'How long do you give this marriage then?'

Nobody was prepared to bet on it. The unsuitable, hasty match continued to baffle them. Thornton in particular was non-committal. Lately he had settled on an unspoken truce with his daughter and did not want to spoil things. Whatever disappointment he felt he had learned to keep to himself. Only Savitha knew of it. Only she saw how the events of the last year, the marriage and Aloysius's death, had aged him.

So a quieter, less robust Meeka, more subdued than before, came home to eat her mother's comforting boiled rice, her crab curry and her *brora*. To be served string hoppers by Savitha in her grandma Grace's bone china, and to listen to her father play his recording of *The Magic Flute*. Then, barely a year into her marriage, she discovered she was pregnant and everything changed. Little things about her husband that irritated her floated like scum to the surface. The way he sneezed for instance, wiping his hands all the way down his trousers.

Disgusting! she thought. She began to hate the way he prefixed the word 'is' before anything beginning with 's'.

'I will drive you is-slowly to the is-station,' he said.

It made her want to scream. She decided she did not much like his mouth either or the way he spat into the washbasin every night before they went to bed. She made a list of her dislikes. Her husband, on the other hand, hardly speaking, hardly noticing, took to coming home early to prepare the meals she did not cook. He suggested that now that she was about to become a mother, she should start wearing a sari again. Meeka stared at him. Was he mad?

A strange in-between time began. Meeka did what she pleased. Sometimes she cooked. Sometimes she went into the town window-shopping, half-heartedly gorging on ice cream, dimly aware of an increasing well of loneliness. The one real pleasure she had was in playing her piano. During the day, when Naringer was at work, she lifted the lid and the rich dark tones poured through the tiny house, but at night, when he returned, the house was silent. She began to phone her mother more often. Savitha, aware of her daugher's need, knowing that many changes lay ahead, talked to Anna-Meeka endlessly in a way she had not done since she had been a little girl. What she had been waiting for was emerging slowly. At last, her daughter was growing up.

For Meeka, however, time ceased to have any meaning. She existed in a somnambulant state with the piano and her conversations with her mother as her anchor. Thornton, noting the frequency of the phone calls and his wife's laughter on the phone, was surprised.

'What's the joke?' he asked Savitha after a particularly long conversation.

Savitha folded her lips and refused to speak.

'Heh?' persisted Thornton. 'What's she say?'

'Nothing,' Savitha said, suppressing a laugh.

'What about that husband of hers?'

'What about him?'

'Well, you know his ears are pasted. That's not a good thing. In Jaffna –'

'Yes, yes, I know. In Jaffna they say you can't trust a man with pasted ears.'

Savitha was laughing openly. Thornton gave up. I'm glad they're getting on so well, he thought, a little jealously. His poor, dead father had been right. Women were all the same in the end. Mistaking his daughter's state of mind for contentment, he was marginally relieved. At least, he thought, Meeka is settling down. Maybe the fellow with the lobeless ears isn't so bad after all.

'Pregnancy!' he declared, folding his newspaper. 'I told you, didn't I, that's what she needed. No?'

Savitha grunted. It was not the new baby she was waiting for. It was something more elusive, something she was not prepared to discuss with her husband.

As the summer wore on Meeka began to garden. She bought climbing roses and honeysuckles, clematis and foxglove seeds. Next she bought an ornamental cherry. Soon her garden began to take on the appearance of a tumbling chaos of greenery. The month of October drew to a close. Meeka's baby was born just as the leaves began to fall, during the November rain. A little girl with dark eyes that shone like beacons in the night. She called the baby Isabella. Her parents filled her house with flowers. Savitha made tiny clothes, sewing soft cotton cloth by hand. Thornton was starry-eyed and ready to forgive Naringer, almost prepared to call him by his name. He was unable to keep away from his precious granddaughter. Christopher snorted and, as a joke, sent the baby her own book on imperialism. He meant it as a warning for her parents.

Jacob visited once but he was busy. These days Jacob was trying to distance himself from his family. They were too difficult and his hands were full with Geraldine and the twins. Geraldine wanted them to go back to Ireland. She hated it here in England and continued to dislike his relatives. In the end, thought Jacob, Anna-Meeka is just another ordinary Asian girl, marrying, having children, living an unremarkable life. What a disappointment!

'I have become a realist,' he told Christopher privately.

'Don't you mean a capitalist, men?' was all Christopher said in response.

Jacob shook his head at the predictability of the remark. He no longer got any pleasure from the trips to the pub. He was tired of Christopher's drunkenness.

'Thornton's become a different person,' Jacob told Geraldine, determined to slowly distance himself from his brothers. It was, he felt, best all round.

Alicia, abroad for the third time in a year, sent Anna-Meeka music by Saint-Saëns and an exquisite christening gown. She seemed happy.

I have a wonderful little flat overlooking the canal, she wrote to Savitha. *And there's even a piano. Would you believe, I've started playing again!*

Frieda, working in the orphanage and unable to send presents, phoned the new mother. Ranjith Pieris, hearing the news, had visited her and sat for a long time talking about the past. He had looked so desolate that Frieda had asked him to stay for dinner.

But they could not flourish. Too much had grown the way it wanted. Too much needed cutting back. It would need more than pruning shears, it would need an axe. Savitha, baking her cake, icing it with royal icing, finishing it off with pink rosebuds on top, travelled up by train from Paddington and watched. Thornton watched without knowing what it was exactly he watched. He took his wife's word that changes were afoot and came with his spade to dig a hole, to plant an apple tree and a rose bush.

Before the baby was born Naringer had been optimistic that Meeka would change. That change had not come. Except when his mother-in-law was visiting, the house was filthy; there were soaking nappy buckets, piles of unwashed dishes, and terrible meals. Naringer placed a statue of the goddess Kali in the hall; it stared at him every time he came home from work. On a bad day he confused Kali with his wife. He felt he was carrying them both on his back. He felt the filth in the house was worse than the stink of Calcutta. He was drowning in it. There was only so much a man could take. Naringer was a man of science. He had a logical mind and he was able to admit defeat. It was probably the saving of him.

One afternoon he returned home early and packed a bag. He found his passport. He informed Anna-Meeka he was leaving. He had had enough. He was going back to the purple water hyacinths that grew beside the canal where he had been born. Savitha, feeling as though she had been waiting for a bus to arrive, now stopped waiting.

'Well, it's no loss,' said Christopher when he heard.

'She'll find someone else, soon enough,' Jacob said consolingly.

And Geraldine, putting aside years of grievances, agreed. 'Poor thing, it'll be tough to start with but she'll manage,' she said, thinking how large-hearted and forgiving she was in spite of how she had been treated by this wretched family. Thinking of all the things she might have said, thinking what a stuck-up little madam Meeka had always been, thinking how the girl's husband must have suffered (no one, after all, had asked *him* for his side of things), thinking how Savitha ought to feel shame but being Savitha she would not.

'Poor love,' said Mrs Smith when she heard. 'Give her a hug from me when you next see her, ducks.'

Meeka had a vague idea of what was being said about her. She felt the pity, but a glimmer of something else, some small defiant spark, began to glow within her. She painted the inside of her house a sparkling blue. She painted gold stars on the ceiling. It reminded her of the ruined chapel in the House of Many Balconies. Her parents were regular visitors now, along with her uncle Christopher. Even Uncle Jacob came on one occasion to help. Her aunt Alicia, having acquired a contentment hard to believe, sent her loving messages, telling her to play the piano as much as she could. What a change is here, thought Savitha, must be a man somewhere.

Meeka was grateful for any support. Her brief and confusing married life receded. All that remained was the piano, its black lacquered presence impossible to ignore. It stood now in a room stripped bare of distractions, its polished surface reflecting moments of passing light. Savitha, watching her daughter as she played, listened to the music from her childhood float tenderly across the house. Listening, she was glad that at last they were close. It had taken many years, but they had come through. Her daughter was happier than she had seen her for years.

When Isabella was two Savitha and Thornton squabbled about going back home for a holiday.

'Are you crazy?' bellowed Thornton. 'There's a civil war on, people in the government are still being assassinated, there is still a curfew, it isn't safe to walk on the streets. And you want to go back now?'

But Savitha longed for the sun. She longed for her home. It was *still* her home. Nothing had changed that. Nothing would. It was something deep and necessary, something connected with the land itself. Try as she might, the longing had never gone away. She had swaddled her homesickness within her for too long. Meeka was a single mother but stronger, better able to cope, argued Savitha. And Isabella was an easy baby. But Thornton continued to refuse to go. He would not risk their both leaving Meeka.

'What if we can't get back? What if we're *both* killed? Who will Meeka turn to?' Their little granddaughter would be without grandparents.

In the end Savitha, agreeing with him, bought just one ticket. She would travel alone, she would visit Frieda, take her all their news. It would be a short trip, she would return in two weeks' time. One evening, a week before she was due to leave, she baked a cake. It was the best cake she had ever made; the icing was pink, and the rosebuds were perfect. She placed it on her mother-in-law's Hartley cake dish. She washed the Venetian glasses, the plates and the cutlery. She covered the leftover curry and swept the kitchen. Her husband smelt of whisky. What on earth was he reading now? He was getting old. It has not been easy for him, she thought, with unusual softness. Even though he would not go back, even though he always said there was nothing to go back to, he felt their losses keenly.

She would not be away for long. She knew he could not manage without her. Tomorrow morning, she told herself, she would go to her daughter's bright blue house and take the cake for her little granddaughter. Savitha smiled to herself. The child was exquisite. When she returned to the island, she would buy Isabella some sovereign-gold bangles.

Tomorrow, she thought with eager anticipation, she would see Anna-Meeka and the baby again. Savitha's heart lifted with joy. Telling her husband she was going to bed, she stepped out of her shoes. And out of her life.

*   *   *

Sitting on the InterCity train, with Isabella beside her, Anna-Meeka watched the fields rush past raked bare by the beginnings of autumn. A simple wreath of white roses had gone before her. A piece of music she had never heard before filled her head. Softly, gathering momentum, it rose above the darkening sky. Struggling to make sense of her grief, she heard it very clearly, cascading around her on this, her last journey to see her mother. The light outside cast long, luminous shadows across the thinning trees. Abandoned farm buildings with darkened windows sprang swiftly into view only to vanish again over the crest of a hill. In the twilight flocks of birds stretched endlessly; dark semiquavers across the telegraph poles, poised and motionless as though waiting to be played. They were heading south on a long flight back to find the sun.

Beginnings

23

TIME PASSED. MANY SPRINGS, MANY SUMMERS, many years passed. The weeks and the months ran seamlessly into each other and in this way eighteen years went by. With time, the house on the estate where Anna-Meeka lived became shabby, its pebble-dash dark and discoloured. There was never enough money for whitewash but it did not matter. Anna-Meeka grew Albertine roses and ivy across the worst of it. The newness of the estate wore off but her own garden remained a tumbling mass of green in summer and untamed branches in winter, tapping against the windows. Like the garden, tended for so long, so too was Isabella nurtured.

Many voices came down to her, Grace's voice and Savitha's and Thornton's. All this Meeka gave Isabella.

Before Savitha died, soon after Isabella's second birthday, she had made a cake. It was from an old recipe. She had made it with rulang and sultanas, raisins and pumpkin preserve, rose water and many eggs. It had been found the next day, resting on a blue-and-white cake stand.

Sometimes on a warm summer's night as Isabella slept,

Meeka caught the scent of jasmine growing beside the open window. It had been her father's favourite flower; and also, surprisingly, her uncle Christopher's. Fragments of memory, like shards of mirror glass, illuminated her thoughts and in these moments it seemed to her that other sounds, other voices, other hands, invaded the music she played. She played her piano nearly all the time now.

Thornton de Silva died in the fourth summer of Isabella's life. He collapsed on the way to the library and never returned to his council flat in Balham. An elderly friend of his, a woman, rang Meeka. Such a shame, the neighbours said. What a pity he refused to go and live with his daughter, but he would not leave London. What a lovely man, they said. Such a stunning smile.

All through what was left of that summer and during the winter storms that followed, Meeka played Schubert. After her father's death she gave up the job at the hairdresser's and began to teach the piano. This way she was always at home when Isabella returned from school. After she had finished her lessons, she would play her old favourites. She played Beethoven; she played Schubert; she played John Field's nocturnes. Then, softly, she played something of her very own. As yet it had no name. Filled with a new maturity, it carried within its haunting melody those things she had glimpsed many years ago in the head teacher's office. Isabella, drawing on the floor, raised her head and listened.

Frieda de Silva, thin and silver-haired, stooped and sad, lived alone on the island. Like her mother before her she had glaucoma. She lived in the house on Station Road, surrounded by photographs of her absent relatives, in rooms shuttered from the sunlight, with a garden a wilderness of neglect. The house no longer had music within it and the piano ivory had become yellow and broken as ancient teeth. Grace's presence lay silent across the threshold of every room. Frieda wrote when she could to her niece. She told her about the nuns at the orphanage and about Ranjith Pieris, killed by a car bomb as he crossed the road. She wrote of the waste of a whole generation. Ranjith had begun to depend on her, she said. It was a long time since she had felt this kind of affection from a man.

After her father died Anna-Meeka toyed with the idea of visiting Sri Lanka with Isabella. But the war frightened her. She was settled at last and could not bear the thought of being disturbed. With the loss of her father she became reclusive. Small things made her anxious. Once she thought she saw Naringer Gupta in the street. It was her constant fear that he would return and claim Isabella, but Naringer had vanished long ago, back to his water hyacinths.

Nine more years went by. Alicia in Venice, where she now lived, had a bad fall. Isabella was eleven at the time. They had not seen much of Alicia although she never forgot birthdays and Christmas. Isabella loved the presents she sent. Her great-aunt wrote telling them about the concerts she held in her flat and the musicians she entertained. After her fall she became bedridden. Then as Christmas approached she caught an infection and was rushed by water ambulance to the hospital, too late. She died five days into the New Year.

One day, not long after they heard the news, a visitor arrived. He was an elderly gentleman. Winter cut sharply across the air, the evening sky was yellow and icy. Leafless trees dotted with abandoned birds' nests stretched across the horizon. Christmas was over, spring still an impossibility. The visitor stayed to dinner. His name, he told them, was Robert Grant. He had been a very old friend of Alicia's. He had wanted to tell them about himself.

'No one knew,' he said. 'She was the most important person in my life.'

Robert Grant wanted to know about the rest of the family. He had lost touch with them all. Isabella, who had adored Christopher, told him what had happened. He had been staying with them when he collapsed last year.

'He was like Aloysius, I suspect,' Meeka said. 'He was an alcoholic. There was nothing we could do about it. He died as poor as a church mouse having spent all his money on drink.'

'He used to turn up with two bottles of whisky and drink the lot!' said Isabella. 'He'd swear a lot and call us putha, and tell us all about his political rallies. Then he'd start calling Grandpa Thornton an idiot and Mum used to get upset.'

Meeka smiled. 'They never got on, you know,' she said. 'God knows why. Christopher used to say my father was an idiot but it wasn't my fault!'

'He kept saying he wanted Mum to do something wonderful some day,' Isabella said. 'He didn't know what but he always told her she would be the one to keep the family name alive! Didn't he, Mum?'

'Yes,' laughed Anna-Meeka. 'I think he secretly wanted me to be a famous concert pianist like Auntie Alicia. But I was never good enough. It's all down to you now, Isabella, I'm afraid!'

Robert shook his head gently, smiling.

'I am glad to have met you, Isabella,' he said. 'And when the war is over, Meeka, you must visit Sri Lanka. Take Isabella, show her your home, and give her back that part of her history. It belongs to her too. It's important you do.'

He left them, disappearing into the night, an old man now, but still with a trace of boyish charm.

Meeka continued to teach the piano. She had lost touch with

all her old school friends years ago and had not been back to London since her father's death. Only her daughter, her music and the garden held her, only here were the threads that anchored her.

Jacob de Silva, having sold his shop, moved to Ireland with Geraldine. Jacob never kept in touch. He had finally broken with the de Silvas. After Thornton's death he had felt no need for any connection with his niece.

'Too many years have passed,' Meeka told Isabella whenever the subject of returning to Sri Lanka came up. Her childhood and its unwitting choices continued to cast their long shadows over her. Memories drifted aimlessly, mingling with the sounds of the piano. They mixed with the sunshine on yet another ordinary summer's day and greeted Isabella as she walked up the garden on her way home from school.

So they did not go back. And the past with its stone gods and its impossible dreams remained untouched, like unused sheets on a bed. Occasionally, the island appeared on the news as a small item. Western reporters did not go there much, not after the planes were blown up on the tarmac of the international airport. Ceasefires came and went, human rights organisations protested about the atrocities, but largely this was a forgotten war within a flawed paradise, with nothing to offer that warranted salvation. So that the violence breeding more violence locked into the land and the island waited while a force worked invisibly.

At eighteen, Isabella was offered a place at Cambridge to read English. Anna-Meeka was filled with pride. Suddenly, she saw that from now on she would be alone.

'Oh, Mum!' said Isabella. 'The terms are short! I'll be back sooner than you think. And next year we *must* go back to Sri Lanka. I'm going to make you! You need to see the place again.

We'll go together. I'm going to write about the war. I'm going to make people notice what's going on there.'

Looking at Isabella and seeing her younger, stubborn self, Meeka was glad. Soon it was time for Isabella to leave. On her last night at home Anna-Meeka sat on the end of her daughter's bed thinking how well they had done together.

'You should go out more, Mum,' Isabella told her. 'Instead of just playing the piano all the time. Go out and make some friends for heaven's sake! I wish you would meet a nice man. Perhaps if we go back to Sri Lanka you will meet someone like Auntie Alicia's Sunil.'

'Oh God! You sound like your grandfather,' said Meeka. 'That's just the sort of thing he would have said!' She laughed, for she could not have Isabella worrying about her.

But then, on a light summer evening when it was least expected, fate stepped in and took a hand in things.

It began with Philippa Davidson, who had been at school with Meeka. Philippa did not think she would meet anyone of interest on a Saturday walking through the centre of Oxford. Hordes of shoppers, youths munching burgers, tattoo artists peddling their skills, buskers with their sleeping dogs, homeless beggars, just like Calcutta, thought Philippa Davidson. She had never been to Calcutta. It was at that moment that she saw Meeka (hadn't she married someone from the very place?) walking towards her totally unchanged.

This was not strictly true of course, she thought later. Of course Meeka was changed, but she was also entirely recognisable. And just as lovely.

Philippa was on her way back from the covered market. She was carrying a shopping bag full of fresh fish and cheeses. She was en route to the French baker for her walnut loaf, for she was having some friends to supper. She was flabbergasted to see Meeka.

'It is you, Meeka, isn't it?' she asked, peering at her, standing in the middle of the street with the man selling mobile-phone covers and the buskers' dogs sniffing around. Her dimple flashed in and out and she tucked her hair behind an ear, showing a small pearl earring. Afterwards Meeka thanked God for that dimple. It was the only bit of Philippa that she recognised.

'I can't *believe* it's you!' said Philippa, and she bent and kissed her on both cheeks with a gesture of such genuine warmth that Anna-Meeka was taken aback. She had never really known Philippa.

They had coffee together. Philippa insisted on it. There was so much to talk about.

'You must come to supper,' exclaimed Philippa, halfway through their conversation. 'Now I've found you I don't want to lose you again!'

Meeka was startled. The last time they had met was at her ridiculous wedding. Remembering how she had shown off, Meeka winced. What, she wondered, had happened to Philippa's parents and the wonderful sports car? She didn't ask. She was cautious. Philippa too was remembering. She remembered Meeka's dazzling father. Everyone had known how much he adored his daughter. What a stunning pair they had made. How ordinary her own family had seemed by comparison, how boring!

'You were the most exotic girl in our year,' she told Meeka. 'You never gave a damn about anything. I so envied you!' She laughed with delight, remembering.

Anna-Meeka stared. What on earth was Philippa talking about? She had been filled with angst, riddled with uncertainties and unhappy.

Pippa, as she called herself now, lived with her two cats in a wonderfully neat little village near Oxford. Anna-Meeka wondered why had she never married, or had children. Pippa answered all these questions with an open friendliness that drew Meeka instantly to her. She had cut her long straight hair. It was still blonde but now it had help from a bottle. Meeka could tell; she had not been a hairdresser all those years for nothing. They were the same age but Meeka looked ten or even fifteen years younger. Neither of them cared. It was as though all the indifference of their childhood had dispersed. Or maybe it was simply that Anna-Meeka was ready to give it room. Whatever it was, something affectionate rose up between them. Although Pippa lived alone she was very sociable. Her friends were a constant presence in her life, dropping in, teasing her, inviting her to the opera and crying on her shoulder. Meeka, listening to her stories, was mesmerised.

'Oh well,' said Pippa easily, 'I don't have a lovely family like yours. I don't have a *daughter*. So my friends are my family.'

Meeka was staggered. Pippa Davidson smiled at her. She had no idea she used to make Meeka feel inadequate. She had always liked her. Seeing the loneliness that lurked in her old friend's face, Pippa's heart went out to her. If she was puzzled by the change in the once headstrong Anna-Meeka she kept these thoughts to herself. Instead, with characteristic generosity, she decided to take Meeka under her wing.

'Do you still play the piano? I remember you were brilliant at music,' she said.

'It was the only subject I was any good at,' said Meeka ruefully. 'I was rubbish at everything else!'

'Come to supper on Saturday,' Pippa said. 'I want you to meet a friend of mine, whom you might find interesting.'

'Who?' asked Meeka suspiciously.

'His name is Henry,' Pippa said. 'And he teaches here at the university. In between conducting the Birmingham Symphony Orchestra. Wasn't your aunt a concert pianist or something?'

Meeka looked wary. She felt cornered. Later she rang Isabella and told her.

'Well, why don't you?' asked Isabella. 'Go on, Mum. Go out for once! Get dressed up. You look great when you do. For goodness' sake, what have you got to lose? If she's an old school friend, what harm is there in it? He might be interesting. You can talk about music. You'll *love* that.'

Meeka continued to make excuses but Isabella would have none of it.

'Ring me tomorrow and tell me all about it.'

Meeka sighed. Her garden was looking wonderful. Years of planting and pruning had given it a wild, magnificent look. She would have liked to stay at home and enjoy it. But she went all the same, dragging her heels a little, because she had promised, and heard Henry Middleton's laughter drifting through the open French windows. Some laugh, thought Meeka, hesitating at the front door, instantly wanting to go home. She might even have done so, had it not been for the fact that Pippa opened the door so quickly.

Well, thought Henry, what have we here? Where's this one from?

Life for Henry Middleton had not been without its struggles. It had tried to knock the edges off him but with little success. Henry always resisted. When his wife left him for a wealthier man, taking the contents of the house with her in an enormous removal van, he stood in the empty drawing room and observed the sunlight flickering on the bare floorboards. When he discovered the note informing him their joint account was now empty he had laughed out loud. His laughter echoed hollowly through the empty rooms. The day she left him he found his love melting away like the snow that covered the ground. But he was not an ungenerous man, far from it. He was not a man to bear a grudge. So when she invited him to visit her in her new home he did so without bitterness, driving through the gilded gates, made, it seemed, for giants, to wish her well. Having tried marriage and failed to understand it, he decided it was not for him. If at times he was lonely, if there were moments when he wondered what it might be like to find a love of his own, he brushed these thoughts aside, considering them sentimental. Instead he concentrated on distractions, of which there were many, for Henry Middleton was a man that women liked. For eleven years he had lived like this, the life and soul of many dinner parties.

'Henry's such fun!' his friends said. 'We *must* invite him.'

'There's someone we want you to meet, Henry!' they cried.

'You're sure to like her. She's pretty.'

And Henry would turn up for supper wearing his outrageously colourful clothes, laughing his delightful laugh, looking deep into the eyes of whoever it might be this evening, flattering her with his attentiveness, *enjoying* her. Although always, on the next day, or the day after that, he would drive her regretfully home, for had he not eschewed love forever? So, as the beginnings of middle age turned his hair to silver, he hid his loneliness with perfect ease, for Henry Middleton had many good friends. Pippa Davidson was one of them. She was always trying to find someone for him. She told him nothing about Anna-Meeka before he met her, wanting an element of surprise.

'Where did you find *her*?' he asked afterwards, not being one to beat about the bush. 'She doesn't look too happy.'

Pippa had been surprised by Meeka's silence. Perhaps she

had disliked Henry, she thought. Or maybe it was simply that she was shy.

'Sulky,' Henry observed, with a short laugh.

She was not his type. Yet something about her interested him. Perhaps it was those dark eyes. So, thinking it best to keep these thoughts to himself, he found a way to bump into her in the music section of the lending library where Meeka had said she often went. This happened several times in a casual, oh-my-goodness-fancy-meeting-you-again, sort of way. Meeka believed it to be a coincidence. She was not interested in him. She did not have any interest in men. Once bitten, twice shy, she believed. Henry, on the other hand, was enthusiastically friendly and in a desire to make himself more interesting, invited her to have coffee with him so that he could tell her a some-what exaggerated version of his life. He meant it as a joke, these stories of his conquests (the Greek, the German, the two Italian students, to name but a few), but Meeka, he noticed, was mesmerised. Although she had no personal interest in him, she listened. How did he do it? Henry sighed. It was hard to explain. With his engaging approach to life, having caught her atten-tion Henry felt it was his duty to entertain her. Eventually, on their third encounter it was assumed he would come over to her house for supper.

He hadn't learned much about her as yet, so throwing caution to the wind he went. But first, being an excellent cook, he offered to bring the pudding. He made a fruit salad in an old chipped blue-and-white china bowl. It had belonged to his mother and would have been worth something had he not chipped it (but then Henry was always careless with the washing-up). He wore a shirt that matched his eyes, which were of a particular sharply defined blue. It was a glorious evening; the spring flowers were out as he set forth on his adventure, whistling to himself. The estate where Meeka lived was thrown into sharp contrast by the light. When he found number 11 Henry was pleasantly surprised. The house stood on the curve of a cul-de-sac covered in a bower of greenery. Bluebells lined the path. Small delicate flowers sprang up everywhere. His own shop-bought offering seemed out of place. Bending low under the branches that would soon cascade with roses, he found the front door and was charmed. It was painted dark green; a wind chime moved gently in the breeze. Dimly, through the glass, he saw the outline of a grand piano. Someone began to play a slow three-octave scale. It rose to the top without a pause before descending. Henry hesitated, listening intently. Then he rang the bell.

'Goodness!' he said joyfully, by way of greeting, handing Meeka the flowers. Then he laughed uproariously as though at some joke of his own. Meeka frowned. She recognised that laugh but could not place it.

'Well,' said Henry, conversationally, 'we could stay out here all evening, or you could ask me in?'

And then he handed her the bowl of fruit salad, stepping inside unasked and making for the piano.

'Can you *really* play this thing,' he asked, teasingly, 'or is it just an ornament?'

For a moment it was as though someone had put the clock back and Meeka felt she was riding the District Line on the Underground in the school holidays with Gillian and Susan and Jennifer.

'Oh, get lost!' she said crossly before she could stop herself, making Henry roar with laughter.

It was not an auspicious start. Things could only get better. Isabella, when her mother rang her the next day, was outraged. She thought Henry sounded like a madman.

'What d'you mean he offered you lessons? How dare he be

so condescending just because he's a conductor,' she said, appalled by such arrogance. 'Who the hell does he think he is? I've never even heard of him.'

Too late, Meeka wished she had kept her mouth shut. Something about Henry, his ridiculous boasting ways, his impossible clothes, or maybe it was simply his irritating laugh, stirred a half-hidden memory. There was a vague familiarity to his behaviour.

A few nights later Henry appeared unannounced just as Anna-Meeka was about to eat supper. He looked enquiringly at her and, rather reluctantly, she invited him to join her. He had been away for a few days rehearsing Mahler in Birmingham.

'It's coming on nicely,' he said yawning, helping himself unasked to some raw carrots.

Then he opened his bottle of wine and went in search of two glasses. Meeka frowned. Once again, his behaviour stirred a long-forgotten memory. Who did he remind her of?

'It's hard work but exciting,' he shouted from the kitchen.

'Make yourself at home,' Meeka said, irritated.

'Thanks,' Henry called out.

He brought in two glasses of wine. 'Here,' he said, not noticing the look on her face, 'try this.'

Meeka ignored him.

'I've got an incredible first violinist,' Henry told her, tucking into the salad. He cut himself a piece of bread. 'I've coaxed her to come over from Berlin,' he said, talking fast with his mouth full.

Again Meeka frowned. Naturally the violinist *would* be a woman.

'Her name is Greta. I've been wanting to work with her for a long time.'

He grinned at Meeka, who listened while trying hard to look uninterested. There was nothing she could contribute to the conversation. Suddenly a feeling of shame enveloped her. She felt hopelessly ignorant. With a flash of insight she understood how her father had felt when she had first brought Naringer home. It had been the way she felt whenever she used to meet Pippa. Then suddenly she remembered Alicia's recording.

'Would you like to listen to my aunt's recording?' she asked when she could get a word in edgeways.

To her surprise Henry was instantly enthusiastic. At first they were both silent. Alicia's magic touch was unchanged by time. When it was over Henry hummed a few bars, drumming his fingers absent-mindedly on the arm of his chair. Meeka said nothing.

'Beautiful,' murmured Henry. 'I'd like to hear her play Beethoven. With a talent like that why on earth didn't she go back to it? That last movement was superb!'

'It wasn't that simple,' Meeka said at last. 'She loved my uncle Sunil. Life wasn't worth living after that.'

'But you said she was all right later on?'

'Oh yes. Much later. She found someone else. She used to play for him.'

'There you are then!' Henry said, satisfied.

Meeka was sitting beside a small table lamp, half in shadows, not looking at Henry. 'I think,' she said hesitantly, 'everything that was happening in the country at the time was too much to bear. You know, the Sinhalese discriminated against my father's people. They had been wealthy once but then overnight they were nobody.' She struggled to explain herself. 'After my uncle was killed the whole family was petrified. That's why my parents wanted to leave. They were frightened for my future. They stayed frightened for the rest of their lives. Not understanding anything about this country. England was too much. In fact . . .' She paused. She had never had this kind of conversation with anyone before. 'I could have helped more, but well . . .' She shrugged. 'All I was interested in was integrating with the other children. Making friends, losing my accent! Without meaning to I broke their hearts, I suppose,' she said softly. 'Leaving Sri Lanka unsettled them more than they realised. My mother used to say the civil war was the invisible story of the British Empire.'

'They certainly paid a high price,' Henry said quietly. 'I wouldn't blame yourself. You were just a child.'

Meeka glanced at him sharply, uncertain if he was laughing at her. But Henry was looking a little solemn. With the oddest expression in his salt-blue eyes.

The next day when he visited Pippa, Henry could talk of nothing else but Meeka.

'Why does she act as though she's crushed?' he asked. He had a funny feeling Anna-Meeka was different underneath.

'Well,' said Pippa doubtfully, 'perhaps she *is* crushed. Have you thought of that? Being an immigrant in the sixties, and having parents who never fitted in couldn't have been easy for her. I think she struggled with them.' She paused.

Henry didn't seem to be listening.

'She was telling me about her aunt,' he said. 'You know she was a professional pianist? Then her husband was killed and she never played seriously again.' Pippa shook her head. She had not known any of this.

'We didn't have a lot to do with each other at school,' she said. 'Meeka was awfully pretty and very remote.'

Still is, thought Henry.

'You should have seen her father. He was very handsome. He adored her of course.'

387

Of course, thought Henry, drumming his fingers. Pippa looked at her friend. Usually within days of meeting someone new he was bored. She was delighted to see him so preoccupied. Henry, unaware of her thoughts, was whistling absent-mindedly under his breath. He whistled a few bars from *The Magic Flute*. Fully alert to all possibilities, he was making plans.

He decided to move things along, pull Meeka's leg a little, see what happened. With this in mind, throughout what remained of the spring, he conducted his investigations. Being Henry he went about it in his own way. He told Meeka stories about his former wife, hoping to keep her keen.

'She was very blonde,' he said, closing his eyes with what appeared to be ecstasy. 'And stunningly beautiful.'

Meeka glared at him. Sensing he had got her attention he told her about his last girlfriend.

'Francesca was really talented,' he said, shaking his head as though with amazement. 'I was staggered the first time I heard her play the flute.'

Anna-Meeka narrowed her eyes. As far as she could see, *all* Henry's women were either goddesses or geniuses. What was he doing spending time with her?

'Well, why doesn't he bloody well go back to them?' snapped Isabella crossly when her mother rang her.

Meeka vowed to show no interest. Henry Middleton was getting on her nerves; she began to feel the stirrings of summer within her, smell the warm air. Henry had better watch out, thought Pippa Davidson, wondering what the devil he was up to. Like the cow-parsley that seeded itself, Henry seemed to be everywhere. Snooping into Meeka's life, invading her space, smitten. Watch out, Henry, thought Pippa, don't overdo it. Remember they don't usually understand your humour. But Henry Middleton didn't care. That was part of his trouble. And possibly also his charm.

A few months went by. It was high summer now, and the roses were out. Every time he saw Meeka, Henry was aware of experiencing all sorts of interesting emotions. Sally Dance, the well-known archaeologist, thought it hugely funny when she heard. She was one of Henry's closest friends. She had thought he had been a bit silent for some time. Now she knew why.

'Henry's met his Waterloo,' cried Sally. 'She looks young enough to be his daughter!'

'I hope he doesn't annoy her,' said Pippa. 'You know what he's like.'

'Oh I know. I think he's trying to be endearing,' said Sally Dance. 'Why are men so clueless!'

'She sounds weird,' said Henry's ex-wife, when she heard. 'I think she's after his money.'

The cat was well and truly stalking the pigeons. On close observation Henry could see that Meeka was thawing out nicely. He was pleased to see more than a hint of spirit whenever he teased her. Good, he thought. Good, good.

'I'd tone down your past,' advised his lodger Dill. 'Women don't like to hear about old girlfriends.'

But Henry grinned, unrepentant. Careful, Henry, thought Pippa again. She didn't say it but, more and more, she felt he was pushing his luck.

'What *is* the matter with him?' she said to Sally. 'This isn't how he usually behaves. He's not *that* funny.'

Sally Dance agreed. 'I think he's scared,' she said shrewdly, enjoying it all. 'He's scared he's falling for her!'

No one knew what might happen next. Only time would tell.

Henry too was surprised by how much he was enjoying himself. He waited, as one waits for a train that's late. He was discovering there was more to Anna-Meeka than even he had first thought. He began to visit her once a week, in the evening, a bottle of fine wine tucked under his arm. Bringing his stories with him, ready for more sport.

'I bumped into my ex again, today,' he told her cheerily, pouring out some wine.

'Really?' asked Meeka, covering her glass with her hand.

Henry didn't seem to notice.

'She's invited me to one of her big dinner parties. Aren't you having any more wine?' he asked again.

Oh my God! thought Anna-Meeka, staring at him. She'd remembered! Henry was showing off like her father. Unaware of her thoughts, Henry continued.

'She has these black-tie dinners about once a month,' he was saying. 'She always wants me there.'

As for that laugh, thought Meeka. I know exactly who his laugh reminds me of. And she remembered how her uncle Christopher had behaved at her wedding.

'Henry,' she said, experimentally, 'I know you were very hurt when your wife left you, but, you know, I think you're simply stuck in your own groove.'

Henry was taken aback. He poured himself a drop more wine.

'What was that you were playing, when I came in?' he asked, changing the subject, knowing she was reluctant to talk about her music.

So, she composed music. As well as playing the piano. Hmm, he thought. That night, just before he left, shamelessly, he stole some of the sheet music lying around. He wanted to take a good look at it without Meeka knowing. The next day he examined her composition. Pursing his lips, he sat down at the piano and played a few bars. He raised an eyebrow, playing slowly, groping his way, trying to illuminate the texture of the music, to understand the underlying structure of the composition. He could hear a number of voices, rising together and falling away one by one. Thinking about the music, following Anna-Meeka's score, he made a few notes in red ink. Then he played it again, bringing out the tenderness within the melody. The sounds dropped note by note into his mind. Poco vivace and exuberant at first, then drifting into a brooding C minor. He could hear her voice through his fingers; her presence in the music. He felt a strong sense of her personality, lifting off the manuscript. The sunshine from the window fell softly like candlelight against the piano keys. There were small particles of dust moving slowly in the light, but Henry never noticed. He wore a strange lost smile of appreciation. An inner world of extraordinary integrity and balance was being revealed to him. The music came to its gentle insistent closure; after the last chord he did not take his hands away from the keyboard. He did not stir. It was as though he was under a spell. Staring out of the window, his face unusually serious, he wondered what he should do. Suddenly he was a little frightened. There was no doubt in his mind: the music was astonishing. She had not studied composition, her notations were not always correct. Yet the structure was clear. There was a tension within that went all the way through the piece, a connection that never once let up. Still Henry hesitated, not wanting to do the wrong thing.

'Beautiful,' he said, sotto voice, playing some of the phrases again and again, listening to the cadence and resolution, the way it developed both emotionally and intellectually.

'Early twentieth-century English composers,' he mumbled to himself.

And someone else. Messiaen, he thought, shaking his head, amazed. Probably she didn't even realise it. An extraordinary woman, he thought. So much locked away, undiscovered. What on earth was she ashamed of that she wouldn't speak to him about it? He wondered how much more she had written, knowing it was too soon to ask. Lost in thought, he began to play once more. Then he reached for the phone. What he really wanted was a second opinion.

Two days later Henry visited Meeka again. He had several plots to thicken. On this occasion he recited poetry to her. Browning and then Tennyson, and after that Yeats. Yeats always came last in his opinion. Meeka flattened her ears as a cat might flatten them when it was confused. Heavens! she thought, remembering her mother had been crazy about Yeats. What would she have said if she heard all this? Henry, observing her reaction, smiled with secret satisfaction. The thaw had settled in nicely. Of late his eyes were the colour of blue lagoons.

'Oh no!' said Sally Dance seeing the seriousness of what was happening. 'I do hope he doesn't get hurt.'

'Listen, Henry, don't keep mentioning your ex,' urged his lodger. 'She won't find it amusing.'

But Henry didn't seem to hear. He was preoccupied with thoughts of his own and was just off for a swim. At his age, he informed his lodger, he needed to keep himself in trim. Besides, it was time to invite Meeka to his house, for a candlelit supper.

Sally Dance and Pippa offered to bleach his tablecloth and make him a summer pudding.

'We'll eat alfresco,' he declared, 'beside the fountain and next to the statue of Venus.'

Lavender grew among the rosemary. The scents mingled with

the Dijon Rose petals falling softly onto the ground like confetti. Henry placed the speakers outside. They would listen to Bach, he decided. The backdrop was perfect.

Then disaster struck. Just as he was chopping the garlic for the *melanzane alla parmigiana*, the doorbell rang.

'*Caro* Henry. *Ciao, caro!*' said a voice.

Shit! thought Henry. Shit, shit! It was Francesca the flautist.

'*Stai bene*, Henry?' she said, slinking in.

Francesca followed him into the kitchen.

'How sweet, you make-a my favourite dish-a!' And she started nibbling the cheese.

There was nothing for it, Henry gave her a large grappa and lured her into his study upstairs.

'Now you just stay here, Francesca,' he said. 'I shan't be long, well, not too long. I'm sorry to keep you out of the way like this, but I don't have much time. It's just a business meeting, that's all, you know what these musicians are like . . . I must go,' he added, as the doorbell rang. Hastily (he could smell the oven from where they stood), thrusting the bottle of grappa into Francesca's hand, he rushed downstairs, taking care to close the study door, remembering to check his face for lipstick. He felt unaccountably hot.

It was an uneasy evening. Meeka had brought a dish that was perfumed with almonds and rose water but Henry's food was burnt and the wine corked. He opened another bottle. Every time he glanced up at the house he could see Francesca prowling around. The light was on. What on earth was she doing? Henry reached for the bottle of newly opened wine, helping himself liberally.

'My goodness, is that the time?' he asked, yawning loudly, glancing at his watch.

He had an early start the next day. Meeka agreed; it was time to go home. She had not drunk much but she decided to use the bathroom before she left.

'No!' shouted Henry, adding more quietly, 'It's just that the bathroom isn't awfully nice, I mean, the light doesn't work.' The bathroom light had just come on; he could hear Francesca flushing the toilet.

'Don't worry,' said Meeka, 'I don't mind.'

'No!' said Henry, standing up in alarm, barring her way back into the house. 'No, I mean, why don't you wait until I take you back? You can't be that desperate? Can you?' he pleaded.

Anna-Meeka was looking at him strangely.

'Henry,' she said patiently, as though she were speaking to a child, 'may I use your bathroom please? You needn't worry, I'm not going to pinch anything.'

Pushing past him she went into the house. Henry watched her go. Francesca, all kitten heels and not much else, watched from above as Meeka went, head down, determinedly up the stairs.

'You *are* an idiot, Henry,' said Pippa, shaking her head at his nerve. Why did he always ruin everything?

Sally Dance couldn't stop laughing. 'I could have told you that would happen,' she said, wiping her eyes. She could hardly speak. 'Oh, Henry! She must have been livid!'

Henry did not bother to answer her. He was still clearing up the mess. The *melanzane* was everywhere.

'I've had enough,' said Dill the lodger. 'There are too many women in this bloody house.'

Henry said nothing. He would have to repaint the wall.

'I've told you,' said Isabella down the phone, 'the man's a madman! Get rid of him.' Her mother was hopeless when it came to men. Perhaps she ought to come home and sort it all out. No wonder Grandpa Thornton used to worry about her so much. 'Get rid of him, do you understand? I'm going to ring you tomorrow to check you have.'

But Isabella had worried too much. She had forgotten how stubborn her mother was. She had forgotten what happened when her mother made up her mind. She had not heard her grandma Savitha on *that* subject. Anna-Meeka unplugged the telephone. She closed the curtains, and turned out the lights. Then she settled down to wait. Had her father been alive, had her mother been there, had her uncles been around, they would have instantly recognised the look in her eyes.

That October was the best ever. From Broad Street, behind the high blue-crested gates of the college, Michaelmas spread its autumn crocuses. The air thickened with damp bonfires and the beginnings of river mist. The Oxford skyline was tinted once again in gentle late-afternoon light, while the college walls near the Martyrs' Memorial in St Giles shed their crimson foliage leaving a pencilled scribble of bare branches across the yellowing stone. Bicycles, moving like furious insects, crossed and recrossed cobbled streets, and evensong in the cathedral swelled with its term-time choir. Henry Middleton had had an astonishing summer. When he was not mowing Meeka's lawn or tying her unruly honeysuckle back, he was playing on her beautiful piano. He took her punting on the river. He poured the finest champagne into his mother's old crystal glasses and toasted her health. He pedalled across Oxford with flowers for her. He invited her to listen to him conduct Mahler and then he took her to dinner to meet his friends. He watched her smile. And he felt his heart turn over with a long-forgotten emotion. Sally Dance and Pippa were delighted. Like the roses, Henry was flourishing. Isabella watched her mother with amazement;

she had never seen her look so happy. She thought Henry was *so* sweet.

'Oh Mum, he's *lovely*,' she said in astonishment. 'He's such a tease! And crazy about you.'

The house just now was filled with life. Cars parked outside, visitors came and went; Meeka and Henry played duets together on the piano laughing, and arguing with one another.

During the second week of term Henry Middleton took Meeka to a piano recital. In all her years living near Oxford, Meeka had never once ventured inside a college. Henry was delighted to be the one to take her. She had met the concert pianist Carl Schiller at a party with Henry. Now he had come to Oxford. Their footsteps crunched on the gravel. The women all wore black. Pippa Davidson was excited. Sally Dance had come too. She would not have missed tonight for the world. Isabella had come home for the weekend. She and Henry had become the best of friends. Several of Henry's friends were present, including the music critic Adrian Taylor. Henry introduced Meeka to him. Even Dill the lodger came. He was glad Henry had painted the wall on the landing. It looked as good as new. Only a slight mark remained. Dill fancied that sometimes, depending on the light or the time of day, it glowed like an old war wound.

'Wear one of your saris,' Henry had said. 'The blue-and-gold one, the one your aunt Alicia gave you.'

He had been unusually insistent. So Meeka wore the blue-and-gold sari.

The air quivered with a sense of expectancy. Meeka, sipping her wine, watched the audience as they arrived. She noticed Henry looking around the room and wondered when his Venetian friend or his former wife would pop up. But Henry, it was clear, was playing safe tonight. Sally Dance had brought her man with her. He grinned at Meeka.

'How're you getting on with Henry then?' he asked loudly. 'I hear he's behaving himself these days!'

'Shut *up*, Matthew,' Sally hissed. When all was said and done, Henry was still her friend, even if he sometimes made mistakes. Besides, she did not want to ruin his big evening.

'What's happening?' asked Matthew, who had no idea why he was here.

'Shh!' said Sally Dance. 'You'll see in a minute.'

Soon the auditorium began to fill up. Meeka gazed in delight at her surroundings, unaware of Henry's anxious glances as he introduced her to some of his colleagues, some members from his orchestra, a journalist and a producer from Radio 3. A flash went off nearby and Meeka blinked. Conversation spun in the air. There were so many people who knew Henry. She lost track of how many hands she shook or how many of these women were Henry's old 'friends'. She wished she had not worn her sari. She almost wished she had not come.

'Stop fussing, Mum,' said Isabella as though she had read her mind.

Suddenly, for no reason, Meeka thought of her grandmother. The sari she was wearing had belonged to her once and she took some small comfort, a feeling of who she was, from the thought. Pippa Davidson, glancing across at Meeka and Isabella, was reminded of the dashing Mr de Silva. The family likeness was very apparent tonight. Sally Dance was busy watching Henry, magnificent in his dinner jacket.

'He's as nervous as a cat,' she whispered to Pippa. Henry was fidgeting.

'I'm not surprised,' Pippa whispered back. 'It's making me nervous too!'

Sally giggled.

'Stop it,' Pippa said. 'I can't bear this suspense.'

The last of the audience took their seats. Then suddenly the lights were dimmed. Swiftly, with the speed of tropical darkness, silence descended in tiers around the room. Only a small spotlight illuminated the grand piano. Carl Schiller, fine-boned and delicate as porcelain, came onstage. He bowed once and sat down, pausing, looking down at the keyboard. In the dark his hands glowed white. All around the room the silence was velvet. Meeka felt her hands become moist with sympathy. Was this how her aunt Alicia used to feel when she had played in public?

Carl Schiller began to play. His slender fingers formed a chord, they ran headlong across the keys, clear and unhesitating. The sounds fell into the darkened room, parting the silence as though it were an overgrown path. They cascaded in a waterfall of notes, overlaying each other, dissolving gently, phrase echoing phrase. Fluid, haunting and unending. He played with a piercing yearning, turning inexorably, just as you thought he might pause, into a minor key and then back again, before being lifted by the music somewhere else entirely. The sounds moved across the room, unstoppable now, effortless and breathtakingly lovely.

A soft rustle went through the audience. Whose music was this? How astonishingly beautiful! How it sparked, how it lilted, how it turned on a chord, unpredictable and always with the melody never far away. A distant voice from long ago returning again, when it was least expected, brushing lightly against them.

Here was how it was, the music seemed to say. Of these things were our lives made. Here was the substance of our sorrows and our joy. Exactly like yours. How we laughed, and how we loved, in the place that was once our home. With its coconut palms, its sun-washed beaches, its ancient tea-covered hills. This land of ours where all our earliest desires are housed, and which, however far we may roam, will remain with us forever. For like you, we carry our youth in our hearts.

On and on the music flowed, brimming over in the oak-panelled room, telling of these things; new longings joining the others that the centuries had absorbed. Pressing insistently into the memory of this new space, crossing continents, moving boundaries, connecting. In a language without barriers, in ways that could no longer be denied.

In the darkness, above the familiar sounds, Anna-Meeka looked at Henry Middleton. He sat with her hand tightly in his, watching her, no longer able to hide his tenderness, his pride in her. Wishing that her father, and her mother, and her grandmother, all of them, all those people he had only heard about, could see just how long the journey had been, how far her music had brought her.

And, thought Meeka, looking at him now with eyes that shone, for all his paleness and all his Englishness, still, his ears were not pasted. His lobes hung freely! Happiness welled up in her, rising from a new depth. How pleased her father would have been. For what difference was there in the end? she wondered, smiling at him. There *was* no difference. People were people. Only their fears had made them struggle. And then, suddenly, she knew. In that moment, as the sounds of her music, submerged for so long, cascaded around her, she knew. With all the clarity that had been missing on the evening in the head teacher's office so many years ago, she knew what she must do. She needed to see her home once more. She needed to see that long-forgotten place, with its sweet, soft sound of the ocean, its wide sweep of beaches, and its clear tropical skies. That place, lodged forever within her heart, where the heat of the day glistened and trailed far into the night. Where her aunt Frieda waited so patiently with her moth-dusty sorrow for the past to be dispelled. For clearly she saw it, in spite of the shock, she saw that the things that had been mislaid, the history that had been buried and the memories no longer spoken of, all these things, were somehow being given back to her. And she saw too, at last, that here within this remarkable Englishman, with his sense of the ridiculous, his understanding and his love for her, was something of her beloved family. Returning again.

Far away in the distance, as a dream realised at last, came the rush of thunderous applause, rising and falling like surf-green waves, crashing against her and catching the dazzling sea light.

ACKNOWLEDGEMENTS

I would like to thank my agent Felicity Bryan, for her unfailing encouragement and kindness to me; Kathy van Praag, also, for her endorsement of the book; and of course Clare Smith, my inspired editor at HarperPress.

Thanks to Michele Topham from the Felicity Bryan Agency for her hours of endless discussion; and to Mally Foster and Annabel Wright from HarperPress for their humour and support throughout.

Also to Richard Blackford, who talked to me about musical composition; Maureen Lake, my long-suffering piano teacher; my friends Tessa Farmer and Jane Garnett, who read the manuscript in single, swift sittings; and my brother-in-law Paul, who pleased me by laughing uproariously while reading the manuscript but then informed me it was my spelling that amused him.

I would like to pay special tribute to the rest of my family, to whom this book is dedicated. Like the passengers of a very large and boisterous ocean liner ploughing the seas, it was they who provided the environment in which I could write.

Thank you.